THE
HIT

D1437997

Anna Smith has been a journalist for over twenty years and is a former chief reporter for the *Daily Record* in Glasgow. She has covered wars across the world as well as major investigations and news stories from Dunblane to Kosovo to 9/11. Anna spends her time between Lanarkshire and Dingle in the west of Ireland, as well as in Spain to escape the British weather.

Also by Anna Smith

The Dead Won't Sleep
To Tell the Truth
Screams in the Dark
Betrayed
A Cold Killing
Rough Cut
Kill Me Twice
Death Trap

THE
HIT
ANNA SMITH

Quercus

First published in Great Britain in 2017 by

Quercus Editions Ltd
Carmelite House
50 Victoria Embankment
London EC4Y 0DZ

An Hachette UK company

A CIP catalogue record for this book is available
from the British Library

PB ISBN 978 1 78429 485 4

10 9 8 7 6 5

Typeset by Jouve (UK), Milton Keynes

Printed and bound in Great Britain by Clays Ltd, Elcograf S.p.A.

For Thea – 'the wee rock'.
Her courage humbled and inspired us all.

PROLOGUE

Glasgow, February 2001

There was always the chance of betrayal. Any fool could have seen that. But Helen had been so blinded. Now, the waiting was almost over.

Like a burglar, she stepped softly around her bedroom, closing the doors of the wardrobes she'd emptied earlier. The contents were now in the Louis Vuitton suitcase in her bedroom. She locked the bedroom door, cursing her trembling fingers as she turned the key, and listened for his footsteps in the tiled entrance outside her luxury flat. Nothing. As she walked past the hallway mirror, she glimpsed her reflection, but didn't linger on the empty eyes staring back at her. There was no point in asking herself how it had come to this. She was as guilty of murder as the hitman she'd hired, who was now about to knock on her door with his latest blackmail demand. More money. No amount would ever be enough for him, and Helen should have known that the first time she paid him off. But she'd taken naivety to a whole new level by also becoming his lover. It didn't get much more stupid than that. She'd been devastated at his betrayal, but more angry with herself for believing they could actually make a life together. Now he wanted everything – all the money she'd squirrelled away for both of them, and more. He wanted everything. What a fool she'd been.

She jumped at the knock on the door. She pressed her fingers to her eyes and smudged her mascara a little to make it look as though she'd been crying, in the forlorn hope he might show her a scrap of sympathy. Then she went across to the door, and opened it. Frankie Mallon stood there, and looked her up and down, his dark eyes resting for a second on the top of her breasts poking out of her tight black zipped top. Then he walked past her into the hall and stood, legs apart, as she turned to face him.

'You got everything?'

Helen met his gaze fleetingly, and went towards the kitchen.

'In here. It's in a bag for you. It's everything I have.'

'Don't give me your shit, Helen. You know there's plenty more where that came from.'

'There isn't. Everything else is tied up in these complicated accounts of Alan's. I told you that. You knew that.'

'Then uncomplicate it. You have all the passwords. You told me *that* – remember? You've been shifting his fucking money around for years, hiding it away. So don't give me any of your crap.' He grabbed her by the arm, squeezing it tight. 'I'm telling you now. There had better be plenty in this bag, or when I walk out of here, I make a call to the cops in the next ten minutes. Tell them what you did.'

'You mean what you did,' she spat.

'They'll never know that. I'm not that stupid. I'm just going to drop you right in the shite. See how you bear up when the cops start probing for details, asking you about Alan's disappearance. You . . . the heartbroken fucking wife.'

'Christ, Frankie! Stop with your empty fucking threats. I was interviewed by the police at the time. I wasn't even in the same country as Alan was when he went missing. I'm whiter than white.'

'Aye. That'll be right.'

Helen lifted a fat bag from the worktop and thrust it towards him.

'Take this and get the fuck out of my life.'

Frankie glanced at her, then opened the zip in the bag. He pulled out a wedge of money, fifty-pound notes, and rummaged around the bundles. Helen knew there was five thousand pounds in there. She'd counted it herself again after the bank handed it over to her.

'Fuck this! This is no good!' He slung the bag onto the worktop.

'Take it and go. Don't make any more trouble for yourself.'

Before she could move, he grabbed her by the throat and pushed her against the cupboard.

'Trouble? You bitch! You don't know what trouble is.'

He pulled her hair back, and she heard his breath quicken. And even now, even though he was here to take her money, threatening to ruin her, she couldn't resist him. He pushed himself against her, and kissed her so hard she could feel her teeth crushing against her lips.

'This is what you want, isn't it?'

He was hard already, and Helen felt weak and angry with herself for how much she wanted him. He pulled her skirt up and tugged her pants as he pushed his hand inside.

'Stop!'

'Doesn't feel like you want me to stop.' He was undoing his jeans and pushing himself against her. Then he suddenly froze, and took a step back, his lips curling into a sarcastic smile. 'Oh, you want it, all right. But tell you what. I'm giving you two more days to get all the money together – and I might even give you a shag for old times' sake when I come back.' He took the bag from the worktop and turned.

As he walked out of the kitchen, Helen knew it was now or never. She fumbled in the drawer, and as he was about to open the front door, she pulled out a small revolver she'd found among Alan's things. She took three steps towards him, worried she might miss, and fired a shot into his back. Then two more. He half-turned as he keeled over, his eyes wide in disbelief. Helen stood for a moment, rooted, as blood spread across his shirt and formed a pool on the floor. Still holding the gun, she went into the kitchen and filled a glass of water, her hand trembling, as she watched the blood spread across the light grey carpet. She had to get out of here. Right now. She hurried to the bedroom and dragged her suitcase out towards the front door. She stuffed the money bag inside it. Suddenly, she heard the lock turn as though a key had gone into it. She watched, barely breathing. The door opened slowly. She stepped back towards the kitchen, steadied herself on the worktop. It was a ghost. It must be. But it wasn't. Beneath the beard, the long straggly grey hair and the hollow cheeks, it was Alan. Back from the dead.

'A . . .' Helen couldn't get the word out. 'Al . . .?'

Alan looked down at Frankie's body, realising his feet were in the pool of blood seeping around him. He took a step back, still scanning the body. Then he looked at Helen.

'You killed him? You sent him to kill me, and now you've killed him?'

'H-he attacked me. He wanted all my money.'

Alan puffed and almost smiled. 'Your money? *Your* money? You don't have a fucking penny to your name, Helen. You never had. All you have is what you stole from me. I gave you everything you have, and you stole from me.' His voice quivered a little as he glanced at

Frankie. 'And you sent this piece of shit you were shagging to kill me?'

Helen could see the hurt in his eyes, and somewhere inside there was a pang of guilt, of sympathy for the scrawny, broken figure standing before her. But she blinked it away.

'No. It wasn't like that. We . . . we fell . . .'

Alan threw his head back. 'Aw, don't tell me you fell for this chancer. Christ almighty! Spare me the details. You sent him to kill me, Helen!' He paused, swallowed. 'Why would you do that?'

'I . . . I didn't. I didn't know what happened to you. I was looking for you. Everywhere. Police . . . everyone was searching for you.'

'Aye. But only you and Frankie knew the truth.'

'I didn't know. I . . . I only found out when he told me what he did,' she lied.

'Liar!' His voice strained as he tried to shout. 'You thought I was dead and you were taking everything I have.' He ran his hand over his face. 'But you know what? I survived. Frankie thought I was dead, but I wasn't.'

'What happened?'

'Don't give me your crap. You know what happened. You just can't believe I'm standing here. And I'll tell you what. I'm not going away.'

Helen felt her fingers tighten around the gun.

'What the fuck are you doing, Helen?' He took a step towards her. 'Put down the gun.'

'Don't come any closer,' Helen blurted. 'I'll shoot you. Don't come any closer. If you move, I'll kill you, Alan.'

'You already did, or so you thought. Put down the gun. You don't know what you're getting yourself into. You can't get away with this.'

She said nothing, still pointing the gun. She began to walk towards the door, giving Frankie's body a wide berth.

'Don't come near me, Alan. Stay where you are. You'll never see me again. Ever.'

She opened the door. She didn't look back. If she had, she'd have seen the tears in her husband's eyes.

CHAPTER ONE

It was only when the stench of the dead body eventually polluted the other flats that one of the residents called the police. A rotting corpse wouldn't normally bring Rosie Gilmour to the West End of Glasgow to investigate. Even the fact that it was the corpse of Frankie Mallon – a two-bob conman who would knife you just for fun – would barely get a few paragraphs in the *Post*. But it was the place where he had bled to death from gunshot wounds that interested her. What the hell was a lowlife thug like Mallon doing in the flat of Helen Lewis? she pondered, as she stood across the road watching the white-boiler-suited officers of Strathclyde Police forensic team go in and out of the three-storey sandstone building. Rosie had been up here before, six months ago, as she'd tried to get a handle on the disappearance of wealthy accountant Alan Lewis. He'd gone missing somewhere in Romania where he apparently owned a holiday home, and had some kind of business interest in the country's growing wine export industry. His disappearance had a whiff of mystery about it, but Rosie could find nothing to go on, and her editor, Mick McGuire, didn't want her to go traipsing all over Romania unless Lewis turned up dead somewhere. At the time, she'd come up to the luxury flats in Park Circus, hoping to speak to his wife Helen, but she was never home, and repeated attempts to contact her had been met with the curt reply that she was too upset and worried over her husband's disappearance to talk to the press. She said she had nothing to say. Rosie was always suspicious when people in the middle of a drama had nothing to say, and her gut instinct told her Helen was hiding something. But you can't keep badgering someone for information if you don't have anything to go on. The wife had given no interviews, or made any appeal for information on the whereabouts of her husband. She'd been silent. Too silent for Rosie's liking. And now this; pond life Frankie Mallon lying stiff in her flat, with no sign or sight of her in the past few days. Nobody saw her leave, and the last time a neighbour did see her at the flat was over a month ago, and she'd only stayed a couple of nights. Helen Lewis was a bit of a mystery herself. On paper, the forty-year-old wife of the wealthy accountant enjoyed the good life – cruises with her husband, dining in the best restaurants, exotic holidays in far-flung lands. But it hadn't always been like this. She'd come from nothing, from the notorious Gorbals council housing scheme in

Glasgow, but she'd quietly buried her past a very long time ago while she pursued the life of a rich wife. Fur coat and no knickers was how one of Rosie's cop pals described her.

Her mobile rang, and McGuire's name came up.

'Anything fresh?'

Rosie chortled. 'Are you kidding me? Mallon's been lying dead for days. There's absolutely nothing fresh. I can smell him from here.'

'You know what I mean. How much do we know about Mallon?'

'A couple of cop contacts tell me he's been a con artist all his life. He'd sell his granny, and probably has twice over. That kind of guy. He gets a bit of a using from time to time by the big boys, but they know they can't trust him as far as they can throw him. I'm told he has, or had, a violent streak in him.'

'So was he shagging Helen Lewis? Maybe she liked a bit of rough.'

'Who knows? But she *is* rough anyway. All the jewellery and the fast cars, it's all a front. She's a wee hairy from the Gorbals.'

'How did she land a guy like Lewis?'

'Don't know. But if you remember her pictures when Alan went missing, she's a looker – even now. They've been married around ten years, so she was probably even better-looking in her thirties.' Rosie gazed across at a stretcher with a black body bag on it being brought down the steps and placed into the waiting vehicle. 'Anyway, it's anyone's guess why he was in her flat. But that's him being taken to the morgue now.'

'Do you think she's shot him?'

'I don't know, Mick. I just don't know enough about her. But tell you what, Frankie Mallon turning up dead in her flat changes things. What the Christ was he doing there? I'm going to have a run at trying to find out what's going on.'

'We need to find Helen Lewis.'

'Oh, good thinking. That hadn't occurred to me,' she said, sarcastic.

'Don't give us your patter, Gilmour. I'll see you when you get back. I'm doing page one, four and five on this. I've got Declan ploughing through the cuts on Alan Lewis's disappearance, so we can revisit that. We'll see where we go with it.' He hung up.

Rosie stood for a few moments watching as a well-dressed older woman came out of the building with what looked like a couple of plain-clothes policemen, one of them carrying a clipboard. They stood on the pavement chatting before the woman turned and walked down the hill towards Woodlands Road. Rosie waited until the policemen went into their cars and drove off, then she went in the direction she could see the woman going in. She followed the woman as she stopped at the bottom of the road, then went into the Grassroots Café. Rosie walked past the window and saw her sitting in the corner, taking her coat off, and talking to one of the waitresses. It might be easier approaching her later at her flat, rather than in the café, risking a public knock-back. But she decided that the woman looked quite civilised, and if she was going to say no, then she didn't seem the type to make a scene. Rosie went in and sat at a table close to where the woman sat sipping a café latte. She made brief eye contact when she sat down. Rosie ordered a decaff latte from the waitress, and when she sat down, she took a sip, and turned around to the woman. Rosie's flat in St George's Mansions was right at the end of this building, and she wondered if the woman might have seen her before in the street. This side of the West End was either young professionals or older residents who'd lived there for years, and while it was a friendly, much-sought-after area, it still wasn't the kind of place where people told each other their life stories. To Rosie's surprise, it was the woman who spoke first.

'I saw you up in Park Circus, did I not? I thought I saw you from my window. Do you live around here? Terrible business that . . .' Her voice trailed off.

Rosie turned to face her. 'Yes. I live nearby,' she said. 'Guy found shot in one of the flats. Not what you'd normally see around this neck of the woods.'

'Exactly.' She sipped her coffee. 'But that's the problem these days. It used to be a good class of people who lived in these flats and this area, but now it's all that new money. People can buy anything, and the area's not as pleasant as it was.' Her accent was posh Glasgow West End.

'Did you know your neighbour – in the flats where the body was found?' Rosie ventured, thinking that if she was getting away with it so far she'd keep it simple, not admitting that she was a reporter.

The woman rolled her eyes to the ceiling.

'*Her*?' She sniffed. 'Nobody really knew *her*. Or him, for that matter. Not the dead man. I mean her husband. That bloke who went missing – the accountant. They've only been here about five years. They lived down below me, but I wouldn't say I knew them. Mind you, some of the fights . . .'

'What, fights between the woman and her husband?'

'Yes. Before he went missing. I reckon he just did a runner to get out of her way. She's a bit of a lowlife. Bit rough. She's got a mouth on her like a sewer.'

'Really?'

'Yes. And that bloody bloke she'd been knocking around with.'

'Who?'

'The guy they found in the flat. The one who got shot? Frankie, his name was, I think.'

'You've met him?' Rosie hoped she wasn't wide-eyed.

'Just on the stairs. He's only been on the scene for the last year. He was never in the house when the husband was there, as far as I know. But I used to see him picking her up outside, in a car, when her man was at work. She was obviously at it with him.'

Rosie tried to keep her face straight. Who needed a newspaper, when you could get a running commentary like this? God bless nosy neighbours.

'Really? That's interesting. It's Lewis, isn't it? Helen Lewis.'

'Yes. That's it.'

'They say he's been lying there for a few days – the dead guy.'

'I know. It was me who phoned. The last day or so, the stink in the place. It would have turned your stomach. I phoned the police this morning. Of course the last thing I expected was someone lying dead with a gunshot wound. It's like a bloody film.' She dabbed at her mouth with a napkin.

'I suppose the police were asking you to make statements and stuff.'

'Yes. But what can I say? I just told them everything I knew over the last few months. She was hardly ever there. I think they might have a house in Spain or somewhere. Or maybe up north. But she'd be there one day and not the next. She doesn't even work, to my knowledge, so I don't know where she goes.' She paused. 'But the last week or so, I heard her and him – the dead guy – shouting and bawling at each other. And one time I looked out of the window and saw them in the street – he grabbed her and she seemed to be trying to get away from him.'

Rosie nodded, enjoying how much the woman was

relishing the drama. She'd barely asked a question, and now she had enough for an exclusive splash. No doubt the woman would have told the police everything she'd relayed to her, but the cops wouldn't be putting this kind of stuff out to the press. So unless any other reporters were fortunate enough to get this woman on the doorstep, she'd have it all her own way. But Rosie's forever guilty conscience was beginning to niggle, and if she was going to blast this background information all over the front page tomorrow, she might at least come clean. She wouldn't be attributing her comments to anyone in particular, but the woman might recognise some of her words, and you never knew when you might need someone again. Best to be honest. At least she hoped so. Rosie took a breath.

'Look,' she glanced over her shoulder at the half-empty café, 'I would have said to you earlier, but I didn't get the chance. I'm actually a journalist.' She paused for a reaction.

'A journalist?' The woman's eyes narrowed. 'But I assumed you lived here.'

'I do. But I'm also a reporter. From the *Post*. My name is Rosie Gilmour.' Rosie stretched out her hand.

'Oh,' the woman said, taking her hand, but looking a little sheepish. 'And here's me running off at the mouth. I . . . I shouldn't have said so much. Look, I hope you're not going to quote me.'

'Of course not,' Rosie said. 'I don't even know your name.

The street and the building is big enough for me to attribute your comments to anyone, But I do think something stinks up there – and I don't just mean the dead body.' She leaned in conspiratorially, sussing that the woman would like this. She did.

'Yes. You and me both.' She nodded. 'But really. Don't be quoting me in the papers. I mean, I'm just trying to mind my own business. It's not my fault if I hear all that shouting and arguments. This place used to be so quiet. It's people like them who are ruining it for the decent folk.'

'Don't worry. I totally understand.'

As the woman stood up, Rosie drained her cup, left two pounds on the table and got up.

'Do you think we could have another chat some time? I'm going to be working on this story. And, actually, I already was investigating Alan Lewis's disappearance, but got nowhere. I'd like to get a bit more background, on both him and his wife.'

The woman shrugged, looked a little uncertain. 'Well. I don't know that much. Only what I see and hear. And that Alan bloke. He was away a lot too. I think he kept some dodgy company. I saw people picking him up in a car a few times. Foreign-looking people.'

'Really?'

The woman pulled on her coat. 'I have to go just now. I have a dental appointment down the road. So do you have a card or anything?'

'Yes.' Rosie fished out her card and handed it to her. 'If you're free, give me a call. Or, can I have your phone number? I don't even know your name.'

'Elizabeth,' she said. 'Elizabeth Baxter. I'm retired now. I was a dance teacher. I'm out quite a bit during the day.' She reeled off her number.

'Do you mind if I give you a call later today, and maybe we could have a coffee tomorrow? Or I could come to your flat?'

She frowned. 'No. Don't come to the flat. There might be police about. I mean, I've nothing to hide, and I've told them everything I know, but I don't want to be seen talking to a reporter.'

'No problem,' Rosie said.

They walked out of the café together, the woman tucking her red cashmere scarf into her coat.

'Thanks for your help, Elizabeth. I really appreciate you being so frank. I'll call you later.'

'I should keep my mouth shut sometimes.' She smiled. 'My husband used to say that to me, God rest him.'

She walked away, and Rosie watched as she disappeared around the corner and crossed the road towards the city centre.

CHAPTER TWO

Helen Lewis was still reeling from seeing Alan walking into her flat, so much so that she could barely string a coherent thought together. She was holed up in a hotel next to Waterloo Station. She must have been on automatic pilot all the way down on the train from Glasgow, because right now she could barely remember anything about the journey south, as though she'd done the whole thing in shock. In fact, shock didn't even cover it. No wonder. It's not every day your dead husband walks back into your flat, seconds after you've just pumped several bullets into the guy you'd hired to kill him. Jesus wept! How the fuck could that have happened? She cracked the seal on the third miniature of Jack Daniel's from the hotel minibar and poured in some Coke and ice.

She lay back on the bed, glancing at the blonde wig beside her, and felt her face smile a little.

The whole wig as a disguise idea had come to her as she'd

planned her getaway. And even if it did feel a bit ridiculous, it had to be done – for the moment anyway. It actually looked quite good on her, like the real thing, and enhanced her high cheekbones and full lips. She might make it a more permanent fixture. She swirled the ice in the glass and swallowed another mouthful, puffing on her cigarette and letting out a trail of smoke.

She'd planned this to the letter. Of course, all the plans were those she'd actually made a month ago, while she was still besotted with that arsehole Frankie Mallon. But they had to be binned once she realised, first, that he was giving her the heave-ho, and second, that he intended to hump her out of every crooked penny her husband had ever earned. What a bastard.

Frankie and her went back a long way, and were cut from the same cloth, even though they hadn't known each other back then. She was older than him, but she remembered him as a figure in the Gorbals where they grew up. He was a known kleptomaniac, who could tell a lie that would get you hanged. Shoplifting at twelve, and then a fraudster by the time he was fourteen, always managing to stay one step ahead of Borstal. Frankie brought a whole new meaning to the word 'chancer', and gangsters often used him as a front man in mortgage frauds because he was the kind of smiling, drop-dead gorgeous charmer who could walk into a building society, armed only with a fake ID and wage slips, and waltz back out with a hundred-grand mortgage in his back pocket.

But by the time Helen met Frankie again, she'd long since left the world of the Gorbals and its stinking poverty behind her. She'd bagged an accountant. Crooked or not, didn't matter a shite to her. Alan Lewis was loaded. And she liked loaded. She'd been conscious of her stunning beauty from an early age, and it had been her saving grace. It gave her power she wouldn't have had, coming from the kind of background she did, where she had no right to have the expectations she had. Once she met Alan Lewis, she knew she wouldn't have to do much to have him following her around like a lapdog, and in months he had proposed to her. This was the good life, travelling, best restaurants, meeting his posh public-schoolboy mates and their horrendously boring, naff wives. She didn't fit in, but she could do a great Oscar-winning performance if she needed to. She'd been royally pissed off when he bought a lavish villa in the countryside in Romania, instead of Marbella where Helen felt truly at home among the designer shops and teeming wealth of Puerto Banus. But Alan had assured her the property – set in the spectacular hills of Moldavia – was a huge investment, dirt cheap, because he'd got in on the ground floor after the country's dictator was ousted. Romania was the future, he'd declared, and soon everyone would want property and business there. And he threw even more money at investing into a wine-importing business. But Helen was bored rigid with the place after a few months of visits. She was in the middle of bloody nowhere. Alan was out doing business most of the time. Some of the guys he mixed with looked like they would tear your head off, so Helen always made herself scarce when they were around; she knew thugs when she saw them, and these guys were thugs. But money was pouring in from the wine business, and Alan was organising the accounts of his associates. Yeah, sure you are, she thought privately. Laundering their money, more like. He was even involved in doing the accounts of some UK charity who brought clothes and aid to Romanian orphans, for Christ's sake. Mother Fucking Teresa she wasn't, so she steered well clear of that as much as she could. But there were no flies on Helen either, because despite leaving school at sixteen, she'd excelled at bookkeeping. And it had come in handy when she began to unravel Alan's accounts one time when he was away on business and she had the place to herself. He'd come to trust her implicitly, and he had so much money, he didn't seem to miss the few grand she was moving around every couple of months. She couldn't believe how easy it was. She would have kept it that way, saved up for the inevitable rainy day when she got older and he got tired of her, trading her in for a younger version. But things changed. Alan came home from one trip to Bucharest and gave her a dose of gonorrhoea, no doubt picked up from one of the hookers who hung around the hotels. He begged her forgiveness and while she told him she accepted his apology, it was the final nail in his coffin. She'd always been planning to get out, from the moment she saw how filthy rich he was. It had only been a matter of time. But it was triggered by the chance meeting of an old Gorbals chancer.

When Frankie Mallon had turned up at a posh accountants' dinner in a Glasgow hotel, he took her breath away. At first she didn't recognise him, but had been stunned by the handsome smouldering hunk dressed in a black suit and shining like a new pin. He was introduced to her as a business associate who was a property developer, but as soon as he said his name she nearly dropped out of her chair. She managed not to show any reaction, and if Frankie recognised her, he didn't show it either. But later that evening, when Alan had gone to the bar to talk to another associate, Frankie had sidled over to her table, leaned in and whispered to her.

'You've done fucking well for yourself, for a wee tart from the Gorbals.'

'And you're still a chancing bastard, Frankie Mallon.'

He'd grinned and clinked champagne glasses with her, and it was as though there and then the seeds of the plot were sown.

Helen puffed up her pillow on the bed, recollecting how she and Frankie had planned Alan's murder to a T. It had started off as a quip by Frankie one night when they were both high on champagne and cocaine. But as soon as he said it, a light went off in her head and all sorts of pictures of a future without Alan suddenly appeared possible. If she was a widow, she could have his money, the trappings of his wealth, and live happily ever after with Frankie. She owed it to herself, she convinced herself over the few days that followed. Frankie hadn't mentioned it again, so it had been she who brought it up. She'd asked him about getting rid of Alan, what it would take. He said people could do that, no problem, the circles he moved in. Then they hatched the plot. He would do it himself. Had he ever killed before? she asked, but he wouldn't say. She suspected he had. The decision was made. It would have to be abroad, they decided – in Romania. And that was it.

When it was done, Frankie returned to Glasgow, and Helen arrived from Spain where she'd gone to cover her tracks so she could be nowhere near Romania when it happened. He'd told her how he did it. They'd gone out fishing, and had a few drinks. He'd hit Alan on the back of the head and pushed him over the side of the boat. He watched him disappear under the water and when he didn't resurface, Frankie started the engine of the boat and headed back to shore. He didn't look back. How had Alan got out of that? Helen thought now as she lay there. Frankie said his head injury knocked him clean out and blood was pumping from his head. How the Christ had he survived? Now she was thinking that Frankie had lied to her all along. Knowing him for the scheming bastard he was, she wouldn't have put it past him to double-cross her. Perhaps he even told Alan she'd sent him to murder him, and maybe Alan promised him more money to let him go. Anything was possible. But it didn't do him any good, because now he was lying stiff. Fuck him!

Helen picked up the remote control and switched it to the news, staring at the television, half listening. Then she heard the Scottish news leading with a story about the body of a man found in a Glasgow flat. She perked up, shook her head to clear it for a moment, put the glass down as she turned up the volume. Frankie Mallon's body had been found in the flat of a woman whose husband went missing in Romania several months ago. Police will not say if there is any connection, but are following up all lines of enquiry and appealing for anyone to come forward who was in the vicinity of the apartment and who may have seen someone enter or leave a few days ago . . . Helen watched as Frankie's body was stretchered out to a waiting hearse, the few cops and locals hanging around like ghouls. They were anxious to trace Helen Lewis, who lived at the flat, but who had not been seen for several days. They would not say if she was a suspect, but wanted to talk to her.

'Fat chance,' Helen muttered as she got off the bed, went into the bathroom and ran a bath.

She came back out and opened her small airline carry-on bag and pulled out one of her passports. She had three, and all of them were fake, courtesy of Frankie's mate. But the one she was using was in the name of Linda Barnet, and she'd be out of the country before the cops could get off their arses and do any more digging. She swigged the dregs of her drink, then took off her clothes and stood naked, gazing at herself in the mirror. Icy blue eyes stared back, and she narrowed her gaze. She felt nothing. She just wanted to get as far away from here as possible. By tomorrow morning she'd be in Paris, and from there she had a flight booked to the Cayman Islands, where she'd spirited away plenty of Alan's money in the past few months. For an accountant, he was so wrapped up in whatever shit he was in, he hadn't even noticed. She raised her glass and thought of what Frankie had said that first night she met him and fell for him.

'Not bad for a wee tart from the Gorbals.'

Helen stepped out of the old hotel with her suitcase on a trolley and into the chilly morning air, then walked across the concourse and into Waterloo Station, where she stood looking up at the board. Then she put her bags through Security on the other side with the rest of the waiting passengers. She had thirty minutes to her Eurostar train, so she crossed to the coffee shop and sat down, her eyes on the magazine she'd picked up in the hotel foyer. But she was not really reading it. She looked around at the business executives and travellers and the air of tranquillity around the station and congratulated herself that she'd decided not to fly. Security was so simple here. A man reading a newspaper came over and sat a distance away from her, but she caught him looking at her. He was dark, Slaviclooking or Balkan, and not unattractive. She glanced back at the magazine. Then the train was called and it was time to board. She made her way to the queue and on to the train. It was her first time and she was more than impressed by the luxury. She settled into her seat and closed her eyes. During the journey she got up only once to go to the toilet, noticing most of the other passengers asleep or reading, and she saw the same man who'd been opposite her in the café. He didn't look in her direction. When she finally got off and decided to have the evening in Paris, she thought she saw him again, but decided it must have been her imagination. Enough of the paranoia, she told herself.

CHAPTER THREE

'She can't have just vanished into thin air.' McGuire peered over the top of his reading glasses as he glanced from his screen to Rosie. 'What are the cops saying?'

'Not a lot.' Rosie sighed. 'I get the impression they took their eyes off the ball a bit when Alan Lewis went missing.'

Rosie missed her close friend and police detective contact Sergeant Don Elliot at times like this. Since his death in a car crash a few months ago, she was using other police contacts, but she didn't have the same rapport that she'd had with Don.

'What do you mean?'

'Well, one guy I talked to told me they didn't send any officers over to Romania when Lewis went missing, even to have a conversation on the ground with local cops in the area where his house was. Or to find out about his business there. They basically did bugger all. It probably wouldn't have achieved much, though, given that Romanian police don't exactly have the reputation for being efficient or cooperative.'

'But I suppose our cops could argue that people go missing all the time, and the fact that he went missing in Romania where he has a holiday home didn't automatically make it mysterious.'

'I know,' Rosie agreed. 'But to me, they should have been digging a bit deeper into his affairs. Lewis is not your average missing man. He's a wealthy accountant, and maybe there's no connection between his disappearance and his job at all, but what if he annoyed some of his clients? Maybe not all of his business was whiter than white. There are a lot of gangsters in Glasgow who could use someone clever to money-launder for them. We got no leads on that at the time, but the cops didn't seem to be busting a gut to solve his disappearance.'

'So what else does your man say?'

'He told me the fraud squad are getting their arses kicked by the bosses because Lewis wasn't on their radar. One or two accountants in Glasgow or Edinburgh are known to the fraud squad, and they try to keep tabs on them, but Lewis hadn't surfaced anywhere. So on the face of it, he was legit. Now they're scrambling around all over the place trying to find out more about him. A bit late.'

'We need to get more on him. But the suddenly vanishing wife with the dead body in her flat is the story. What the Christ is she all about? What do you know about her?'

'We've had a couple of calls, which I'm going to follow up. People who knew her years ago. She's from the Gorbals, and so was Frankie Mallon. But I'd have thought she'd have buried all the traces of her early life when she hit the big time, marrying a rich accountant.'

Rosie's gut feeling told her that Helen Lewis was up to her neck in not only her husband's disappearance, but Frankie Mallon's death.

'I bet she's bumped Mallon off,' the editor said. 'So it's up to you to find her before the cops do, Gilmour. Or at least get something so that we can point the finger at her being dodgy.'

'Aye, no pressure there then, Mick.' Rosie gave him a sarcastic smile but she knew that, wild and unfounded as the allegation was, McGuire was already seeing it all over his front page. 'Put it this way, we might be a wee bit away from *that* story.'

'Have the cops got nothing on her? No trace of her since she left? She must have booked into a hotel, bought petrol, got on a flight or something. You can't just vanish.'

'Maybe she didn't kill Mallon, and someone else was in the flat who did, then took her. Kidnapped her.'

McGuire sat back, and nodded his head slowly. 'I like the sound of that.'

'Me too, but it's fiction.'

McGuire stood up, and Rosie knew he was finished with theorising for the moment.

'Well. Let's see where we go. The splash was great today, that old busybody telling us chapter and verse. She'll be sitting up there like Miss Marple. But we need something more.'

Rosie headed for the door. 'Declan is going through the ring-ins, and we both might hit a few doors.'

'Good. Keep me posted.' He picked up his papers and sat back. 'Not that you will.'

CHAPTER FOUR

Rosie drove to the unit for the homeless up in Springburn on the north side of the city to meet the young woman who'd phoned the *Post* claiming to be Frankie Mallon's ex-girlfriend with the familiar sinking feeling she always got when she went to this area. The whole landscape changed so swiftly from the chic, trendy backdrop of the city centre with its designer shops, upmarket bars and restaurants, to this dismal, dank area that screamed of poverty and lack of hope. It was the same in so many housing schemes a stone's throw from the centre, but Rosie never got used to how it affected her mood. It took her back to her own early life growing up in the tenements where there was never enough of anything, and the odd glimpse of wealth when her mother took her to some big fancy department store only underlined their own poverty. She blinked away the images. Don't go there today, she told herself. It was the anniversary of her mother's death, and though years of telling herself to try to focus on the good things that she could pick from her early life, on a day like this, in a place like this, the blackness always crept in. 'Christ, Gilmour,' she murmured. 'Get on with it.' She consoled herself with the thought that her mother, wherever she was, would be smiling on her, glad that she had overcome so many of her early difficulties and turned her life into something good. And she had, really, considering her beginnings.

She slowed down as she approached the homeless unit – a grim red sandstone tenement building in the middle of a long road that led to the equally grim housing schemes of Possil on one side and Springburn on the other. She could see a woman with a young baby in a pushchair standing outside. She looked cold, shivering in the drizzle. The girl bent her head a little and raised a tentative hand in acknowledgement. This must be her, Rosie thought, glad that she didn't have to go into the homeless place to talk to her. She'd been there too many times, working and interviewing people, and no matter how good the carers made it look, it was what it was: a homeless unit. For people who had nothing. A refuge for the battered wives who had nowhere else to go, a bed and some heat for a young mother who might also be a drug addict. A place of refuge for victims, because at the end of the day they were all victims. However good it was for the people who were glad to take refuge there, for Rosie it was one of the most depressing places on earth. When you were in the unit for the homeless, it was staring you in the face that it had come to this. Whether through bad choices or desperation, you'd ended up at rock bottom, and the struggle from here was all uphill. Rosie slowed to a halt, and a brief glimpse at the skinny girl's hollow cheeks and frame told her that at some stage her bad choices had included heroin. But she wasn't here to judge.

'Hi,' Rosie said, smiling as she dropped the passenger-side window. 'Donna?'

'Aye. You Rosie?'

'Yep.' Rosie leaned across and opened the door. 'Come on in, I'll take you for a cup of tea.'

'Right, okay.' She began unhitching the baby strapped into the pushchair and folded it. 'Maybe better if I go in the back, with the wean.'

'Sure. We'll not be going far.'

Rosie watched in her rear-view mirror as she got in and propped the toddler down beside her. She caught the little one's eye and smiled. The kid looked up, little dark circles under her eyes.

'Who's this wee one?' Rosie asked brightly.

'Amy. She's two and a half.'

'Amy,' the little girl repeated softly.

Rosie turned her body around to face them.

'You're a lovely girl, Amy.'

Rosie smiled to the mum who drew back her lips a little and smiled back. But not with her eyes. The eyes were somewhere else.

'You all right to go to a café?'

'Café,' the kid repeated.

'Well, somebody wants to go anyway.' Rosie grinned in the rear-view mirror as she drove off.

'Aw, she's full of patter, this one. I think she's been here before.'

'Very cute,' Rosie said.

'I know. I adore her. Yeah. We'd love to go for a cup of tea.'

Rosie drove to the top of the city and pulled into a café she knew that was old-fashioned and off the beaten track, so wouldn't be full of the lunchtime sandwich run. They could find some place to talk.

Inside, she was glad the place was warm, because the girl didn't have enough clothes on for the icy rain outside. She rubbed her hands together as she sat the toddler up on a chair.

'You hungry?' Rosie asked. 'Why don't you have something to eat.' She reached her hand across the table and took the girl's ice-cold hand. 'Good to meet you, Donna.'

Donna glanced around the café at the few customers eating soup and pastries.

'I'm starving, actually. Would it be okay to have a fried-egg roll?' She looked at her little girl. 'She'll have some scrambled eggs on toast. And some milk.' She looked down at the table. 'We haven't had any breakfast.'

Rosie looked at both of them for a long moment and could see that despite their circumstances they were a little family unit. She watched Donna for any signs that she was on drugs right now and was glad that it looked like she wasn't.

'Sure. Whatever you like.' She waved the waitress across.

Rosie gave things a few seconds to settle as Donna pulled off Amy's jacket and settled her down, pushing the salt and pepper and napkins out of her reach. She put a little doll on the table and the kid started playing with it.

'So, Donna.' Rosie looked her in the eye. 'You and Frankie Mallon.' She glanced at the toddler. 'Is Amy his?'

She nodded, but said nothing, bit her lip. Rosie let the silence hang for a moment.

'Had you been split up for long?'

'Aye. Since she was four months old. In fact, we were never really together. Frankie never lived with me. He . . .' She paused. 'He just used me.'

'How did you meet him?'

'I knew him from years ago. We grew up in the Gorbals. But he's older than me. About nine years. He made a bit of money, no doubt conning people because that's all he ever was. And then I met him a couple of years ago by chance, in a bar.' She touched her face. 'I looked better than I do now. It was before . . .' Her voice trailed off. 'Before the drugs.'

Rosie's heart sank even further.

'Heroin?'

'Aye. Smoking it. But that was after the wean was born. I was depressed and then I couldn't cope, but I'm off it now.

On the methadone. Less and less meth every day. I'm going to get clean. Definitely. I'll soon be off it altogether. My social worker is dead pleased.'

Rosie had heard it all before. But this girl wasn't rattling like the junkies she had often encountered in bars or cafés or places where they'd pitched up with information, usually looking for some money.

'Good,' Rosie said. 'I hope so.' She glanced at Amy. 'For both of you.'

'Definitely.'

'So, what about Frankie? What can you tell me about him? And did you know Helen Lewis? She grew up in the Gorbals too.'

The food arrived and the waitress set down the tray. Rosie decided to wait until Donna had at least broken her fast before badgering her with questions.

'Tell you what, Donna. Get some food into you, and then we'll talk.'

Donna didn't answer, and was already one bite ahead in her fried-egg roll. Rosie sipped her tea and watched them as they ate. When they she had finished, Donna wiped her mouth and turned to Amy, making sure she finished her food.

'Okay,' she said. 'That Helen Lewis. She was a hooker, you know. When she was about fourteen. Did you know that?'

Rosie had to be careful how she reacted to this, because if she admitted she hadn't a clue about it, Donna might ask for some money and up the ante, though she hadn't shown any indication of that so far.

'I didn't think she'd always been whiter than white,' she said vaguely. 'She's got a past. We've had a couple of phone calls. How do you know about the teenage hooker stuff?'

'I just do. It was known in the scheme. She was beautiful, Helen. Some guy – don't know who he was; older; a pimp – put her on the game. I heard her ma was in on it too. I don't think Helen was long on it, but she definitely was a teenage prostitute. And after that, I think before she got married, she did a lot of coke, dealt in it, I was told. I think she also went to London one time for a while. But I'm not all that sure.'

'Who told you all this?'

'Frankie.'

'Frankie Mallon told you all this? Why?'

She shrugged. 'He just did. He was full of it one night – loads of nights actually. Coke and drink. He blabbed a lot.'

'It's not something that will be easy to prove.'

'True,' Donna conceded. 'You'll never prove it. But if you find her, you should ask her.'

'Oh, I will.' Rosie wished it was as easy as that. 'So what about Frankie and her? How come he's been found dead in her flat?'

Donna glanced over her shoulder, then leaned in across the table. 'He was blackmailing her.'

'Blackmailing her?'

'Aye.' She lowered her voice. 'And I'll tell you something else. Frankie killed her husband.' She nodded knowingly. 'He told me. She hired him to do it.'

Rosie looked her straight in the eyes. 'Frankie, a hitman?'

'I know. I didn't think he'd have the bottle to be a hitman. Christ! Maybe it was made easy, I don't know. But he did tell me that. He was off his tits on coke one night he came up here to see the wean and then spilled it all out. Maybe he was making it up. But why do that?'

This was crazy. McGuire would love it, but the lawyers would have a stroke.

'Why would Frankie tell you all that – you know, if he's killed someone? It's not very smart.'

'He was out of his nut on coke, I told you. I'm not making it up, Rosie. Whether it's true or not I don't know, but that's what he told me. He was shagging her. Probably just to con her out of her money. And he said he was blackmailing her. He told me when he got a big payoff from her, he would see me and the wean all right. I didn't believe it for a minute. He's an arsehole – was. Good riddance to him.' She patted Amy's head. 'We'll be better off without him.'

'I take it you haven't spoken to the police about this?'

She shook her head. 'No. I don't see the point. What good will it do?'

'It might help them nail Helen Lewis, if they ever manage to find her. If she did kill Frankie and arrange her husband's murder, she's a criminal.' Rosie thought for a moment. 'I'm not sure how much of what you tell me I can use in the newspaper. Maybe not even any of it. I'll have to talk to my editor.'

'You can't name me in anything in the paper. I don't know who Frankie was mixed up with. Maybe there are others involved. I don't want my name in the paper.'

'Don't worry, I don't have to. There are ways round it.'

Amy sat back and smiled as she finished the last of her food.

'She was hungry,' Rosie said.

'She's always hungry.' Donna smiled. 'She's like a wee Hoover with food.' She looked down at the table. 'My social is hardly enough to cover our dinners and stuff. I'm hoping to get a council flat soon. But there's never any money. I'm always skint.'

Rosie waited, knowing what was coming next.

'Look, Rosie, I didn't phone you so I could get money. Honestly. That's not my thing. I was just so shocked by what happened, before I knew where I was I was calling the paper. I'm not asking for money, but would the paper pay for any of the information I've told you?'

Rosie's heart always sank when people asked for money, but it was the way things were these days. Donna seemed genuine enough, and Rosie felt sorry for the hand she'd been dealt.

'Yeah. We can pay you something. Not right now though.

I'll speak to the editor and we'll sort something out. Maybe I'll meet you in a day or so and have some money for you. We don't pay a lot though.'

'Anything would be good. I should get word about the flat this week, so I'll want to move in and get settled.'

Rosie nodded. They got up to leave and as they left the café, Rosie went to open the car door.

'Nah.' Donna looked up at the grey sky. 'The rain's stopped. I think we'll go for a wee walk. I hate being in that place all day. It's depressing.'

Rosie looked at her. 'Okay. I'll give you a phone call and we can meet here if you want.'

'Thanks.' She buttoned her thin jacket. 'And remember, no name.'

Rosie drove off, watching in the rear-view mirror as they walked towards the shopping centre. As she did so she thought of Mags Gillick, the prostitute, who had helped her and paid for it with her life, throat slashed in a Glasgow side street. It would haunt her forever. But Donna was different. However frail and troubled she looked, there was hope somewhere. Her mobile rang and she didn't recognise the number.

'Is that Rosie?'

She didn't recognise the voice. 'Who's this?'

'Rosie. My name is Christy Larkin. You might remember me from the Glasgow refugee council a couple of years ago?'

Rosie brightened. Of course she remembered Christy. Everything about him at the time had spoken of hope, among the wrecked and damaged people he encountered while he worked processing refugees in Glasgow. He'd been planning to go travelling, give up the job.

'Of course I do, Christy. I thought you were travelling the world?'

'Yeah,' he said. 'I was. Did a bit of that, but ended up working for a charity.' There was a pause. 'Look, Rosie. That's what I wanted to talk to you about. I've seen your stories the last couple of days about that guy dead in Glasgow, and also the name of Alan Lewis – the accountant. Are you around sometime for a chat?'

Rosie wanted to say, Are you kidding me, I'll be there in a flash, but she held back.

'Sure. Any time, Christy. Anywhere. You have something on Lewis?'

'I don't want to talk on the phone. Can we meet?'

'Of course. Where and when? You tell me.'

'How about same place as the last time? It's handy for my train. About six tonight?'

'I'll be there. Great to hear from you, Christy.'

He hung up. Rosie's day had just got a whole lot brighter.

CHAPTER FIVE

From the café off the Champs-Elysées, Helen watched the buzz of the city, the tourists, lovers young and old, feeling like she was watching an old movie. Paris was one of her favourite places in the world, and she used to sit in cafés and bars around here with Alan, marvelling at how far she'd come in her life. She'd never dwelt on how she'd got there. Soul-searching wasn't her thing. It was here in Paris that Alan had proposed to her, and if she was really honest, that had been the best moment of her life. A moment of triumph, when she knew she was made. She'd known exactly what he would do when he whisked her away that weekend – that she was about to nail down her meal ticket for life. But deep down, the thought stirred her even now, because at the time she'd never felt more wanted, cherished: feelings she'd never experienced before. And even recollecting that made her feel surprisingly emotional. She'd been truly happy at that moment, despite her scheming. What had brought the lump to her throat that night was that somebody like Alan Lewis, a successful, wealthy accountant, would fall for her. He was from a different world, raised with all the privileges and opportunities people like Helen knew were not for them. Ever since she was old enough to work anything out as a kid, she'd sussed that there was a them and us. There always would be. And she was part of the bones-on-your-arse group who were never expected to amount to anything. She hated that. Growing up in the Gorbals in itself was a tag you would carry around with you all your life, like a stamp on your forehead. The name was synonymous with trouble, gangsters, hard men and hard women. You had to be tough to survive, and Helen learned very quickly in her life that she could be the toughest of them all.

Her alcoholic, prostitute mother used to bring men back to the house. But worse than that, she used to charge them for touching her little girl. That was the first betrayal, she recollected, and it burned her for life. It was probably there and then, Helen thought, whenever she actually looked back, that her life was decided. To survive that shit, you had to either get out as a youngster or fight like hell. And she wasn't getting out. She was on the streets at fourteen – her mother knew and even encouraged it. She was as bold as brass, gorgeous and mouthy, and the men loved that character as much as her shock of long black hair and her steely blue eyes. What they didn't see were her private tears when she was alone or if she ever took the time to reflect on her life. She was miserable, so miserable that one night, as she stood on the Jamaica Bridge, she thought of just throwing herself off. She was only sixteen. But she didn't. She decided there and then to survive. She stopped crying, and she told herself she *could* have everything she wanted. She would just take it.

She packed her bags and left the Gorbals on a rainy morning and boarded a bus for London. She had twenty quid in her purse, no idea what she was going to do, but only that she was getting the hell out of there. On her first night, she was robbed in the hostel she'd found, and it was only later the following afternoon that she was picked up by a woman who saw her outside in the street begging. Instinct told her the woman was a hooker, and when the woman offered to put her up for a few nights, her suspicions were confirmed. She was being pimped out by the end of the week. Older men mostly, business types in fine suits, smelling of cigars and expensive aftershave. But suddenly she found she wasn't miserable any more. She was making money. She sold coke to punters as a sideline. She had bundles of notes in a stash below her bed. Yes, Helen Lewis was doing all right for a wee tart from the Gorbals.

Helen finished the dregs of her drink and sat back, smoking a cigarette, as the memories came flooding back. She saw herself on the day she came back to Glasgow, by this time working not as a hooker but as a receptionist in one of the city's slicker hotels. That was where she met Alan Lewis, who was at some business function – he was bladdered and chatting her up. She was in his bed by midnight and living in his flat before the week was out. She quickly lost her rough Glasgow accent in London, and invented a different story than her real life, which Alan had swallowed happily, so wrapped up was he in their wild passion. Life was good. Things were happening. She could see that he was wealthy beyond anything she had ever dreamed of.

Even before he'd asked her to marry him, he was so swept away with her, and blinded, that he began to bring her into some of his business dealings. She'd told him that she'd had an aptitude for bookkeeping at school, and he'd been impressed at how quickly she picked things up. He asked her to help him, and one night, after too much wine, he showed her the sets of books he kept: the one that was completely separate from his business, and the one he showed the tax man. At first, she couldn't make head nor tail of it, as it was simply a lot of names and money and where he'd put it. The format wasn't as clear as the conventional way she'd been taught at school, but once she scrutinised the information, Helen's sharp brain began to get around it. Some were abroad, companies set up, businesses created and then later dissolved. Property had been bought and resold. She wasn't that daft. She could see money-laundering from a mile away. One or two of the clients she didn't recognise, but she later saw their names in the newspaper, linked to criminal activity. Alan was a crook with a clipped accent. But what the hell did she care? She was living the life. She began to help him; he trusted her more than anyone else. She moved his money around from one account to another, learning fast how to hide it away. She had her fast car, her gym membership, the trips to the Costa del Sol, the fancy house in Romania. She went along with all of it. She had no plans, nothing to scheme about at that time.

But that all changed when Frankie Mallon walked over to their table at a function and sat down. When Alan had introduced him to her, it was as though a spark caught fire: she fell for him. She should have steered clear. It began as sex – that's all it should ever have been. But Frankie told her that he really had feelings for her, that they could have a proper relationship. He coaxed her to leave Alan, take what she could. But she told him there would be so much more if she stuck around for a bit. She didn't want to risk having to work or go back to poverty. When she left, she would take it all. Poor Alan. He hadn't a clue. He was more involved in business and travelling abroad – and whatever other kicks he got from his foreign hookers.

That was when they hatched the plot. When Frankie came back from Romania, with the job done, he was triumphant at first. They planned how she would play the heartbroken wife when she reported her husband missing. She would bide her time, and then they would move to

Spain or some far-off land. The police search came and went, and it seemed they had got away with it. But then Frankie changed. One night he told her it was over. He had never wanted her in the first place. She was a means to an end. I want your money, he told her. All of it – it's what I do, he said, with a grin on his face that she could still see now. I love you, she told him. Tough shit, he'd said, for falling for my charm. She shuddered at her stupidity. Fuck him. He deserved what he got. Blackmailing her, threatening her, he'd already taken nine grand from her, and demanded everything else she had. Well, nobody fucked with Helen Lewis. If Frankie Mallon thought he was hard, he wasn't even in the same street as her.

Helen steeled herself with these thoughts when she felt lonely. She drove herself on, convincing herself that everything she did, she did to survive. It was dog eat dog. She knew no other way. She shook off the shoddy ghosts from her past. Her new life started here.

Helen walked back to her hotel slowly, enjoying the cool of the night and the beauty of Paris. The streets were busy, and even in the side street where she crossed to her hotel there were people in the pavement cafés. She toyed with the idea of having one for the road, but decided to call it a night. She had a flight to Grand Cayman tomorrow morning from Charles de Gaulle airport, and she wanted to be fresh for the journey. As she passed the café she thought she saw a man look at her, and for a moment thought she recognised him. But she couldn't have. She didn't know anyone here. It was only when she was in the lobby of her hotel and climbing the stairs to the first floor that she suddenly remembered the face. He was the guy from the café in London, the one she'd also seen on the Eurostar. Coincidence, she told herself. Was he following her? Christ! She was being paranoid. She opened the hotel bedroom door, glanced back in the darkened corridor, and quickly went inside and locked the door.

She prepared her case for the morning, took off her make-up and was about to get undressed when she heard footsteps in the corridor. Then they stopped. Outside her door. She held her breath. Christ, for a tough bird, she was jumpy tonight. It was all part of the stress of the last couple of days. She needed to get away. She listened at the door again, and heard the footsteps move on, fade. She stood at the window smoking a cigarette. Then a few moments later, under the lamp post, she saw the man from the restaurant looking up.

CHAPTER SIX

Rosie had to take a closer look when the tall young man came through the swing doors of the bar and glanced around. At first she didn't recognise Christy Larkin without his glasses, and his hair was closely cropped, instead of the mid-length, foppish style it had had when she met him the last time. He spotted her from across the room and came striding towards her with a big smile.

'Hi, Rosie. Good to see you.'

She stood up, and shook his hand, then to her surprise, he leaned in for a bit of a hug. She put her arms around him in the kind of friendly hug you would give to your favourite cousin. When they parted, he studied her face.

'I saw that story about the serial killer, and the other one, earlier, when you were in Pakistan. You've been up to the capers, Rosie. I'm glad you're still alive.' He put his hand up for a high five. 'But big respect for your work. You sail a bit close to the wind.'

Rosie smiled. She liked this boy. He was like a breath of fresh air the way he breezed in, and his face spoke of youth, and the enthusiasm of a bright person with his whole life in front of him.

'It's all good fun really,' she joked. 'Sit down, I'll buy you a drink and you can tell me about your travels.'

When she returned from the bar with a pint of Guinness for Christy and a glass of red wine for herself, she was prepared for some small talk. She didn't want to delve straight in and ask why he wanted to talk to her.

'So where have you been since I last saw you? It's nearly two years, isn't it?'

'Yeah. Just about. That's what I wanted to talk to you about, Rosie.' He took a long drink of his pint. 'Actually, I felt like phoning you a few months ago, but I was waiting to get a bit more information.'

'I'm intrigued,' Rosie said. 'Where did you get to?'

'I was a lot of places. Did that gap year thing, Australia, Indonesia and stuff, then I came back and went to France for a bit. But one of my pals I met on my travels had worked as an aid worker, you know, an NGO, with some charity in Romania, and he was telling me about it.' He looked at Rosie. 'I think I'm a bit like you in some ways, I get a feeling for things like that. You know, with the refugees and stuff, up at the council? The way you had an instinct. I always feel really touched by refugees and people like that.' He paused, stretched his long legs out. 'Anyway, my mate, who's

English, said it was great working over there, that it was tough, but you really thought you were doing something good, because you were on the ground in these orphanages. So I decided to give it a try. Kind of get it out of my system.'

Rosie looked at him, full of admiration. So many lads his age would be thinking only of having fun and making their way in the world. She'd always admired aid workers wherever she met them, because they put themselves in all sorts of difficult circumstances. But she also recalled that the trouble with them was that they found it almost impossible to fit into normal life back home. Once you'd seen the grim reality of the refugee camps – the sickness and death – and lived with the people and witnessed their suffering, the kind of things that pissed people off back home just seemed so trite that most of the aid workers she'd encountered went back time and again, often from one trouble spot to another. It was as though they couldn't fit back in to normal life at home. A bit like her, she'd supposed, only more so.

'Good for you, Christy. You're a better man than me,' she joked. 'I've done more than my share of refugee camps over the years, but I was only in and out. I always admired the guys like you who stayed on and did the nitty-gritty day in, day out. So how was it? I was there myself a few years ago, in these Romanian orphanages. It's awful, toddlers hanging onto you, desperate for a hug, any kind of touch at all. Heartbreaking.'

Rosie didn't want to say she'd always felt guilty the way they moved in and out of these kids' lives, tormenting herself that they probably believed that this stranger in their midst was actually going to make their lives better. But all she was doing was highlighting their plight. Visiting the orphanages after the fall of the dictator, Nicolae Ceau-şescu, had been one of the most difficult jobs she'd ever done, and their little faces had stayed with her for years.

'Yeah, it's tough. I think probably when you go in temporarily, like you or other media, or even doctors from abroad and stuff, you get really affected by it. But when you're working there on a daily basis, you're too busy to get upset by it. You just do the stuff you have to get through, and there's shedloads of work, to be honest.'

'How long did you stay? When did you get back?'

'I've been back six weeks now. I was there for nearly eighteen months, but I felt it was time to move on. But I saw some horrible sights, and I was told about other things that I can't prove. But there's bad stuff going on. So that's why you came into my mind.'

Rosie leaned across closer to him. 'I'm intrigued, Christy. The country was a mess when I was there, ripe for the corruption that followed. Gangsters running the show now.'

'Exactly. And exploitation.' He shook his head. 'Of the kids. That's what I want to talk to you about. But it's going to be really hard to get to grips with.'

'Well, let's hear it. Everything is hard at the beginning,

but if there's a way to do it, then I'll find it.' She looked at him. 'What's the Alan Lewis connection? I know he had business interests there. A vineyard and wine importing.'

'Yeah. That's right. But that's not the full story. I was away from the UK when he disappeared, and other than seeing something on the TV that a Brit had disappeared, I didn't see much news or bother with it over in Bucharest as I was so busy all the time. But it's only when I came back and I heard the news the other day there about his wife being missing, and then your piece on the background, that I thought, this stinks.'

'I couldn't agree more.'

'But tell you what. As soon as I saw his name in your story, I remembered that I recognised it. From Bucharest.'

'How come?'

'I saw some papers while I was over there, someone showed me them one time, on kids that were being adopted.' He made inverted commas with his hands as he said 'adopted'. 'But in fact they weren't being adopted, they were being sold. It was around that time I saw his name on a document I was shown in relation to a charity, and some other known figures – Romanian and also Russian. I even thought of getting in touch with you at the time, because I had suspicions then. But I had nothing much to go on apart from what someone was telling me and I didn't want to waste your time. Look, Rosie, I might sound crazy at the moment, and this could be a wild allegation, but I think Alan Lewis and this charity, or someone putting themselves across as a charity, was involved with gangsters over there, and they were selling children. Maybe they still are.'

'Christ almighty! Seriously?'

'That's what it looks like to me. Proving it is a different matter.'

'Jesus! Maybe there's more to his disappearance in Romania than we thought.' She couldn't mention what she'd been told in her conversation with Donna – that Helen Lewis had sent Frankie Mallon to kill him. But if he was linked to selling orphans, this was a much bigger story than a greedy wife wanting rid of a boring husband.

'I think there *is* more to it,' Christy said. 'He could have been bumped off, or something. I've no idea about anything like that. But all I have on him is this . . .'

He reached into his inside pocket and brought out a sheet of A4 paper. He slid it across the table to Rosie and she strained her eyes in the half-light. It looked like a whole list of payments and names of people and a charity, Hands Across Europe. Alan Lewis's name was on their list of trustees as Director of Accounts.

'I've heard of this Hands Across Europe charity. I'm sure they have some kind of base in Scotland as well as down south. I wish you'd called me, Christy. You should never worry about wasting my time with a tip-off like that. Even if it turned out to be way off the mark, I'd rather hear than not hear.'

He nodded. 'Okay. I'll remember the next time.'

She looked up from the sheet of paper. 'Where did you get this, Christy?' She put a hand up. 'I don't mean you to name names, but I mean, I have to have an idea of where it came from – to make sure it's authentic. You understand?'

He nodded confidently. 'Sure. Obviously I can't say who gave me it, but it came from people involved in the orphanages and who are in the know. I can vouch for them, they're trustworthy people. They came across it, and, well, let's just say they shouldn't have.' He grimaced. 'And they shouldn't have copied it and given it to me. But things are going on there that need to be looked at. And by the look of this, Alan Lewis's name is all over it.'

Rosie scanned the document again.

'I remember the charity used to go over with aid packages and clothes. Some guy called Robert Morgan is the big boss, but I don't know anything about him. Convoys of trucks. Loads of other charities did the same,' she said.

'I know,' Christy replied. 'I even know the charity myself, and they did good work. But there were things going on over there that probably people here had no idea about.'

'You mean actually selling orphans?'

He nodded his head slowly. 'And not just orphans, Rosie.' He lowered his voice to a whisper. 'I've heard of instances where a mother's child was taken from her at birth in the hospital. She'd be told it had died, and didn't even see it in some cases. The babies were taken and sold.'

'Jesus wept! Sold to who?'

'Wealthy couples. Americans, Russians. The baby would be taken from the mother, and the other organisations then took over. I don't know much about that. But my friend – a Romanian girl I went out with for a few months – told me about it. She was working for one of the aid agencies out there and she told me this had happened. She told me she even knew one of the mothers whose baby was taken. The mother was told it was dead, but she never actually saw it.'

'That's unbelievable! Absolutely awful! Do you think the people who run the charity know about it?' Rosie sighed. 'How the hell do I get to grips with this? I really want to get this story, Christy. More than anything.'

He puffed out a sigh. 'I do too, Rosie. Maybe I can help a bit. I can ask my ex-girlfriend if she can help. We're still friends, just not really together. I think we both knew it wouldn't last, but I really like her, and we get on well. So she might see what she can do, make a few discreet enquiries. But if you were really going to look at it, I think you'd have to go there. I don't know if any of the bosses know about it, but if they don't you'd want to ask why.'

'That won't be a problem.' Rosie knew she could convince McGuire, and she was already thinking of her Bosnian friend Adrian as back-up, and Matt, the *Post*'s photographer, to work with her.

'Okay. You can let me know if you do plan to go, and I can try to arrange things.'

Rosie looked at him. Having someone on the ground over there would be a huge bonus rather than going in blind to some ex-girlfriend whom she didn't know if she could trust completely.

'Do you think your ex-girlfriend will help us? It would probably be better if you were there, but I don't think my editor would wear that, and I wouldn't want to put you in any danger.'

He took a long drink of his pint. 'I understand. I don't think I'd be ready for getting involved in the kind of dust-ups you do anyway, Rosie. But I'll help you every way I can, and I think my ex-girlfriend will too. I think she would like you. She's got the same kind of beliefs you have, if you know what I mean.'

Rosie took it as a compliment, but said nothing. She finished her wine and stood up.

'Okay, Christy. If you can talk to your friend on the phone tonight, see how it goes, I'd be looking to get over there as soon as possible – in the next twenty-four hours.'

'Really? As fast as that?'

'Yep. That's how I do business. I don't hang around.'

He stood up, gave her a hug, and they walked out of the bar together.

CHAPTER SEVEN

McGuire was looking at Rosie, his eyes narrowed in concentration, as she reeled off the details of her meeting with Donna, and also with Christy. BABIES FOR SALE was all he could see. Rosie could read his mind. The story was growing, but they both knew they were miles away from having anything they could put in the newspaper.

'You know, Gilmour, this Romanian babies for sale puts everything else in the shade. A story like that could go worldwide. Groundbreaking. Given what we know, that Romania has been overrun by gangsters since that bastard Ceaușescu was executed, I don't suppose we should be surprised that the fuckers are making money out of orphans. But all those images of children when the Romanian orphanages scandal first broke years ago, they still tear people apart.'

'I know. I saw them, Mick. They still tear *me* apart,' Rosie said, glad he was as hooked as she was. 'And I agree.

We need to get into this. And now that we know Alan Lewis and this charity may be linked to the whole thing, it's a belter.'

McGuire bit the inside of his jaw. 'I'd love to get both of the stories and link it all up, but if I'm putting resources into this, then I want to get to the heart of the baby trade.' He put his hand up as though to silence Rosie. 'And before you ask, you don't even have to talk me into letting you go there.'

'Well that's a first.'

'I want this story. I want to put flesh on it. Get me a mum whose baby was stolen – that kind of stuff. I know it won't be easy, but I want us all over this – boots and saddles. Just get me a costing. How do you want to play it?'

Rosie had thought this through in bed most of last night, before she'd dropped into a fevered sleep full of wailing Romanian orphans being dragged from their stinking cots by thugs, and abandoned on freezing hillsides. And when she woke this morning, TJ, her friend and on/off lover, who'd stayed over after dinner, had told her she was ranting in her sleep – again.

She knew McGuire would love the story, but she hadn't expected him to be so eager to throw everything at it. She wanted the story even more than him but, if she was honest with herself, now that it was on, part of her didn't know if she was quite ready to be propelled into the midst of another danger zone. It was only a few months since she'd escaped the psycho serial killer who'd left her to drown in

a pit of rats and rotting body parts, and she had been trying to deal with the consequent trauma. She'd even had a
couple of curries with the friendly psychologist she'd interviewed while investigating the killer, and he was gently
counselling her. But even the four-week break she'd had in
the south of Spain, sunning herself, hadn't been as relax-
ing as she needed. The truth was, she hadn't really relaxed
deeply since it happened. Her worry in the immediate
aftermath of the anxiety attacks was that the fear was
going to be permanent. But the psychologist assured her it
wouldn't be, that she would learn to deal with the panic
attacks and trivialise them when they happened. And she
did, but there was always the dread that she could fall off
the edge lurking in the background. Fortunately, most of
the time, her anxieties came out in her nightmares, so she
could keep a lid on them. But she found that these days she
looked over her shoulder more, examined her mail deliver-
ies with more care before she opened them, took time to
lock doors of her flat four and five times over. She knew
she was getting better, and it would pass, but throwing
herself into the zone again so soon would be challenging.
Not that she was going to admit any of this to McGuire.

'I was thinking to involve big Adrian. Just for a bit of
extra muscle. God knows, we've been grateful for him on
enough of our trips. He's not a million miles away from the
area, and I think he'd be good to have with us. I'd want to
take Matt, since we've always had such great holidays

together in the arseholes of the empire – as he keeps saying,' she joked.

'This is my main worry, Rosie. Sending you over there into something we have very little knowledge of, and nobody really on the ground.'

'We have Christy Larkin's girlfriend. So, she'll be there and speaks the language as well as great English. She knows the orphanages and the geography. But we'll need plenty of cash with us, Mick. Money talks all over Romania, and I remember last time I was there the corruption was everywhere: from the border cops to the people who worked in the orphanages. Everything can be bought. That's why we probably shouldn't be surprised they're selling orphans. They've got plenty of them to sell.'

McGuire stood up. 'Right. Okay. Get me a costing, and let me get my head around it. See when you want to go and get Marion to organise it.' He picked up his papers from the desk. 'I'm going into conference now. What kind of story can we write on the bird Donna's claims? I know they're a bit outlandish without proof, but we need something, not attributable to her, about background on Helen Lewis.'

'She might sue us if we say she was a teenage hooker who went on to have her husband bumped off.'

McGuire smiled. 'Aye. You might want to tone that down. But work out something to write. I want to drip-feed this story. And by the time the cops track Helen Lewis down, a story in the *Post* will be the least of her worries. Get some words over to me and I'll get the lawyers to have a look.'

As she got into her car, Rosie's mobile rang and she put the phone to her ear as she pushed the key into the ignition.

'Christy. Howsit going?'

'Good, Rosie. I wanted to let you know that I talked to my ex today, and she's keen to help if she can. She's a bit wary, but she'll meet you if you go over.'

'Brilliant. I'll call you in the morning to let you know. We'll be going over in the next day or so, so it would be great to meet her in Bucharest.'

'No worries. I'll sort it.'

He hung up and Rosie smiled a little at his enthusiasm. She might even make a reporter out of him yet.

CHAPTER EIGHT

Helen woke up with the same niggling unease that had kept her from sleeping. It wasn't a guilty conscience, or any of that crap. She'd long since convinced herself that she deserved everything she had, everything she took. No. She didn't feel guilty at all. Not about shooting the scheming, blackmailing bastard Frankie Mallon, who would have left her with nothing. And not about organising her husband's murder. He was only ever a means to an end, a convenient meal ticket until she could have plenty of money to stand on her own two feet. Though the fact that Alan had come back from the dead was driving her crazy, as much with curiosity as with the cold dread that he could find a way to claw back all the money she'd moved out of his accounts. It was six months since his disappearance. For him to survive with the head injury, he must have got out of the water fairly quickly, got to the shore, and found some kind of help. So he'd been around for months, yet hadn't made any attempt to look at his bank accounts – as far as she knew. She wrestled with the thought. He couldn't have. If he had, he'd have noticed they were all closed, officially by his own signature, forged by her own hand. So what had he been doing for these past months, and why wait until now to get in touch? He was an accountant, for Christ's sake. He must have known straight away that she'd taken his money. She was baffled, and anxious. She looked at her watch. It was time to go. She checked her image in the mirror, the blonde wig and her dark glasses, full of Parisian chic. She zipped up the suitcase, then she eased her way out of the bedroom, wheeling her case along the corridor towards the lift. When the lift doors opened, she suspiciously eyed the two well-dressed men already in it. They looked flatly at her, and for a second she almost didn't get in. Get a grip, she told herself, and struggled in with her cases. The lobby was bustling with guests checking out and arriving, and she swiftly perused the area, in case the man from last night was lurking. He wasn't. She cursed herself for beginning to feel like the fugitive she was. Calm down, she told herself. Nobody is hunting for you. Nobody has a clue who you are or where you are going. Outside, the taxis were busy, but one with a light on was sitting just at the edge of the lanes of traffic. She waved to it, and was relieved when it started towards her. She really wanted out of here. The driver got out of his car, took her bags and placed them in the boot. Then he opened the door for her and she got in the back. She breathed a sigh of relief.

'*L'aéroport Charles de Gaulle, s'il vous plaît,*' Helen said in her best French.

He didn't reply as he put the car in gear and drove off. She sat back, thankful, and gazed out of the window. Then she heard the voice. For a moment, she thought it was in her head.

'Hello, Helen . . . or Linda . . . or whoever you are this day.'

It was like a gun going off in her head, and she turned quickly to see a man in the front passenger seat turned and facing her, an icy smirk on his sallow face. It was him. The man from last night, the man from the Eurostar. How the Christ had he got in here? How could she have missed him when she got into the back seat? Panic coursed through her, and her head swam.

'What the fuck!' She glanced from the man to the back of the driver's head. 'What the fuck's going on?'

She caught the driver's deadpan expression in the rear-view mirror as he kept driving.

'What is this? Who the fuck are you?'

Automatically, her hand went to the door handle and she pulled it. She would throw herself out before they hit the motorway. Fuck! It was locked. She threw herself across the back and tried the other one. Locked.

'Stop!' she commanded. 'Stop! Let me out of here.'

She tried to roll down the window, but it too was locked. She was trapped. The man in the passenger seat kept his gaze on her.

'What are you doing? Who are you? You're kidnapping me? Stop the car now!'

'Why don't you call the police?' the man said, toying with her in a voiced laced with Eastern European tones. 'I'm sure they'd love to hear from you.' He turned away and faced the front.

She could hear her heartbeat. She slumped back, choking with fear. She wanted to ask where they were taking her, but she was too scared. In her gut, she knew that wherever they were taking her, she wasn't coming back. The game was up.

Helen came to in the pitch black, with the chill of a cold metal floor on her back. She blinked, but could see nothing. She moved her body a little and there was no pain, so she hadn't been beaten. Her hands and feet weren't tied, and she could move freely. Whatever she was in was being transported. It was noisy and bumpy. She put her hand behind her back and felt cold ridged steel. She was in some kind of container. What the fuck! Where were they taking her? Even if she could see the walls, there was no point in crying out or banging on them. There was nobody to hear. Whoever had taken her was in the truck cab in front. She sat up, and her head throbbed. She had a blurred recollection of being dragged out of the taxi in a darkened multistorey car park by some fat bloke in a leather jacket. She could hear voices, Slavic or Eastern European. Then a hand from behind had covered her mouth, and she felt a needle in her neck. That was the last thing she remembered. She hadn't a clue how long she'd been out. Sick with fear, she crawled around on her hands and knees until she touched the wall of the container. She pulled herself into a sitting position with her back against the wall, and tried to take deep breaths to relax and think straight. She brushed her fingertip against the pinprick in her neck, which was a little tender, and wondered how long she'd been travelling. If she'd been out for a while she could be anywhere in the middle of Europe. There were no English voices among the men who had snatched her, so she had to assume she was being taken somewhere in Eastern Europe. But she couldn't understand why. For sure, Alan had been involved with some Eastern Europeans in this Romanian wine-importing business, where he was moving a lot of money. She remembered seeing the names of several companies in the secret ledger he kept, which she had hidden in her flat, but she had no idea what they were. When she'd quizzed Alan about them as she was helping him with his administration he'd told her they were some small companies he'd put some capital into because he wanted to be in on the ground floor in a part of Europe that was growing fast now that the Communist regime was dead and buried. One of the companies was also connected to a UK charity whose accounts he did. Hands Across Europe or something, she thought they were called. She remembered the names of the charity bosses from the UK and Romania, both of whom she had met when they were over in Bucharest dealing with charity business. Helen had moved the money from all the small companies apart from the charity into another private account in the name of a company she had set up in Jersey and the Cayman Islands, and she was the only signatory. She had a cold feeling in the pit of her stomach that she'd been rumbled, and now these companies wanted their money back.

The truck seemed to be slowing down and she could sense from the movement and trying to keep her balance that it seemed to be turning a corner. Then a few moments later, it came to a halt, and there was the shuddering and hissing of brakes. She sat, holding her breath. There was no sound outside at first, then she heard muffled voices and what seemed like a couple of car doors being closed. Locks and heavy metal bolts were being hit with something, then one of the doors was dragged open. Helen could feel her whole body trembling, her eyes wide, ready to adjust to the changing light. But there wasn't much difference. She felt the icy blast from outside, but it was still dark. Somewhere in the distance there was a light, maybe the motorway or whatever road they'd just left. A foreign voice barked instructions and she heard someone scrambling on to the container. A torch was shone in her face and she blinked, her eyes smarting in the harsh light. She was pulled roughly to her feet, and as she opened her mouth to say something she was dragged to the door. Outside she could see another man on the ground, and as the man behind her pushed her down the step from the container, he caught her. She looked around, anxious to see where she was. Then, from the darkness, a tall figure in a black coat stepped forward, but he wasn't close enough for her to see.

'Well, well, Helen. You haven't half fucked things up.'

She knew the voice immediately. Ricky Thomson. Ricky fucking Thomson. One of the hardest men in Glasgow. She'd seen him with Alan at a couple of dinners and had kept out of his way because he knew her history better than anyone. Alan had done some work for him in the past – laundering his money, no doubt – and just this second she remembered where else she had seen his name. Fuck! When she'd seen the name Richard Thomson, she hadn't twigged. It was on the list of directors in one of the companies Alan had set up in Romania, and where most of the money had been stashed. Jesus Christ!

'Where am I?'

There was a pause.

'Well. You're not in the fucking Cayman Islands.'

CHAPTER NINE

Rosie could feel that familiar little punch of adrenalin she got when she was on a big story abroad. As she'd been packing her bag and saying goodbye to TJ in the last twenty-four hours, she'd been more nervous than normal, and had to dig in to prepare herself mentally for the job. She hadn't had to do that in a long time, but this was her first out-of-town investigation since her near-fatal brush with serial killer Thomas Boag. So it was a test she couldn't afford to fail. Getting back firmly in the saddle was how to banish the anxiety, she told herself, and she knew she was right. The butterflies in her stomach would go once she had more pressing business to occupy her mind. At least that's what she hoped as she stepped out of the glass swing doors at the Intercontinental Hotel in Bucharest into the chilly, grey afternoon. She watched the taxis come and go, her eyes peering, awaiting Adrian's arrival. In seconds, the gypsy kids were around her like flies, smiling, 'Hello, beautiful lady', grimy hands out, begging for money.

'Flattery will get you nowhere, guys,' Rosie chirped, placing her back firmly against the hotel wall as the doorman shooed the children away.

She knew from her last trip here, some six years earlier, that while two of the little charmers were smiling hopefully at her one of their mates was trying to dip into her back pocket. It was pointless giving them anything as it would only attract droves the next time she came out. But she still felt heartless as they stepped back a few yards, leaving one little boy sitting on the wall, staring up at her with big, doleful eyes. Rosie turned away from him, because she knew she had to. She'd learned that you had to do that a lot in Romania. She was glad when the taxi drew up, and she caught a glimpse of Adrian in the front seat. She waved, smiling, and he nodded back, the way he did, something close to a smile breaking over his face. He got out of the car and handed the driver some cash, then he slung his rucksack over his shoulder and walked towards her.

'Rosie.' He held out his arms. 'Good to see you.'

Rosie took his hands, and for a second hesitated, not quite sure whether to embrace him. He looked at her for a moment, and then eased her into his arms.

'How are you, my friend?'

'Great, Adrian. I'm so glad you said you would come. I wasn't sure if you'd want to.'

He puffed an exaggerated surprise. 'But of course, Rosie. I

will always be here for you. I told you many times. When you need me, for anything, I will be there.' He looked beyond her at the children swarming around. 'And this investigation you tell me about on the phone. It makes me sick. I want to help you find these people and make your story.'

'Thanks. That's good to hear.'

As they walked together into the hotel, he touched her shoulder.

'But how are you really? I didn't hear from you, except only one phone call after that last time, with that bastard Boag. You are still troubled by this?'

Rosie tried to look nonchalant. 'A little. But it's getting better.'

Adrian nodded. 'I could see it. From the taxi, I spotted you before you saw me. You looked far away.'

He really did see her so well, Rosie thought, and met his eyes. 'Yes. I suppose. But I've been here before, you know, during the Romanian orphanages scandal a few years ago. So some thoughts come back to me of how that was.' She changed the subject. 'Go on. Get yourself checked in. Then we'll go out for some coffee and lunch. I wanted to meet you first on my own, but Matt's here, and we're going to meet this young woman here in the old city. Hopefully, she'll be our person on the ground.'

'Good.'

Adrian went towards the reception.

*

An hour later, as they strolled along the cobblestones of the old city's narrow streets, Rosie was mesmerised at the change in the place in just a few short years. When she'd last been here, a few months after the dictator Ceauşescu and his wife were shot by a firing squad as the city descended into mayhem, Bucharest was a hotbed of unrest, and every day she'd stood on the streets as people marched against poverty and for workers' rights. You would be hard pushed to find a coffee shop with anything other than a couple of tables, because there would be barely any coffee or drinks in stock to serve. The shops were empty. Now, the bustling street was lined with pavement cafés with colourful umbrellas and trendy wooden tables and chairs where locals sat sipping their drinks. It could have been any modern European city, and in the wider streets away from the old town it was every bit as stunning as Paris. She suspected that a few hours' drive from here there would be the same square blocks of flats from the old Communist regime where people eked out an existence in poverty, but this was perfect, and though it was chilly to sit outside, they were well wrapped up.

As they got to the café where they'd arranged to meet Ariana, Christy's ex-girlfriend, they stopped and looked around, as many of the tables were occupied. A young woman stood up, caught Rosie's eye, and tentatively made her way towards them.

'Rosie?'

'Yes,' Rosie replied. 'Ariana?'

The girl in tight jeans and a leather jacket looked barely out of her teens. But Christy had told Rosie she was twenty-four. She smiled, liquid brown eyes lighting up beneath a lush fringe of dark hair. She looked like a model who'd been done up for the tousled casual look.

'Yes. I'm Ariana. I am pleased to see you.' She stretched out her hand.

'Great. How do you do?' Rosie said, her handshake firm. 'I really appreciate you agreeing to see us. Christy spoke very highly of you.'

Ariana smiled a little shyly. 'He is a good boy, Christy. I like him a lot.'

She beckoned them to sit at her table, pulling over another couple of chairs for Adrian and Matt. Rosie did the introductions, and they ordered coffee.

'I've been in Romania before,' Rosie said to her, 'and I know how difficult it is to work without someone local translating and preparing the ground. So it's great to be met by someone who knows the landscape.'

'Christy told me you had been here. He said you do a lot of good work for your newspapers on exposing the bad people. I hope I can help you.'

'I hope so too,' Rosie said as steaming mugs of coffee arrived. 'And your English is much better than my Romanian.'

Ariana smiled and lit a cigarette, telling them that the café served terrific home-cooked food, but it was best to eat inside as it was getting chilly. For the moment, Rosie was glad they could just be here and take in the atmosphere of the city. Or perhaps it was the protective presence of Adrian at her side that was making her happy. Once the coffees were drunk, they ordered wine and beers, and some small talk followed about the work Ariana did in orphanages and how she and Christy worked together. Rosie told her some stories of her own experiences reporting from various depressing places where children were held in horrendous conditions. She wanted to get a handle on Ariana's personality and a bit of her background, before they went any further. The more they talked, the more Rosie liked what she heard. It was time to get down to business.

'Ariana, you know that Christy has talked to me a little of the suspicions you had about babies and children being sold. And also about this Scottish accountant, Alan Lewis.' Rosie looked at the others. 'I'd like to talk about that, so we can see what we do next.'

'Of course,' Ariana replied, drawing her chair a little closer to the table. 'I can tell you what I know, and what I suspect.' She took a breath. 'Christy told me about the wife of this Alan Lewis going missing, which is very strange. As you know, he disappeared in Romania some time ago.'

'Was there much on television or in the newspapers about his disappearance? Much from the police about the search?' Rosie asked.

Ariana shrugged. 'Not much. I don't think the police really did much apart from have some kind of search of the area where he lived, and around the lake not too far from his villa. But it wasn't like a big manhunt, or something that would be on television all the time. It was on the national news at first, because he was a Brit who disappeared. But there were no reporters or media over here from the UK asking questions. I think there was perhaps the view that he maybe disappeared and took his own life, and that one day his remains will be found.' She puffed. 'As you know, the police here have a hard time investigating anything. If it was a child who went missing they would perhaps make a big fuss about searching, but they would not keep it up for long.' She shook her head. 'I'm sad to say that the cities and towns – in fact the whole country – is run by gangsters these days. The mafia is everywhere. Lot of Russians.'

Rosie glanced at Adrian, and they both nodded in agreement.

'It's the same everywhere,' Adrian said. 'In my country, it is getting a little better, but the mafia and the Russian criminals always muscle in. And the Albanians. They are everywhere.'

Ariana nodded, taking one of Adrian's cigarettes and lighting it, inhaling deeply. Rosie declined the offer of a cigarette.

'So, before we talk about anything else, Ariana, what do

you know of Lewis's role here? He's an accountant. But was he ever in the orphanages, to your knowledge?'

'No.' She shook her head. 'Not that I know of. The only time I saw him was at a small function organised by the UK charity – Hands Across Europe – and he turned up there. I thought it was because he had a villa here and because he was friends with the boss of the charity, who would be in and out of Bucharest a lot. The charity would come with convoys of aid – you know, clothing, food for babies, lots of things like that. And once they touched base in Bucharest, they would then go north to places like Cluj, Suceava and around Bacău – these are places where the orphanages were particularly in need, where they have nothing. They took a lot of good aid and supplies to these places. I went with them a couple of times, and so did Christy, so I saw it for myself.'

Rosie told her that when she went to an orphanage with an aid convoy, she had witnessed the clothing going in the front door, and half an hour later being taken out of the back in a horse-drawn wagon, no doubt to be sold. Corruption was at every level.

'I am not surprised at that,' Ariana agreed. 'I have seen this happen too. Is all corrupt. And to be honest, I can see why some of the people who operate in these orphanages steal some of the clothes, because the reality is they have so little themselves. Of course, they are taking from orphans, much worse off than them. But this is human nature.'

Rosie was impressed by Ariana's knowledge and attitude. There was a bit of steel about her.

'Of course,' she said. 'But all of that pales into insignificance when you look at the trade of babies. That is a different story altogether. Tell me, Ariana, how much do you know about the boss of the UK charity? Do you think he could possibly have been in on this? His charity is very respected, and though there isn't a lot about him in the newspapers, it's widely believed that the work of the charity is genuine.'

Ariana nodded her head vigorously. 'Yes. I'm sure that is true. But . . .' She paused. 'I cannot say for certain that he was involved, not actively anyway. But there is such a thing as turning a blind eye.' She spread her hands, as though explaining. 'You see, in adopting a baby, especially in the north of the country, where laws may be overlooked and money can buy just about anyone's agreement, then a lot of decisions are left up to the head of any particular orphanage. If they are the kind of person open to corruption, then that is why the trade in babies has been allowed to operate. And I can tell you that it has.' She stubbed her cigarette out. 'I am making some very discreet enquiries, and they have to be discreet, of course, but I am trying to trace a mother whose baby was taken from her. They told her the baby had died. And this was not in an orphanage. This was in the maternity unit of a hospital. So it is more widespread. But someone has told a friend of mine that this baby wasn't dead, and that it was taken away and sold to someone. The problem is, there is no way of tracing where the baby went. It was a few months ago. It would be impossible, unless someone on the ground could tell us. That is the kind of thing we are faced with.'

'Do you think there is much chance of tracing the mother?'

Ariana nodded. 'I think it is a good possibility. I am working on it, and have someone trying to find where she is. It is somewhere north of here. Up in Bacău area and Botoșani. I'm thinking we should go there tomorrow if you want?'

Rosie nodded. 'Sure, if you think that's the best place to start.'

'That is where my best contacts are, and it is in this region that a lot of the trade goes on. People are so poor there. They have nothing.'

Rosie glanced at Matt and Adrian, then spoke. 'Ariana, do you think if an ordinary couple from, say, a foreign country, went or were put in contact with someone in the baby trade, they could buy a baby from them? I know it sounds a bit off the scale. But what do you think?'

Ariana crossed her long legs and sighed. 'That is a different matter, Rosie. That is very dangerous. If someone discovered that the people trying to buy a baby were not genuine, well, I wouldn't want to think of what would happen.'

Adrian's face was deadpan as ever, so you never really knew what he was thinking. But Matt rolled his eyes.

'Christ, Rosie. Can we not have a few days' holiday first, before you get us killed?'

Everyone burst out laughing, as much to ease the tension of a long day and heavy discussion as the fear of what tomorrow might bring.

CHAPTER TEN

'So where is he? Where the fuck is Alan? And more to the point, where is his fucking money?' Ricky Thomson growled at Helen from across his desk. 'And listen, ya wee tart. I'm not going to sit here all day coaxing this out of you.' He glanced up at the big thickset minder in the leather jacket who stood at the door with his arms folded. 'I have people who do that for me. So it's up to you.'

Helen really didn't know how she was going to answer him. But she knew Ricky Thomson from way back. He would cut your throat just for fun, and as a teenager throwing his weight around the Gorbals, he often did. But usually if Ricky cut you up, it was for money, or, more accurately, because you hadn't paid your debt. Back then, he'd been an enforcer for one of the biggest moneylenders in Glasgow, and it was working as muscle for him that got him noticed by the big boys. Ricky hadn't the brains to be a big-time Charlie, but he had the brawn. And that got him through the ranks when fear and power ran the show. How the Christ he'd got involved with Alan Lewis was beyond her. But now that her brain was bouncing off the inside of her head trying to work things out, she thought back to the time when she found out Alan was involved with Frankie Mallon and how surprised she'd been then. So anything was possible. She was desperate to ask questions. Somehow Ricky had discovered there was no money in Alan's accounts, so it looked like he was blaming Alan. But Alan had been missing for months. Why had he not come after her before? Helen wondered why Alan hadn't contacted whoever Ricky worked for to tell him the money had gone and it was nothing to do with him. But he'd probably been too scared to risk that. Christ, this whole thing was a mess and she didn't know where to start. But one thing she couldn't do was tell him she'd had Alan murdered – or thought she had. He wouldn't believe it, for a start, and the fact that Alan had landed back at her house would have made her sound crazy. No. She had no idea how she was going to get out of this one. Best to say as little as possible.

'Look, Ricky. I'm being honest with you. I've no idea where Alan is. I wouldn't lie to you. He disappeared off the face of the earth. Do I think he's alive? I honestly don't know.' She swallowed. 'I don't know anything about his finances. He was the accountant. Do you seriously think he's going to tell me anything about his business?'

Ricky listened, but he didn't look as though he believed her.

'So what about Frankie Mallon? Did you kill him?'

Helen looked as surprised as she could muster.

'Kill him? Are you kidding me? How could I kill him? Where was I going to get a fucking gun, Ricky? I'm not living in the same world as you.'

'Aye. But you come from the same world as me, ya wee hairy.'

Helen sighed. So far, no punch in the face, so that was a bonus. She looked him in the eye, crossed her legs, knowing he was watching her skirt ride up her thighs. Ricky would have fancied her back in the day as much as the rest of the boys, but she hadn't been remotely interested in him or any of the others.

'I never said I don't come from the same world as you, Ricky. I know who I am and where I came from and I'm not ashamed of it. But I left all that behind.'

'You were a wee fucking prostitute at fourteen.'

Helen swallowed the sting.

'Aye. I was. And it was a shite life, let me tell you. But I knew I was getting out of there as soon as any chance presented itself. Listen, Ricky. Please. You must believe me. I'm just a bird who got out of the mire and did all right. I had no idea that my husband was involved with guys like you.' She managed to make her voice wobble with emotion at the end of the sentence. She might even tear up at this rate. But Ricky was barely buying it.

'So what was Frankie Mallon doing in your flat?'

'Who knows? Maybe he was looking for Alan too. Or his money, or his books or something. I don't know.'

'So who shot him?'

Quick as a flash, Helen concocted a scenario.

'Look. Here's what happened. And this is the truth. I was in the bedroom, I heard noises – the door being forced, footsteps. I thought it was a break-in. Suddenly, I see these two men. Frankie and some other guy. They were shouting to me, Where's the money – just like you are. But I didn't know what they were on about. They started arguing and one thing led to another, then this guy was shouting at Frankie that he was trying to double-cross him. I didn't know what they were on about. Then, all of a sudden the second guy pulled out a gun and shot Frankie. I think the two of them were out of their box on coke. Maybe somebody sent them. I just haven't a clue.'

'What guy was with him?'

'I don't know. I've never seen him before. I've only seen Frankie once, at a dinner with Alan, and I met him.'

'Frankie must have remembered you.'

'Yeah. He did. We said hello. But we didn't actually reminisce about the good times. I met him once. That's all.'

'I don't believe you.'

'Well, I'd tell you to ask him, but it's a bit late for that.'

'So what happened? You just did a runner?'

'I was leaving anyway. Hence the packed bag. I was going to the Cayman Islands. You're right. Alan had put money in a joint account over there for us, and we sometimes went on holiday there. It wasn't much, Ricky. I can show you the account. There's all of twenty grand in it. I was going to have to get a job over there as soon as I was settled. Alan has obviously disappeared, or maybe even been bumped off. Who knows, the people he was involved with? But I just decided I'd had enough. I wanted to start a new life.'

'Well. We don't think Alan's dead.'

Helen's stomach turned over.

'You mean he's alive? What makes you think that?' She hoped she looked genuinely concerned, even excited.

'Because someone's moved our fucking money into another account. The banks won't tell us the name, obviously, for fucking security reasons. But they say the account of Alan Lewis doesn't exist any more. It's been closed down, and the money moved to another account. That's why we know. He's fucked off with all the money. They have his signature on the account that he moved.' He got up and walked over to her and held her face in his hands. 'Maybe the cunt's in the Cayman Islands waiting for you with our money.'

Helen looked up at him, her eyes filling with tears. She had to look the part, but inside her she felt like punching the air at the fact that the bank told them nothing.

'Jesus, Ricky. Don't say that. If Alan was alive he would have got in touch with me. He wouldn't just disappear to the Cayman Islands and then tell me to get a flight out.

Christ's sake! He's been missing for over six months and I haven't heard a fucking sound from him. Honestly. I'm not lying.' She paused for breath. 'I don't know what he's done with your money. I wish I did, because I would tell you right now, and maybe you would let me go. This has nothing to do with me. He never told me anything about his work.'

Ricky looked down at her, not convinced.

'We'll see.'

He walked towards the door.

'What are you going to do? Just leave me here? Ricky. Please. Don't just leave me here. I've got nothing to do with this.'

He walked out of the door and left her with the big guy in the leather jacket. She gazed up at him, catching his eye, and knew he was ogling her cleavage. She touched it a little and crossed her legs again.

CHAPTER ELEVEN

They had been driving for almost four hours, and Rosie was thankful she'd decided to hire the biggest car the rental company at the hotel could provide. The last time she'd driven hundreds of miles across Romania it was in a tiny cramped car which had caught fire in the middle of nowhere, leaving her and the driver stranded in a thunderstorm. Memories of eventually being picked up by a tractor and taken to the nearest town where they had to spend the night in the single, dilapidated hotel, were still burned in her memory – how she'd lain awake in bed in the room with no lock, a wooden chair jamming the door handle shut. The worst thing that would probably have happened was that she'd have been robbed, because criminal gangs were always on the lookout for easy pickings. But it had not been a good start to a trip that got more depressing by the day.

And this journey looked no different – in every town they drove through, there were the same rows of grim blocks of flats, typical all over Eastern Europe, where people had lived in poverty for generations while their Communist leaders lapped up the splendour of gilded palaces. If ever there was a monument to how Communism had failed, then these concrete slabs were it. And, she recalled, as they drove through another town and past a man lying comatose at the side of the road, nearly everyone was drunk. No wonder.

Ariana was driving and giving them a guided tour of each town, and told them they were heading up to the Bacău area, where some of the villages hadn't changed for generations and people eked out a living from the land or in nearby industrial towns under a dense cloud of choking pollution. Most of the younger people were leaving and a lot had already gone, seeking jobs in Western Europe. Often children were left with older relatives, and some would end up in orphanages, where despite all the publicity at the time, the improvements had been minimal. Children were still trapped in desperate environments, even though some places were now a little more enlightened. But in spite of all that and the government supposedly watching things, still the trade in orphans went on, seemingly unnoticed. Or, as Ariana said, perhaps in collaboration. Rosie gazed out of the windscreen, thinking how incredible it would be if she could nail down a story like that, involving government collusion. But for now, she'd be happy just to get some inroads into the baby trade.

It was late afternoon when they drove into the sprawling

industrialised town of Bacău, nearly two hundred miles to the north of Bucharest. They checked into their hotel, the dimly lit foyer as drab as any other Eastern bloc hotel Rosie had ever been to. What was it with this one bulb for the entire reception area? It was always the same in the bed-rooms too, where, even if the table lamp in the bedroom worked, the place was dark and eerie and made you want to get out of it the moment you put your bags down. Rosie, Matt and Adrian walked along the gloomy corridor on the second floor and she was glad to see their rooms were all next to each other. Handy, Rosie thought, if anything bad happens. The last time she'd been in Belgrade, in Serbia, in a similarly dreary hotel, she was dragged out of her room, down the fire escape and kidnapped before anyone could see her. She pushed the flashback away as she closed the door in her cheerless room and put her bag on to the bed.

The bar where they'd arranged to meet Ariana's contact was close by, so they all walked together. If you'd done that eight or nine years ago in an area like this, you would stick out like a sore thumb, but it was clear that Western influence had reached as far up as Bacău. Street corners had Coca-Cola umbrellas and fast-food cafés, unheard of a few years ago. Rosie wondered who was cashing in, because it was a fair bet it was the gangsters and not some local, hard-working busi-nessman. It was cold and they went into the bar – again only half-lit – where Ariana spotted her friend at the far side.

'Is Nicu. I see him.'

As they approached, Nicu stood up, dark shaggy hair and pot-bellied figure, dressed in corduroys and a V-neck sweater and shirt. He had at least a day's stubble and dark circles and bags under his eyes. Rosie saw him wiping the palms of his hands on his jeans, and thought he looked a little edgy, his hands trembling a little. She wondered how he lived his life, and if the edginess about him was to do with drink, because alcohol was such a huge problem in all walks of life in the country. She chided herself for being uncharitable, given the fact that he was here to impart information to them that could get him killed; he had every right to be edgy. His eyes darted warily around the group as he embraced Ariana. Rosie motioned them all to sit rather than stand around looking like some official delegation. The waiter came across in an instant and they ordered beers. Then Ariana did the introductions in English, explaining that Nicu spoke the language and had worked with many British expats in the orphanages.

He shook Rosie's hand and his face softened as he looked at her. 'I did get to meet some journalists when they came to the orphanages in the beginning – after Ceauşescu.' He shook his head. 'It was a grim time for everyone.'

'I know,' Rosie agreed. 'It was grim enough just witnessing it.'

He nodded. 'So much pressure being put on the orphanages and people working in them. But the truth is that we could do nothing but try to make these places work. With no money, nothing, and always under the threat of, well, anything, if we spoke out.' He shook his head. 'I know a lot of people who suffered from terrible stress long before the revolution and couldn't work in the conditions, but some of us stayed. What else could we do?' He spread his hands to explain. 'You see, under Ceauşescu, abortion and birth control were banned. He demanded that all women have at least five children. It was all about creating "workers" for the greater good of Communism. Often the government spies even came into workplaces to track how many babies women were producing. The women were told that if so many babies were a problem, then the government would take them and look after them. That is why so many women, who couldn't cope, were happy to hand their children to the authorities. This is when it all fell apart. So many babies were abandoned, and there was no money to support the orphanages. The children were living in what was really poor conditions. Hard to work in. But if everyone left because they cannot cope, then who will look after the orphans? Was terrible.'

'It's better now, though? From what I read and see on television,' Rosie asked.

'Yes. Much better. But still very many orphans, and still they grow up with nowhere to go when they leave.'

They sat in silence as the waiter brought the beers and then Ariana spoke.

'You know, Nicu, that Rosie wants to look at the baby trade.' She lowered her voice almost to a whisper.

Nicu looked at Rosie, and nodded with a half-shrug. 'I can help. I have some names. People you can talk to.'

'Is it happening in a lot of orphanages, Nicu?' Rosie asked, leaning closer to the table.

'A few. But these are only the ones I know. Could be happening all over Bucharest and other cities, for all I know. I would be surprised if it isn't.'

'So can you explain to me how it happens? How can a child just disappear who has been in the orphanage? Surely the managers and government officials would have to sign papers.'

'Yes. There is official ways and that does happen a lot too. Many Romanian children go to Germany, to America, to UK. They go through the courts. It takes a long time. The courts are still busy with applications and that I think is part of the problem. While all this is going on, the people in the homes don't know who has paperwork and who has not. Only the managers of the homes know that, and they tell the staff nothing. So in the places that this is involved – in the corruption, I mean – the managers of the home are part of the operation. It is disgusting.'

'You mean they are tied in with the gangsters?'

'Yes. They must be. How else can a child just vanish from a home? For example, I cannot go into my boss's office in an orphanage and ask, Is he certain there were official papers for the adoption of a child, and ask, Can I see them. That is not how it works. The manager is the boss. He just tells us that papers have arrived from the courts and that the child can go. And sometimes I'm sure it is a child with the correct paperwork, but others I don't think they have proper paperwork.'

Rosie shook her head. 'Awful. And do the parents ever come back to the home to visit their children?'

'Not many. Mostly not. A lot of them are alcoholics and some die in their thirties and forties or have moved away for work. It's always been the way here.'

Ariana looked at Nicu. 'And, Nicu, Rosie is also, as I told you, interested in the babies who are taken from the maternity unit.'

'Yes. That is the worst. I know for sure this happens. Because I know the woman who lost her baby.'

Rosie stomach tightened. 'You do? Would she talk to us?'

He shook his head, stubbed his cigarette out.

'Not for the papers and a photograph. For sure, she will say no to that.'

'But would she talk to us without naming her?'

He looked at Ariana. 'Yes. I spoke to her this morning. She told me she will talk in private. But you must not reveal her name. She will tell you everything.'

'When can we see her?' Rosie hoped she didn't sound as keen as she was. 'I mean, we will only be here for a limited time, and if I could talk to her, then it would be a start, and I could pursue or try to track down the people involved. I also want to talk to you about Alan Lewis and his charity.'

He shook his head and his mouth tightened.

'Yes. They are gangsters. The company – the adoption firm – is set up for the smuggling of children. That is what I hear. Alan Lewis is the man who does the accounts for them, I am told, but as you know he is missing. I don't know if he is part of the whole thing, but he is a director in the business so he must have known. Or maybe they didn't tell him. Who knows?'

'Do you know the people behind it?'

'I know they are Russians. That much I know. And very dangerous.'

'Do you have names and anyone we can see if we decide to do that?'

'What do you mean, "see"?'

Rosie glanced at Adrian. 'I mean, do you think it would be possible for me and, say, Adrian here, to go undercover? Like pretend we are a married couple who want a baby?'

He let out a long sigh. 'It is going very close to the fire to do that, Rosie.'

'I know. But I can't see how we do it any other way, if we want to get inside it.'

'I agree. We can talk about it.'

'We'll have dinner after this and we can talk further. '

CHAPTER TWELVE

The address was somewhere in a clutch of bleak-looking blocks of flats on the outskirts of the town. Nicu had suggested it would be better if only he, Rosie and Ariana went along to meet the woman whose child had been stolen in the maternity ward. He didn't want to make her feel under threat with a lot of people coming at once. It had taken a bit of persuasion from Rosie for her to be able to bring Matt along, even though they knew that the woman did not want her picture in the paper if the story ever got that far. They needed some kind of image, Rosie insisted, if only of the area, or even some kind of backshot or silhouette so her image wouldn't be identifiable. She promised that if the woman didn't agree, they wouldn't push her. Nicu hadn't been convinced, but reluctantly agreed, and was a little huffy at first until Rosie explained to him how these things worked.

He drove off the main road and down the side street to

the rear entrance at the block of flats and parked their car. Three scruffy kids came up straight away and Nicu said something to them in a stern voice and they stood back a little. In the back courts, washing fluttered from clothes lines, some of the flats had broken windows with grimy curtains poking through the shattered glass, and a few women stood chatting and smoking at the entrance, their faces wearing the same resigned expression Rosie had seen everywhere since she got off the plane. The new freedom and affluence that was growing in the towns and cities hadn't reached the backstreets, where people would probably never get out of the mire. The women watched them as they filtered past into the entrance, and Nicu took the lead while they climbed the stone stairs. He turned to Rosie.

'Madelina will be a little nervous, Rosie. And she may even have had a drink, as that is her life these days. So we have to be very gentle with her. I'm sure you understand.'

'Don't worry, Nicu. Of course, I understand.'

On the second floor, Nicu knocked on the door and they stood waiting. No answer. He knocked again, a little harder, but still no answer. He shrugged.

'Maybe she went out. We can come back.'

Rosie's heart sank. First door-knock, and getting nowhere. Then, as they turned to go back downstairs, they heard a lock being turned. The door opened on a chain, and a face peered through.

'Madelina,' Nicu said. Then he spoke in Romanian, gesturing towards Rosie and Ariana.

The door opened and the woman stood back and beckoned them in. They all filed down the short narrow hallway to a tiny living room. Rosie glanced around at the neat, sparsely furnished room. Nicu introduced everyone, and Madelina nodded and shook hands, her small clammy hand feeling cold in Rosie's. Rosie made eye contact with her, and could see the bloodshot eyes and puffy complexion of a drinker. She held her hand a little longer than was necessary, hoping to convey her sympathy.

Ariana spoke in Romanian to the woman, who seemed to nod in agreement.

'I am going to make some coffee for us, and we can sit down and talk,' Ariana said.

Madelina motioned to Rosie to sit on the thin, wooden-legged sofa, the kind she hadn't seen back home since the seventies. Madelina sat on a matching armchair next to the wooden fireplace, and Nicu sat opposite her. He turned to Rosie.

'I have already told her yesterday that you may be coming, and I will explain more to her now. So if you want to say something to her, I will translate.'

'Okay.' Rosie nodded, taking a deep breath. She looked at the woman as she spoke. 'Madelina. Thank you for seeing me and allowing me this time. I really appreciate it. As Nicu explained, I am a journalist and I am investigating claims that Romanian babies and orphans are being sold, often abroad. Nicu has told me that you have been a victim of this terrible crime, and I want to talk to you about it. But we will not identify you in any way, and I want you to understand that.'

Rosie nodded to Nicu to translate and watched Madelina as he spoke, his voice gentle. She could see her face twitch a little, and she swallowed and bit her lip. Rosie's heart went out to her as she glanced around this tiny, impoverished room, trying to imagine the pain for this young woman, going through a pregnancy and then coming back into this place without her baby. It was unthinkable. She listened as Madelina responded, then Nicu turned to Rosie.

'She will tell you what happened. But she is afraid. Because the people who did this must be very powerful. She says she thinks that her husband, who left her two months before the baby was due, had maybe been behind this. He is an alcoholic and a bad man. She thinks maybe he went to these people and sold their baby for money.'

Rosie glanced at Matt and shook her head in disbelief. And deep down, she chided the journalist in her for knowing that this story was getting even better. She asked Nicu if it was possible for Madelina to talk them through what she recalled of that morning, and about her life since. Ariana came in from the kitchen with coffee and a tray of cups, and handed them out. Then Madelina sipped from hers, her hand trembling as she held it, and began her story.

Rosie watched while Madelina, her soft voice in the still-ness of the room, told her story. And as she broke down, wiping her tears with her sleeve, they all sat awkwardly until she stopped weeping and continued. It was hard going, and even without understanding a word the pain of what Madelina had gone through was palpable. Then Nicu turned to Rosie and translated.

'Madelina is telling me what happened. And as you can see, she is very upset. It is almost a year ago, but it is still so fresh in her mind and always will be.'

Rosie produced a tape recorder from her bag and set her notebook on her lap.

'Is it okay if I use this to tape the conversation?'

Madelina nodded her agreement, and Rosie switched it on as Nicu began to translate her story.

'It was to be her first baby, and she was very excited about it, even though her marriage was not good. Her hus-band, Eadbert, had been involved with some of the local gangsters – as you know, there are more of them in recent years. They take money from the bars – protection money and things like that. And sometimes he would go away for days at a time. So things were not good between them. He was also a drunk and sometimes he would beat her, even when she was pregnant. Eadbert said he didn't want a baby, even though in the beginning he had seemed pleased. By the time she was eight months pregnant, he said he was leav-ing. One morning Eadbert got up, packed his things and left her. She was very upset. She had nobody to turn to, as her parents are both dead, and the only people she had were the few friends around here in the flats. She had very little to prepare for the baby's arrival, but one of her friends gave her a crib.' Nicu gestured behind him towards the hall, where the bedrooms were. 'She still has it in the bedroom.'

Rosie could sense Matt seeing a picture opportunity for later, but for now she wanted to hear all of this. Nicu went on. 'In the hospital, her labour was normal until the last stages and it seemed a little difficult for the baby to come out. That is how Madelina put it to me. But when she was born, a little girl, they showed her to her briefly but had to take her to another room, they said, to resuscitate her. They didn't allow Madelina to hold the baby. They said they will come back with her in a few minutes when the baby is breathing. Madelina was a little worried about the baby, but was happy that she had given birth. She waited. And waited for a long time, then asked the nurse where the baby was. But she seemed to avoid coming to her bed, then eventually another nurse came in and told her the baby had died, that they were very sorry. Madelina couldn't believe them and she, as you can imagine, was so upset. She asked to see her baby, but they told her that was not possible or even advisable, that the baby was dead. Like stillborn. But Madelina knew that the baby was moving when they showed her to her in the beginning. She thought they must be lying, but why would they? She was in a maternity hospital and people were here to deliver babies, so she knew she had to believe them. She knew nothing of whether they allowed you to see your baby if it has died. The hospital said that is their policy because a mother is in a very upset state mentally and seeing the corpse of their newborn baby would be even more traumatic.'

Rosie could barely believe what she was hearing. She tried to imagine what it must be like to be denied even a glimpse of your baby at that moment, and to have nobody around her to comfort you. They sat in silence for a moment, and then Nicu continued.

'When Madelina came out of the hospital the following day, she pleaded with them to tell her what had happened, but they just explained that the baby wasn't breathing and had died, and it happens. There was nothing they could do. She even asked if she could have the body so she could bury her, but was told she already had been cremated. That was hospital policy, they said. They gave her the death certificate. All it said was the baby's name, Iasius, and the name of the parents. She still has it. She could not believe or understand this cruelty. She walked out of the hospital that day and her life, she has told me, has ended since then. She came home to the apartment here and sat in a kind of shock for a few days, crying and in a terrible state. One of her friends has helped her a little and made some food for her. So that is how her life became. But her friend told her it would be easier to sleep if she had a drink of vodka in the night, and so that is how she started drinking. Now, she says to me, she is an alcoholic. She admits that the alcohol does help and that every day, she must take some alcohol to get her through the day and that then she doesn't cry so much. She said some days she feels she cannot put one foot in front of the other to walk because she is so sad and so desperate.'

Rosie didn't know what to say as she looked at Madelina, who was weeping and shaking. She waited a moment until she had regained her composure.

'I know this is painful for her, Nicu,' Rosie said. 'But can you ask her if I can see the death certificate?'

Nicu spoke to Madelina and she got up and went into a bedroom. She returned with an official document. On it was the name of a baby, Iasius Onescu.

'What does it say, Nicu?'

Nicu read it. 'It gives the name of the parents and the baby. It says stillborn. But that is not true, as we know from Madelina. Because she says the baby was moving when she was born.'

'Jesus,' Rosie murmured. 'Nicu, can you also ask her this: how did she get the information that perhaps her baby had been sold? Where did that come from?'

Nicu asked her and then translated.

'It was one of her friends who works in the bar a couple of blocks away from here. Madelina hasn't seen her husband since the day he left, but the barmaid in that place said she had spoken to someone who knew him and that he seen him in another bar in a town not too far from here, and that her husband had told the person that he had made a deal to sell their baby. He was drunk one time and said he didn't want a baby and it was best for Madelina now that he had gone that she wasn't saddled with a baby. But he is just evil for what he did. If he did do it, it wasn't for Madelina or anyone except for himself and for money. She said she wanted to go to the authorities, to the police, but with what evidence? Who will listen to her? Who will believe her? And now, so many months later, as she is drinking, who is going to listen to a woman who is drunk?'

For a moment, Rosie had to keep her eye on her notebook.

'Tell her I believe her, Nicu.' Rosie swallowed, looking at Madelina. 'Tell her I will do everything I can to find out what happened to her baby. Everything. I cannot say what will happen, but please tell her she has a friend in us, and we will not stop until we find out the truth.'

Nicu nodded and translated what Rosie had said. As he did so, Madelina wiped away her tears with her hands, saying thank you. Rosie knew that she could promise no more than what she had, but she resolved there and then that if she did nothing else in her life, she would find out what had happened to that baby and where she was now.

CHAPTER THIRTEEN

For the first few minutes of the journey back to the hotel, nobody spoke. Rosie gazed through the windscreen as they drove through the rundown streets where the few shops and cafés that looked open were mostly empty. She could still feel the firm grasp of Madelina's hand in hers when they were leaving the apartment, and hear her pleading with Nicu to find the truth of what happened to her baby. If her daughter was happy now with someone else, she told Nicu, then she would have to accept it. She was a pitiful sight, her face blotchy, and by now, Rosie thought, she was probably topping up her cup with neat vodka to get through the rest of her day. Madelina had been willing to have a silhouette picture taken of her with her back to the crib, and that was as good as it was going to get. Matt was happy enough to have been able to get a picture of the birth certificate and any shots inside the house, and he took some snaps of the building and the general landscapes on the way to the car. McGuire would be delighted, but they were a long way from getting the story Rosie wanted. They were here to pursue the story of Alan Lewis's links with the baby trade, but right now, if she could find out what had happened to Madelina's baby that would be just about enough, she thought, as they drove into the hotel car park.

In the bar, she relayed Madelina's story to Adrian, and she knew that – although it was always hard to work out what was in his mind – this time she could see the disbelief and anger in his eyes.

'The father sold his own daughter?'

Rosie nodded. 'We don't know that for sure, but that is what Madelina has been told.' She looked at all of them. 'We have to find him. He's the key to a lot of this, and if we find him, and apparently he's some drunk, then we can maybe get something out of him without blowing our cover.'

'Do we know anything about where he might be?'

'Not really, but we know the bar where Madelina was told he was talking about it that night. I think if we go there, discreetly, we may be able to get a lead.' She turned to Nicu. 'What do you think, Nicu?'

He nodded, his mouth downturned. 'Is a possibility. But not you, Rosie. You cannot go in and ask questions in an area like that. Would have to be me.' He looked at Adrian. 'And perhaps you, my friend?'

'Of course,' Adrian said. 'I can go with you.'

'Money talks everywhere in Romania. So if we can find

the barmaid that Madelina told us about, we can get more information. If we can give her some money.'

'Are you sure you are okay to work with us on this, Nicu? I mean, being so upfront?'

'It's okay for me. I work mostly in Bucharest and I can keep my head down for a while if this becomes a story. But I want to try. I was very sad to hear the details from Madelina today.'

Adrian said nothing, and Rosie could read his thoughts. The idea of selling your own child would be so abhorrent to someone like him, who had lost his own unborn son after Serb soldiers tore him from the womb of his pregnant wife.

'I think we should get moving on this. I don't want to hang around now that we've been to see Madelina,' Rosie said.

Nicu drained his cup. 'Then we should go now.'

'We'll go behind you,' Rosie said. 'I'll be with Ariana, but we'll be in a café as far away from the area as need be. But it would be good if Matt could be in the same café as you. He has good camera equipment that can film discreetly. Whatever happens here, I want to have an image of Madelina's husband. So if the barmaid gives you a direction or a place we can find him, I need Matt to be there.'

'Okay. I think we can do that.'

They all stood up, and Rosie could feel that little dig of nerves in her gut that told her things were about to happen. They had a long way to go, but she hoped they were going in the right direction.

*

Rosie kept checking her mobile in the café while she and Ariana waited for a call from Adrian or Nicu. Nicu had called nearly three hours ago to say they had a lead on where the husband drank and were heading there. They were now on their third cup of tea, having grazed through all of the snacks on offer. It was beginning to get dark outside, but she was relieved that the café was reasonably busy with people who looked like they'd been working or were out for an early evening drink. She noted there were a few foreigners in the place – they looked Scandinavian or German, probably tourists, or ex-pats working in the various charity organisations dotted around the region. Rosie was ashamed to admit to herself that she always felt edgy in foreign lands, and was always glad when there were some other people she could assume were tourists. It wasn't that she was racist, or afraid of foreigners, but she had so many close calls happen to her on foreign turf that she preferred to remain close to a big city when abroad. And as she wasn't in a city, she preferred to have someone like Adrian at her side.

Eventually, Rosie's mobile rang and it was Nicu.

'Nicu. How did it go?' she asked.

'It was good.'

'Was he there? Did you get to talk to him?'

'Yes.'

'Excellent. Can you give us a call when you get close to here? Then we'll all head back to the hotel.'

Ariana looked enquiringly at her.

'Nicu says it's gone well,' Rosie said.

'He was there? They met Eadbert?' asked Ariana.

'So it seems. Nicu and Adrian are on their way back with Matt. We'll hear it all when we're back at the hotel.'

Ariana nodded. 'Your friend Adrian – he doesn't say very much.'

Rosie smiled. 'No. He doesn't. But tell you what, though, Ariana. If you were ever in a corner and you needed a hand, you'd want him to be close by.'

'You've known him long?'

'Yeah,' Rosie said. 'A long time. We're old friends.'

Ariana nodded and asked no more, and Rosie was glad not to get drawn into a conversation about Adrian.

In the hotel bar, they found a quiet corner and ordered beers from the waiter, while they listened to Nicu and Adrian talk.

'What's he like?' Rosie asked.

'He's a drunk,' Nicu said. 'He was already a bit drunk when he came into the bar. That made it a bit easier. Eadbert's a stupid man. Boasting about connections. He is the kind of man that the people he deals with would think nothing of just getting rid of him.'

'I agree,' Adrian said. 'He was stupid enough to brag to us that he knew all the people who sell the babies.'

'He actually said that?' Rosie turned to Nicu. 'You have that on tape?'

'He sure does,' Matt said. 'I had a listen to it on the way back. I've no idea what he says, but Nicu says he is confirming that he is involved. But I managed to get a snatch pic of him anyway, and it's not bad.'

Rather than listen to the tape right now, Rosie asked them to talk her through it.

'When we went to the first bar, as you know the lady pointed us . . .' Nicu said, 'we were in there for nearly an hour when he came in. Eadbert was a bit drunk and went straight to the bar and ordered a beer. The bar was not very busy and he was looking at the few people who were in. But nobody talked to him. I saw him scraping up coins for his next beer when I was at the bar, and I smiled to him and asked did he want a beer. I made some excuse about directions and we struck up a conversation. I told him we are looking at business ventures here. And that was it. He came and sat beside us, and started talking.'

At one stage, Nicu said, they started talking about the orphans, and about the red tape for couples trying to adopt. Then, to their astonishment, the drunk started spilling out about how he knew a company who operates very discreetly and doesn't advertise, but people like him can put couples in touch with them. This adoption company, he told them, gets babies for couples who cannot get through the red tape. Eadbert said the red tape is just stupid, that everyone wants a chance of a good life, that this company is doing Romania a great service. He then went on to describe even newborn babies can be sold. When they expressed disbelief, he described much of what Madelina had said. And when they said it was hard to believe, Eadbert then said that he knows better than anyone, because he did it himself.

'Christ,' Rosie said. 'He must be completely stupid to admit that to total strangers.'

'He was drunk by this time. He'd had four beers and a whisky on top of what he'd already had.'

'He could say it was the drink talking,' Matt said.

Rosie knew that. 'Yes. But we already have a story of a woman saying it had happened to her, and that her husband might have been involved. If we have that kind of evidence, it might be enough to go to the authorities with. To the police.'

Nicu sighed. 'The police are corrupt, Rosie. As corrupt as the gangsters.'

'They can't all be corrupt,' Rosie said.

Nicu shrugged, but didn't answer.

'Well,' Rosie said. 'We can go to the British embassy. If we can nail the name of the company and connect it to Alan Lewis, a British citizen, then that makes it our business.'

Nicu nodded. 'Is true. Is worth a try.'

CHAPTER FOURTEEN

Helen knew that seducing Ricky Thomson would be the easy part. The problem was going to be getting out of his clutches – smartish. She didn't have time on her side. As she lay wide awake in the darkness watching him snoring like a bull next to her, she re-ran the past few hours.

She knew Ricky would be stupid enough to let his guard down if she showed the least bit of interest in him. So for the last day, while she was a prisoner in this apartment, she'd made sure he'd be putty in her hands. She knew she was halfway there when he appeared last night and told the knuckle-trailer who'd been guarding her that he could beat it for the night. So when he cracked open a bottle of Jack Daniel's, Helen decided this was it. Halfway down the bottle, Ricky was relaxed and telling her how he'd always fantasised about her while they were teenagers back in the Gorbals, but he'd always thought she was out of his reach. Nonsense, Helen purred as she'd reached across and caressed his thigh. He'd given her a couple of drinks, and she'd been feeling relaxed too. Two-thirds of the way down the bottle and Ricky started blabbing that he'd heard that Alan was involved with some heavies abroad who were involved in selling Romanian babies. Helen thought he must be raving. She'd always known Alan was a money-grabbing bastard in his job and she sussed early on that he was laundering money. But selling weans? That wasn't his bag. The Alan she knew couldn't do anything like that. She wanted to push Ricky for more information, but was too afraid to make an issue out of it in case he thought she was fishing. She wondered if it was anything to do with the Romanian export business she'd seen him named in as a director. But if it *was* true, and Alan was involved in selling babies, there wasn't much she could do about it now. She had her own shit to deal with, and right now she had to deal with this prick Ricky. But the more he drank, the more he talked. He even told her it hadn't been his idea to kidnap her, but he was only doing what he was told by some foreign guy – Russian, he thought – who'd been in business with Alan. It was his mob's money that had gone missing when the accounts had been closed, and he wanted to question Helen himself. He'd be arriving the next after-noon. Ricky told her that if this guy believed her then she'd be free to go. That'll be right, Helen thought sarcastically. She knew it was now or never. She had to get the hell out of here before some Russian thug came kicking the door in, punching answers out of her pretty face. If she told him what she'd done, she'd be in the bottom of the River Clyde before the day was out. If she kept up her lie, she'd get a hiding and a lot worse. It was a no-brainer. Ricky was her only option. All the crap he'd been shouting at the start that it was his money had been bullshit. Ricky was the enforcer – same as he'd always been. He talked a good game. He might have moved around with all the hard men, but he was just the same thick muscle he'd been for the various toerags they'd all known back in the Gorbals. Around midnight, she'd asked him to pour her another Jack Daniel's while she went to the bathroom. And when she emerged a couple of minutes later, stark naked, his jaw just about hit the floor. He was out of his clothes in a flash, and across the room lifting her up, Helen wrapping her legs around him as though she'd been waiting for this moment all her life. Despite the amount of alcohol Ricky had knocked back, he was inside her before they even hit the bed.

Now, she slipped out of the bed, hurriedly got dressed and crept from the room. She had no idea where she was going, but Ricky and the thug who had been guarding her had been stupid enough to leave her case and her handbag in the hallway. They clearly hadn't reckoned on her having the balls or being stupid enough to attempt an escape. But they were wrong. This was about survival now, and Helen knew if some Russian gangster was going to ask her questions then she'd get a bullet in the head no matter what her answers were. She gently eased open the door of the flat and tiptoed into the hall, carrying her suitcases and bag behind her. She got downstairs as fast as she could and out of the front door. Never in her life had she been as glad to step into the buzz of Glasgow centre with early-morning traffic everywhere. She spotted a black cab with its light on two cars back and waved furiously. It pulled in and she rushed forward, and more or less threw herself in the back seat, hurling her bags in first.

'Where to, darlin'?' The driver looked in the rear-view mirror.

For a second, she didn't know what to say, because she hadn't a clue where the hell she was headed. But she had to get out of the city fast. Her mind was a blur. She couldn't go to Glasgow airport as that might be the first place they'd look. And they'd be looking soon.

'Can you take me to Edinburgh? To the train station. Waverley?'

His eyes widened. 'Sure, darlin'. But it'll cost you. Listen, I don't want to do myself out of a fare, but Queen Street station is just around the corner, and you'll get a train every half-hour.'

'No,' Helen snapped. 'Just take me to Edinburgh. I'm in a hurry. Could you just go now? Please. I need to move fast.'

The taxi pulled out onto the street.

'Sure. No problem. It's your money, doll.'

CHAPTER FIFTEEN

The meeting place was in a block of flats, and Rosie was already uneasy about it. Even the fact Nicu had established that the offices of the charity were on the ground floor did not make her feel any more confident. You could go into one of these dreary buildings along this side street and never come out, she'd remarked to Adrian as they drove from the hotel. Not surprisingly, he hadn't reacted, just wore the deadpan expression he always did when he was going into something unknown. She knew he'd be considering all the dangers and, knowing him, he was already working on a worst-case scenario. Sometimes you had to grit your teeth and get on with it, she told herself as they turned off the main street. Nicu had already made a discreet recce of the street to see if he could gather any more useful intelligence on the business. But the fact that the charity's office was situated at the back of a wine-importing firm ticked all the right boxes for Rosie. From what she'd seen in the documents Nicu had provided, Alan Lewis was a director of this firm, and also a director of the charity. If he didn't know exactly what they were up to, if they *were* selling babies, then he should have. She was getting closer to the truth, and it kept her going.

Last night over dinner, the decision had been made that it would be better if Rosie and Adrian posed as a couple, rather than her and Matt. As far as Nicu could gather, most of the people who had bought children and babies were from Germany or the Netherlands, so the Romanians might react better to a couple who weren't exclusively Brits. At least they hoped so. Nicu and Ariana, along with Matt, were in another car and were hanging around near enough so that Matt could snatch some shots if Rosie got lucky and the director of the adoption agency whom she was meeting came out of the building along with her at the end. It was a long shot. But even just knowing they were there was a little comfort, because right now her gut was in knots.

Adrian pulled the car up to the kerb and turned to her as he switched off the engine.

'You are all right, Rosie? You have been quiet.'

She nodded. 'I'm nervous.' She attempted a half-smile. 'You've seen me like this before. But I'll be all right. I can do this.' She knew she sounded as though she was trying to convince herself.

Adrian watched as she pulled her bag onto her shoulder. He reached across and touched her arm.

'Rosie. I know you are nervous – especially after what happened to you in Glasgow a few months ago with Thomas Boag. Is difficult to come back from that, as I told you at the time. But you will be fine. These people will not suspect anything. I am sure of that. We are just a couple who want to have a baby. That's what we have to believe.'

She looked at his pale face for a second, knowing that for him, anyway, this investigation meant so much more.

'I know, I know. It's the first time for months I've done anything that might be dangerous. Once we get in, I'll be fine.' She opened the door. She didn't want to analyse this any more. Just get on with it. Rosie switched on her tape and the hidden camera. 'C'mon. Let's go.'

Inside the dark green gloomy hallway, they saw the wine-importing business's façade. Large images of sun-kissed vineyards and some earthy-looking figures working with casks of wine. Another with a glass of red. They walked past the door towards the charity of Hands Across Europe, which Rosie had seen in the news, over the years, going from Glasgow to London to Romania, as they loaded up trucks with clothes and aid for stricken orphans. They knocked on the glass door and through the frosted panel they could see someone who looked like a woman sitting at an old desktop computer. She glanced up, her expression not changing, then stood up and came towards them. She opened the door.

'We have an appointment. With Mr Georgescu. I am Ditmir Ahmeti and this is my wife, Elizabeth,' Adrian said.

Rosie smiled, hoping she looked the part.

The woman nodded, said nothing, and stepped back to allow them in.

'Wait here.'

She disappeared along a narrow corridor and Rosie watched as she knocked on a door, then opened it and stuck her head inside. She said something in Romanian and they heard a gruff voice answer. She came back halfway down the corridor and beckoned to them.

'Come.'

Rosie felt a dryness in her mouth from tension as they walked along and she took as deep a breath as she could. She felt Adrian's hand in hers. He didn't even look at her.

The door opened, and as they stepped in Rosie saw a bald, squat man get up from behind a desk. Another man sat on a chair next to the wall, staring straight ahead.

'Hello, hello. Welcome.'

The man came forward and shook their hands. Rosie felt the fleshy sweaty palm and hoped hers wasn't just as cold and clammy.

'I am Alex Georgescu. Sit. Please.' He jerked his head towards the figure sitting against the wall. 'My assistant Bogdan. He helps with the families.'

He didn't stand up, but one quick glance at the build of him and Rosie sensed he wasn't a fairy godmother – he was the muscle in case anything went wrong.

'You want to adopt a child? Is good news for us, and for Romanian children. So let us begin.'

'Thank you,' Rosie said, clearing her throat. 'I hope you can help us. We have looked for some time, and the red tape makes everything so complicated.'

He spread his hands. 'I know. But it should not be like that. We are here to help people like you, and to help the children. Abandoned children. They would have nothing if it wasn't for people like us. So much goes on with the court and the paperwork, often people like you give up. But we can make it easier.'

'Thank you.' Rosie smiled hopefully into his eyes. 'But how?'

The man looked at her, narrowing his eyes, and then to Adrian. He leaned forward and sighed wearily.

'You see, Romania is a very corrupt regime. Even now. After the dictator is dead, it is still corrupt at the top. People do not care for the children. They don't care how many in the orphanages. We know what is best and how to give the children a better life.' He paused. 'But to do that, and to get over the red tape, we must deal with these people. I will put it blunt for you, for both of you. Here in Romania, you must pay for everything. It is sad, but it is true.'

Rosie nodded, hoping her tape was picking this up.

'We understand that,' Adrian said. 'We know what happens, and we want to go ahead with our plan. We are prepared for that. If you can help us to look after one of the children from here and make our own family, we will be so grateful.'

He nodded, looking pleased. He shuffled some papers on his desk as he glanced from Rosie to Adrian.

'Now. You are quite young people, so do you want a new baby, or are you looking for a small child, like two or three years old?'

Rosie was wide-eyed. 'You mean you can get us a new-born baby?' She looked at Adrian, nonplussed. 'It would be amazing also to look at that possibility. We were thinking of a young child, from the orphanages. We had assumed it was impossible to get a small baby. How are you able to do that? Are they in the orphanages as well?'

Silence, and Rosie hoped she hadn't asked too many questions.

'It is not so easy for a new baby. But they are there. It is possible.' He leaned across his desk and clasped his hands. 'Can I tell you something? Sometimes a woman is pregnant and maybe there is no money and she already has a child. Maybe the husband is drunk or not in the home. She wants the baby to have a good home and she cannot give it. So she comes to us. And we make it better for her.'

'She gives the baby to you?'

He nodded reassuringly, as though it was commonplace.

'Yes. We make her life a little better, and she knows the baby will have also the chance of a better life.'

Rosie nodded. 'And will this baby have papers and a birth certificate, all the documents we need to take him or her home, if that is what we decide?'

'Yes. Papers will be provided – official adoption paper-work.'

'But it takes months with the courts.'

'Not if you know the right people.' He raised his eye-brows a little to emphasise his point.

'So you would be able to do this in how long?'

'Maybe in one or two weeks. We have babies coming in the next few days, but people from other places have made arrangements for them.'

To buy them, Rosie was thinking. They have already been ordered, like going to a high street store and ordering a piece of furniture. Jesus! This was dynamite and she prayed once more that her tape was working.

'Thank you. And if we wanted to look at a small child, like one or two years old, or maybe a little older, how diffi-cult is that?'

His demeanour was almost clerical.

'Is easier. Much easier. The orphanages are full of chil-dren desperate for love. Nobody has the time to give them love here, and the place is not much staff and terrible conditions – even with the changes and improvements. It is very sad. But these kind of children can be made availa-ble very quickly. In a matter of days.'

'Really? That's incredible.'

'Incredible. But sad.' He took a breath and let it out slowly. 'You want we can take you to an orphanage this day and you can have a look at some toddlers and some children?'

'You can actually do that today?' Rosie enthused, looking at Adrian. 'That would be fantastic.'

'Is no problem to do. But you must prepare yourself because it is difficult to see children in these conditions. Every one of them wants to go home with you. You understand what I mean. The children, especially the small ones, they will follow you everywhere.'

'Yes. Yes, I do.'

'So it is not an easy thing to do, walk into these places, and walk away.'

'I know.' She looked at Adrian. He spoke up:

'We would like to go today, if it is possible.'

The man looked at his henchman and spoke in Romanian.

'My assistant here will take you. I have some people to meet, but he will take you and let you see.'

This was all happening so fast. But there had been no mention of money.

'Can you tell me . . . if we decide to do this. You see, we don't really know how it works, or if we have to pay for documents, you know, to make it flow easier.'

He waved his hands. 'You don't have to worry or go to court or any of that. I will organise all that. But it is necessary to pay me, because I must make the way easier. You know. To make the way smooth. For example, from the boss of the home, to the people in the courts, and maybe for the parents to sign the baby over. Everything is money.'

'You pay the parents?'

'Well. We need to have a signature from them. Most of them don't even visit their children. They are abandoned. But we still must have their approval. It is easy.'

'So you pay them a lot of money?'

'Not a lot. But there are other people in the chain who must be paid. So it will cost two thousand pounds. Do you understand that?'

'And for that I will have a baby I can take home?'

He shook his head. 'No. For a baby is more. It is three thousand and five hundred. Maybe a little more. The children from the orphanage are cheaper because there are so many of them. Not many babies. So they are more expensive.'

Like an exclusive sale in a big store, Rosie thought. Disgust rose in her throat. She could almost feel it coming off Adrian, who managed to look accepting nonetheless.

'We are fine with that kind of money,' Adrian said. 'But I think we want to see the children in the orphanage first.'

'Good. Then come. My assistant will take you. Then we can talk.'

CHAPTER SIXTEEN

The woman from the front of the office accompanied them on the trip to the orphanage. She sat in the front seat, exchanging a little conversation with the driver, but saying nothing at all to Adrian and Rosie, who were in the back. Rosie had nipped to the toilet before they left the office, to check that her wire and tape recorder were working, to see how much tape she had used and to insert a new tape. She wasn't sure what form the orphanage visit would take or how long it would be. As Adrian took hold of her hand in the back of the car, she could tell from his look that he wanted them to look authentic as an ordinary couple: a little nervous and excited, in a foreign land, trying to adopt. She smiled, like the eager wife she was supposed to be. The only conversation they had was to remark on the lush scenery once they'd left the town, where the road became more rural and less populated. It stretched for miles, just a few houses and isolated smallholdings, and seemingly endless sweeping fields. They reached the turn-off for the orphanage. There was a long, tree-lined gravel drive full of potholes up the gradual slope to where a large, long, low, faded cream building stood. There was a play area outside with a couple of swings and a merry-go-round, and a small slide. The swing doors suddenly opened and half a dozen excited children aged around three or four came scampering out accompanied by a young woman in a green overall holding the hand of a little girl. As the car pulled up, some of them started to run towards it, but the woman shooed them towards the play area. All except one of them followed her as she ushered them, but a little boy still stood there, wide-eyed, watching as the car doors opened. Rosie got out of the back seat with the bag over her shoulder and looked down at him.

'Hello, wee guy,' she said as she closed the car door.

He stood for a second, fiddled shyly with his hands behind his back, his dark eyes liquid brown, his unkempt hair shimmering in the sun. He was wearing a checked shirt like a cowboy's and a holster with a toy gun. Then he took two steps towards her and to her surprise threw his arms around her legs, clutching her tight. She reached down and ruffled his hair, knowing from experience in these places that you had to get away from that as quick as possible – for the child's sake. They would cling to anything and anyone who they met, desperate for the hugs and human touch they so seldom received. The young woman shouted a name, and he turned around, easing his grasp. She was issuing an instruction. The driver got out and shooed him towards the park, as you would an errant puppy. He walked backwards, still smiling, then took his toy gun out, closed one eye, and pretended to shoot as he turned and ran towards the other children. Rosie looked at Adrian, who had been watching it with his arms folded, and she could almost see his mind turning over, wondering what it would have been like to have had a boy like that if his own had been allowed to live.

'The kids are always like that in these places, Adrian, so prepare yourself,' Rosie said quietly.

He nodded but said nothing.

'Come this way, please.' The woman from the office beckoned to them as she walked towards the swing doors.

They stood in the entrance hall, a huge circular foyer with a polished floor and the almost overpowering smell of cleaning fluids. The shiny walls were pale green, adorned with some watercolour prints of cartoon characters. The place was eerily quiet, and Rosie glanced across to where there was an entrance to what looked like a corridor where she assumed the toddlers' and babies' rooms must be. A door opened off the hallway and a tall, heavy man appeared, smartly dressed in an open-neck, pale-blue shirt. His looked down at them with soft blue eyes.

'Hello. I am Dorian Borsan. Mr Georgescu telephone to say you are coming. I am pleased to meet you.'

Adrian stepped forward. 'I'm Ditmir, and this is my wife, Elizabeth. Pleased to meet you too. Thank you for seeing us so quickly.'

He waved his hand, dismissively. 'No problem. Of course, is always good to meet people who are interested in our children. Anything we can do to help is all we want.'

A woman appeared at his side from the same office and he spoke to her. They all shook hands.

'Okay,' he said. 'Maria can give you some information about the children as we go around, and if you have any questions, then please ask. She knows more about the children than anyone, and is like the only mother they have ever known.' He paused. 'But as you will see in a moment, is difficult to be a mother to so many . . .' He stretched his arm out towards the corridor. 'Please, come with us.'

Adrian and Rosie walked behind them, glancing briefly at each other as they went through the doors and down the long dim corridor.

'How many children do you have in the orphanage?' Rosie asked, knowing she would need to dig out a lot of information from this one visit.

'We have eighty-five children in total. You will see, some very young, under one year old until two, and then some older children, three to five years old and older. The children stay with us until they are eleven, then they go to another place.'

'Good,' Rosie said, hoping she just sounded interested and not too probing. 'And do you have a lot adopted every year?'

He sighed. 'Sometimes. In the beginning, yes, there were more. But because of some bad things in the newspapers years later, not so many. But each year, because we are able to work very hard and talk to the right people, we can sometimes give twelve or thirteen children a good home. That is our aim. That is the most important thing for us.'

'Of course,' Rosie said. 'It's a difficult job you do.' She made eye contact with him, and she wondered if he was driven by the money he was given to smooth things over, or if he was genuinely driven to help these children. He didn't look or sound like a conman. She would have loved to have talked to him away from a place like this, but there was no chance of that as he was probably deep in with the men behind the babies for sale. Who knew? If he was, perhaps he was motivated by wanting to find homes for the children, legal or not.

As they got to the end of the corridor, the sound of babies howling filled the air and once the woman had opened the door there Rosie felt herself wince as the cries grew louder. Rosie glanced at Adrian as they both recognised the smell of stale urine in the thick, humid atmosphere. They stepped in. At first there was the shock at seeing the rows upon rows of iron cots and so many children. It was hard to take in. Rosie's eyes darted around the room. Some of them were sleeping, others just sitting, staring, and some rocking backwards and forwards. There were stains on the cot mattresses. One or two children were standing up, wailing, and these were the worst because now that they had seen the visitors they were reaching out their arms, desperate to be picked up. Rosie and Adrian stopped short for a moment, taking in the scene.

'I know this must be a little shocking for you, but I'm afraid this is how it is. We cannot be a mother and father to all of them, so we have to do what we can,' Maria said.

Rosie nodded, a little choked, and she caught Adrian's pale expression, his eyes hard as he looked around the room.

'I understand,' she murmured. 'So many children, it is so difficult.' She looked at Maria. 'Do their parents visit? Or have they been abandoned completely?'

The woman let out a resigned sigh. 'Some come back at first after they bring the children here, maybe as one- or two-year-olds, or even younger. They visit for a few months, always planning to take them back home some day. But then the visits get less and less, and then they stop. It is always the way.'

'And all of these children . . . Have they not had visits from their mother or father in a long time?'

'The younger ones, maybe every few months, but the bigger ones – you see them standing in the cot? They have not seen their parents for over a year now. Is very difficult to deal with them because in the beginning they are so . . . so . . . dis . . . I cannot remember the word.'

'Distraught,' Rosie said.

'Yes. Distraught. But after a while, they become like they accept it. When we come into the room, they light up and we can do things with them, they smile and get used to it. In their little minds, they seem to know this is their life, in their own way. It is how things are.'

Rosie nodded. 'It must be very difficult for you to work here and do what you do.' She glanced from Maria to Dorian.

'Yes.' Maria nodded, holding Rosie's gaze for a long moment. 'It is very difficult, but like the children, we must get used to it. We are all they have now.'

Dorian nodded. 'But now and again, some people like you come along, and a child's life suddenly becomes great. That is what we hope for. I wish there were more people like you.'

Rosie and Adrian nodded, and he clasped her hand tight.

'I will take you around each child and tell you what we know, and please ask if you have any questions.'

Rosie said nothing and they followed her as she stopped at each one, briefly explaining their background. The bleakness was almost overwhelming as she gazed around at the children's pale faces, some fast asleep on the mattress, snot caked to their faces, some just staring blankly, picking at the blankets. But each child had a life, a history, a story of how they got there. Even though Rosie had seen this before, she could feel herself choking with emotion. Child after child, a similar story, the parents poor, the marriage split, a young mother and an unwanted child. All of them abandoned, left to survive here in this stench and the heavy, choking loneliness of being one of so many little souls who would grow up not knowing what love or touch or relationships were, other than what they had found here in this regimented, sterile environment that passed for life. Who would make them understand as they grew up – perhaps angry and dysfunctional – that their beginnings were so very different from those of the people they would encounter as they were released into the world? The lucky ones were sold to parents who weren't even checked out and it didn't bear thinking about what their future might be. No doubt, most of them would be happy or at least have a chance of being happy, but the fact that it was built around a system of money meant there were no guarantees. Inside, she felt like screaming about the injustice of it all, and she glanced at Adrian, whose face didn't change, but whose eyes were dark and shocked. She'd seen this before when they'd found the children trapped in that hellhole in Morocco a couple of years ago. But there had only been a few of them. Here, there were at least twenty. Rosie listened while Maria described the children's daily life, their diet, how the workers tried to play with them and take them out in the garden in good weather. It wasn't an ugly, horrible life all the time, she stressed. But it was sad nonetheless, she said.

Then, to Rosie's surprise, Dorian said to them, 'We will go for a couple minutes and leave you together to look at the children. Maybe you will see a particular child you are interested in. Sometimes parents just naturally fall for one child. Everyone is different.'

Rosie and Adrian nodded their thanks and watched as they left the room.

They stood for a moment in silence, looking around the place, then each other. Then Rosie whispered, 'That's a result, leaving us here like this. I'm just going to walk around here, Adrian, and hope the camera has been taking everything in. The images won't be perfect, but hopefully we can use them.'

Adrian said nothing as he walked between the cots, looking at the children, not touching or reaching out as though he was afraid to go there. One child was standing up, smiling, reaching his arms out. A little boy, light hair and blue eyes, nappy soaked. Rosie walked along to where he stood. His name on the cot.

'Hello, Jabir,' she said, looking at him.

Adrian smiled at her. 'How beautiful he is.'

The little boy banged on the cot and grabbed for Adrian's arm. He didn't touch him. Rosie knew from the look in his eyes that he longed to pick the boy up and hold him in his arms, but there was no point. They'd be out of here in the next few minutes and this child would be bawling after them. They couldn't afford to touch or pick up or hold any of them. She was glad when the doors opened and Maria and Dorian came back in.

'You see all the children. Did you pick any of them up?'

'No, we didn't want to unsettle them.'

He nodded his understanding.

'Did you see any particular child you may be interested in?'

Rosie looked at Adrian, not quite sure what to say, but she knew they would have to respond.

'The little boy . . .' She pointed to the one still bouncing on his cot. 'Jabir is very beautiful. How long has he been here?'

'Since he was ten months old. He is now . . .' He turned to the woman.

'Two and a half,' she said. 'The mother was a teenager and abandoned him. She has never been back to see him. He is a good little boy. Bright and funny. And very mischievous.'

'Jabir,' Adrian said. 'He is a very beautiful little boy.' He did his best to smile as he glanced at Rosie. 'He is a lovely boy, Elizabeth. Yes?'

'Yes.' She could read the pain in his eyes. 'I don't think we can make our mind up quickly, but if it was possible, how long do you think the paperwork would take for a boy like this?'

'Not long. Two weeks. Maybe less. Depends. But you could ask the agency about that.'

Rosie instinctively knew she wanted a picture with this little boy in it so she could feature him, but didn't want to raise any suspicions. She couldn't have taken a picture of Adrian with him as he had to remain unidentified. But at least they had an image of the boy in his cot and it would have to do. She wanted to get out of here as soon as possible.

They took them to another room. It was all babies, around eight or nine of them, some only weeks old. The place was peaceful, with blinds drawn, all of them sound asleep, not knowing what was ahead of them, and perhaps just as well. She listened while the woman whispered their stories. They walked around, Rosie hoping the images would be good in the light.

'And how much more difficult to adopt a little baby?'

'Depends. Some of them still have visits from their mother, so they are not all abandoned. But usually they will be after a while. But is more difficult because it is only a few months since they came. But you must ask the agency.'

When they emerged from the room, they turned down the offer of a coffee as Rosie wanted to be out and away in case there were any problems or slip-ups. The longer you were in a situation like this, she thought, the more chance there was of saying the wrong thing, or being asked a question you couldn't answer, or them becoming suspicious. They had what they had and it would be good enough. They shook hands with the staff, said they would be in touch with the agency and thanked them.

'I hope your visit here was good, and that you are

successful,' Dorian said. 'You look like you would make very good parents. Very good indeed, I think.'

Rosie and Adrian glanced at each other and half smiled.

'Thank you. You have been very helpful.'

'We do the best we can for the children here. Everything I do is for them. I can promise you that.'

Rosie sensed a little edge to his voice and wondered if he wanted to convey that perhaps she already suspected he was involved in the money chain, but was attempting to justify his role in it. And the thing was, she believed him.

They drove off and nobody spoke all the way back to the office. When they got out of the car, they shook hands and told the adoption agency lady they would be in touch. They walked around to their own car. It had been a major result, she would have pictures, hopefully, of the place, and a recording of the full conversations in the agency and the orphanage. She could go home tomorrow if necessary, with a splash and a couple of spreads in the bag. But Rosie's heart was heavy from what they'd witnessed and she knew by the images of the cots and the children and the little boy desperate to be picked up would haunt her. And on top of that, she knew that not too far away was a woman whose newborn baby child had been torn from her. She should go now; Quit while you're ahead, she could hear McGuire saying. But she couldn't.

CHAPTER SEVENTEEN

Helen asked the taxi to drop her outside the Caledonian Hotel in Princes Street, rather than go to the train station, as she didn't know where she was headed. She handed the driver an extra fiver on top of the forty quid for the run through from Glasgow. She thought she saw a look in his eye as though he detected that she was in a lot of trouble.

'Listen, sweetheart,' the driver said as he put her suitcase beside her. 'It's none of my business, but I'll be honest with you, it looks like you're on the run or something. Are you all right? Is there anything I can do to help you?'

Helen gave him a long look, partly grateful but also part of her wondering if he was on the make – a lonely woman on her own, with plenty of money. He looked quite genuine, but she didn't need any more people in her life right now, and she wasn't daft enough to take a complete stranger into her confidence.

'Thanks for your concern. But, I'm all right. I've just got some things I need to straighten out in my mind – that's all.'

She took hold of her suitcase and pulled her bag over her shoulder.

'Good luck to you then,' he said, stepping back.

'Thanks,' she said. Luck had never featured much in her life so far, but she could sure use some now.

The driver turned towards his car and opened the door, and she could feel his eyes on her as she approached the revolving doors of the Caledonian Hotel, with absolutely no idea what her next move would be.

Helen had been sitting in the bar at a table in the corner, watching it fill up, empty, then fill up again with the various tourists, business people and general traffic you got on Princes Street at one of the city's well-known and stylish haunts. She was still on her first glass of white wine, and had picked at a chicken salad as she sat watching. She felt desolate, empty and lonely. It was as though all the adrenalin of the last few days – from the moment Frankie had come into her flat, until she'd escaped from Ricky Thomson's clutches – had all been a blur. She'd been kicking her way through everything that was in front of her, determined nothing would keep her down. She'd been like that all her life. That was the reason she was in the financial position she was in right now, with bank accounts chock-full of Alan Lewis's money. With the amount of dosh she had stashed away – it was over £800,000 – she could go anywhere in the world, or that's how she'd thought it would work out. Until Frankie had started blackmailing her, until she decided she had to eliminate him, and until Ricky Thomson had tracked her down for some Russian bastard who, unknown to her, seemed up to his eyes in some kind of shit with Alan Lewis. All she really knew about Alan's business was what she saw on the accounts and the money they brought in. She knew about the wine-importing business and that he did the accounts for the charity. And she'd already figured out that he must be money-laundering for gangsters. But she didn't know who the figures or personalities were, and she hadn't even bothered to ask questions before as she'd enjoyed the champagne lifestyle. But now, there was nothing. Just a pile of money, and every fucker from Moscow to Glasgow was looking for her – including the bloody cops.

She scrolled down her phone contacts. There was one person she could contact, but she was loth to do it. One person, who knew what she was, who knew her every move, and who could tell her what she was thinking even before she thought it. Her mother. She looked at her name and her mobile number. She hadn't spoken to her ma in five years. She'd left all that shit behind without so much as a backwards glance. They never spoke, she'd stopped answering her ma's calls, they lost touch. Christ, she didn't even know if she was still alive. But knowing the vicious bastard that her ma was, she'd be surviving somewhere, doing someone out of money, conning her way through life as she'd always done. She almost smiled at the thought. The apple doesn't fall far from the tree. And yet, she was all she had. Even with her drunkenness, the smell of her, the cut of her and the complete arseholes she had brought into their lives, Helen had loved her. She had cried her eyes out when her ma kicked her out for stealing from her.. And then months later when her mother had tried to contact her, leaving messages on her phone, Helen had refused to answer. It would be the same old story, the same old apology. Abuse and apologise. She'd had enough of it. She was making enough money on her own by then, in London, in the profession her mother had more or less set her up in. But she wouldn't be some street hooker or some two-bob whore who brought men to their home. She would use her assets to move on to greater things. She never once even gave that a second thought, or the morality of it. She had one goal: to get out of the shit. And once she'd hooked Alan Lewis, she had completely airbrushed her mother out of her life. Now she needed help, a place to hide, somewhere she could take refuge. She looked at the number again. What would her mother do? Tell her to fuck off? Perhaps. But by this time she'd have read in the papers about Frankie's murder and she would know that if her daughter had been married to a wealthy accountant, she'd have money. That would be all that mattered. Helen scrolled down to the number again, then hit the Call key, listening to the phone ringing.

Two, three, four rings, then the unmistakable rasping voice of her mother, clearly still with her thirty-a-day habit.

'Ma. It's me.'

Silence.

'Are you there, Ma?'

'I'm here.'

'I need help.'

Silence, then a wheeze. 'I saw the papers.'

Helen let it hang for a second, wondering stupidly if she would even ask her how she was.

'What do you want?'

'I . . .' Helen felt surprisingly choked. She remembered early days as a little girl, when her mum came into bed beside her and they snuggled in and she could still smell her perfume and the cigarettes and alcohol on her breath, but it was warm and secure. 'I . . . I just don't want to be alone. I'm scared. Can I come and see you?'

Silence, and the sound of a deep breath and a long sigh.

'Where are you?'

'Edinburgh.'

'What the fuck are you doing there?'

'I ran away. They kidnapped me.'

'Who?'

'I don't know. Some gangsters. I don't know. It's something to do with Alan.'

'Your husband. The guy who's gone missing? What the Christ are you up to your arse in?'

'It's a mess.'

'And you want to bring your shit to my doorstep? After five bloody years?'

Helen didn't know what to say.

'I didn't think you'd want to talk to me. After . . . after the way I didn't answer your calls and just ignored you.'

'You were right. I didn't. You're a conniving wee bitch.'

Her words and the way she spat them out stung Helen to the core, even though they shouldn't have. Because her mother was right. She *was* a conniving bitch.

'Okay,' Helen said, swallowing. She wasn't going to beg. Half the reason she had turned into the kind of woman she was was because of the shit dealt out to her as a kid. Or so her therapist had once told her. 'I'm sorry I called you.'

There was a long moment where nothing was said, and Helen could hear her mother breathing.

'Get on the train. Meet me at Queen Street. Phone me before you arrive.'

She was about to say 'Thanks, Mum', but her mother had already hung up.

Helen looked out of the train window at the grey fine rain sweeping across the fields. She didn't know what to think. Her mother had agreed to meet her off the train, but she wouldn't be expecting her to stand there with open arms and misty eyes. It might have been five years since they last saw each other, but this was not a welcome home party.

She hadn't even agreed to help her. Janey McCann would meet her daughter, listen to what she had to say, and then make up her mind. And Helen knew that her decision on whether to help would be based on what was in it for her. That's how it always was. She'd never done anyone a turn in her life that didn't benefit herself. Especially if there was money in it. Sometimes Helen thought that her mother's obsession with money and getting as much of it as possible was the reason *she* was so greedy and worshipped money. Or perhaps it was the security it brought. The doors it opened. If you had money, you didn't have to sell your daughter for sex. You didn't have to open your house and your legs to all the useless, scummy bastards of the day to make a living. In her darker times, Helen used to wonder why her mother couldn't just go out and work like everyone else – take in ironing, do washing, find a cleaning job. Being a prostitute was *her* decision. And then, it was her own. She hated herself for it. And if she was honest with herself, she'd never really got away from being a hooker. Everything she had achieved, she'd got on her back – including Alan Lewis's fortune, and including securing her recent escape from Ricky Thomson's clutches. Who are you to judge your own mother? she told herself. You're the very same.

Helen dragged her suitcases to the door as they approached Queen Street. She pulled her collar up to hide most of her face, and straightened herself up. She'd taken the wig off, and was wearing a hat with her hair tucked in.

When she got off the train, she walked briskly behind the commuters and tourists along the concourse, her eyes scanning the people milling around. Then she spotted her, the auburn hair coiffed and full, framing her face. From this distance, she looked like an ageing screen goddess, at least that was the look her mother had always tried to achieve. But now, as she got a little closer behind the crowd, Helen could see the make-up and the hardness in her blue eyes as they also scanned the crowd. Then she caught her mother's eye. Nothing. Just the slightest raise of her chin to acknowledge her. Helen almost stopped in her tracks. She didn't even know if she could trust her own mother. But she pressed on, and now she could see a black wool over-coat and a jade green scarf wrapped around her mother's neck. Whatever she was up to these days, she wasn't skint. As she stood there, two feet away, Helen stopped and put her suitcase down, not sure what to do. They stood looking at each other, not a word; Helen searched her mother's face, but not a sign of a crack. Still hard, cold eyes. Or was she wrong, was there a little flicker there of regret, or sorrow? She was thinner, but not frail.

'All right, Ma?'

'Aye.' She glanced down at her daughter's bags. 'Right. Come on. We'll get a taxi.' Then she turned her back and walked away. Helen picked up her bags and followed her.

CHAPTER EIGHTEEN

'So how much proof do we have of Alan Lewis's involvement in the baby racket? And I mean *proof*, Gilmour.'

Rosie listened as McGuire probed every detail from the other end of the phone, as she knew he would. While there was a general belief that Lewis was missing, presumed dead, and therefore wouldn't come and sue them, the editor was playing cautious.

'Well, we have him as a named director of the wine-importing business. And he's also a director of the charity. And the managing director of the wine-importing business is also named as a director of the charity.'

'You have that in actual black and white.'

'Yes. I got the documents tonight from a contact over here. So whatever we say about selling, we can link him to Hands Across Europe. No question about that. I'm not even worried.'

'But I want you to say he's behind it.'

'We can't say that unless we have someone in the organisation saying it. And that will be impossible. I don't even want to go there. We're posing as a couple looking to adopt a kid, remember, so asking questions like that would be crazy.'

He paused and thought. 'I know, Gilmour. I'm not daft. I'm just thinking of another way. We have to find another way.'

'Unless it came from someone in Scotland. And that's not going to happen. It's not as if selling babies – if he does know about it – is something he'd be talking about at dinner parties.'

'But he's been raising money here – well, the charity has anyway. So maybe someone involved in that knows about it.'

'It's a possibility, but a long shot.'

'So what do you think? I know you have that other story about the Romanian mother and the snatched baby. I love that. Where are we with it? And how dangerous is it?'

'I've now got the address of the people who were given the baby – well, they must have bought her, actually. I have to go there, Mick. I can't not go. You know that.'

'It would be a belter if we already have the bastards at the adoption charity saying they can get a baby, and suddenly we can produce evidence of a stolen one. I mean the whole story about how we tracked them down and stuff – it's dynamite. But would you propose to put it to the couple that you know their seemingly adopted baby was in fact stolen?'

'I'll think of something.'

'Like what?'

'I don't know. I'll let you know when it comes to me.'

'No. You mean you'll let me know once you've done it. Listen, Rosie, I want to know what you do *before* you do it. Are we clear?'

'Sure.'

'Aye, right. Call me in the morning, let me know your thoughts.'

What Rosie hadn't told McGuire was that she was already on her way to the address of the couple who had bought the baby. She was afraid he would tell her to leave it for a night and think about it again tomorrow. But after the visit to the orphanage, Rosie had decided they didn't have a lot of time to hang around here. They'd already shown the so-called adoption agency their interest, and they'd expect to hear from them one way or another in the next couple of days, and she still wasn't even sure how they'd pursue that. But in case they had to get out of Romania quickly, she had to hit the adoptive couple's address straight away. Even if it was only to establish that the baby was really there. She had to admit to herself that she didn't really know how they were going to handle it if the couple came to the door and confirmed that they had an adopted baby. Earlier on, over coffee, she and Adrian had decided to wing it, and to say they were thinking of adopting a newborn baby, and that friends of theirs had told them that this couple had already adopted one and might be able to help them with the right sort of information. Rosie was worried it didn't sound very convincing, and she wasn't even convinced herself. But another reason they were going tonight was that the address was only half an hour's drive away, on the edge of Bucharest, so they wouldn't have far to travel.

She was in the front seat, with Adrian driving, and Ariana and Matt in the back. Nicu was back at the hotel, and Rosie had suggested he keep a watch on the adoption agency comings and goings from a distance, and if possible follow the boss. She now wished she hadn't asked Nicu to go on the spying mission in case they all got rumbled.

Ariana leaned forward in between the two seats, and pointed to a street off to the left of the road they were in.

'This next turn is the address we are looking for. See on the right?'

'I see,' Adrian mumbled and pulled the car over.

Rosie glanced up at the block of flats, which looked slightly less drab than some of the others, and the area looked a little better.

'The apartment is on the second floor, Ariana. But I think before we go straight to the house, we should maybe try a neighbour. Make sure we're in the right place.'

'Sure.' Ariana shrugged, as though she didn't really understand. 'If you think is best.'

'I'm just a little bit wary of going knocking on the door

like this, with no real story that sounds convincing, and I'm worried the couple might be suspicious and get back to the adoption agency. Then we're in trouble.'

'Yes. I see now. Okay. We will go to the neighbour first.'

As they got out of the car, Matt was discreetly taking pictures of the area and the apartment block, and also the foyer inside. They climbed the stairs and there was no name on the door of the apartment number they'd been given. Rosie looked at Ariana and jerked her head to indicate that she should knock on the other door. Matt and Adrian had stayed on the first floor, waiting. Ariana knocked on the door and they waited a few moments. Nothing. Then Rosie knocked, and another few moments. Nothing.

'Should we try upstairs perhaps?'

Ariana nodded, but suddenly the door opened a little, and through the small gap they could see an old woman. Ariana spoke in Romanian to her. The woman shook her head, and then opened the door fully. She looked Rosie up and down and then back to Ariana. Her hands were raised in surprise, and when she spoke she sounded sad and a little agitated. Rosie waited, anxious to hear the translation. Ariana turned to her.

'She is saying the couple, the Ginescas, who we are looking for . . . the husband was killed in an accident at work. A truck hit him. And the wife, she can no longer cope with a small baby, because her life is very difficult without the husband.'

'Is she saying anything about the baby? Did they adopt her?'

'Yes, she is saying they had just adopted a newborn baby and were very happy. She seems a bit upset. She has known them a few years.'

'So what happened?'

Ariana turned to the old lady again and continued asking questions. The old woman spoke again, wringing her hands like a baby rocking, her eyes filling up.

'She is saying it was a terrible tragedy, all of it. The mother went to pieces and the baby needed looking after, but she couldn't cope. She says that some days she was left with the baby and the mother was always crying and not able to go to the shops. After a few weeks, she decided to give the baby back up to an orphanage. The mother is gone now, to another town, to where her sister lives, and she is not coming back.'

'Jesus,' Rosie said. 'That's unbelievable.'

'I know. But she is telling the truth, I think. She would have no reason to say this, and you can see how upset she is.'

'I believe her all right.' Rosie lowered her voice. 'But the poor baby. Can you ask her does she have any idea which orphanage the couple used or did anyone come to collect the baby?'

Ariana spoke to the woman again, and Rosie watched as she answered.

'She doesn't remember anyone coming. Only a friend of the woman who helped her pack up and the day they left with the baby in the pram. She said she watched from the window, them putting the baby in the car, and she could hear her crying. It was so sad. That was the last time she saw them.'

Rosie stood for a moment. 'Ariana,' she said, 'can you ask the lady if she has any photographs of the woman or the baby, or even any of them together with the husband? And also, the name of the baby, the name they gave her?'

Ariana spoke again to the woman, and she looked surprised. Then she nodded and closed the door a little and they could see her going down the hall.

'She has one photograph she can show us, of the baby and the couple. They had a celebration a few weeks after they got the baby and everyone was so happy.'

Rosie's journalist brain was screaming 'Result!', but her heart sank for the poor baby ripped from its natural mother to be sold by criminals and now dumped in an orphanage, Christ knew where. The woman appeared with a photograph in a frame and her trembling hands held it up.

'Beautiful,' Rosie said. 'What a lovely picture. Everyone is so happy.'

'She said she was like the baby's grandmother, and that now she is so sad. But also her heart is broken for the mother.'

'Can you ask her if it is possible for us to take a photograph of the picture? I can get Matt up here to do it. We really need this picture, Ariana.'

Ariana nodded, but her expression was flat.

'I will ask, but she might wonder who you are.'

'Tell her I'm someone who is trying to trace the baby. She's an old woman, and the business with the agency and this family was over months ago. It's not as though they're going to come back here and start asking questions. Just please tell her I'm trying to trace the baby for the real mother.'

Rosie couldn't translate, but she watched Ariana explaining everything to the old woman, and she could see her face light up when she mentioned that perhaps the real mother and the baby might be reunited. She nodded in agreement, and Rosie leaned over the banister and called down to Matt.

'Make this quick, Matt. We don't want to hang around here longer than is necessary.'

Matt got Ariana to hold the picture and snapped several times.

'Done and dusted.'

'Now can you ask her if she still keeps in touch with her neighbour?'

'Are you sure?' Ariana seemed reluctant.

'Yes,' Rosie said without even needing to consider it. 'I'm going with my gut on this. I think she's a genuinely caring old woman.'

Ariana spoke to the woman, then turned to Rosie.

'She last spoke to the woman a couple of months ago, but she doesn't talk to her very much.'

'I was thinking if it would be possible for her to phone the woman and maybe talk to her about the baby and where it went to.'

'I can ask her that, Rosie, but I think it wouldn't be a good idea. It doesn't strike me that she keeps in touch that much and would have the kind of relationship to go back and talk about the baby.'

'Okay. Leave it. But will you ask her if she knows if the mother was taking the baby to an orphanage where her sister lives? Or is it in this area?'

Ariana was talking to the woman.

'She said the woman was taking the baby to an orphanage in Bucharest. She mentioned the name. I know this place. I can check the name.'

'Excellent. Okay. Ariana, can you tell her thanks so much for her assistance, and find a way to hint to her that it would be better if she didn't say anything to anyone about our meeting? Should I give her some money? I don't want to insult her, but can you suggest I give her something just as a token to help her? She's an old woman. She won't have much.'

Ariana nodded and spoke to the woman. She put her hands up, in protest.

'She said it is not necessary. She doesn't have much, but

she is okay. She will be happy if the baby finds her mother. She asks one thing only. If the baby and the mother are reunited, she asks could I come and tell her if that happens. That's all. She would just like to know.'

'Tell her yes, you will, if it happens.'

CHAPTER NINETEEN

Back at the hotel, Rosie listened in disbelief as Ariana told her what she'd discovered after a lengthy search at the registry office in Bucharest. There was no record of a baby named Iasius Onescu born at the hospital to Madelina and Eadbert, and no record of a death registered in that name. So the document Madelina had been given by the hospital had been a fake. They hadn't registered the baby's birth or death. The baby simply disappeared. The adoption agency had taken crooked to a whole new level. Not only were they stealing newborn babies, they were able to issue fake death certificates, and somehow able to make sure the child was not even registered as having been born to its biological parents. Surely this had to involve not just one person at the hospital, but several? Rosie asked Ariana.

'That is something we may not be able to find out. But in the hospital, there will be a key person who is responsible for registering the births on any day or week, and that information will be passed on to the registry department in the city. But it is looking as though while they register most of the babies, there must be one or two that go missing. They tell the mother the baby has died, then produce a death certificate. They cannot do this with several babies a week or even in a month, but it can be done with one or two babies every couple of months. Stillbirths happen a lot in this country, and no poor, uneducated mother is going to argue with a doctor or a nurse who is telling them their baby has died. But the person at the hospital who is registering the babies must be in on the scam. We'll probably never be able to find out who that is.'

'So where do we go from here?' Nicu asked as they sat drinking coffee in the hotel bar.

Everyone sat for a few moments, then Rosie put down her cup.

'I have an idea. What we know at the moment, though we have no definite proof, is that a UK citizen is a director of a wine-importing company and also a director of this UK-based charity Hands Across Europe. We have established, or pretty much established, that this charity also operates a babies-for-sale racket. We have our meeting with them on tape and on film. So I think we go to the British embassy. We take the mother with us and her baby's fake death certificate, and we tell them what is going on.'

'But the woman who is affected isn't British, so I'm not sure the embassy would be interested,' Nicu said.

'They'd have to at least initiate some kind of investigation. Especially if we have a story, either in the paper or ready to go, exposing a huge level of corruption. As the British embassy, with a possible Brit at the centre of criminal activity, they have to ask some questions in high places of their Romanians counterparts.'

Nicu nodded. 'But then if your British diplomats start asking questions, you might find everything closes up and perhaps the child at the centre of your investigation will go missing. We know where she is at the moment, but we have no proof that she is this woman's child. And, as Ariana has already established, the child with the name on the fake document doesn't exist at the registry office. And if she doesn't exist there, they will simply close the doors. I know what they are like.'

Rosie glanced at Adrian, who was listening, but saying nothing.

'Then we must find a way to take the child with the woman to the British embassy,' she said. 'We can put her story and her case to them, and plead to them to ask questions because a Brit is at the heart of serious criminal activity.'

'I agree with you, Rosie,' Adrian said. 'But I think we must find the husband who sold the baby and get him to admit what he did to the embassy and police.'

'There's not much chance of Eadbert coming along to that party, Adrian.'

'We can try to persuade him,' he said, deadpan.

'But do you think the British embassy will even be that interested? Do you know anyone there?' Nicu asked. He was beginning to look at Rosie and Adrian as though they were a little unhinged.

Rosie thought of the Scots diplomat in the British embassy in Pakistan who'd pulled her out of a hole last year in Islamabad after she'd escaped with a teenage bride whose father was about to marry her off to an old man. He was a solid, senior contact, and she was sure he'd at least listen.

'No, I don't know anyone at the embassy here,' Rosie said, 'but I know a man who just might.' She stood up. 'Let me make a phone call.'

'But how are we going to be able to take the baby from the orphanage to the British embassy?' Nicu asked. 'We cannot just steal her.'

Rosie looked at Adrian, but didn't answer. From the corner of her eye, she could see Matt put his head in his hands.

They had established, through Ariana's contacts, that the baby Iasius was now called Ioana and was indeed in the orphanage the old woman had suggested she might have been taken to. It was the most practical choice and closest to where they'd lived, and by this time, with her name having been changed, there would be no chance of the real mother tracking her down. In fact, Ariana had told them, the baby that was in that orphanage now would have no papers or history of her real name or origin. Ariana had one contact in that orphanage – a girl who went to university with her – and she told Rosie she trusted her enough to confide in her about the baby. Rosie was sceptical, given that there were few people she could trust in this whole country, but Ariana had been on the ball up until now, so she told her to go ahead. Rosie had spent the last couple of hours in her hotel room, trying to work out the best way ahead. She'd phoned her contact in Pakistan, Gerry, who was glad to hear from her, and he listened to her story. He promised he would do what he could. One iron was already in the fire. Ariana had gone to Madelina to tell her that there was a possibility that they had traced her baby. And at some stage, though she did not know when, Adrian would find the husband and bring him to the British Embassy. Best not to dwell on how Adrian was planning to manage that. It was all getting a little wildly out of control for Rosie's nerves, and she'd no idea how she'd be able to break any of this to McGuire. She felt tired, partly from the exhaustion of running around since she got here, and partly from the fact that she'd complicated things by being determined to help the woman whose baby had been stolen. She lay on the bed and was beginning to drift off when she heard a soft knock at the door. She got up and opened it, and Ariana stood there. Rosie beckoned her in.

'Ariana,' she said rubbing her eyes. 'Sorry, I was almost asleep there. I'm tired today.'

Ariana nodded, but didn't look at all tired herself.

'Sorry to disturb you, Rosie, but I have some news about the baby.'

Rosie was suddenly alert as they sat down on the chairs by the window.

'I called my friend on the phone. I trust her and I asked her some questions about this baby. First, did she know if a baby of that name was there, and what circumstances she was brought in.'

'Good.' Rosie was impressed. This girl was efficient.

Ariana nodded enthusiastically, then went on. 'She has told me, Yes, the baby with the name Ioana, she was brought in by the mother who adopted her, and she also give me her name. It is the same name as we were told. It is Iasius.'

'Excellent. Great work, Ariana. You've done really well for us since we got here, but it's fantastic to have found this out.'

She was keen to go on.

'But, Rosie. I'm afraid there is a problem with this child.'

Rosie heart sank.

'What problem?'

'The health is not good. The baby has had some fits, convulsions, and they do not know what is wrong. But the doctors examine her and still doing tests. But here and in an orphanage is difficult.'

'How ill is the baby? Is she going to die?'

'My friend doesn't know, but she doesn't think so. The baby might have a heart problem or even more complications. But she said, If this is the case, then this baby will never be adopted. Nobody wants a baby who is sick.'

Rosie nodded. 'And what did she say when you told her about the baby being stolen from the real mother?'

'She is shocked about it, and very angry. My friend, like me, has heard about these things, but didn't know of anyone it happened to. She knows that some charity buys and sells children from orphanages, and knows it will always happen because of the corruption in this country at so many levels. But stealing a newborn baby is wrong. She will help us.'

Rosie thought for a moment. 'If we gave her a camera, could she take some pictures of the baby? If she is alone with her at some time?'

Ariana shrugged. 'I will ask.'

'I want to try to get the baby to the British embassy, but I think this will be impossible, unless we steal her and that would cause all sorts of trouble. It could get us in jail. So we'll have to think of another way.'

Ariana stood up and went towards the door.

'I will call my friend and arrange to meet her with the camera.'

'Good. If she's able to take the picture today, we can take it with us to the embassy.'

Ariana left. Rosie stood by the window, watching the traffic below and the children in the street running up to every car that pulled up to the outside of the hotel. A little baby with health problems stuck in an orphanage. She didn't have much chance even if she was with her real mother. But in the orphanage she had none.

CHAPTER TWENTY

When the taxi crossed the Jamaica Bridge and headed past the Glasgow Sheriff Court, Helen felt her heart sink a little further.

'Still in the same house?'

Her mother glared at her then looked out of the side window.

'What did you expect? I didn't get any superannuation in my job.'

Helen half smiled despite the gloom. Janey could always deliver a one-liner with the kind of deadpan expression that would have given Lauren Bacall a run for her money in an old Humphrey Bogart black-and-white movie. In a momentary reverie the thought sent her back to watching the black-and-white telly in their living room three floors up in the Gorbals' high flats. Helen had dreamed of being in those movies – the glam dresses, the sweeping hairstyles – the starlets all reminded her of her mother, how she used to watch her as a little girl, getting all dolled up as though she were a movie star. Helen used to dream she would be a film star one day in her little world of make-believe. Until night fell and she could hear her mother coming home from wherever she'd been, with some oily guy in tow, smelling of drink.

Her ma hadn't even asked her any questions yet on how it had come to this. When they'd got into the car and Helen had told her she'd was in a right mess, Janey told her to button it. Save it, she'd said. Till we get to the house. Walls have ears, or have you learned nothing in the big wide glam world? It was going to be a long night. Darkness was already coming down like a cloak on the deserted streets, the grubby flats, some with windows boarded up, adding to her depression. The taxi dropped them off, and Helen got out with her bags, traipsing behind her mother after she was left to pay the driver. She knew where she was going. A couple of teenage boys stood in the close's entrance, drinking cheap Buckfast wine, faces flushed. Inside, it smelled the same as always – a smell she could conjure up wherever she was in the world, whether she was in Monaco or Puerto Banus. She could call up that smell as a reminder to herself never to fuck up her life so much that she ended up back here. Yet here she was, tail between her legs, getting into the lift as it stuttered to the third floor, doors opening on to a hallway with a flickering light. Her mother unlocked the door and they went into her flat's hall, neatly carpeted and smelling fresh and welcoming, the way it always did. Her mother had always been fastidious about cleanliness, as though she was trying to clean and polish some respectability into her scummy life. As she walked down the hallway Janey silently pushed open Helen's old bedroom door. She gathered she was meant to put her stuff in there, so she did, walking in, switching on the light. As she entered, she could see it hadn't been touched. Nothing had been moved: the perfume, the dressing table, her hair-brush, comb, and little things she'd had to make her room girly. The small jewellery box that she'd covered with sea-shells. The bed with its pink duvet and small table lamps on either side. It looked as though it was lovingly cleaned and polished every day, like the rest of the house. Helen instantly felt tears coming to her eyes, but she bit them back, looking at the bed, remembering the things that she'd had to do there. She'd learned to live with that a long time ago, and it didn't shock or frighten her any more. It had taken her on a road to prostitution and it had helped her bag a rich man. And now she was rich. But the image she still saw was the little girl of thirteen the first time. She blinked away the picture and sat on the bed. She had to work something out. And soon. She didn't want to stay here any more than her mother would want her to, so there had to be some plan to get the hell out.

She went into the kitchen as she heard the kettle click

off, and found her mother making tea. Helen sat down at the kitchen table, as she had done all her life – except her life had been so different in the past five years. She thought she had left all this behind, including Janey, who was taking two mugs out of the cupboard and milk from the fridge. She put milk in her own tea and left Helen's black. That she remembered small things like that should have touched her, but the two of them had become so remote to each other long before her walk-out. In fact, as Helen had grown into her late teens and got out of the game and moved on, she'd begun to hate her mother. Yet, looking at her now, across the table, she thought there was a tiny tremor in her mother's hand as she poured the tea, and she saw the concentration in her mother's face as she sat down and pushed a mug of tea towards her.

'I'll phone for a Chinese in a wee while. Are you hungry?'

Helen shrugged. 'I will be.' She wanted to say, Thanks, but the word caught in her throat. Thanks for what? For making her who she was? Stop with the blaming, she chided herself.

'So tell me . . .' Janey sipped her tea and lit a cigarette. She inhaled and coughed, her eyes watering. 'Did you shoot Frankie?'

Helen didn't answer for a second as she recalled the image of Frankie's shocked expression a second before he'd hit the floor.

'Aye,' she nodded, 'it was him or me.'

'Aye. That would have sounded quite convincing in the High Court,' her mother said, sarcastic. 'So if it was self-defence, why did you bugger off and leave him lying there?'

Helen waited a moment, deciding how she should answer this. 'I was leaving anyway. I had already packed. My case was at the door. Frankie was just being a bastard. He came to take all my money. He came to . . . to . . .'

'To what?' Her mother looked her in the eye.

Helen decided to tell her. This might well be her next big mistake, but she couldn't keep it in.

'He was blackmailing me.'

'Blackmailing you?' She gave her a sly look. 'Were you shagging him?'

Helen nodded.

Janey shook her head and let out a long sigh.

'You're a stupid bastard. But you always were. Frankie is the biggest robbing chancer in the Gorbals. Only got away with it because of the way he looked – some kind of roguish charm, they might call it. Fucking conman from the day he was born, like his da.' She paused. 'Do you know he's got a girlfriend, and a wee daughter? A baby?'

Helen dropped her eyes to the table. 'No. I didn't.'

'Probably wouldn't have bloody mattered. Well he has, or had. A wee lassie up in Springburn. A junkie, or reformed junkie – which is what they all say till they're found face down in a close.'

'How do you know this?'

'Because I know the girl's ma. She's from here. You know her. Donna Malone, the girl's name is. Younger than you. So you might not remember her.'

Helen tried to place the name, but her mind was a blur. Apart from anything else, she'd killed Frankie and left a little girl without a father – even a bastard of a father like Frankie Mallon.

'I can't say I know her.'

'Well. Doesn't matter now.' She drew on her fag. 'So why was he blackmailing you?'

Helen said nothing.

Then Janey looked like a penny had dropped.

'Don't tell me that this missing husband of yours I read about in the papers, this fancy accountant who hasn't been seen for eight months . . . Don't tell me Frankie had anything to do with this . . . had he?'

Helen waited a long moment, then she nodded.

Her mother shook her head. 'Fuck me! Did Frankie bump him off? He's got quite good at that, I heard. Doing people's dirty work.'

Helen nodded. 'That's what I thought,' she said.

'What do you mean, that's what you thought?' She looked a little confused, and then amused. 'Fuck me! Don't tell me you got Frankie to bump off your man. Aw, for fuck's sake, Helen!'

Helen didn't answer.

'Where did this happen? I read he was in Romania.'

Helen nodded, then looked away.

'Frankie bumped him off in Romania?' Her mother's voice went up an octave. 'Who the Christ do you think you are – in one of these old movies we used to watch? You got a hitman to kill your bloody husband? Oh, Jesus protect us! Why? Greed. Of course. Greed. You could never get enough. I knew you'd be like that, given half a chance.'

Helen felt her face flush. 'Given half a chance? Given half a chance I might have been a different girl, a different woman.'

Her remark stung her mother and her face fell. They sat in stony silence for a moment, and Janey drew deep on her cigarette, her face like flint.

'Aye,' she said finally. 'You might be right about that.'

'Ma—'

'Shut it! Tell me what happened.'

'I paid Frankie to kill him in Romania. And he came back and told me he had. Then I was leaving to start a new life. I was getting the hell out of here forever. That was my plan. Yes, I did have an affair with Frankie, but he was just using me. So I was fucking off forever.'

'No doubt with your poor late murdered husband's money.'

'He was a crook. Laundering money for gangsters.'

'Oh, and that bothered you, did it? I bet it didn't bother you when you stuffed it into your Louis Vuitton suitcase.'

She almost smiled, jerking her eyes in the direction of the bedroom where Helen had put her bags.

Helen almost smiled too. 'Alan's not dead.'

'What?'

'After . . . After Frankie came to my flat. It was like this . . . There was a struggle, and I shot Frankie. He was lying there with blood pouring out of him. He was dead. The next thing was the key turned in the door, and Alan walked in.' She raised her eyebrows. 'You can imagine my surprise, to put it mildly.'

'Fuck me! Like Lazarus?'

'Yeah. Looking rough, bearded, thinner, crazy, but definitely Alan.'

'Jesus wept, so what did you do?'

'I told him to get out of my way. I had a gun pointed at him and told him I would use it. He stepped aside and I left. He told me I was making a huge mistake and that people would come after me. But he didn't follow.'

'But somebody did come after you.'

Helen nodded.

'And they're still after you?'

Helen nodded. 'I escaped. So I'm here now.'

Janey stubbed out her cigarette in the ashtray and got up and emptied it in the bin, then ran the ashtray under the tap like some kind of obsessive compulsive ritual. She sat back and stretched out her legs.

'Well. You are in plenty of trouble now, aren't you?'

Helen nodded. She didn't feel like crying. She was just glad it was out, and she could see in her mother's face something between pride that her daughter had been so bold, and gladness that she was needed.

CHAPTER TWENTY-ONE

As Rosie listened to McGuire, her mobile pressed to her ear, she pictured him pacing up and down the office, waving his hands for emphasis as though she was sitting opposite him.

'You know something, Gilmour, I might be just imagining this . . . In fact, I'd better be just imagining this. But what you've just told me, about this stolen baby now being in an orphanage and your plans to contact the British embassy . . . Well, I'm getting a wee niggle in my stomach that you might even be thinking about stealing this fucking baby out of that orphanage. Please tell me I'm wrong about that.'

Rosie could feel her face smile, but she knew he was deadly serious. Of course, finding a way to get the baby out of the orphanage had crossed her mind several times, and she had no doubt that Adrian would be considering stealing her. But that would be a bridge too far.

'I'm not entirely reckless, Mick. I'm not going to steal a baby from an orphanage, for Christ's sake.'

'Are you sure about that?'

Rosie hesitated. 'Yes.'

'And what about that big Bosnian? He's not going to steal this baby on your behalf, Gilmour, is he? Because if we end up in some Romanian court because my investigations editor is swanning around Bucharest stealing weans, well . . . it really doesn't bear thinking about. You actually might get put up against a wall and shot – and that would only be when you walked in here.'

Rosie chuckled. 'Don't be daft. I have to admit though, it did cross my mind. I mean, things are so corrupt over here that stealing babies, selling kids, bunging officials to smooth the way is all fairly normal. But I wouldn't want to get involved in that. I'm still thinking of the way ahead. But going to the embassy with the woman and the husband, as well as getting our story ready for the paper, will put a bit of pressure on – I hope.'

McGuire was silent for a moment, then he said, 'Right. That's made my mind up. Get Matt to send everything you have over in the next couple of hours. It's only lunchtime here, so I can splash this tomorrow, once the lawyers have seen it. Go and sit somewhere and write up your spread about Alan Lewis and the charity – the way we discussed it the other day. We don't need to implicate him, but we've got enough to write a good splash and spread, especially given that his wife has gone missing after the stiff was found on her living room floor.'

'I agree. And you never know, maybe it will flush something else out, once it goes in the paper.'

'That's why I want you back here as soon as possible.'

'I will be. As soon as I can. A couple of days, I think. But in the meantime, I'll put my story together and send it soon as I can.'

'Fine. But let me know what you're doing next. And I'll say it again – don't phone me from a police cell saying you're getting done for kidnapping, because I'll leave you there, Gilmour, I bloody will.'

'Don't worry,' Rosie said.

'Aye, right.' He hung up.

Rosie was pleasantly surprised that the meeting at the embassy was to be in the evening on the following day. She spent most of the day making sure Ariana would definitely be able to bring a nervous Madelina with them. She hadn't even seen her splash in this morning's *Post*. It was supposed to have been faxed to her, but the hotel's fax machine was on the blink, so she'd had to settle for her colleague Declan reading the headlines and the gist of it over to her. She was well pleased that the lawyers hadn't cut it to pieces. McGuire had also called to say well done. So far, so good.

It was already getting dark by the time Rosie, Nicu and Adrian headed out towards the town where they'd located

Madelina's husband. She felt uneasy, not just from being away from the city and not knowing anything about the lie of the land here. She waited with Nicu in the car outside the bar as Adrian looked in through the door. He told her it was busy and Madelina's husband was standing at the bar. He said he looked as though he was finishing his drink. They waited, but Eadbert didn't emerge for another twenty minutes, then they saw him come out, a little unsteady on his feet, a cigarette dangling between his lips. He walked along the road and headed towards the blocks of flats in the area they'd just driven through. Nicu drove slowly a few yards behind him.

'Stop here, please,' Adrian said. 'I will go to him now and talk to him. See if he remembers me.'

'What are you going to do, Adrian?' Nicu asked.

'I am bringing him back to the car. To take with us to the embassy.' Adrian looked surprised that Nicu would even question it. He glanced at Rosie. 'You want him to be there, don't you, Rosie, so he can admit what he did?'

'Yes. If possible,' Rosie said, glancing at Nicu who looked a little perplexed.

Adrian got out of the car and walked slowly behind Eadbert. Nicu kept the car crawling a few yards behind. Then they watched as suddenly Adrian went ahead and down a darkened alley situated between street lamps. They could see the man looking up, a little startled and unsteady. Adrian took hold of his arm, but he jerked it away. Adrian grabbed it again and firmly turned him around to face the car. Then Rosie saw him put something into the man's back. She assumed it was a gun, but told herself she hadn't seen that. It might not have been. Adrian ushered him towards the car and Rosie opened the back door. He pushed him in, husband babbling in Romanian.

'Shit,' Nicu said. 'We are taking him? Kidnapping him?'

'He's a criminal, Nicu,' Rosie said.

'I know. But he is saying he knows all these people – gangsters. He is making threats here. Says he can get us all killed – that we will die for this.'

'Don't worry,' Adrian said. 'Is just stupid threats. He is a drunk.'

Rosie turned to Nicu.

'When we get to the embassy, Nicu, maybe you should leave us. I don't want to involve you too deeply by you putting your head above the parapet in an official way.'

'No, Rosie, I want to be involved. I want to see someone stopping what is going on. I don't mind going to the embassy and the police if we get some protection. But the thing is, we have taken a man from the street.'

'Well, if it goes well, and the embassy really does intervene and the Romanian authorities react, then maybe this bastard will end up behind bars where he belongs. He sold his own baby.'

Nicu drove the rest of the way in silence. Rosie was glad when she saw the lights of the embassy, and the car with

Ariana and Matt inside. She could see the silhouette of Madelina in the back seat. Nicu pulled up, and Rosie got out, keying a number into her mobile.

'We are outside now,' she said into it.

In a few moments, the iron gates of the embassy opened.

'Here goes.' She got back into the car and they drove past the British soldiers and into the compound.

The massive mahogany carved doors were opened and they stepped into a vast hallway of marble pillars and pale stone-coloured walls adorned with paintings and tapestries. Rosie gazed around at the lights and chandeliers and could see Ariana and Nicu doing the same, probably thinking about the splendour of the Ceauşescu palaces that were exposed to the public in the days of the revolution, and how he had lived in opulence while his country had existed in abject poverty for generations. As they all stood, a little awkward, nobody speaking, Rosie squeezed Madelina's arm and nodded to Ariana. Ariana said something to Madelina in Romanian.

'Madelina says she feels sick with nerves. I think seeing her husband is also making her feel physically sick, after what he did.'

He had obviously heard that and stood there, head bowed. Rosie hoped he was ready to tell the truth. They could hear the clatter of shoes on the tiled floor and from the swing doors to the left emerged a tall, reedy, sandy-haired young man. He looked around at everyone, his eyes finally resting on Rosie.

'Rosie Gilmour?'

'Yes.' She smiled. 'I'm Rosie.'

'Desmond Fairlie. I'm the assistant in the office and will take you through now to see the ambassador. I deal with all the press enquiries that come into the embassy.' He stopped walking and touched Rosie's arm. 'I have already had your story faxed over to us, and the ambassador has seen it. Pretty horrific stuff. I should let you know that he has already informed his Romanian counterpart, as well as the chief of police. They are both here in the office and are keen to meet you.'

Rosie was wide-eyed. 'That's quick work, Desmond. More than I could have imagined. Normally everything takes forever in this country. And I cannot believe how corrupt it is.'

He lowered his voice. 'Well, you don't want to be saying that when you go in there – at least not in front of the Romanian hierarchy. They know the score, though, and to be honest, the reason they got here so swiftly is that the boss has made them very aware of the power of the press, and that this revelation does not make the new Romania look good in the eyes of the rest of the European Union. They are only just recovering from the last big wave of stories on the orphanages and the international adoptions scandal, but this is a whole new level.'

'Well, I hope they can help this poor woman.' She jerked her head towards Madelina, who was behind her. 'That's the most important thing. And, of course, run this mob into the ground.'

They reached the end of the corridor and were facing another large carved door, which Desmond tapped on softly. A voice called him to come in. He turned to Rosie.

'Rosie, I think for the first couple of minutes it should just be yourself. We have an interpreter, and there are a few people here, so let's just you and I go in, and we'll touch base, and then you can bring in the others. You okay with that?'

She turned to Adrian and Nicu as Ariana explained to Madelina. She nodded, her hands shaky.

'But when we do go in, Desmond, I want to bring Nicu and Ariana in. They have been instrumental in helping us get this matter exposed, so I want to make sure they get their points across.'

'Of course.' He held the door open, and beckoned her forward.

Inside the large, airy office, the ambassador's desk was as big as McGuire's conference table, which seated about fifteen people. Behind the desk, a slim man with a pale complexion and salt-and-pepper hair got to his feet.

'Ah. You must be Rosie Gilmour.' He came around from his chair, soft grey eyes studying her. 'I'm Martin Porter-Brown, the British ambassador to Romania. I've just been reading your exposé in the *Post* and had it translated to my colleagues here. Very shocking indeed. I do hope we can all help each other here.'

'Thank you,' Rosie said. 'I'm hoping there is a lot more to come out of this investigation.'

'Quite,' he said.

He stood in front of Rosie and shook her hand warmly. Next he introduced her to the chief of police, the interior minister, then the Romanian ambassador and a local politician. All of them wore the same expression, flat, resigned, no friendly faces here. Rosie nodded her greeting to each of them, eager to get on with it. They all sat down in chairs opposite the desk.

'I see from your story you have the name of the organisation.' Porter-Brown glanced at the police chief. 'We are already in the area and picking up the people you have spoken about in the story – the people you recorded.'

Rosie looked around the room, then at the ambassador.

He spoke to Rosie again. 'I think it would be good to bring the others who are with you in here now, if you don't mind. I don't want to be going over the same thing again, and it's important we hear from the mother herself, and the father. Because we need to act fast to get this baby back to her.'

He nodded slowly and looked at the translator, who addressed the others. Their expressions never shifted. The ambassador nodded in the direction of Desmond, who got to his feet and went to the door. Rosie watched as they all shuffled in – the young woman, shaking and with her face pale, and the grey-faced husband looking as though he was being dragged to the gallows.

'I think we should hear from the mother first,' the ambassador said.

Madelina's voice shook in the beginning. But she managed to compose herself and spoke slowly and in a measured way, going through everything – Nicu translating as she was speaking. Rosie sat and listened again, pleased that Madelina was being strong enough. Her husband stood, head bowed, as the police chief glared at him. There was a lot of talking among the Romanians, and this was also translated to the ambassador. Rosie was glad with the way it was going. Eventually, the ambassador leaned across the desk.

'Rosie, I would like our involvement in this kept at a minimum, despite what has gone on here today. As you know, we are only involved because of this Alan Lewis character, and the charity that is based in the UK. We know of Lewis, but didn't know about the charity's involvement when he went missing, and the news story surrounding him seems to have disappeared. But the fact that he is a director of this charity is what has got us involved – so you made the right call there by contacting us. The police chief and interior minister will be instructing people at the orphanage to hand over the baby to a place of safety at the moment, and then there will be blood tests to prove her parentage. This is indeed a mess, and there are a whole lot of heads that will be rolling in the next few days. So I do thank you for your help in this.'

'So when will the baby be given back?'

'As soon as possible. I think in the next few days. But wherever she is being held, the mother will be able to be there too, alongside. They have arranged for that.'

Madelina bit back her emotion as this was translated to her. Then, as the officials all stood up about to leave, the door opened, and two uniformed police officers came into the room and handcuffed her husband. Madelina glared at him but he didn't even raise his eyes to look at her. Everyone watched as he was marched through the doors.

Porter-Brown came out from behind his desk and shook hands with Rosie, telling her he was glad she had got in touch, and reminiscing about his old friend in the embassy in Pakistan who had contacted him on Rosie's behalf. They lived in another world, Rosie thought, but was glad they were open to her.

They left and headed towards the car, with Matt, who had waited for then there, taking pictures. Suddenly Rosie turned around to see where Adrian was. But his car wasn't there.

'Where's Adrian?' she asked. 'Did anyone see the car he was in when we came out?'

Everyone shook their heads, and Rosie felt a sudden jolt in her gut. Adrian wouldn't have gone anywhere. He had been outside, a few yards from the entrance on the other side of the road. This was not good. She looked at her mobile and saw missed calls.

'Shit!' she said, noticing that her mobile was on Silent. She must have done that automatically before the meeting started. 'Shit! He's called me twice in the last ten minutes.' She looked at Nicu.

'Let's go, Nicu. I'll call him now, on the way to the hotel.'

CHAPTER TWENTY-TWO

Adrian answered after two rings.

'Adrian. Sorry I missed your call. My phone was on Silent. Where are you?'

'Rosie, listen. There is a problem. I had to leave in a hurry.'

'What? What happened? Where are you now?'

'I'm following the car with Madelina's husband in it.'

'The police car?'

'Yes. I tell you what happened. I'm in my car but nobody can see me, and then I saw the police come out with the husband in handcuffs, so I'm thinking it's good that he is arrested.'

'He was arrested. It went well at the embassy and the police took him away. Everyone is helping. They even had the interior minister there and they said are going to get the baby out of the orphanage. The ambassador was great. So the husband is going to jail.'

'I don't think so, Rosie.'

'What?'

'Because, I see him going in the car with the police, and then I see another car come up the road, so I watched it for a moment. I thought I recognised the man who drove us to the orphanage, Mr Georgescu's assistant. From the adoption agency. Then I see that it *is* him.'

'Jesus! Really?'

'Yes. So I follow the police car for little bit, and then they get out and bring the husband from the back seat and they hand him over to the guy – the guy who drove us. It was him. I am sure. And another two men.'

Rosie knew Adrian didn't make elementary mistakes. If he had recognised him, you could be sure he had studied every feature of his face on their first meeting.

'So then what happened?'

'The police handed him over to this guy. They punch him in the face and bundle him into the back of the car. They are part of it, Rosie. The police are part of the corruption.'

'Jesus Christ, Adrian! That's unbelievable. They just walked out of the embassy two minutes before, with the interior minister summoning them and assuring us that there would be justice all round. Then the cops just walk out and hand this guy over to the bloody criminals?'

'That is what happened. They must be in the pay of the gangsters.'

Rosie's mind was a blur. 'They can't all be in the pay of the gangsters – not the government people, surely? And definitely not the British embassy officials.'

'Shit, Adrian. I feel I should go back into the embassy and tell them what happened. But I'm scared now in case it's all some kind of cover-up. I can't believe the Brits would be involved in that.'

'Maybe they are not. But all I can say is that the police are.'

'So where are you now?'

'I am three cars behind them, but it looks to me that they are going back to the town where I picked up Eadbert and maybe they will dump him. But I don't think so. He knows too much, now that they have been discovered. They will have to kill him.'

Rosie pressed the phone to her ear.

'This means everyone is in danger now, Adrian. Especially Madelina, and her baby.'

'We need to get the baby out now, Rosie. Tonight, if possible.'

Rosie looked around at the darkness falling, heard the buzz of the traffic. She didn't know how she was going to tell Madelina what had happened. She hadn't even broken the news to Madelina yet that her baby was ill with some possible heart condition. And now this. She knocked on the door of the window and beckoned Ariana out. She came towards her, a concerned look on her face.

'Ariana, we have a problem.' She explained what had happened. 'So we need to get the baby out now. And we need to keep the wife away or they will get her, because now that we have made an official complaint she will be on the list of witnesses. Her husband will no doubt be dead before the morning.' She shook her head as Ariana looked at her in disbelief. 'Ariana, we need to get that baby out tonight. We cannot trust anyone else in this organisation. The police are in on it, so they may tell the gangsters to do what they have to do.'

Ariana puffed out her cheeks and ran her hand through her hair.

'My God, Rosie. What a mess.'

'I know. I don't think everyone is in on it – I mean, that would be too crazy. But the police are, and it might be them who would be instructed to take the baby from the orphanage that she's in, so we cannot wait around for this. Who knows? Maybe the manager of the orphanage is also on the payroll of the gangsters and he will do what he is told.'

'I don't think he is, Rosie. My friend Jaana has been there three years, and she says the bosses are all good, and there are no babies or children disappearing there. Everything takes forever, she says, for adoptions, so I don't think this is happening here.'

'But how can we be sure?'

'We can't be.'

'Can you ask Jaana to help? Do you think it would be safe

for her to tell her boss what is going on and what may happen?'

'I don't know. I will have to ask her.'

Rosie felt sick. What if they'd got it wrong, and the boss was also in on it? What if the criminals got there first?

'Can you phone her now? We may not have much time.'

Ariana looked at her watch. 'Jaana will be home now. But she lives nearby. I will ask her and see what she thinks is best. Is it okay for me to tell her everything that has happened today?'

'Yes. Of course. You trust her, don't you?'

'Yes. If she can get the baby out, she will. But I must talk to her first.'

Matt and Nicu got out of the car.

'What is going on?' Nicu lit up a cigarette.

Rosie shook her head. 'It's all gone crazy, Nicu.' She glanced at Matt. 'Adrian saw the policeman hand Madelina's husband over to the thug from the other day – the driver of the agency boss who took us to the orphanage. They must all be in on it.'

'Shit,' Nicu spat. 'This bloody country. So much corruption. Shit! But the government ministers, they were so helpful. I'm sure they don't know, Rosie.'

'I agree. But the police seem to be a law unto themselves.'

'It has always been the way. They turn the blind eye all the time. So what now?'

'Well, everyone is in danger now. Madelina's husband no doubt will be history by the morning, but they will be after Madelina, and maybe the baby too now. They need to remove all evidence. Even though the baby has a different name and is in an orphanage, they still have to get rid of her as evidence now that we have tracked her down. The interior minister said there would be blood tests to determine that Madelina is really the mother, so they have to get rid of the baby.'

He drew on his cigarette, his face pale.

'All of us are in danger now, Rosie. We must do something.'

'We need to get the baby out, and then I can talk to the embassy.'

'You don't think you should talk to them now?'

'I'm not sure how much time we have. I think the priority is to get the baby and hide somewhere until I get to the embassy in the morning.'

'What is Ariana doing?'

'She is talking to her friend Jaana, who works in the orphanage. And the orphanage boss. We must try to get the baby tonight.' She paused. 'Nicu. Do you know anywhere we can go to hide until tomorrow? Not too far.'

He thought for a moment, then nodded. 'I know a place. It's is in the countryside. But it is dark already and the road is not good. My friend lives there in a small farm. They have not much, though, but I know he will help us.'

Ariana came off her mobile and turned to them.

'Jaana is at the orphanage, and she has spoken to her boss. They are expecting us. I think everything will be okay.'

The road into the orphanage was dark and eerily quiet through the tall trees; dogs were barking somewhere in the distance. They had no idea what was on the other side of the trees on the road leading up to the orphanage. Adrian drove Rosie, Matt and Ariana up the tiny narrow track and they could see some lights in the building, but couldn't make out how big or long it was. Nicu was following them in a separate car, and he was going to park it a little distance away from the orphanage so he could take them to his friend's farm. That wasn't much comfort now, though. Rosie's heart was thumping in her chest, but at least she felt as though she was doing something rather than sitting around waiting for the morning. Jaana had been more than cooperative and had told Ariana that she would speak to her boss, assuring them that he was not the kind of man to get involved with criminals. He had children of his own and had worked all his life trying to place children with the right parents, or working to improve conditions for the children. She said it was one of the better orphanages in the region. He had been horrified when he was told the story, but insisted on meeting Rosie the reporter and Ariana as he wanted to make sure himself that they were genuine. And he wanted to meet the mother too. Rosie had been reluctant to bring Madelina but she had no choice.

Adrian drove the car up to and parked outside what looked like the building's main entrance, with a single light. Suddenly, one or two more lights came on and the door opened.

'I see my friend, Jaana,' Ariana said. 'The man with her must be her boss.'

They piled out of the car quietly and he ushered them in to a small side room. Ariana introduced everyone and they shook hands. She told them they did not have much time. The orphanage boss asked to see Rosie's credentials and Matt's and also Ariana's. Then he asked Madelina some questions, and seemed to ponder and consider her answers. Rosie shifted around on her feet, silently willing him to get on with his questions. Eventually he took a deep breath and spoke to Madelina. Ariana translated.

'He is saying he is sorry this has happened to the mother and knows she must be in pain. He is worried he might be in trouble by doing what they ask. He says that the baby is not well and tests were being done on her heart. She will need to be taken care of in a hospital in the coming days. But he will give the baby over now, and tomorrow he hopes that Rosie will, as she promised, go to the authorities and they will come here to speak to him. He only wants to do the right thing.'

Madelina's face fell when she learned her baby was ill, and Ariana touched her arm to comfort her.

Rosie told Ariana to reassure the orphanage boss that he was doing the right thing, that though she was certain that the police were in with the criminals, the other government figures she had met today were not. She hoped to Christ they weren't, but she couldn't admit that. He nodded to Jaana and she disappeared out of the room. They stood in a kind of edgy, sweaty silence in the half-light. There was no sound of babies crying, just a thick, hot, humid smell. Then the door opened and Jaana came back with a baby in her arms, wrapped up in a blanket. Madelina looked at everyone in disbelief. She stepped forward and stretched her arms out as the girl handed her the baby. Then she crumbled and sobbed so much she had to sit down, cradling the baby to her chest.

'This is her things. Some food and clothes, nappies. She doesn't have much. You should go now,' Jaana said.

The boss shook Rosie's hand and held it.

'Good luck. I hope to speak to you tomorrow. I must speak to you.' Jaana went back into the office and he showed them out.

Rosie ushered Madelina and her baby to the car. Ariana and Matt were standing next to it. Adrian was standing nearby, but in the shadows. Suddenly, another car pulled up, headlights blinding. Rosie pushed Madelina into the back of their car, got in to the passenger seat herself and closed the door. Two men got out of the other car, and she could see the metal of a gun in the headlights. They shouted something in Romanian, and pushed the orphanage boss inside their car at gunpoint and closed the door. Rosie could still see Adrian in the shadows, but she could do nothing. She was afraid to move.

Rosie saw Ariana and Matt, now both crouched down next to her side of the car, and she heard Ariana whispering. Ariana whispered, 'They are saying to hand over the baby and the mother. They are taking them away, they said.'

Rosie couldn't speak. She looked over to Matt, saw panic in his face. One of the men approached the other side of the car and pointed the gun at the rear back seat-window where Madelina sat clutching her baby. Suddenly there was a gunshot, and he dropped to the ground. Then several more gunshots, and Ariana fell to the ground too, clasping her stomach. Rosie braced herself for the next shot. But when it came, it was Adrian who came out of the bushes as the other man fell to the ground. He ushered Matt into the car, then picked up Ariana carefully and placed her in the back seat across Matt's lap.

'Let's go quickly. We must go,' Adrian said, as he got into the driving seat.

Rosie's hands shook as she phoned Nicu. His phone was answered immediately.

'Nicu. We are out. Where are you?'

But there was no answer, and his phone cut off.

CHAPTER TWENTY-THREE

'Shit!' Rosie said. 'Someone answered Nicu's phone but didn't speak. Something's happened.'

Adrian drove through the potholes past the edge of the wooded narrow road away from the orphanage.

'We will be there in a moment. We have to get out of here.' He didn't glance at Rosie. 'But it might be a trap.'

Rosie's heart accelerated. She turned around to look at Ariana, slumped in the back seat clutching her stomach, her T-shirt soaked in blood. Next to her, Madelina sat holding her baby, who was fast asleep.

'Ariana, how bad is it?' Rosie asked.

'I'm bleeding. I don't know. I don't feel pain though.'

'Matt, can you take a look?' Rosie said.

'I can't see a lot for the blood on her T-shirt. It's not pumping out, Rosie, but we need to get it fixed soon.'

They drove out of the clearing and on to the main road, where a car blocked their way out. Rosie could also see

Nicu's car, and in the headlights she saw he was slumped in the driver's seat, blood coming from his forehead.

'Christ!' she murmured. 'Nicu's been shot. Maybe they've been following us.'

There was an anguished groan from Ariana in the back seat. Rosie looked at Adrian.

'We have to get him, Adrian. Maybe he's still alive.'

Adrian gave her a bleak look that said he thought he was dead.

Rosie touched his arm. 'We need to check. Maybe we can save him. We have to do something. If Nicu's dead, then he died helping us.' Guilt washed over her.

'I will go,' Adrian said, softly opening the door.

He crouched down and went across to Nicu's car and crept inside. Rosie could see him lifting Nicu's head back and placing his fingers on his neck to feel for a pulse. Then he rested Nicu's head back on the seat, and crept back to their car.

'I'm sorry. He is dead.'

'Oh, Nicu.' Ariana started to cry and Matt put his arm around her.

They sat for a moment in silence, staring into the dark, watching the car close to Nicu's blocking the road. But there was nobody in it.

'They are out there,' Adrian whispered. 'In the trees, I think.' He reached for the door handle as he turned to Rosie, and she could see perspiration on his pale face in the moonlight. 'I'm going to draw them out, Rosie. Lock the doors and everyone lie down as low as you can, so you are not near the windows.'

'Jesus, Adrian! You can't go out there and look for them. That's what they want. We should phone the embassy.'

'There is no time. Just do as I say. Please, Rosie.' He turned to Matt. 'Please.'

She saw him reach inside his jacket and bring out a gun. Then he softly opened the door and rolled on to the ground. In the darkness, Rosie slumped down in the driver's seat, barely breathing, cold sweat trickling down her back. In the silence she could hear the shuffling sound of Adrian crawling towards the back of the car. They waited. Trapped. It seemed like an age, but after a few seconds Rosie heard something rustling in the trees. Then the sound of gunfire – one shot. She quickly popped her head up and saw Adrian get up to a crouching position and fire into the trees. She thought she saw a figure fall in the shadows. Then Adrian was on his belly again, crawling, waiting. She lost sight of him for a moment, then saw him again going towards the passenger side of the car. Then more gunshots. They hit the car that was blocking them, bouncing off the bonnet, followed by the hissing of punctured tyres, and the plinking sound of the headlamp glass shattering. Then angry, rasping voices were shouting, and people rushing from the trees. Rosie could see two burly men, shooting wildly, coming their way.

'Christ, Rosie,' Matt's muffled voice, 'what the fuck's happening?'

'I think Adrian shot one of them, then he's hit the car, done the tyres. But more are after him. Christ almighty! Just keep down.'

Rosie eased herself up a little and watched from her wing mirror as the two men went to their car and kicked the tyres in frustration, then began to prowl around. They came towards the car they were in. She could no longer see Adrian. Shit! They were getting closer, then there was gunfire and one of them collapsed, clutching his leg. Adrian was out there somewhere. But where the hell was he? Another gunshot, then one of the men hunkered down and fired several shots under the car. Rosie could hear shuffling and groaning. Adrian had been hit. Then suddenly, more gunshots, three very rapid, and the other man keeled over. Rosie waited, terrified, watching the trees for more gunmen.

'What's happened?' Matt asked.

'Two more down, I think Adrian is under the car, and he's been hit.'

They waited for a few more moments.

'I'm going out to see.'

'You can't go out there, Rosie. Fuck's sake! There might be more of them.'

'I think Adrian's hurt, Matt. We can't just stay here. I have to see.'

Rosie opened the door and slipped out on to the dirt on all fours. She looked below the car and saw that Adrian was on the other side, groaning.

'Jesus, Adrian! You got hit.'

'Two shots, hit me. My stomach,' he gasped. 'Rosie,' he struggled to speak, 'we have to go. Now!'

Suddenly a car came racing down the road they'd just come from, headlights flashing. In the glare, Rosie could see blood spreading across Adrian's shirt. She stuck her head above the side of the car as it came towards her, then relief flooded through her. It was Ariana's friend, Jaana.

The car screeched to a halt and she jumped out as Rosie stood up.

'My God! What's happened? They were here too? My boss just arrived back in the orphanage, he said there was shooting. He said I should find you,' Jaana said.

'Yes, Jaana. We have to get out of here. Nicu is dead in his car. My friend Adrian is badly hurt, and Ariana too. We have to get help.'

'We have to move this car blocking us.'

Matt got out and he and Rosie rushed to the car as Jaana got into the driving seat.

'Matt,' Rosie said, 'just push it enough for us to get past.' They pressed their shoulder to it, and pushed with all their strength. The car slowly moved to the side, its wheels hanging over a ditch.

'You have to get away from here. Quickly,' Jaana said.

'I have to get in touch with the embassy,' Rosie said. 'I'm scared to phone the police because they must be in on this.'

She looked at Adrian on the ground trying to sit up, but blood was pumping from his stomach.

'He is in bad way,' Jaana said. 'He needs a hospital.'

'We can't risk it.'

Jaana went to her own car and brought out a black medical box with a red cross on it. She put it in the footwell of Rosie's car, went to Ariana and looked at her wound.

'Ariana, it looks like maybe just flesh wound. Don't worry. But you need to get away. Can you go to my cousins? You know, in the countryside? Are you okay to tell them where it is, can you sit up?'

Ariana groaned. 'Yes.'

Jaana looked at Adrian.

'We must get him in the car.'

Between them, and with Adrian gasping for breath and blood dripping, they got him to his knees and helped him into the front passenger seat of Rosie's car.

'Can you drive, Matt?'

Rosie was not confident about her driving in the pitch black on these roads.

'I'm going to have to,' Matt said. 'You're all right, Adrian,' he said as he got into the driving seat. 'Don't worry, big man. We'll get you sorted.'

Rosie climbed into the back seat and rolled down the window.

'Thanks, Jaana. We probably owe you our lives for this.'

The girl reached in and squeezed Ariana's hand, then ran her finger over the forehead of the sleeping baby.

'Hurry. It is only twenty minutes away. I will phone her. She was also a nurse, so she will be ready.'

'What about Nicu?' Ariana asked.

'I'm sorry, Ariana. Is too late for him. I will phone the police in a few hours. We will tell them we found the body and the car here and no idea who it was. Gangsters are always having shoot-outs. They won't think anything.'

Matt drove out of the tight country road and on to the main road, Ariana leaning forward enough to instruct him to turn left and go straight for a few miles. Adrian was silent and Rosie leaned over from the back, holding her jacket to his stomach to try to stem the blood flow. There was fear in his eyes and she had seen that only once before. She prayed under her breath. His eyelids were heavy and he seemed to be drifting in and out of consciousness, his hand on hers, blood coming through both of them. She saw Matt's sidewards glance at the blood, then he caught her eye in the rear-view mirror.

'He'll be all right, Rosie. We'll be there in no time.'

Despite her despair and fear and hopelessness as she watched the blood and the colour drain from Adrian, she was impressed by Matt's determination and the way he had stepped up to the situation. She knew he was a lot stronger and braver than some people gave him credit for.

'Left here, Matt, and then go straight up the road,' said Ariana. 'Just keep following. It is potholes and dirt track. You will see a small house on the right side. Wooden. There is a well outside.'

The road was pitch black. Adrian's eyes were flickering, and Rosie leaned over, stroking his head. The baby was beginning to stir in her mother's arms. Finally, after what seemed like forever, they could see a light in a window and the headlights fell on a well. They drove through the potholes, Adrian's body jerking every time the car jolted over them. Then a woman and a man emerged from the house. Matt pulled in and they came towards them, speaking in Romanian as Ariana rolled down the window. The man was built like a tank, and he opened the door and leaned in towards Adrian, as Matt got out of the car and came around to help him. Between them, they got Adrian to his feet, and more or less dragged him to the front door. Rosie helped Ariana out, and she limped into the house. Madelina came in behind them, the baby waking up and smiling, her little innocent face lit up by the fire burning in the hearth. The big man almost lifted Adrian onto a wooden kitchen table as his wife opened medical boxes and began to work in the gloom of one light bulb strung on a wire across the single room that was their home.

CHAPTER TWENTY-FOUR

Rosie stirred, feeling the icy chill, every bone in her body aching. She'd barely slept more than an hour at a time, sitting up in the uncomfortable wooden chair next to Adrian still lying on the kitchen table, with a grey blanket over him. A few times in the night she'd woken, her face numb with the cold, and in her exhausted stupor, thought she was actually sleeping outside. She opened one eye, and could hear the man of the house snapping twigs as he knelt by the fire, blowing into the blackness, coaxing the fire back to life. He was cursing under his breath, as the fire must have gone out overnight. She sat up a little and pulled her coat around her shoulders as she looked at Adrian. He was sound asleep, his chest rising and falling, his face the colour of death, the dark smudges under his eyes looking even blacker. He looked like a corpse, and Rosie turned away, feeling tears spring to her eyes. Last night, Jaana's nurse friend had told them he might not make it through the night. If he did, there was a chance he would survive. But he had lost so much blood, and they had no idea of the damage that had been done internally by the second bullet. Rosie had watched as Adrian lay unconscious while they bathed and cleaned his wound, the nurse pointing out where the bullets had gone straight through and out the other side. He was lucky, she said. It didn't look that way right now, Rosie thought. But he had made it through the night.

She gazed around the small, sparsely furnished room. It was still dark outside, and Matt was asleep propped up against his camera bag, a blanket over him. Madelina and her baby lay covered with blankets and hot water bottles on a mattress behind a wooden frame, where she was, hopefully, warmer. How could anyone live like this? Rosie didn't even know the names of any of the people in the house, and she couldn't even remember in the chaos of last night if they had been introduced. Yet here they were, these total strangers, who had taken them in when all was lost. The act of kindness made her chest ache with emotion. Rosie felt miserable, exhausted. Back home in Glasgow people had so much, everything they needed, yet here, not too far from the bars and the trendy cafés in what was the new Romania, families still lived as they did a hundred years ago, existing off the land or whatever meagre jobs they could find. No wonder they wanted to leave this place in search of a better life. She looked up when she heard the wife coming in, her feet shuffling on the stone floor as she went to the cooker and switched on the one ring they had. She filled a cooking pot with water and looked across at Rosie, a thin, tired smile on her face. She glanced at Adrian for a moment, then gave Rosie an encouraging nod. Where did they go from here? Rosie wondered. She was exhausted, she barely had the energy to work out what would happen next. Her phone was low on battery. She had to do something. She needed to get out of here, but she couldn't bear the thought of leaving Adrian like this. The silence was filled with the sound of the baby's wakening cries, and in a few seconds, everyone was awake, and Adrian's eyes were beginning to flicker. Rosie stood up and reached for his hand, relieved that it wasn't stone cold.

'Adrian,' she whispered. 'Can you hear me?' She brushed her fingers across his forehead. 'It's Rosie.'

Relief flooded through her when he squeezed her hand, and she swallowed hard. She leaned closer to his face, feeling her cold cheek on his. He opened his eyes a little.

'Rosie.'

Her chest ached with emotion.

'Adrian! Thank God, you've made it through the night. Are you in pain?'

He moved a little and grimaced, nodding.

'Don't move. Just rest.' She squeezed his hand. 'You saved us. Everyone. I'm so sorry you're hurt.'

His lips moved but she couldn't hear him. She leaned closer.

'The baby?' he murmured.

'She's okay. With the mother here. These people are looking after us. The woman is a nurse and she looked after you last night. But she said you need a hospital.'

Adrian shook his head. 'No hospital.' His voice was barely audible. Then he opened his eyes wider, and held Rosie's wrist. 'Rosie. Phone my friend. Risto. In Sarajevo. Tell him he must come. He will bring me home.'

Rosie didn't know what to say. Sarajevo was a three-hour flight away, and Adrian was in no shape to be going on a plane. The only other way to get back was by car – too long – or by train – almost two days. He wasn't fit to travel right now.

'Adrian, you cannot go anywhere until you are more stable.'

He nodded. 'Please call him, Rosie.'

Rosie knew she had to talk to McGuire. They had to get him out of here, whatever the cost to the newspaper. She checked her phone again – it was only five thirty back in Glasgow. But she had to make the call now before her battery died.

'Okay. Just rest. I will phone your friend. I will get you home. Don't worry.'

He squeezed her hand and for the first time in all the years she'd known him, he looked dependent on her. It was a stiff reminder of how much was at stake here. She couldn't lose him, no matter what. She realised for the first time how much she loved him.

Rosie zipped up her jacket and went outside into the half-light, feeling a blast of the windchill from across the fields. She pulled out her mobile and punched in McGuire's number. He'd still be at home. But he answered after two rings.

'Gilmour. This can only be bad news. I'm just out of my bed.'

Rosie took a breath, surprised at how emotional she felt.

'Mick.' She cleared her throat to buy herself some time. 'It is bad news. All sorts of shit has happened here. It's . . . it's bad . . .'

'Are you hurt, Rosie? Are you in a hospital?'

'No. But listen. I don't have much phone battery left. So I need to make this quick. Adrian's been shot – twice. It's pretty awful.'

'Fucking hell. What happened?'

'It's too long a story to tell you right now, but he got shot saving all of us.'

'What do you mean, all of us?'

She remembered that she hadn't even had time last night to tell him about the developments with the baby.

'You know how we went to the embassy?'

'Yes. I was waiting to hear about it all night.'

'It went great. Everyone on our side. All that stuff. But then as we left, we discovered the cops were in on it.'

'Fucking Christ! What do you mean, in on it?'

'They handed over the husband who sold the baby to the bloody gangsters.'

'Aw, for Christ's sake! Dirty, thieving, corrupt bastards! So what happened?'

She explained to him that Adrian went after them and what had happened at the orphanage, and how they had to get out fast.

'You what? You kidnapped a fucking baby from the orphanage?'

'It wasn't kidnapping, Mick. The boss of the orphanage handed the baby to her rightful mother. He's on our side.'

'But are you on the run with a stolen baby? Is that what you're telling me? And Adrian's been shot. I mean, how badly is he shot? Is he going to die?'

'Last night we thought he wouldn't make it. There's a nurse at the house where we all are, and she helped him. But Adrian's lost a lot of blood and she thinks he may have internal injuries.' She paused. 'Mick, we need to get Adrian back home to Sarajevo. I've to tell his friend Risto over there to come for him, but we need to arrange something to get him home safely. We can't just leave him here. And we can't stay here. I can't stay here.'

Silence.

'No. You definitely can't stay there. In fact, you need to be back here. Today, if possible.'

'Okay. But I need to get to the embassy again, and get a safe passage out of here. But they don't even know about Adrian. I really need you to get him out of here. Can you do that?'

Silence.

'Leave it with me. Get out of wherever you are. Get your phone juiced up and work out where you should go. I'll get Adrian out.'

Rosie felt choked. 'Thanks, Mick.'

'You're something else, Gilmour. But listen: I want you out of Romania today. Anywhere. Just get on a plane. Talk to Marion. Get it arranged. We'll get Adrian sorted.'

Rosie should have felt relieved, even though she knew McGuire wouldn't be anything less than sympathetic. Just hearing his voice in the middle of all this chaos and crap made her feel like breaking down. She took a deep breath as she saw a couple of stray dogs running around in the dim light. The door opened and Matt came out, scratching his head. He stopped when he looked at her, then came across, put his arms around her. She let him hug her tight.

'Shit, Matt. I'm so scared.'

'Were you talking to McGuire?'

'Yeah. He was great. Wants us out of here today. Any-where, he says. And he'll get Adrian out.' Rosie swallowed. 'I don't want to leave him here like this, Matt. I mean . . . Look at the state of him.'

Matt ruffled her hair, still holding her shoulders.

'I know, Rosie. He's not in good shape, he can't travel today. But people might be looking for us, for him. Christ! What a mess! We need to get out of here.'

'I'm going to talk to the embassy. They need to get the Romanian interior minister again. They have to get 'this sorted, give us assurances. But they can't be involved with Adrian. He won't want that. I know him. He'll want to be left to his own devices.'

'I heard him say to call his mate. Have you done it?'

'No. But I will once I talk to the embassy. Mick will organise a way to get them out.'

'He needs a doctor. Proper medical attention and maybe a look inside to see the damage. He looks terrible.'

'I know. I never thought I'd see him like this – not able to get up and take charge of things.' She shook her head. 'Christ, Matt. If it wasn't for him we could all be dead.'

'I know, pal. I know.'

He put his arm around her shoulder and they stood watching the morning light spread across the fields, their breath steaming in the cold.

CHAPTER TWENTY-FIVE

Helen lay in her single bed, the pink duvet cover pulled up around her. She'd left a little bit of the curtain open the way she'd always done so the room wouldn't be completely dark. The darkness brought too many haunting memories. In the light from the lamp-post outside the flats she could see fine rain and watched it, listening to the sounds of passing cars, then the quietness, then people arguing in the street, a bottle being smashed in anger on the ground. Another car pulled up, and doors were slammed as fighting started. She didn't bother to get up and look out of the window. These were the sounds she'd grown up with; every night another Gorbals drama unfolding. As a child, she used to kneel up at the window and watch the violence as people attacked each other with knives, bats and cleavers. Then it would quieten down again, the blue lights of the police cars flashing in her window, and the sound of people being dragged kicking and screaming into their vans.

Sometimes, if her mother hadn't been out, she would go to sleep early and soundly, not waiting in dread for the noises and lowered voices of the men her mother had brought home with her. They were the best nights, when she could lie and dream, imagine she was somewhere else in the old movies, living in some ranch somewhere, or some townhouse in New York, with the big lifts and the gates around them and people in top hats and uniforms on the door. When she became rich enough, with her own money, or, more accurately, Alan's money, they'd go on holiday to exotic places just like that, and often Helen would lie in the bedroom, enjoying the luxury, the sense of being in the movie she'd always dreamed of. But tonight she couldn't sleep. It wasn't her conscience, she was done with all that shit, though she did feel a pang of guilt that Frankie Mallon's kid was left without a father. If she could find the girl she would make sure she gave her some money for the kid. It was the least she could do. The thought of Frankie's baby brought back a flood of long-buried memories. Now, lying here, she remembered. It had rankled with Helen all her life, the fact that her mother made her have an abortion when she was sixteen. She'd got pregnant by one of the boys in the block, or so she thought. She didn't actually care who the father was, but she was ready to have a baby, and hadn't even thought beyond that; there was a baby growing inside her, and that's why she didn't tell her mother straight away. She knew what would happen. And it did.

When her mother caught her vomiting three mornings in a row, she marched her down to the doctor with a urine sample to confirm her suspicions. Then she took her back up to the house and told her she would arrange it. Helen was hysterical. She wanted the baby, she'd screamed to her mother. You have no idea what to do with a baby, her mother screamed back. I'll learn, Helen had pleaded. But no, it was done, and she was taken to a clinic in a back-street in the West End of Glasgow. And when she came out she was a different girl. If it was a decision she'd made herself and she hadn't wanted the baby, she might still have changed her mind that day, but she wanted this baby, just an instinct. She'd told herself over the years it was for the best that she didn't have it, that it was one of the first times in her life that her mother was actually acting in her best interests. But she never, ever forgave her. And so the hatred began to build. Helen went back on the game, not under the watchful eye of her mother and the pimp, as she had been earlier, but this time with an escort agency. She decided there and then that she would fuck her way out of this shithole. And she did.

Now she closed her eyes to blot it out as she tossed and turned in the bed, then sat up. She thought of what her mother had told her earlier about the junkie girl who'd had Frankie Mallon's baby. It niggled her that the girl would probably have nothing now. She wished she could make that better but knew that she couldn't. She rubbed her eyes as she switched on the bedside lamp. She had heard her mother on the phone half of the evening, then the kettle boiling, and the sound of bottles. Who had she been talking to at this time of night? Eventually she got up, pulled on a sweater and went through to the living room, where her mother was sitting almost in the dark, with only one tiny lamp on and the glow of the fire. She was drinking a glass of red wine.

'What's the matter with you?' Janey glanced up at her and then at the fire.

'I can't sleep.'

'Guilty conscience,' she said, deadpan.

'What's your excuse?' Helen snapped back.

'I've been busy.'

'I heard you on the phone.'

Janey moved her mouth to acknowledge that, but said nothing.

'What have you been doing?'

'I was on the phone. I'm trying to get you out of here. Out of this shit you're in.'

'Ma.' Helen felt a little panicky, 'I hope you've not told anyone I'm here.'

Janey looked up to her, scowling.

'Do I look buttoned up the bloody back?'

'No.'

Helen sat down.

'I'm working on something.'

'What?'

'Get yourself a glass. I'll tell you.'

'I don't want any drink. I'll get some tea.'

Helen went into the kitchen and switched the kettle on, then returned a few moments later with a mug of tea. She sat down, silent, as her mother looked at her, then back at the fire again.

'I do some work for someone,' Janey said.

Helen waited, wondering if she should ask who. 'What do you mean?'

'Listen to me and listen good. Nobody here or anywhere else has a single clue what I do for a living. Okay? Plenty of people may have known years ago, but that's all in the past. I'm too old for all that shit now. So now, I just do one thing. It makes me enough money to keep me going – and a bit more.'

Helen was baffled. In this neck of the woods there was money-lending, but her mother wasn't the type to be involved in that, she'd always hated the parasites who held poor people to ransom. She wondered if she was running an escort agency – she certainly had some experience to put on her CV.

'What do you mean, Ma? Tell me. I'm intrigued.'

'Okay. If I tell you and anyone outside of these four walls ever finds out, then it will be you who's grassed. And the people I deal with won't let you escape. Are you understanding me?'

'Christ. Aye. What's going on?'

'Okay. Every month, sometimes more often, sometimes less, I travel abroad. To Amsterdam, usually. And I deliver money. Cash. A lot of it.'

Alarm bells were going off in Helen's mind.

'Money? To who?'

'Use your loaf. Who do you think?'

'You're a drug dealer? A mule?'

'No. A mule brings the drugs into the country. I just go with the money. Nobody pays any attention to a middle-aged woman going through Security. Except that I'm often carrying up to anything from thirty to eighty grand.'

Helen looked at her in disbelief.

'Christ. How do you get it through?'

'It's easy done. In my small bag. It goes through the X-ray machine but never gets opened. It's a bit risky. But I've been doing it in Amsterdam, Malaga and Istanbul for the past five years. Nobody's cracked a light.'

'Christ almighty. An international smuggler. I'm more than impressed.'

'Not a smuggler. A smuggler brings drugs. I'm only taking money over to business people. What they do with it is their business.'

'Yeah, like you don't know it's drugs.'

'Of course I know, but I don't ask questions. I never have.'

'What if it's heroin? You've seen all the shit around here from that. How could you?'

Janey flashed an angry glare at Helen. 'Don't you attempt to fucking lecture me. So far in my travels, I haven't arranged for a hitman or popped someone in my flat. I'm no killer.'

Helen shrugged. 'So what's this got to do with me?'

'Because I'm going next week. And you're coming with me. We'll travel together. To Amsterdam. Then you can disappear. We might even take a holiday together.'

'Christ. I'm scared to put my nose out the door.'

'Have you got any money. Cash?'

'Yeah.'

'How much?'

'About twenty grand on me. But I've got money in various accounts.'

'Fiddled from your man, who you thought had been bumped off.'

Helen said nothing. She didn't have to.

'Well. You need to get out of the country and start somewhere else. A new life, a new identity.'

'Christ, Ma. You're talking like the Mafia. When I left here you were bringing men in here for money, and now you're some international wheeler and dealer telling me I'll need a new identity. Is this the fucking movies?'

'No. It's actually happening. You called me, remember. You're the one who shot someone. It's you who's in the shit. I can only try to get you out of it.'

Helen sighed. 'Do you think it will work?'

'What do you think I've been doing all night?'

Helen nodded, impressed, and sipped her tea. Things had certainly changed a lot since she left.

'How come you didn't move out of here? With all your money, how come you didn't move to a nicer area?'

'Because they're all full of wankers up to their arse in debt, or crooks. I'd rather be here among my own, including the crooks. This is where I come from. And it's where you come from. You'll never get away from that, and don't you forget it.'

Helen didn't answer, but she could see now that, despite how far she thought she'd come, she'd never really left.

CHAPTER TWENTY-SIX

Helen sat in the kitchen sipping from a mug of coffee, her head groggy, eyes stinging from lack of sleep. She hadn't heard her mother go out, but the house was silent and she wasn't in her bedroom when she'd popped her head round the door. Maybe she'd gone to see whoever she was talking to on the phone last night. Just as she clicked on the remote control, bringing the television mounted on the wall to life, she heard the key in the front door. She automatically flinched, still traumatised and flashing back to the moment when Alan had walked into her flat. She stood up.

'That you, Ma?'

'No, it's the Holy Ghost.'

Helen knew she wasn't expected to answer. She sat back down as the kitchen door was pushed open and her mother came in with a plastic carrier bag, her face flushed and her eyes blazing. She pulled out a copy of the *Post* newspaper from the bag and slapped it on the table.

'So this is how your man made his money?'

Confused, Helen looked at her, and then her eyes scanned the newspaper's front page. It was Alan's picture she noticed first, and then one of her. Then the headline. MISSING ACCOUNTANT IN ROMANIAN BABIES-FOR-SALE RACKET. Below, a smaller strap headline across the top of the story: MYSTERY DEEPENS OVER SCOTS MONEY MAN AND HIS WIFE – ALREADY AT THE CENTRE OF A SHOOT-ING IN THEIR HOME.

'What the fuck . . .?' Helen picked up the paper and sat down, her legs shaky. She began to read, her mouth drop-ping open.

Missing accountant Alan Lewis was the director of a UK charity linked to the sale of Romanian orphans, the Post can today reveal. The charity – Hands Across Europe – has links to gangsters who sell children to buyers from all over the world, and who want to bypass the red tape involved in legitimate Romanian adoption. We can also reveal newborn babies are snatched from mothers in hospital maternity wards, after the heartbroken mum has been told their child died at birth. The Post has travelled across Romania investi-gating the scandal, and today we can name and shame the men behind this racket. We have now passed our dossier to police in Bucharest and the UK. Our revelations come just weeks after

Lewis's wife Helen vanished after a notorious Glasgow gangster was found dead from gunshot wounds in her plush city flat. Police are hunting for her, and insiders have told us that they cannot rule out that she may have been part of the babies-for-sale scandal.

Helen looked up at her mother. 'In the name of Christ! What the hell is this all about?' She put her hands up pleadingly. 'Honestly, Ma, I don't know what the fuck this is. It's the first I've heard of it.' She suddenly felt choked. 'I'd never in a million years get involved in anything like this. And I'm sure Alan wouldn't either.'

'Read the story. It says his name is on the directors' list of the charity and the wine business. And it's the same name on the adoption agency. They have it in black and white.'

Helen didn't look further at the story – she was too dizzy with shock to take it in. She shook her head, trying to picture the various documents she had seen over the years as she snooped in his files. She knew Alan did the books for this charity, but that was all.

'B-But . . . I can't understand. I know he was in this wine-importing business. I've seen some documents over the years. And I remember seeing that he was director of a charity. But I've never looked closely at his correspondence with them.' She ran her hand through her hair, frustrated. 'Christ! Maybe I've got some in my case. But I can't believe Alan would be involved in stuff like this. He just wouldn't.

I mean, I know he was dodgy, laundering money for gangsters. But selling babies? No way, Ma. No way.'

Her mother took off her jacket, draped it over a chair and sat down at the table, flicking the pages of the newspaper. Helen could see the story ran across two pages: pictures of orphanages, of the charity office and of a baby being reunited with its mother.

'This is just crazy, Ma. Alan would not be mixed up in this. I think he must have been in that charity as a tax saving thing, because he wasn't the kind of man to be getting into charitable causes. He didn't do anything with it. He probably doesn't even know who runs it.'

Janey grabbed her by the wrist. 'You listen to me, Helen. Look me in the eye, and tell me the truth. Because so help me, I will do you in myself if I find out you're lying . . . if you're a part of this.'

'Ma,' Helen pleaded, 'you've got to believe me. I don't know anything about it. I bet Alan doesn't either. Christ. What can I say? I promise you. I . . . I love weans. I'd never be bad to a wean, or sell it or any shit like that.' To Helen's surprise, tears sprang to her eyes. 'You have to believe me.'

They sat in silence, Helen staring at the pages of the *Post* as her mother sat, her face set hard, glowering at her daughter.

'Well, you're up to your arse in shit now, all right. So you'll need to work out what you're going to do about it.'

'I don't know what to do, Ma. I . . . I'm trapped. Everywhere I look, there's no way out.'

Her mother stood up and poured hot water over a teabag in a mug.

'Well, you might have been in a lot less trouble if you'd just have asked your husband for a divorce instead of getting that dick Frankie Mallon to murder him – or not murder him, as it turned out.' She paused and sighed. 'You've got two choices, the way I see it. You need to get out of here, or you go to the police. Tell them everything.'

'B-But they'll lock me up. I can't do that. I'm not involved in this babies thing. Nobody will ever know about Alan and what Frankie did to him out there in Romania. Frankie's not here to tell about it, and who's going to believe Alan even if he was to talk? He's not going to talk now if this is all over the paper implicating him. He'll stay missing.'

'Maybe you should talk to the paper. That reporter whose name is on it. Clear your name – if you're brave enough.'

'But what's the point?'

'You'd have your say, then you could fuck off somewhere and never be heard tell of. That's if these bastards who are looking for you don't get you first.'

Helen shook her head. 'Ma, you're not helping here. I need to do something.'

'Aye. You do.'

CHAPTER TWENTY-SEVEN

Rosie barely spoke all the way from their hotel to the airport. When she and Matt had climbed into the British embassy diplomatic car outside the Intercontinental, she sank back into the leather seat and let out a long sigh. She should have felt relieved, elated, full of the sense of freedom and achievement that she had done the right thing. She had reunited a baby stolen at birth with her real mother, and she and Matt had made a couple of groundbreaking splashes and spreads for the *Post*, exposing the inside story of the babies-for-sale racket. And she was being protected by the British embassy all the way onto the tarmac of Bucharest airport. Ordinarily, she'd have been punching the air with excitement and satisfaction at a job well done. But right now she was deflated, shattered, and she couldn't get Adrian out of her mind. She sat back in the passenger seat and replayed the last frantic few hours.

*

Rosie's anxious phone call to the ambassador's assistant at the British embassy had put in motion a chain of events much more swifly than she'd expected. He'd been shocked and furious to find out what had happened once they'd left the British embassy, and that the Romanian police had played such a dirty role. He'd instructed her to remain where she was, asked to speak to the man of the house and got the address, and assured them assistance would be on its way promptly. Rosie was panicking in case somehow all of them ended up in police custody. She'd rushed outside the house when she heard the cars, as well as an ambulance, coming up the driveway.

'Rosie.' The ambassador's assistant got out of the Mercedes to greet her. 'What an unbelievable mess.'

Another Mercedes car with blacked-out windows pulled up, and two well-dressed Romanians got out. Rosie knew nothing about the secret police or security organisations in the country, but the embassy man introduced them as from the interior ministry who would be taking over the case. Rosie explained to all of them what had happened, watching as the translator relayed it to the Romanians, whose worried faces showed they were aware that once again the country had been plunged into an orphans scandal splashed all over a British newspaper. Another car arrived, and two medics got out and went straight inside to see to Adrian and Ariana. A woman who was with them was introduced as a social worker to see to the mother and baby.

The embassy man took her to one side for a moment.

'So, this Adrian chap . . . He wasn't with you in the embassy, was he?'

'No. He was outside.'

'Can I ask you who he is? Is he a journalist?'

'No. He's from Bosnia. I've known him for years. We work together on investigations from time to time in Glasgow and abroad. He lives in Sarajevo, and my editor is arranging for him to travel back home. His friend is on his way from Sarajevo to be with him.'

He looked serious. 'It's just that, well, there's a few loose ends here for the Romanians. They have two dead bodies outside the orphanage. Fair enough, they were gangsters –' he lowered his voice conspiratorially – 'and between you and me, completely off the record, the nation will be all the better without them. But the police will need to file some kind of report. I take it the Bosnian was the one who shot them?'

'I didn't see what happened, and that's the truth,' Rosie said. 'We were all in the car with our heads down as these men began shooting, except Adrian. I didn't see what happened after that, I only heard gunshots. But these men were shooting at him, and the car. They came there to kill us, and take the baby. And they came to kill the mother of the baby because she could have given evidence against them. If they'd got her, she'd have had the same fate as her husband. I'm sure his body will be found somewhere soon.'

He nodded in slight agreement. 'I do see your point, Rosie, but they will need some kind of statement from your Bosnian friend, and they will have to investigate.'

'I hope they're not going to charge him with anything. Whatever happened at the orphanage was self-defence. Everything I've described to you is because of these gangsters, and because of the corruption at the heart of the police force. I hope they're not going to get all high-handed now.'

His mouth twitched a little. He was a diplomat, and trained to find a compromise, a way out, and perhaps Rosie's tone was more aggressive than he liked.

'I understand how you feel, Rosie, but—'

'Can I tell you something?' Rosie interrupted. 'About the police, even before I came here this time? Years ago, after Ceaușescu, I was over here with a charity and there was some altercation and one of our party was stabbed by a gypsy. Stabbed in the back. The lights had gone out and the whole place was in chaos. But then the police arrived, and they captured the man who'd done it. I watched them as they dragged him out, and then I followed them to the police van. They dragged him into the back and six of them stamped on his head. There was blood everywhere. It was awful. I watched them kick this man to death, well, kick him until he wasn't moving. Then when I spoke to the police chief on the ground a few minutes later, and told him what I'd seen, he told me to get back behind the police lines and that I had seen no such thing. They'd just killed a man. That's how they do justice, so I won't stand here and let them mess me around. I'm sorry. I really appreciate everything you are doing, please don't get me wrong. I do. But these security guys have to understand that they have gangsters all over the police force.'

He sighed, glancing at the officers.

'I'm sure they know that already, Rosie. Okay, let's see what we can do here. The thing is, we want to get you and Matt back to the UK pronto, and the authorities are here to make sure this woman is fine and looked after.'

'That's if they are genuine.'

'Oh, I'm sure they are. The interior ministry has been left in no doubt that there is a daily newspaper about to launch an exposé and dig even deeper into this scandal, and how the Romanians are seen to deal with it is crucial to how they are viewed by the rest of Europe. So I don't think you have to worry about the mother and her baby.' He paused. 'And if I may say so, I think you have done a fantastic job on that – above and beyond the call of duty.'

Rosie managed a half-smile. 'My editor always says I'm a bleeding heart. I think he's probably right.'

The medics came back out and reported that Adrian was conscious and speaking, and that he was determined he was not going to a hospital. He said he was going home.

They told him it was risky to travel, and he had to rest for at least twenty-four hours, with some medical assistance as well. He promised them he would. Rosie watched as the police security people and the embassy staff spoke together, then went in to Adrian. She was relieved to see him propped up, his face as bright as it was ever going to be.

'Thank God, to see you awake.' Rosie sat at his bedside. 'I thought we were going to lose you last night.'

He shook his head. 'I am okay. I feel better. I am going home. Risto is coming. He phoned me.' He paused, took her hand. 'You must go now, Rosie. Go back to Glasgow. Tell everyone what has happened. You have a very good story, I think.'

Rosie shook her head. 'I don't want to leave you here, like this.'

He held her hand tight and ran his other hand over her hair.

'Rosie. Listen to me. I will be fine. I will be home in a couple of days. I will call you. Please. You must go. The longer you are in this country, the more dangerous for you. These gangsters, there are more than just the ones from yesterday. People will be looking for you, and for me.'

'My editor says he will get you out. Whatever the cost.' Rosie knew he hadn't said, Whatever the cost, but she was determined to cover it.

'Don't worry. Risto will get me home.'

'No. My editor wants to pay for it. You can fly or take the

train, or rent a car or get someone to drive you to Sarajevo.'

'I hope I can fly by tomorrow.'

'Okay. You must tell me how you are and I will arrange it. I will give your number to the editor's secretary and she will fix everything for you and for Risto.'

'Okay, Rosie. Thank you.' He squeezed her hand. 'Now go. Please. I will be okay.'

Rosie stood up and for a moment she didn't want to leave. He was weak and vulnerable, reassuring her all the time, but he was extremely tired. She leaned down and kissed his cheek, then kissed him on the lips.

'Go, Rosie.'

'Thank you, Adrian. For everything.'

'Goodbye, Rosie. Take care.'

She swallowed hard as she left the room and went outside, where Matt gave her a sympathetic glance. The Romanian couple who had given them shelter stood shyly in the background, looking overwhelmed by all the activity and cars. Rosie went across to them, and stretched out a hand to each of them. They shook her hand, then she found herself embracing them, and being hugged back by both of them. She asked the translator to thank them from the bottom of her heart, that they had saved her friend Adrian's life. As she said goodbyes to Madelina and her baby, the young mother clung to her, thanking her several times. Rosie told her through the translator that she would see that she was looked after, and she would be talking to her editor soon, and that they would make sure she was in a position to get medical treatment for her little daughter.

The embassy car took them to the hospital where Ariana was to remain for a few days for her gunshot wound. When Rosie walked into the small side room where she lay propped up, her face pale and her eyes ringed with dark circles, Ariana turned to her and seemed to force a smile.

'Ariana,' Rosie said as she went over to the bed. 'My God! I'm so sorry about Nicu. I feel so responsible. I got both of you involved in all of this to help me.' She shook her head, and took Ariana's hand. 'I'm so very sorry.'

Tears trickled out of Ariana's eyes and she sniffed as she squeezed Rosie's hand.

'I know, Rosie. It's okay. I . . . I am so sad because Nicu is gone. He was one of my closest friends. We had known each other, worked together so many times over the years. He was a good man. He cared so much.'

'I wish there was something I could do for him. For both of you.' Rosie hoped it didn't sound trite. 'I feel so helpless now. And I have to go back home. I've left Adrian with the family of your friend, and he is very badly hurt. He told me I must go. But I am arranging for him to get back home to Bosnia.' She sighed. 'It's such a mess.'

Ariana nodded. 'Yes. But listen, Rosie. Nicu has lost his

life, and I lose also a little bit of my heart. But it is because of his work that Madelina has her baby back. That is worth so much. I know it would have been worth so much to him.' Tears came again. 'I wish he could have been here to share their joy.'

Rosie bit her lip. She didn't know what else to say. She intended asking McGuire to make sure Ariana and Nicu were looked after, as well as all the others who had helped, and who had so little. But this wasn't the moment to discuss it.

'Did Nicu have a wife?' Rosie asked, tentatively. 'A family?'

'Only his mother,' Ariana said. 'She is very old. Lives in the countryside. A widow.'

Rosie nodded. 'Have the police spoken to you about protection?'

Ariana looked at her. 'All they told me was that they would look after me, not to worry, I would be safe. I'm not sure how much of that I trust. So much of it is corrupt.'

'I will speak to the embassy here to make sure they talk to their counterparts in Bucharest and ensure your safety.'

'Thank you,' Ariana said. 'You must go now, Rosie. You must go home, and tell the world your story.'

'Our story,' Rosie said.

Ariana smiled and rested her head back.

'Our story.'

Rosie leaned down and brushed her cheek with hers.

'I will be in touch soon, Ariana. I promise.'

'Of course. We can speak soon.'

Rosie stepped back from the bed, then turned away and left the room.

The embassy car with diplomatic plates pulled up close to the plane and they got out. As they climbed the stairs, Rosie looked back. Her mobile rang.

'Where are you, Rosie?' a familiar voice asked her.

'I'm boarding a plane, Mick. To Vienna, then a connecting flight to London. I should be in Glasgow by tonight.' Just saying it made Rosie feel emotional. Sometimes she ached for the sight of Glasgow – to feel she was home safe.

'Good. That's a relief. If you're not too tired, see how much you can write on the plane. I want to go big on this over the next couple of days.'

'Sure,' Rosie said, 'no problem.' She was going home. Already, her mind was focused on the piece she would write.

CHAPTER TWENTY-EIGHT

Rosie drove to the office, feeling brighter than she should have been, given yesterday's twelve hours' travelling. Between flying to Vienna and waiting hours for the connecting flights to London, then Glasgow, she was so jaded she dropped into a hot bath as soon as she got into the house. She'd lain there, exhausted, staring at the tiles, watching the path of the steam trickling in rivulets down them. She kept seeing Adrian's face, flashbacks of seeing him crawling around while the Romanian thugs fired shots from the darkness. Guilt washed over her. It was only months since he'd been stabbed by the serial killer, Thomas Boag, who took her prisoner, and here he was again, almost killed helping another of Rosie's investigations. It was *she* who put him in this situation. If she didn't call him, he wouldn't be there, she told herself. Simple as that. She could make a decision now, and that would be it. No more calling on Adrian to protect her. But then what? Could they be friends, someone she could visit in Sarajevo for a break sometimes? Typical Rosie, wanting without committing – not that she'd ever seriously considered a commitment with Adrian, even if he would want it. But what she felt right now was deeper than ever, and watching him yesterday, unconscious, not sure if he was going to make it, had somehow changed things. All the way home on the plane she'd kept thinking about him, couldn't get him out of her mind. It was more than just the worry that he might not make it. There was a moment as he'd lain there when she had realised how deep her feelings were for him, and no matter how she pushed them away, they kept coming back. She couldn't get involved in this. She'd already made her mind up about that a long time ago, and lately there had been nothing but friendship between them. A friendship forged the way theirs was meant they would always be close no matter what, and Adrian too, it seemed, had decided that this was how it was. Why the hell was she even thinking this way? They hadn't even properly discussed or entertained the notion they could be together. They couldn't be. It was impossible. He lived in Sarajevo, she lived in Glasgow. There was no future in it. He was so damaged by his past that he would never escape it. It was doomed, and best to stay away. And there was always the guilt that she was even having these thoughts. TJ was in London for the next few months, on and off, and might even be going on tour with the jazz singer's backing band he'd joined. He was the happiest she'd ever seen him, enjoying the working and touring, and coming home to be with her. She loved him, that much she knew. Adrian had been a mistake, a distraction almost, something that had got out of control, and thankfully they'd put it to an end over a year ago, before it really began. But now it felt different. Her mobile on the passenger seat rang and she picked it up. She recognised the number, but there was no name.

'Rosie?'

'Who's this?'

'Rosie, it's me. Donna. Remember we were up at the caf—'

Rosie interrupted her. 'Of course. Sorry, Donna. I've been away for a week or so on a job abroad and my head is all over the place. Sorry. How are you?'

'I'm all right. I've got a house from the council. Move in next week. So it's good. And the wean is going into the nursery school.'

'You keeping well too?'

'Aye. No drugs, if that's what you mean. I'm finished with that, Rosie. Definitely.'

Rosie wondered why she'd phoned her and guessed it wasn't for a chat, or maybe it was? Perhaps a casual friend like her was all she had. So she'd keep up this small talk as long as necessary. But then Donna spoke again.

'Rosie. I've got something to tell you.'

'Yeah?'

'Aye. About that Helen Lewis.'

'Really?'

'She came to see me. Out of the blue.'

'Helen Lewis came to see you?'

'Aye. She got in touch. Well, her ma got in touch. And she came to see me. I'll tell you about it. Can we meet?'

'Of course. Any time. I've got to check into the office first and see the editor to offload some stuff that happened when I was away. But I'll call you shortly.'

Pause. Silence. Rosie hoped she hadn't upset her because she wasn't coming to see her straight away.

'She gave me money. Five grand. Cash.'

'What? Why?'

'Dunno. Well, she said it was to look after Frankie's wee one.'

Rosie felt like turning her car around and going to meet her now, but she knew McGuire would be waiting to see her, and she had to talk about today's business.

'Give me an hour or so, and I'll call you. That okay?'

'Aye. Great. Talk to you later.'

She hung up.

Rosie pushed in the revolving doors as Jean on the reception was hanging up on a call. She beamed as she walked towards her.

'Some story over there, Rosie. Those poor bloody weans. I'd take those bastards out and shoot them.'

Rosie wanted to smile and say, 'Actually, that's what did happen,' but she couldn't.

'I know, Jean. As if things aren't bad enough over there in the orphanages for these wee kids, people are making money out of them. And, stealing weans from their mothers as they're born, I mean, what kind of mentality does that?'

'Would make you sick. Have you more to come?'

Rosie winked. 'I hope so.'

Part of the buzz of working for a daily newspaper for Rosie wasn't always about the editorial floor and chasing stories, the excitement of watching them go in the paper, and waiting for the fireworks the next day. It was the family aspect of the whole place. It wasn't something you could explain to people outside who might have thought of reporters as being hard-bitten drunkards, hidden behind a cloud of smoke all day. Sure, there had always been an element of that. But what Rosie loved about the place was that any time she went to the canteen or into a lift, everyone knew each other. From the library to the accounts to the publicity people, there was a shared excitement when the paper broke a story like this. Things were changing on the editorial floor – no doubt about that, with cutbacks and restraints. But she hoped the camaraderie of it all would remain the same. It was hard to understand the black humour of journalists in the middle of a major unfolding drama or tragedy. And there were plenty of egos around newspapers who revelled in the glory of breaking a big story. Rosie wasn't one of them, even though she'd always loved the moment when her story was all over the front page. She loved the chase of it all, the tearing down the walls of injustice. But once the story was in the paper, you moved on. Most of the time. Unless it was something like this, where the image of a toddler clinging to your thigh as you leave them in an orphanage remained with you for a very long time, as did so many more haunting memories. It was all part of the package.

When she stepped onto the editorial floor, a few of the reporters looked up from their phone calls or notebooks or screens and gave her a wave or a thumbs up. She could see Marion clock her arrival and buzz through to McGuire to say she was in. Marion caught her eye and waved to her to come through.

McGuire was on his feet and coming out from behind his desk to greet her.

'Gilmour! Thank Christ to see you in one piece. Every time you've walked in that door for the past while, I haven't known what to expect.'

'Well, as you see, Mick, I'm alive and kicking.' He motioned her to sit down by the coffee table and joined her in a chair opposite.

'You want some tea?'

'That'd be great. I'm a bit knackered. Long day yesterday.'

McGuire got up and put his head around the door and asked Marion to bring tea, then he sat back down.

'So tell me what happened. Blow by blow . . . And how's the big Bosnian?'

Rosie let out a tired sigh, picturing his face as she left.

'I've no idea. I've been trying to call him, so I'm guessing when he's able to he'll get back to me. When I left him, the embassy were taking him to a hospital and patching him up until he gets this flight home today that Marion booked for him. Hope he gets it.' She paused. 'And, Mick, thanks for sorting that. I know the bean counters don't like this, but they're going to have to brace themselves to be parting with a lot more money.' She paused, seeing McGuire puff his cheeks. 'Seriously, Mick. I think we should speak to our insurance guys. We need to compensate Adrian. He took two bullets for us to get us out of there. If it wasn't for him, we'd all have been killed. It could have been a bloodbath.' She shook her head. 'Wee baby caught up in the midst of it. Adrian was a real hero, and I want him sorted.'

'I'll talk to them.'

'Make them understand how important this is, will you? And another thing. We need to be parting with a few quid for other people who helped.'

'Oh Christ, here we go.'

'I mean it. Look what we've got so far in the paper. World exclusive baby-selling racket involving Romanian and UK gangsters and even the bloody Romanian cops and authorities. Any newspaper would have paid a fortune to have that. And we're sharing it with our sister paper in London, so we need to get them to fork out. They splashed it too, I take it?'

'Yep. They did.' He sipped his tea. 'I'll talk to them. Who else do we need to pay?'

'Well, the mother of the baby. We got that great exclusive from her, and fair enough, I helped track down her baby and get her back, but she didn't need to talk to us. She's got nothing, and by the sounds of things her baby's going to need some serious medical treatment. Part of the whole mess of that place and the reason for so much criminality is because people have nothing. So I want us throwing a few quid at her – a right few quid. I can work out a way to get it to her. Also, Ariana. She got shot too. So we need to sort her. The work she did for us on the ground was immense. Totally. Oh, and the family who took us in when we were in the middle of nowhere and blood was pouring out of Adrian and Ariana. I need to get something to them.'

'So who got killed? What was his name?'

'Nicu. He worked really hard to help us, but he wasn't hired, as such, the way Adrian was, so the insurance won't wear that. He wasn't married, so I don't know what we do there. But he died helping us.' She stopped as the words stung her, and she swallowed hard. She'd been talking and demanding for five minutes, but suddenly the emotion got to her. Change the subject a little, she told herself, before you blub.

'You all right?'

'I'm fine.' Rosie didn't look at him. 'Anyway. Here's the

latest situation.' She sat back and stretched out her legs. 'You remember the girl, the ex-junkie, who's the mother of Frankie Mallon's kid?'

'Yeah.'

'She's just called me as I was pulling up in the car park. She says Helen Lewis phoned her and they met. And, wait for this, she gave her five grand.'

'What?'

'Yep. She handed her the money and said to look after the wee one. What does that tell you?'

'It tells me she's guilty as fuck.'

'Yep. Smoking gun. It was her who shot Frankie, for whatever reason. I think we knew that anyway, but the fact that she's done a runner and can't be found means it wasn't a mistake. She knew what she was doing.'

'You bet. What are you going to do with her?'

'I don't know yet. But first, I want to talk to a senior cop. A DI – I've met him before. You might remember. DI James Morton. He's the guy who was in here after Don was killed. He's a bit of a hard guy, but I want to see if I can strike up some kind of contact with him. Maybe work with him on this. To be honest, I'm not sure he'll be up for it, but I want to see what he's about. I did say to him when I saw him after the Boag drama that we'd meet for a drink or a coffee.'

'Good. But be careful what you do.'

The silence hung for a moment, both of their minds ticking over.

'The other thing, Rosie. The British embassy and the Romanians. I mean, that was some farce that the cops just moved in and handed the guy over when you'd left the embassy. Where are we on that?'

Rosie felt a little uncomfortable.

'Okay. Well I had a conversation with the embassy press guy, and remember, he did open all the doors for us, got us out of the country – effectively saved our lives. So we owe them a bit.'

'What do you mean?'

'Before I left, we had a meeting in his office. He's not daft, he knows that the part about the Romanians and the corruption that we witnessed at first-hand is a great tabloid story. But he wants us to tone it down. Obviously he's acting on the instructions of the embassy. A bit of diplomacy in the background.'

'What? Christ's sake.'

'Yeah. I know. But maybe we should look at it. We can still write about the corruption, and he accepts that. But he doesn't want the Romanian authorities to come out as though they are corrupt bastards across the board, willing to sell children. They're trying to get into the European Union, and I think what he's getting at is that they don't want to be painted totally black.'

'But they are bloody black.'

'Agreed. But not all of them. The interior minister who came to the embassy that day did everything in good faith.

It's lower down the food chain – like the cops – that is the problem.'

McGuire nodded his head slowly, tapped his fingers on the cup.

'Well, you go back and tell him that we hear what he's saying and we understand. We'll bear it in mind, but we tell our story all guns blazing. If they want to come up with some statement of damage limitation from the Romanians then we'll use that and give it a decent show – say that there are bad apples and they are being rooted out.'

Rosie nodded. 'I think that's the way to handle it.'

McGuire gave her a sarcastic look. 'That's why I'm the editor.' He looked at his watch. 'Right. I'm going up to see the managing editor to talk this money stuff through with him. You go ahead and do what you've to do. Good luck with your DI.'

The meeting was over. She got up and left.

CHAPTER TWENTY-NINE

Rosie headed for a café at the Charing Cross end of Sauchie-hall Street, frequented by people looking for a fast blood-sugar hit on a low budget. It was mostly bagels they sold at the counter for people on the run, and the tiny café had only a few thin tables that looked as though they'd been thrown together in haste. Outside, it had two of the same wooden and steel bistro tables, more in hope than in expectation of al fresco dining. Rosie looked up at the leaden sky. Not in this town, Toto. It wasn't the kind of place she usually ate in, because she could never see the point of bagels, no matter what they loaded them up with, and nothing in the glass counter would ever tempt her to order a bagel with her coffee. But the latte was great, and she liked the Irish guy who owned the place. In a quiet afternoon one time after it opened a couple of years ago, he'd told Rosie the story of his life, and made her laugh when he confessed to her that he couldn't see the point of bagels either. But he'd spent fifteen years in New York, where they sold by the millions, and were beginning to get more popular in the UK. He was right. Cheap and cheerful stodge, food of students, buskers and busy shoppers who just wanted a quick fix. Or posh ones for upwardly mobile office workers.

'Hey, Rosie. Long time no see,' said Mikey Joe, with a twang somewhere between Kerry and the gangster movie *Goodfellas*.

'I've been up to my eyes, Mikey Joe. You know how it is.'

'I do. I've been reading your stuff in the *Post*. Christ, Rosie! You don't half get up to some shit out there. You wanna be careful, girl.' He stacked a few more bagels in the glass case. 'I don't suppose I can tempt you with any of these?'

Rosie smiled at the twinkle in his eye.

'No thanks, pal. Just the latte, the perfect way you always do it.'

'Comin' right up.' Again with the transatlantic drawl.

Rosie sat at the furthest table, which was squeezed into the corner at the back, but where she could still see part of the glass door. She watched as Mikey Joe prepared her coffee and dealt with two studenty types at the bar ordering some takeaway bagels. He gave her a wink as he pushed them into the bag and handed them to the young women. Then he came over to Rosie, carrying her coffee.

'So, how you doing? Business good?' Rosie asked.

'Not too bad, thanks. Always on the go.'

He placed the glass latte cup with the steel handle on the table, and turned as the ping of the door opening sounded. Two more customers at the counter. Behind them, Rosie saw the big cop coming past the window and looking curiously at the shop and the glass door as though he wasn't sure he was in the right place.

'Jesus!' the DI said as he approached her. 'You reporters can dig out the places.' He sat down opposite her and looked around the place.

'You fancy a bagel?'

'A bagel? No thanks. I'm not the bagel type.'

Rosie smiled. 'Me neither. Coffee? Tea?'

'Tea please. Black.'

Rosie got up and went to the counter. 'Can you bring a black tea, please?' Then she went back to the table, and sat down.

'I thought you liked O'Brien's bar, schmoozing around in there,' said the DI.

'Not at this time of the day. This is one of my haunts. I like cafés – all kinds of cafés. That's where you see a lot.' She smiled. 'But I like O'Brien's too.'

Rosie was a little surprised that her old friend Don must have told James Morton he used to meet a reporter at O'Brien's for drinks. The cop gave her a long look and a half smile.

'Don told me he used to meet up with you.' He put a hand

up. 'Don't worry. He didn't share any details about how close you were.'

Rosie glared at him. 'We were friends. That's all. Good, close friends, who had a lot of respect for each other.'

'Of course. I'm not suggesting anything else, so spare me the indignant look.' He glared back at Rosie, then his face softened. 'I didn't mind that he'd a pal in the press. Not at all. The opposite, in fact. I came through the ranks at a time when cops and the press could be found together in bars all the time. But there were some rogues out there, back in the day.'

Now Rosie smiled. 'You mean cops?'

'Aye. Them too.' He allowed her to score the point. 'But a few of our boys got their fingers burned dealing with reporters. It's not all of them you can trust.'

'I know. Goes both ways. Don was somebody I knew for a very long time. And it worked for us. We were mates as well. Sometimes we'd get the calls the police wouldn't, but I knew when I gave him a lead, or helped him with a case, that he would look after me when it came to doing the story. He sometimes gave me a heads-up – but never compromised himself.'

'I know that too. And often it was a bit irregular. You got away with a lot, Rosie.'

'Sure I did. But my priority was my story. That's how it is.' She knew he was studying her and she felt she had him on her side. 'I'm kind of hoping that we can have a bit of a similar rapport. You know. I help you where I can, you help me. How do you feel about that?'

'Is that why you asked me to come here?' He sat back, mock-indignant. 'You might at least have bought me a decent lunch.'

Rosie smiled and the atmosphere relaxed between them. She liked this guy, despite his attempts to pull rank the couple of times when they'd encountered each other before. He couldn't yet be the big friend that Don had been – that would take time. But she hoped they could build up some mutual trust.

'Actually, no. I didn't bring you here to chat you up, James. I might have something for you. I'm sure you'll be interested.'

'I'm all ears.'

'Helen Lewis.'

'That wildcat.'

'Yeah. I think I can bring her to you.' She watched his eyebrows go up. 'I've got a source who may be able to lead me to her. And if I do actually get to meet her . . . who knows, once I sound her out and get my story out of her, I might be able to talk her into handing herself in.'

He took a long breath and let it out slowly.

'We're pretty sure she shot Frankie Mallon in her flat. We've no smoking gun, but word is he was shagging her – if you'll pardon my French. Frankie was a real womaniser, a bastard of a guy. I don't know what happened that morning in her flat, but I'm sure she pulled the trigger. Why else would she have done a runner?'

'I agree.'

'Has Helen Lewis contacted you?'

'Not exactly. Well, to be honest, not at all. But, as I say, I have a contact who might lead me to her. And that contact would be valuable to you – if she talked.'

'It sure would.' He leaned forwards. 'Do you know, Rosie, reading that stuff of yours, it makes me think that Alan Lewis has done a runner because he was mixed up in something. Maybe hiding out in Romania. Or maybe even been bumped off.'

Rosie nodded. 'Yeah. Well, if I get anywhere, I'll let you know.' She paused. 'We could help each other a bit.'

He said nothing, nodding his head slowly, as though he was trying to process everything she said. Then he leaned forward again.

'Rosie. I'm not going to make any promises to you. But I think you're savvy enough to know that I have a level of respect for you – otherwise I might have locked you up a few months ago when you turned up with that bastard Timmy O'Dwyer in your car. He'd obviously had the shit beaten out of him, and I know I was being kept in the dark. But hey, he's locked up for a long time now and that's one bastard more off the face of the earth. Same goes for Boag turning up dead like that. I suspect you know things that you decided not to share with the police. And I'll be honest with you, I don't want to know. If Jonjo Mulhearn was behind it, then I can sleep at night knowing he had his justice. That's the kind of guy I am.' He paused. 'But it doesn't mean that you get it all your own way here. You need to understand that. You have to be sensible about it. I'm well up in the ranks here, and much as I gave Don plenty of leeway, it's a bit different with the position I'm in. Do you understand that?'

Rosie knew it would not be easy to establish another working relationship with a good, reliable cop like she had with Don. She knew she had to agree to rein things in a bit on how she treated the police, especially a high-ranking DI. It was useful to have someone high up the greasy pole, but it could also work against her. His priority wouldn't be the *Post* story, and she had to accept that, but this was going better than she'd hoped.

'Okay,' she said. 'I understand, and I'll take that on board. I'll be as open as I can with you, but as long as you respect that I won't be able to show you my full hand all the time. But I will put people your way if I can.'

He drained his cup, then stretched his hand across the table and for a second put it on top of hers, surprising her.

'Good. I think we can do business.' He looked her in the eye. 'Will you give me a shout if you get a talk with Helen Lewis? Good luck with that if you do, by the way. She's a hard bitch, by all accounts.'

'Thanks. I'll bear that in mind. I'll talk to you again, James. And thanks for meeting me. I really appreciate it.'

He stood up. 'Aye. Always good to meet the reporter who brought the former Chief Constable down.'

Rosie smiled. 'He deserved it. He had it coming.'

The DI nodded, smiling. 'You're not the Rottweiler they say you are, though.'

He winked, then turned and walked past the counter and out of the café, before she had a chance to answer.

CHAPTER THIRTY

Rosie waited for Jonjo Mulhearn on the bench by the Clyde next to the iconic bronze statue of a famous Spanish Republican heroine, *La Pasionaria*, a monument to the Scots who'd fought in the Spanish Civil War. *Better to die on your feet than live forever on your knees* was the inscription on the base. It was Jonjo's suggestion to meet there, instead of the bar where she'd met him twice before. The old-school gangster was a useful contact and Rosie was hoping to pick his brains on something Christy and Nicu had mentioned: that there was a Russian organised crime connection to the baby selling that possibly stretched all the way to Glasgow. She hadn't spoken to Jonjo since the day she'd left him in the bar, knowing that he'd been behind the butchering of the killer Thomas Boag, who had murdered Jonjo's only son. Jonjo had saved her life after Boag had kidnapped her and left her to drown in a lock-up. If she'd felt bound totally by professional ethics, Rosie would have turned him in to the police when they questioned her. But she made her own rules, and it wasn't just because he saved her life that she didn't stick him to the cops. Deep down she approved of his kind of 'an eye for an eye' justice. Even now, as Rosie gazed out at the murky River Clyde flowing past, she could see herself back in that black pit where Boag had left her to die. The nightmares came crashing in from time to time, but it was still quite early days, the shrink had told her. During their sessions, he'd told her she would learn that the terrors she'd witnessed in her life would always walk beside her, but eventually they wouldn't frighten her so much. He was right, she was coping with it better now. But every time she saw a river or rushing water in a stream, it brought the flashbacks. She sighed, blinking herself out of her gloom. She took her phone out of her pocket and scrolled through the messages. The last one from TJ was from two days ago when she'd come back from Romania. She had answered briefly saying they would talk that night, but he was still in London and told her he was working. She hadn't called him back and he hadn't got in touch. She was surprised at how little it mattered to her these days, but that was for another day. The truth she was trying to avoid was that she couldn't get Adrian out of her mind. He had to be out of Romania by now. She would try to contact him tonight somehow, even if she had to phone the embassy to find out what had happened. She'd been so busy and knackered since she'd got back, there had been barely a moment.

'You're miles away, Rosie Gilmour.'

Rosie flinched at Jonjo Mulhearn's voice. She turned, squinting up in the sunlight to see him standing beside her. He was holding two polystyrene cups, and pushed one towards her.

'I brought you a cup of tea. Black, no sugar, if I remember.'

Rosie smiled. 'Yes. That's very kind of you, Jonjo. I'm sitting here like one of the homeless. Cheers.' She took the tea and shifted up in the seat so he could sit beside her. She turned to him. 'How you doing?''

He nodded, his blue eyes softer than she remembered.

'I'm all right. Not too busy. Just taking things a bit easy over the last few months.'

She wanted to ask him if he'd had any heat from the police about Boag's body, because she knew they would suspect him. But to ask if he had been interviewed by the cops would mean she was complicit in burying the truth. Which she was, but she didn't want to say it out loud. There was a long moment where they said nothing, and Jonjo carefully took the lid off his cup and sat it on the bench beside him.

'What about yourself, Rosie? I see you've been in Romania. Great story that. You did well out there. Sounds a bit hairy, though, at the end of it. You really need to watch yourself. Was that big fella there? Adrian?'

Rosie felt a pang of stress lash across her gut.

'Yes, he was. Saved our lives. But he got shot up quite badly.' She looked out to the river. 'He insisted I leave without him, as we had to get out fast. We are having him looked after, and the editor is sending him money, but he seems to have slipped off the radar. I can't get a hold of him.'

Jonjo gave her a wistful look. 'I wouldn't worry. If the big man is still breathing, he'll get himself out of that. I was very impressed by him. Wish I'd had him by my side years ago.'

Rosie nodded. 'He's very brave. A lot of bad things happened to him and his family in Bosnia during the war. He's got a lot of scars, mentally and physically.'

Jonjo dipped his head in acknowledgement. 'We all have. But that big guy is different. I hope he's all right.'

Rosie said nothing. She knew Jonjo would want to get to the point of their meeting. Sure enough, he sat up straighter and spoke briskly.

'Anyway, how is your investigation going? Are there more fireworks to come?'

'I hope so. Do you know Helen Lewis? Married to that missing accountant?'

'No. But I know Frankie Mallon – well, knew him. Fucking rogue and a coward too. Cardboard gangster. He's wanted shooting for years, so good on her if it was her who did it.'

'I'm looking into some charity the accountant was involved in, as you'll have seen in the paper. There are links to the baby trade in Romania. The charity is Romanian, but also has a base in the UK, but I'm not sure if they would even know about the babies for sale. I can't imagine they did. A couple of contacts told me, it was a Russian guy and the Russian mafia behind this. Do you think they could be connected here too?'

Jonjo shrugged. 'Hard to say without knowing more. I can put some feelers out. I'll let you know.'

'Thanks. I'd really appreciate that.'

They didn't speak for a long moment, the only sound the river and the traffic. She knew nothing of this man other than what she'd read in cuttings about his chequered, violent background. And she'd seen the kind of character he was, the look in his eye that day when he stood over Thomas Boag, revenge burning inside him, an open razor in his hand. She'd known what would happen to Boag, and she'd been glad. Jonjo wasn't her friend, yet there was a kind of unspoken sense that she had some kind of friend in him. And she was sitting here, confiding in him about her work and asking for his help. What did that make her? She'd known and befriended plenty of gangsters over the years and this guy was harder than all of them put together. But despite his tough front, there was a deep sadness in him that was almost palpable in any of the quieter moments when she'd been in his company. He would never really get over the murder of his boy, and not even the butchering of his son's killer would ever bring him back. None of this was really any of Rosie's concern, but somewhere in that bleeding heart of hers she cared about Jonjo. She found herself breaking the silence.

'Are you getting on with things, now, Jonjo? I mean, after everything that's happened? I don't know you at all really, but I hope you are okay.' She stopped herself, wishing she hadn't even broached the subject. His private life was none of her business. What the hell was she doing?

He turned to her with so cold a stare that she thought for a moment he was going to unleash a tirade of abuse. But he didn't.

'The people who ask me things like that, I can count on one hand – all of them I've known for more than thirty years.'

'Sorry . . . I shouldn't have. I just . . .'

He touched her shoulder. 'It's all right, Rosie. Thanks for asking. My life is what it is these days. I'm rich. I can do what I want, go where I want, live how I want. I keep busy, because when I go home at night my wife is there for me, waiting. But she's a shell, and that big house is almost breathing down my neck with its emptiness. But that's what my life is. I knew it would take time, but we'll never be the same without our boy.' He ran a hand across his chin and tightened his jaw. 'Anyway. Life goes on, eh?' He stood up. 'I'll see what I can find out on these Romanian charity bastards.' He looked at his watch. 'I have to get going. Can I give you a lift anywhere?'

'No thanks, Jonjo. I'm going to sit here for a few minutes, enjoy the view, then walk back.'

'Fair enough. I'll give you a shout.'

He turned and walked along the cobblestones and Rosie watched as he approached one of his minders whom she'd seen that day when he'd saved her. She kept watching as they walked across the road and disappeared up a side street.

Rosie's phone buzzed on the bench next to her and she could see it was Declan from the office.

'Hey, Declan. What's happening?'

'Rosie, I've taken a few calls from people about that charity in Glasgow. People saying they went on a trip with them once to look into adopting Romanian babies. It was a couple of years ago, but they thought the guy who ran the show was a chancer. Said he took money off them for accommodation, and that they'd stayed in all sorts of shitholes along the way.'

'Really? That's interesting. Did they get babies to adopt?'

'No. The ones who phoned said it always fell through. Too much red tape.'

'Okay. We should talk further to them anyway.'

'But listen, Rosie. More important than that, I think. I took a call about five minutes ago from some guy. He sounded like a foreigner. Said he knew about the charity, that he'd worked for them. He said he can tell us a lot about them. He'd seen the story in the paper and asked for you.'

Rosie perked up. 'Sounds good. You got a contact number?'

'His mobile.' Declan reeled off the number and Rosie wrote it down. 'Thanks, pal. I'll call him now, set up a meeting. Talk later.'

CHAPTER THIRTY-ONE

Rosie scanned every face who came into the café in the Buchanan Street precinct, convinced it had been a bad idea to arrange to meet someone she'd never seen before in a busy city centre café like this. But it was his suggestion. She'd spoken to him briefly earlier, and now reflected on their conversation. His name was Viktor and he was Albanian.

'I can tell you things about this charity Hands Across Europe – what they do,' he'd said, his accent heavy.

'I'll be glad to meet you, Viktor. Sooner the better. What kind of things do you mean?'

'Things they do. I can't say on the phone. I don't want picture in the newspaper. I want money.'

'Well, we'll see.' Rosie's felt a little deflated. She wondered if he was an illegal immigrant. If he was, it hadn't taken him long to jump onto the chequebook journalism bandwagon he'd probably never heard of back home. 'We do sometimes pay for information. But the kind of story like this – about a charity? Look, I don't want to waste your time, but unless you've got actual proof that they've done something illegal, then honestly, we won't be able to use your information.'

'I have proof.'

Three words. That was enough to bring her here. McGuire had rolled his eyes to the ceiling and told her to phone him the minute she'd talked to him. He'd also suggested taking someone with her, but she'd already agreed to get Matt to sit outside to snatch a picture of him.

The café was busy with shoppers, office workers, tourists, people on their laptops sitting in corners. Rosie was watchful of every foreign-looking face that came in. Eventually, five minutes after the agreed time, she saw a figure stopping briefly at the window and glancing inside, then a man pushed open the door. This looked like it could be him. Tall, slender, olive-skinned. Could be Albanian or Bosnian, it was hard to tell the difference in the Balkans. He stood at the door and glanced around the room. She'd told him she had dark hair and was wearing a light blouse and black jeans. She stood up, looking across to him, and he seemed to acknowledge her, then squeezed his way through the tables towards her.

'Rosie?' His voice was low, dark eyes darting.

She nodded. 'Viktor?' She pulled a chair out for him. 'Thanks for coming. What can I get you?'

'Coffee, please. Black. Lot of sugar, please.'

Rosie quickly ran her eyes over him, the lean, hollow cheeks, pasty complexion, two-day stubble, sniffing a lot. He didn't look as though he was well off enough to afford cocaine, though you never knew these days. The black coffee with lots of sugar would make him even more nervy.

She glanced back from the counter while she was waiting to get served and could see him sitting staring into space. He looked troubled, afraid. Rosie returned with his coffee, plus another tea for herself, and sat down. She watched as he emptied three phials of sugar into the coffee, his hands trembling a little as he lifted the cup. It was either too much coffee, or speed, or something. But his eyes didn't look spaced out.

'You have been in Bucharest. I see in the paper. You did very good story. But is not the full story.'

He wasn't spaced, no way. He wanted to get to the point.

'That's why I'm here, Viktor,' she replied, meeting his gaze. 'Tell me, though. How long have you been here?'

'Three years. I came with the charity. From Bucharest.'

'You worked for them?'

He shrugged. 'I will tell you. But will you pay me money?'

Rosie sat back and puffed out an exaggerated sigh, knowing he was watching her. She had to admire his directness. But she had to let him know this was not how it worked.

'Listen, Viktor, I don't know what you've read in papers or what you've heard about newspapers in this country, but you'd be very wrong if you think you can just turn up and journalists will hand over money to you. That's not how we do things.'

'But newspapers pay money. I see it in the news, in the papers. People sell their story. I have a story to sell.'

He wasn't arrogant or aggressive. More matter-of-fact, even surprised she was questioning him.

'Okay.' Rosie leaned forward. 'I want to be really clear here, so we're not wasting each other's time. I'm really pleased you got in touch, and I'm keen to hear what you've got to tell me. But once we get the information, we have to decide how we pursue it. The way it works is that if we have a story we can publish – and that means going through our strict legal process with lawyers who look at every aspect, every line – then we can put it in the paper. Then, and only then, will we pay a person money. Once we are ready to publish or after we publish. Do you understand that?'

'Yes. I think so. You will pay when the story is in the paper. Is okay. I can wait.'

'Okay.' Rosie spread her hands, a little bemused by this character. 'Then talk to me, Viktor. What can you tell me about the charity that is worth a story for my newspaper?' She was bursting to get the information out of him but she had to get the measure of him. If he was the kind of guy who would take umbrage at the way she talked to him, he'd have been out of here two minutes ago. He looked hungry. He wanted money, and he had information – at least she hoped he had.

Viktor took out a cigarette packet and fiddled with it, turning it one way and another, pushing it as though it was a Rubik's cube. He pulled his chair closer.

'Your story – about the babies being sold. Is all true. I saw it. But there is more than that. They sell people too.'

'People? What do you mean? In Romania?'

'They bring people. Here to the UK from over there. Not just Romania. But from Albania too. And Bosnia. Hungary.'

'Do you mean like slaves?'

He shrugged. 'Kind of like slaves. When you come you are tied with them.' He made a gesture with both wrists, indicating handcuffs. 'You cannot go back until you pay your way. Because they bring you here, and it costs a lot of money. If you have money to pay them, then is fine. But if you come with no money, you must always work for them. But you never pay the debt, because they always tell you it isn't paid yet. No matter how much you pay them.'

Rosie processed the information. People trafficking was getting bigger every year – mostly in prostitution, bringing women in from Eastern Europe and East Asia. The majority of illegal workers she'd encountered before were men who'd been brought over by Indian restaurant owners. But they weren't slaves, they were just toiling for a pittance, living in crap accommodation. None of this was new. But a charity transporting them here was a different ball game.

'You mean Hands Across Europe transports these people over? How? In their trucks?'

He nodded vigorously. 'Yes, yes. You know this already?'

'Not really. Just surmising from what you're saying.'

'Yes. The charity . . . It goes from UK to Romania, to the orphanages, and they bring in the trucks, food and medical supplies, clothes. Once they unload the supplies, the trucks going back here are empty. All empty. So they can bring anything.'

'But what about borders and customs?'

He rubbed his thumb and forefingers. 'Is all money. All corrupt. Everyone gets paid along the way.'

Rosie was conscious that her tape recorder was picking this up. She'd decided not to ask him for permission as he'd been bold enough to ask for money first, so she wanted to get his claims clearly on tape. It wasn't quite honest, but she played by her own rules.

'So are you telling me that this UK charity – Hands Across Europe – goes out there filled with all the supplies donated by the goodwill of people in this country, then their trucks return with migrants in them? And the trucks go through the borders in various countries by paying officials off? I've been through these borders before and it's a nightmare. I was on a bus one time, and they stopped us for hours, going through everything we had.'

His lips curled. 'It is who you know. Is all gangsters. Albanian, mostly who work across the Balkan areas – Hungary,

Bulgaria and places. Some Russians too. The Russians organise everything. They have the money.'

'But what about when they come to the UK? Surely the ports there are more secure?'

He nodded. 'Yes. But by that time, if there are, for example, twelve or twenty immigrants in the trucks, they have all been split up. When the trucks cross into France and Holland, the immigrants go with other people.'

'What other people?'

'Other people in the, I think the word is, network. Is all organised. Some go in vans, in other trucks or in cars. They go to different places in the UK. To London, Manchester, and to Glasgow.'

'All run from this charity?'

'I only know from this charity. I don't know about other charities. But maybe. Is no surprise if more charities do it.'

'So how do you know this for sure?'

He raised his eyebrows in surprise.

'How I know? Because I am one. I come like this. I have no money for my passage here on the trucks, so I have to work for them when I come.'

'For the charity?'

'Yes. I go back with them when they go to Romania with the aid because I know the road and can tell the driver, and I help with things. Then we bring more people up and come back.'

'You do that?'

'Yes.'

'How many times in the past three years?'

He puffed as though he was thinking, touching his fingers.

'I think maybe ten or fifteen times. A lot.'

'Always bringing people back?'

'Yes. Always the same.' He shifted in his seat and leaned across. 'Not just people. Drugs. In Holland, we pick up drugs also. And on two trips, I know that we took also guns. Handguns. I saw them. They were in long boxes in the truck I was in.'

'How may trucks each trip?'

'Two, sometimes three.'

'The drivers. Are they from the UK? From Scotland?'

'Some from Scotland, and others we meet in England. Like two trucks go from Scotland, and on the way to the ferry, we meet the other truck from England. Usually Hull.'

'The charity has a base in Hull?'

He shrugged. 'I suppose. I don't know so much detail like that. I only know where I go and what I bring back.'

'When did you last make a trip?'

'Two months ago.'

'Did you bring people back then?'

'Yes.'

'How many?'

'I think about twelve. Men. Young men like me.'

'Do you know the boss of the charity?'

'I see him. He doesn't come with us. Always if he is going by road, he travels in jeep. Sometimes he flies and I have seen him in Bucharest. With the Russians. At the office you had the photograph of in the paper – the adoption place.' He paused. 'It was very dangerous out there for a journalist to do what you did. You must be brave, Rosie Gilmour. You could have been killed. You also must be careful here in Scotland.'

Rosie felt a sudden knot of nerves in her stomach. It wasn't that she was naive enough to think an organisation that she'd just busted all over the *Post* wouldn't have tentacles that stretched across here, but she'd been so wrapped up in the story, and so glad to be back on her home soil, that she hadn't given her own safety a second thought.

'I will be careful.'

'You have bodyguard?'

Rosie smiled. 'No. No bodyguard. But I am looked after. I'm okay.' She knew she was lying, but that question made her suspicious. If this guy was asking for money and telling her things, how did she know he wasn't sent by the organisation to suss her out, find out where she was? Maybe he was all part of the plan. Paranoia forever lurked on her shoulder – and with good reason. She pushed the niggle away.

'This is all fascinating, Viktor. But as I said, I need proof. What kind of proof do you have? And also, are you still working for them?'

He glanced around the room. 'Okay. I will tell you the truth. I have run away from them. I am hiding from them. I am very angry with them, because they double-cross me. I pay them a lot of money – or they take the money off my wages every week, but always they say I still owe them money. They tell me to wait, that they have a good job for me in time. That I will be working in a good place in their organisation. But it is all bullshit.'

'Where do you live? Do you work every day?'

'I live in Glasgow. But I go to Edinburgh sometimes to work for the charity, to help with the loading of the stuff at the warehouse. Maybe three days a week I am in the warehouse.'

'And how do they pay you?'

'They give me money in an envelope every week. My flat I don't pay for. One other boy is also there.'

'Albanian like you?'

'Yes. But younger. He is twenty. He work delivering drugs and things.'

'Drugs? You mean here in Glasgow?'

'Yes. Look, I don't know. But I think the bosses are working with people in Glasgow. Also in England. I think they work together. But I don't know. I don't want to be a gangster. I just come to get normal job. I want to be a carpenter.'

Rosie watched him closely and could see his face drop a little.

'Sometimes I wish I had stayed back in Albania. But it is shit over there. I grew up in an Albanian orphanage. So I know what it is like to be in these places. I have nobody back there. I thought maybe I would be safe here and could have normal life. That is why I ask to come with these people.'

'Are you not safe here?'

He puffed. 'Not now I'm not. Because they will be looking for me. I have not been to my house or to work for a week.'

'Why did you leave at this time?'

'When I saw your story. They are going crazy at the depot – the bosses. They closed the place down. They shit themselves. I am afraid I will be found as part of it, by the police or something.'

Rosie wanted to say that he *was* part of it, and knowingly went to Romania every time, but she could also see that he didn't have much choice. He wasn't someone who immediately touched her, not like other refugees she'd encountered. He was just one of the people thrown into the mix because he wanted a better life. Of course people made wrong moves and choices when they were in a foreign land not knowing who to trust. It was easy to get caught up in it if you had no money and nowhere to turn to, and you knew from the outset that you'd arrived here illegally. You were trapped before you began. That was the hold these lowlife thugs had over people.

'I understand.' She reached across and touched his wrist, and he seemed to flinch a little.

'I'm sorry.' He swallowed. 'I'm tired. I been sleeping in the street at night and one night in the homeless place. I think now I want to go away. Maybe abroad to somewhere else in Europe and live. I have to go and hide from these people. That is why I was asking for money for the story.'

They sat for a few moments in silence, listening to the cups clinking and chairs being dragged over the floor. Watching people coming and going, the freedom to do these small day-to-day things suddenly struck Rosie as incredibly potent. Whatever we think we don't have, in this society we have this single thing: we are free to do what we want, go where we want, work or not work. We are part of a system, and though it might be groaning under the strain, unless you really messed up, someone would pick you up.

'So, Viktor. What kind of proof? You said you have proof?'

He nodded, and finished his coffee, again playing with the cigarette packet. Then he reached into his pocket and pulled his chair so he was alongside Rosie. She could smell stale sweat, tobacco and grubby clothes. He took out a grimy envelope and opened it, pulling out three photographs. He placed them on the table in front of her, and Rosie's eye immediately went to one of the big charity trucks, 'Hands Across Europe' emblazoned on the side. She scanned the picture, and could see the boss of the charity, Robert Morgan. Then another picture, at a port somewhere, what looked like the Dutch flag fluttering in the distance. The truck was open at the back, and the photograph was of half a dozen or so men crouched in the back, dark eyes, frightened looks. But it proved nothing. It could have been workers taking a break after unloading their cargo. Another picture was of two transit vans, and some people going in the back. He told her he had taken the pictures with a cheap camera he had and had kept them hidden.

'Can you explain the pictures?'

'Yes. You see, here,' he pointed to the charity truck, 'this is the truck after we deliver the aid in Romania. We went to a place called Cluj, and then we go to a place on the border of Romania and Hungary and we pick up some people. Albanians. And the other one is the people in the back of the truck we pick up. The other pictures of the vans are people going in. The same people. You see this? They are all illegal.'

'But it doesn't prove anything really, Viktor. These people could be just workers coming home. Where are they now?'

'I know only three of them who are in Scotland. The others went somewhere in the UK.'

'Do you know their names?'

'Yes. One is in the flat where I lived. But he doesn't know I'm doing this. Another two boys also here, but they don't live with us.'

Rosie's mind was buzzing. If they used the pics and these men's faces they could all be in trouble. They could blank the faces out and tell the story but it still didn't prove anything.

Not enough to make the kind of accusations he was making about corruption on a grand scale. Her heart sank.

'I need more proof, Viktor. It needs to be backed up with someone else talking. What about your friend from the flat? Or the other two?'

'I don't think so. I haven't seen any of them for a week.'

'Are they unhappy?'

'Yes. Like me. They know they will never pay the debt for coming here. They work in the car-wash business. Many car-wash business workers are just the slaves who come here.'

'Would any of them talk to us without being identified?'

'I don't know. Will you pay them money? Maybe they can disappear before the story comes out.'

Again the money. She knew McGuire would be against parting with money, but she also knew that time was not on their side. If they wanted to really go for this story, they had this man on the run to back it up, along with the pictures. If his friends went along off the record, the story was in the bag. But they had to act fast. Also, the more people in the chain who knew about it, the more danger for the informants, especially Viktor.

'Would you consider going to the police?'

'No,' he said quickly. 'Never. I don't want that. If you want the story and the pictures I can speak to my friends on the phone. But they won't want police. You pay us and we go.'

'Can you trust your friends?'

He sighed. 'I hope so. The one who lives with me, I can trust. But we are not gangsters. We are like puppets. They work the strings. We are not free.'

'But can you trust your friends not to inform the bosses?'

He shrugged. 'I don't know about all of them. I speak with the boy in my flat first. But if I tell my two other friends, if I can find them, we have to do things fast.'

'I know. I will speak to my editor.' Rosie finished her tea. 'Where will you be later? Can you talk to your friends and meet me somewhere if any of them agree? Tonight or tomorrow, if possible?'

'I will try. I will talk to them. First the boy in my flat.' He bit his lip and looked at her. 'Rosie, I have nowhere to sleep and nothing to eat. I have no money. I'm sorry. I am not a beggar like some people you see. But can you give me some money to find a hostel or somewhere and get some food? I'm sorry to ask this.'

His face reddened.

'Okay, Viktor. I'll help you out for the moment. But I need to know I can trust you.'

'You can trust me. I came to you. I want to talk. But I need to get away.'

Part of Rosie didn't know if it was an elaborate plan of his to con her out of money. But she found herself reaching into her pocket and fishing out two twenty-pound notes and a tenner. It would be a lot to him back home, but it would barely get him a hostel bed and some food for the next day or so. She needed to keep him onside.

'Take this. Get somewhere cheap to stay. There's a place down near Glasgow Green and it doesn't cost much. I need to be able to speak to you as soon as you talk to any friends. Can you do that today?'

He took the money and scrunched it in his hands before stuffing it in his jeans pocket. 'Yes.'

He collected his pictures and put them in the envelope. Rosie touched his wrist.

'Viktor, I need the pics. Can I keep them till we meet again?'

He blew out a sigh. 'I don't know. Is all I have.'

'If we have trust, mutual trust, you will give me them. Or even if you let me copy them, that's okay.'

'How you mean?'

'I have someone with me. A photographer.'

'What, here? Inside?' He looked shocked.

'No. Outside. Don't worry. He'll take a copy of them. Is that okay?'

'But no picture of me in the newspaper.'

'No. Not if you don't want.'

'I don't want.'

'Okay.' Rosie stood up, and he also got to his feet. She shook his hand, which felt soft and fleshy.

'How old are you, by the way?'

'I am twenty-seven.'

'Okay. I just wondered.' He looked older. 'When we go outside, my friend will come across and take a picture of the photos.'

He nodded, and they walked towards the door.

'Thanks for coming to see me, Viktor. I will do everything I can to tell the story.'

'Is wrong what they do. I know I am wrong too, because I am with them. And I am asking for money. But is not my choice any more. I just want to be free.'

'I understand.' Rosie found herself putting a comforting arm on his shoulder. She glimpsed Matt in a doorway across the precinct and beckoned him over.

CHAPTER THIRTY-TWO

'I know it stinks, Gilmour, but we don't have proof that Hands Across Europe were aware about the selling of orphans, hence the reason we said so in your piece. And right now, we definitely don't have an iota of proof that they're also part of a people-smuggling racket.' McGuire folded his arms across his chest and sat back. 'I know you're well aware of all of that, so what do you want me to do here? We can't even think about publishing allegations made by some random Albanian, who, by his own admission, is a criminal himself.'

When it was laid out like that in front of her by the editor in his usual devil's advocate fashion, Rosie knew it was hard to argue. But she'd known anyway from the moment Viktor showed her the pictures and told her of the people-smuggling that this wasn't proof enough.

'I'm not disputing any of what you're saying, Mick. But if the charity is so innocent, then how come they haven't made a single statement since my story came out? Okay, it didn't accuse them, but their name was all over it, because it was a UK charity and because Alan Lewis is attached to it. Why did they not come out with a statement? What have they got to hide? All the papers followed my story, but still nothing from them. If they had nothing to hide they'd have come out shocked and fighting.'

'What about the boss? Where is he? Robert Morgan, is it?'

'Yes. He's never been seen. I sent Declan there yesterday and the place is all locked up. At the warehouse they use, the workers said they just store clothes in a locked room, but nobody has been around for a couple of weeks. I even got a stringer to check their depots in Hull and Manchester – but nothing. It's all locked up. It's as though they've disappeared.'

'Where does Morgan live?'

'Declan went to his house too. All locked up. No sign of life. No cars. Nothing. It's a bungalow on the outskirts of Glasgow, down towards Helensburgh. He lives by himself. Neighbours haven't seen him since the story hit the paper.'

'That's suspicious in itself. I mean all of it is, and we know that. But maybe Morgan is up to his neck in talks with some lawyer as we speak, trying to find a way to come back at us legally because we've linked his charity to the international baby trade.'

'I wouldn't bank on it. He's done a runner. The smart money is on that.'

McGuire looked pensive as he stared at the blank pages of the dummy newspaper pages on his desk.

'How did you leave it with Viktor or whatever he's called?' He waved a finger. 'I'm not parting with any money until I can get this story past the lawyers at least.'

'I know, I know. I told him there would be no money unless his story can be corroborated. I'm waiting for him to get back to me once he speaks to his mates. But the boy is shitting himself because he knows the gang masters will be looking for him – especially now, when they'll be trying to cover all their tracks.'

'Did you talk amounts with him?'

'No. Not yet. I was going to deal with that when we see what we've got.'

'I'm not giving them a fortune. The bean counters will crap themselves if they know we're paying out to people like that. After all, they are criminals too.'

Rosie ran a hand through her hair.

'You can say criminals, but I'd be more likely to say victims.'

'Aye, of course you would, Gilmour. They're all victims, but they learn pretty fast that being a victim gets them nowhere.'

'You can guarantee that the bastards at the top of this empire won't be the ones dragged into custody. Even in Romania, where the cops are supposed to be trying to bust this criminal gang, the guy whom I spoke to at the adoption agency and his cohorts will be up somewhere well out of the way when the heat is on.'

'They're probably here, or somewhere else in Europe. They're not going to hang around and wait for a corrupt Romanian plod to knock on their door.'

'I know. So that's why we can't let up on this, Mick. We've got a chance here to bust the UK end of this if these guys agree to talk. I'll be honest with you, if it was up to me, and we can get proof from them that will get this story into the papers, I'd be happy to pay them plenty of money.'

'Oh, aye, I'm sure you would. You've been throwing my money up and running under it for years.' He stood up. 'Let's just wait and see what we've got from them before you start changing lives. Now bugger off, I've got a meeting upstairs.'

As Rosie was walking out of the room, she almost bumped into Declan who was looking breathless with excitement.

'Rosie. I was just coming to see you. Morgan's car has been found up in the Old Kilpatrick Hills with a body in it.'

'Christ! Is it him?'

'Don't know yet. Police have just put out a statement on the wires saying a car with a body in it.'

Rosie stuck her head around McGuire's open door.

'I hear it,' he shouted. 'Let's hope it's him. It'll be a great splash tomorrow.'

'I'll make some calls.'

Rosie noticed a missed call from DI Morton and cursed

under her breath when she saw her phone was on Silent. She immediately pressed the callback number.

'Rosie. How are you going to be first with the news if you're not answering your phone?'

'Sorry, James. It was on Silent for some bizarre reason and I missed it. I was in with the editor. I've just been told Morgan's car has been found out in—'

'That's why I was calling you. I was giving you a heads up.'

'I really appreciate that. Sorry I missed your call.' Rosie paused, still annoyed with herself. It didn't look very efficient when she was trying her best to impress a new contact. 'It's on the police wires, but it's not saying whose body. Is it Morgan's?'

'It sure is. Stone cold dead.'

'Suicide? Hosepipe?'

'Nope. From what I hear from our boys, it's a single gunshot to the head.'

'Christ!'

'No weapon found at the scene.'

'Jesus. He's been murdered?'

'Certainly looks like it. Executed. Hard to hide a weapon after you've shot yourself in the head.'

'What do you think?'

'We're all over it. Forensics are out there at the moment combing the car. They'll bring it in, and his body too. They're also at his house, picking up his computer and all his files. Though I wouldn't expect he's going to keep a diary of anything he's involved in that isn't charity work.'

'Astonishing stuff. When will you be confirming it's his body and about the gunshot wound?'

'Well, here's the situation, Rosie. We won't be releasing the details about the gunshot until tomorrow, and definitely not for this evening's news. So you can get first bite. It is, after all, your exposé, so I'm giving you a break.'

Rosie tried to keep the excitement from her voice.

'Really? That's a real turn you're doing me, Jim. My editor will be delighted.'

'Well, make sure you watch how you word it.' He paused. 'It's not something I'd be doing every day for any reporter, and that's the truth. But I can see the work you put in on this, and you've helped bring this case to us if we can get to the bottom of it.'

'I owe you a big dinner.'

'I can't be bought. And certainly not for a bagel. But I'll hold you to that dinner.' Silence for a moment. 'Oh, and Rosie, I hope if you're getting anywhere on this story and anyone else around it, you'll reciprocate the heads up.'

Rosie hesitated a second. 'I will, if I can.'

'Which, translated, means, you'll pass it on to me once you know your story is in the paper.'

Guilt washed over Rosie that she was hoping to meet two men who could be key to this entire operation. But they were terrified of cops and there was no way she was ready to throw them into the mix.

'I'll do what I can. You can count on me for that.'

'I'll talk to you.' He hung up.

Rosie waited in the same café where she'd met Viktor yesterday, her stomach tightening every time the door opened. It was packed out again, but she'd managed to get a table at the back, away from the window, while Matt had come in and taken his coffee outside to his vantage point at the shop doorway. She'd already cleared it with McGuire to give the boys enough money to put them into a reasonable hotel for a couple of nights, if they both spoke out. Things were ratcheting up. McGuire was much more onside now that she'd told him her inside information that Morgan's body had been found with a gunshot wound to the head. He was even more impressed that it would be the *Post*'s exclusive splash. So he was willing to push the boat out a little to accommodate the lads, if she thought Viktor's mate was genuine. Her mobile pinged with a message and she could see it was from Matt.

'Two boys coming your way now.'

Rosie felt a little surge of adrenalin. When she'd spoken to Viktor earlier he'd said his friend was refusing to talk but he'd work on him, and he would meet her anyway, even if it was on his own. It was up to her now to make this happen. She watched the door as it opened and saw Viktor scanning the room until their eyes met. She glimpsed the smaller, skinny, dark-haired boy behind him. He looked young, and was dressed in a tracksuit zip-up top and jeans. He had the haunted look so many of these young men had, when they arrived in a strange country with nothing but hope and the fear they'd be sent back. Viktor came across and sat down at the table as his friend hesitated behind him.

'Sit, Pavil. Is okay.'

He pulled out a chair and gestured to his friend. Rosie looked at Pavil and smiled, but was leaving it to Viktor to introduce them.

'This my friend Pavil,' he almost whispered. 'He is very nervous.'

'I understand,' Rosie said, looking at Pavil long enough for their eyes to meet. 'It's okay, Pavil. Don't be afraid. My name is Rosie.'

Pavil glanced over his shoulder and licked his lips as though his mouth was dry. He nodded.

'Let me get you guys some tea or coffee. Anything to eat?'

'Coffee,' Viktor said, glancing at Pavil. 'Coffee please.'

Rosie went to the counter and ordered a couple of coffees and extra sugar, then two baguettes. Pavil looked like he needed a good feed, but he also looked too nervous to eat. But she still had that urge to mother them when she saw poor vulnerable boys like this. Her bleeding heart. They were part of a people-smuggling operation, she had to remember. Keep it in perspective. She returned with the food and drinks on a tray, and another tea for herself.

'I thought you might be hungry.' She pushed the sandwiches towards them.

Pavil looked at Viktor, then at Rosie, as though waiting for permission to eat.

'Go ahead,' Rosie said.

He tore open the sandwich and took a bite and another, then swigged some coffee. His head was down and both hands were clutching the sandwich as though he was waiting for someone to come in and snatch the food out of his hand. Viktor toyed with his sandwich, slowly unwrapping it. He smiled a little.

'Pavil is always hungry. There is never enough food for him.'

'He's a growing boy.' Rosie smiled, glad of the lightness breaking the ice. 'How old are you, Pavil?'

He looked at Viktor as though waiting for him to give the sign for him to speak.

'Twenty. I am twenty.'

Rosie nodded. 'How long you been here?'

Again, he glanced at Viktor, who blinked his approval.

'I come one year ago.' He tore off a bite of sandwich and chewed it furiously. Rosie watched as he swallowed, his Adam's apple moving in his skinny neck.

They sat for a moment, and Rosie decided to let Pavil finish eating. She hoped he'd feel a little less scared and edgy once he'd got some food into him. After he downed the last of the sandwich, she glanced from one to the other.

'So, Viktor, have you and Pavil talked? You have agreed to tell me your story?'

Viktor looked at Pavil.

'He doesn't speak English like me. But he understands a lot. I have been here longer, and because I work with a lot of the Scottish people longer I can speak not bad.'

'Your English is really very good.'

'Thank you. I am trying.'

Rosie turned to Pavil and spoke slowly. 'So, Pavil. Viktor will have explained to you. I am writing the story of the charity and the people-smuggling. I already did the story in the newspaper about the babies for sale in Romania.'

'I know. I see the story. I am an orphan too. Like Viktor.'

Rosie felt a rush of sympathy for him, for the skinny boy with tired circles around his eyes, and for the way he looked so lost in a place like this, vulnerable, alone, and so desperate that he'd ended up sitting in a café with a reporter he didn't know, hoping she'd have the means to allow him an escape from whatever hell he was in. What a shitty deal to be handed out for so many kids like this around the world.

'Viktor told me about how the charity brings people from Romania once they deliver the food and medical aid. That the trucks are then filled with people – Romanians, Albanians, Hungarians, et cetera. Is that how you came here?'

Pavil nodded, and looked at Viktor.

'You can tell her, Pavil.'

'I am frightened. If they find me talking, they will kill me. They will kill me and Viktor.'

Rosie watched as Viktor spoke to him in Albanian and he took a moment to explain. Eventually, Pavil nodded.

'I have told him that we will be paid money if our story is proof of what happens,' Viktor says. 'If you do the story for the paper we get money. Then we can go.'

'Yes. I have spoken to my editor, as I told you on the phone. They will agree to give you some money on publication.'

'But how much?'

'I don't know about that yet. It depends on what you can tell me, the level of proof, and how much we can use. But we will look after you.'

'We need a lot of money. We have to go to Europe. Find a way so that these people don't find us first.'

'I know. I understand.' Rosie was beginning to feel she was losing the edge here. Pavil was nervous. This could easily slip through her fingers. She had to save it. 'Okay. I understand everything you are saying, and I know how frightened you are, Pavil – both of you. But it is best if you, Pavil, can tell me your story. What is your experience with the charity and your life here, and then once we've got that we can see how we are.'

Viktor nodded to him, and he began to speak, wringing his hands, chewing his grimy fingernails.

'I come here because I want to find my brother. Saban. He also come, but before me. We are in the orphanage together, all the life. But he leave a year before me, and get some job in Tirana and here too. It was him who told me this is what we do.'

'Your brother is also here? In Scotland?'

'No. I don't know. Maybe in England. I have not see him and I been here one year. I talk on phone and he say he is busy working with the business. I don't know what business.'

'With the Albanians?'

'Yes. He worked with them in Tirana, but also in UK.'

Rosie's gut was beginning to sink. What if his brother was well wrapped up and established within the Albanian criminal empire? He must be, or he would have found a way to get to his brother. Perhaps he was protecting him. Her mind buzzed with various gloomy scenarios. Keep to the facts, she told herself.

'Okay. Viktor told me about going back to Romania and picking up people. Is that something you do too?'

'Yes. I go with Viktor most of the time. Some days I work in the warehouse too. But mostly I go on the trucks. I help take things off and load.'

'And you have seen people in the trucks being smuggled through the borders back this way?'

'Yes. I see this.'

'Can you tell me about this?'

He looked at Viktor.

'I go many times with Viktor, and always we bring people back. They go everywhere when trucks come to Holland. They go in vans.' He paused, looked at Viktor, then took a deep breath. 'But one time, I see one of the men. I think he is Hungarian. When we come to Holland, it is the night time and when the truck comes in, there is a big van in the car park. The van is there for the people. But one boy – the Hungarian, tries to run away. He doesn't want to stay with the people. I don't know why. Maybe he is afraid. But they run after him, and bring him back. Then they beat him with sticks many times until he is dead. I see him dead. They put his body in the side of the road, then we drove away. He is lying there. I see from the back window, still he lies there. He is not moving. They killed him.'

'Jesus,' Rosie whispered. 'That's awful.'

Pavil sat saying nothing, the muscles in his jaw tightening.

'I see what they do. That is why I frighten.' He paused and swallowed. 'I want to go. They will beat and kill us for talking like this. But one day, I think they will beat and kill us anyway.'

Rosie listened as he turned to Viktor and spoke animatedly in Albanian, his eyes filling with tears, and Viktor held his arm in a comforting gesture.

'He is afraid. Pavil is young boy and it was difficult in the orphanage. He was beaten before by the people there.

Abused. Like me, he thought we could come here and get a job, but now we are like prisoners. He is asking about the money and how soon can we go.'

Rosie listened and sighed. 'Okay. I know what you're saying, and what Pavil told me is really great for helping with the proof. Can he also identify the photos, and also between you can you name these people, or even say what nationality they are?'

'Yes. We can do that.' Viktor took the envelope from his pocket and laid the pictures on the table.

They went through them.

'This boy, from Romania, and this one too. This one, Hungary, and these two also. But these four boys, they are Albanian. I don't know them but only met on the truck. I can remember some of their names if Pavil does too.'

Rosie wrote the information down beside each picture like a caption, labelling the men from left to right.

'And most of these people? You didn't see them after Holland?'

Viktor scanned the photo again.

'Two of the Albanians – these ones. They stay in Holland, and the Romanians they both come to France because they want go to Spain. But the rest of the people, they all come to England with us. All of them stay in the south of England. I never see them again.'

'Thanks,' Rosie said.

She had enough beefed out information that would also

help with the lawyers, and when the police eventually were given her story, there were photographs of, the young men who'd been trafficked and their basic nationalities for them to go on. What she had here was evidence and corroboration of a criminal gang at work. She would have to talk to McGuire soon and she knew the lawyers would ask for sworn affidavits from the boys. But the problem with these affidavits was that they were really only a comfort to lawyers, and could be blown out of court if it came to it. But on this story, nobody was going to sue the *Post*, Rosie was convinced of that. She had her story. She was ready to pay out and let these boys go.

'Viktor, I asked you yesterday about the possibility of going to the police and you said, No way. I'm asking you again, because I do think it will help put away these people who treat people like you, and all the others who have been smuggled, like slaves.'

'It won't, Rosie. There are too many Albanians now in gangs here. It is very organised. It is not going to help the police or us.'

'But do you have names of the people in charge?'

'Only the names we deal with. That is all. And the charity boss. Morgan. He knows all about this. The police can come and arrest him now. Maybe he will talk.'

She knew that by telling them Robert Morgan was dead they would freak out, feeling the net beginning to close in already. But if she didn't tell them, they'd see it in her story all over the front page tomorrow or the next day. She took a breath, looking from one to the other.

'Listen. I have something to tell you. But I don't want to alarm you, but it is something you need to know.'

Viktor and Pavil glanced at each other anxiously.

'Morgan is dead. He was found earlier today in his car out in the countryside. He has been murdered.'

Both of them blanched and their heads went down. Pavil began to shake.

'This because the story you did?' Pavil cried. 'This is what they do. They are closing all the people down. They will be looking for me more now. We should go, Viktor.'

'No, listen. Wait.' Viktor held Pavil's arm. 'Rosie. We need to get away. When is your story in the paper? Now we have told you everything we know?'

Rosie spread her hands to calm them down.

'Just keep calm for the moment, guys. Honestly, just stay calm. I want to talk to my editor on the phone just now, and I think we can work on the story to get it in the paper in the next two days.'

'But what we do?'

'I can put you in a hotel somewhere in the city. Nobody will know you are there.'

'They will be looking for me. For both of us.' Pavil looked pleadingly at Viktor. 'What do we do?'

'Pavil. I think we listen to Rosie. I think we stay in a hotel and stay in until it is time.' He turned to Rosie. 'When will you know about the money?'

Rosie stood up, reluctant to leave the café but not wanting to discuss with McGuire in front of them.

'Let me make a call to my editor.'

CHAPTER THIRTY-THREE

The splash was written, and Rosie read it over one last time before emailing it across to McGuire. Tomorrow's front page would fly off the shelves, with her exclusive line about Robert Morgan being shot in the head. The TV news at six led with the death of the charity boss whose body was found in his car, days after a newspaper had revealed the charity's link to an orphans-for-sale scandal in Romania. But that was it. No murder line. Rosie had DI James Morton to thank for the break on this one, and she wondered how much cooperation he'd be looking for in return. He would know by this time that she didn't run to the police every time she had a tip on a major criminal activity, but he had enough respect for her to know that now and again she would. She hoped it would work both ways, and this wouldn't be the first big shout he'd give her. She looked at the time on the top of her screen. She and Matt had dropped Viktor and Pavil at the city-centre hotel where she'd booked them a room and told them not to venture outside, and to order everything they needed from room service. They were already scared that they'd come this far, and she hoped they wouldn't do a runner. But if they did, she had their stories on tape and Matt had snatched a photograph of both of them together as they left the café. She needed to get back up there soon, to get better pictures done and, even though she hadn't even written their story up yet, ask them to sign the sworn affidavits the *Post*'s lawyers were insisting on. But she didn't want to argue. McGuire had agreed to pay them five grand for their story. She'd hoped for at least eight, but had had to settle for less. She hadn't broken the news to them yet, so if they were hoping for some kind of jackpot they were going to be disappointed. But five grand would take them a long way. They had no idea where they were headed, but just wanted to get as far away from here as they could. And they had no passports. The gangmaster thugs held on to the passport of every person they smuggled, to make sure they'd be slave labour for the rest of their lives. So Rosie had to make the decision for the boys, and she knew the risks. She'd already sounded out her contact in the north of Spain, Tony, who drove a truck to Europe every couple of weeks. He'd agreed to get them out of the country in his truck. He was even going to make a detour from the north of England to come and pick them up in a motorway service station car park. Rosie knew big Tony would call in the favour another time, and she would return it. She'd also phoned her big ex-cop friend, Bertie Shaw, who now owned a hotel in the Borders where she occasionally hid people from the press pack if the *Post* was on an exclusive. The last time she'd seen him, he'd helped her in an investigation into a child sex abuse ring involving top-level Establishment and showbiz figures. He was glad to get out of the kitchen, he'd told her, and was already on his way to Glasgow to keep an eye on Viktor and Pavil. Rosie hadn't told McGuire any of this. It was her call. She couldn't just leave these guys to wander around the city. As she hit the key sending the story over to McGuire's private email, her mobile rang on the desk. It was Jonjo Mulhearn.

'All right, Rosie?'

'Yep. Working away here, Jonjo.'

'Okay. I won't keep you. But a couple of bits of info from our last chat. Have you got a minute to talk?'

'Of course.'

'That charity you were talking about. I see the boss's car has been found with a body in it. No doubt he's been murdered.'

'I think you'd be right on that one.' Rosie didn't want to give her splash away, even though she had a level of trust with him.

'I put some feelers out on him, relating to your story on the babies in Romania. You're bang on about the charity being linked to this mafia mob in the UK. And also those thug Albanians and Russians who are over here muscling in? It's part of the same grubby empire. The names you've mentioned have come up. And the charity boss was in on it.'

'Really? Have you got people actually saying they know Robert Morgan and that he was working alongside them?'

'So I'm told.'

'What about Alan Lewis? Any word on him knowing all about it?'

'Not as such, to be honest. I was really only asking if the charity was involved with the mob here, and it seems they are. But Lewis was the accountant. He must have known. Tell you what . . . If I was him, I'd stay missing.'

'Thanks, Jonjo. I really appreciate your help.' She pulled on her jacket. 'I have to go now, as the story is growing arms and legs, and I've got a couple of guys I'm looking after who are giving me good information.'

'Good for you. Be careful. If you need any help, give me a shout.'

He hung up.

Rosie and Matt made their way along the quiet hotel corridor to room 212. She'd told Viktor not to answer the door to anyone but her, and she hoped the two of them were sensible enough to stay in the room. She gently knocked on the door. No answer. Matt glanced at her and pursed his lips. She knocked again, and thought she heard movement.

'Hello?' The voice was from inside.

'Viktor? It's Rosie. Can you open the door?'

She heard the chain being slid back and the lock turned, and as the door opened a little she could see Viktor, with Pavil standing behind him.

'Rosie.' He took off the chain and opened the door. 'Come.'

'You all right?' Rosie looked from one to the other. Then she turned to Matt. 'This is Matt. He's a photographer with the paper and we work a lot together.' She could see the worried look on Pavil's face. 'Don't worry. He will not take any pictures of you that can be identified. We will do pics from behind you. Nobody will even see your faces. And you can put on baseball caps or something.'

They both looked at each other and nodded.

'When is the story in the paper? So we can go,' Viktor asked.

Viktor looked more anxious than he did yesterday. Probably being holed up in the room all the time with nothing to think about except getting rumbled was beginning to get on top of them.

'Okay. Here's the situation. I came up to see if you were all right and to tell you the plan.'

'What about the money?' Viktor asked.

'That's what I'm going to talk about. Sit down, guys. Try to relax a bit.'

'I am very frighten. Look.' Pavil held up his mobile phone and scrolled down. 'Many times they called me. And messages too. In Albanian they spoke. My boss. He said I to get back to the flat that they will find me.'

Rosie looked at Viktor, who then said:

'I haven't switched my phone on since yesterday. I don't want to know what they say. It makes me more nervous. We want to get out now. Is dangerous here.'

'Nobody knows you're here, Viktor. In this hotel. If they're looking for you, they know you've no money. They won't even know where to start. Don't worry. I have a plan to get you out of here by tomorrow.' She motioned them to the sofa. 'Come over here. Sit down and we'll we talk a little.'

They sat down and Matt sat at a chair by a writing desk.

'Okay,' Rosie said. 'What we want to do now is take some pictures, then when I go back to the office, I will write your story. It won't go in the paper tomorrow, but it will be in the next day's. The lawyers have to go through it very closely.'

'Why the lawyers?'

'Because we are making allegations that link this char- ity to people-smuggling. It's a big accusation, Viktor, and if we are wrong, then my newspaper will be in trouble.'

'It is not wrong. We tell you the truth. We see it. We were there when they bring the people, as we told you. That is what happens.'

'I know. And we believe you. My editor believes you and that's why we are doing the story. You have been very brave to come and speak to us like this. And when this is all over we will pass the information to the police here and abroad.'

'No police. We not talk to police.'

'I know. You don't have to. They will take my information and everything we have, the pictures and stuff, and they will decide what to do.' She paused and sighed. 'But I honestly think you should talk to the police before we do the story. They will make you safe.'

They both shook their heads vigorously and Pavil got up and sat back down nervously.

'No. No. Because I see a man being killed. I cannot tell police that because they may think I am guilty too. They think "Albanian – he must be a gangster", but is not true. Many Albanians are just poor like us. No police.'

Rosie could see how agitated he was and she put a hand up.

'All right. No police. Don't worry.'

'You promise?'

'Yes. I promise. So,' she continued, 'what I want to do is get you out of the country. But I know you have no passports. So I'm afraid you will have to go out the same way you came in.'

They looked at each other.

'Smuggled?'

'It's your only option because you don't want to go the authorities, and I can understand that. But you cannot buy a plane ticket or a ferry ticket or go through the UK border without a passport. Once you get to France you will be fine. My friend will help you to make your way to the north of Spain. Then it's up to you.'

'What you mean?'

'I mean, I can get you out of the country. I have a contact who takes a lorry over to Spain and delivers things, and he can take you in his truck. He will drive you to Spain, and then you have to try to get some jobs somewhere.' She paused, looked from one to the other. 'I'm sure you know how to do this. There's bar work, labouring jobs. All sorts of things you can do. And you will have money. I will give you the money tomorrow once the lawyers okay the story for the paper. Then you can be on your way.'

'How much money?'

Rosie flicked a glance at Matt.

'Enough to keep you going. Get yourselves a room or apartment in a hostel or something till you get some work. It's the only way.'

'How much money?'

Rosie hesitated, picked her words.

'Okay. I've had a long talk with my editor about this and the managing editor who controls the money. We are pleased to have your story and it will make a difference having had you to talk and back up the allegations along with the photographs you gave us. But we cannot pay a lot of money. When the police start asking questions they will ask if we have paid money, and that is something we have to deal with.'

'You can say no.'

Rosie half smiled, knowing how tricky denying paying money could be once the police got their hooks in. But she was hoping they'd be happy to get their story published rather than chase around counting money the paper might have paid them.

'Yes. We can say no. But don't worry about that.' She took a breath. 'We will pay you five thousand pounds in cash tomorrow.'

Rosie saw Pavil's eyes light up, and Viktor was trying his best not to show anything, but she knew this was more money than they had ever seen in their lives. Whatever they'd heard about newspapers paying money, she'd hoped they weren't expecting twenty grand. And they clearly hadn't been. And the sad irony of the shitty business of paying for stories was that her paper and some of the other tabloids would pay ten and twenty grand on some celebrity's lurid tale of three-in-a-bed sex shame or a drug scandal. Yet people at the sharp end, who could actually tell a story that could net an international smuggling operation, were paid a pittance, if anything.

'I thought it would be more.' Viktor tried to sound disappointed, but it didn't ring true.

'It's what we pay for things like this. A lot of what you hear isn't true.' Rosie hated lying.

They sat for a moment and Rosie glanced at Matt fiddling with his cameras.

Viktor spoke to Pavil in Albanian and they had a conversation for a few seconds while Rosie looked at her watch. She had to get back down to work later, get this story on her screen as it had to be at the lawyers tonight.

Finally, Viktor looked from Pavil to Rosie and they both nodded to her.

'Okay. We agree. If you can get us away from here and to Spain like you say. Pavil?'

Pavil nodded. 'Okay. I am agree.'

'Good.' Rosie looked at Matt. 'Now, Matt will take a couple of photographs of you, but you won't be recognised. Matt?'

'Sure. Don't worry, guys.' He went over to the hotel room window. 'If I can have the two of you here. Looking out of the window. I'll do the pics of the back of you.' He produced a baseball hat and a woolly hat. 'Try it with these too.'

The boys looked at each other and did what they were told. Rosie watched them, wishing she could do more for them, and always with the guilty feeling that she was using them – which she was. It was the nature of the business, and the part of it that always made her feel guilty, especially if people were putting themselves at risk. Don't go there, she told herself. No time for soul-searching. You've got work to do, and a deadline to meet. Her mobile rang and it was Bertie Shaw.

'You've arrived, Bertie. Great. I've booked you in, so check in at the reception and I'll come down in a minute.'

CHAPTER THIRTY-FOUR

Helen was bored out of her skull. It felt as though she'd been here for weeks, holed up in this poky flat, surrounded by the ghosts and images of her childhood and teenage years. Every time she looked out of the window, she saw pictures of herself as a little girl, playing in the street, running around with her band of pals, making mischief. At night as a teenager, or when they skived off school, she'd meet up with her mates and go drinking bottles of cheap wine down in Glasgow Green. And in the Gorbals, nights became a terrifying orgy of gang fights as the scheme's tribalism spilled onto the streets, with young men, armed with knives and baseball bats, on the rampage. She could still hear the smashing of bottles, women weeping angry, frustrated tears, then the wail of police sirens trying to round up the usual suspects. And when she peered out of the window, there would be sudden eerie silence. All the culprits were hiding, probably within earshot of the police, confident the boys in blue wouldn't be brave enough to venture up into the back courts or closes where they might get ambushed. It was a wild, crazy existence, with areas like the Gorbals, Easterhouse and Drumchapel becoming notorious across Britain as the badlands where only the brave or the stupid ventured if they didn't belong. It was no place to bring up a family. And yet there was such camaraderie on the stairs and on the landings, people knew where everyone was, everyone watched each other's back. If something had been blagged by shoplifters or robbers and was being hidden, the neighbours often grouped together when the cops arrived at a suspect's house. Whatever had been thieved had already been passed over the landings and hidden three doors down. Police knew they couldn't win, so they left the Gorbals and areas like it to police themselves. And that's when people like Frankie Mallon and other small-time hoods flourished, running their own little empires. Survival of the fittest, the law of the jungle. Helen thought she'd left it all behind, but here she was, bored rigid, frustrated, and pissed off listening to her mother bitching all day long. She was also scared shitless to leave the house. Especially now, when her ma had just walked in the door with yet another front page in the *Post* spelling more gloom and doom.

She saw the front page picture.

'Fuck's sake, Ma. I know that guy. From the charity.'

'You mean you knew him. He's stone hatchet dead.'

'Christ! It's saying here he was murdered. Shot in the head. Jesus, Ma, what if that means they're doing away with everyone attached to that charity?'

'Who? This mafia mob you keep talking about?'

'I don't know. I think so. I told you. I wasn't involved in all that. I didn't know a bloody thing about it.'

'No. You were just spending the proceeds of your husband's shitty, shameless crimes.'

'Whatever I was doing, I was not part of any racket to sell off poor wee weans. I want nothing to do with this. I told you a few days ago, I need to get out of here. We need to do something.'

'I know.' Her mother stuck on the kettle and took two mugs out of the wall cupboard.

Helen read the front-page story twice, then her gut churned as she flicked inside to see Alan's face looking back out at her and another story recapping how he went missing, and a picture of herself and him at some champagne function before he disappeared. They were rehashing the old story. Then, a picture of Frankie brought her up short and she put the paper down, handed it across the table to her mother.

'I'm going for a shower. You can feast your eyes on this, then cast it up to me what a bitch I am.'

Janey shook her head and didn't answer. She pushed a cigarette into her mouth and lit it, drawing deeply as she sat back on the chair and began reading the newspaper.

A few minutes later, as Helen came into the kitchen, her hair wrapped in a towel, Janey was on her feet clutching the *Post*.

'From what you've said, and the fact that you're shitting your pants about these people, the way I see it, Helen, is we have two choices.'

'Oh really? Let's hear it.'

'Don't be a smartarse – sure, you've been sitting here for nearly two weeks not doing a hand's turn, and all you talk about is how terrible this all is. Well, unless you're waiting for some fairy godmother to come waltzing in here and get you out of this, then you need to get your arse in gear, and think hard.'

'Hold on, Ma. I haven't exactly been sitting on my arse. The only reason I'm here is precisely because I did make a decision to get out of the place, and I ended up getting captured by these bastards and held prisoner – in case you've forgotten. I'm not going to risk that again by putting my head out the door.' She rubbed her hair. 'So what are my options? Let's hear it.'

'Okay. Here's your choices. You either go to the cops, give them the whole shite about self-defence, that Frankie came into your flat and raped you, and you shot him because he was going to shoot you. Then you did a runner because you thought nobody would believe you. You say nothing about Alan, and stick to the original story, that he went missing, and you are, to this day, grieving for him as though he was dead. You're a good enough actress to get away with that.'

Helen was quiet for a moment as she took it all in. Her ma had a point. She could go to the cops, but she could have done that in the first place. She didn't want to be questioned too closely about Alan and about the money. And what if they started examining her bank accounts? What if they had forensic or some other kind of evidence that showed she shot Frankie in cold blood?

'You're forgetting, I shot Frankie in the back.'

'I know you did. Listen, this is not some old Wild West movie, where shooting in the back proves anything. You shot him the moment his back was turned because it was the only chance you had to save yourself.'

'Aye. They'll believe that,' Helen said, sarcastically. 'I don't want to take that chance, Ma.'

'Okay. Up to you, but I think you're wrong. Your other choice is to phone that bird on the paper, the one whose name is on the story. What is it?' She glanced at the paper. 'Rosie Gilmour. Phone her. I told you the other day. That's your best option right now.'

'And say what? I mean, what's the point of that?'

'Tell her your situation. These reporters, they're all the same. They'll bite your hand off for a story, especially a hot one like this. Tell them everything. Tell them about Frankie and how he tried to rape you and he got shot in the struggle.'

'They'll turn me in to the cops.'

'Maybe not. But the most important point you want to talk about is that story about the babies for sale, and to stress that you, and, to your knowledge, Alan, had nothing to do with it. It puts you up there in the clear.'

'I know what you're saying, but I don't really see the point.'

'If the story is in the paper, it gets a message to these bastards who bumped off that charity boss. Maybe it will make them think twice before they come for you. If you're out there in view of the public with your picture in the paper, coming over as all living in fear, then they might think twice. That's all. It buys you some time. But at the end of the day, you need to get out of here. We need to go abroad somewhere. Spain is probably the handiest right now.'

Helen ran the brush through her hair, looking at her image in the mirror, admiring her skin and cheekbones. She could look the part in the paper, play the griev- ing wife now living in fear because her husband had vanished and people attached to the charity are sud- denly being eliminated. That might work. She looked at her mother.

'I might get away with that, Ma. That's not a bad shout from you. But I'd be worried about talking about Frankie and the shooting in my flat.'

'Then just say you weren't there. Stuff it. They can't prove you were there right at that time, can they? Can anyone categorically prove you were in the flat when he got bumped off? No. So just deny it.'

'Okay. I'm willing to give it a try. Will you phone the paper for me?'

'You don't want to phone them yourself?'

'No. Of course not. Sure, I'm living in fear, terrified to make a single phone call.' Helen half smiled. She'd almost convinced herself.

Rosie was in McGuire's office, sitting on the sofa while he read over her copy on the two Albanian runaways. She watched him nodding in approval at various parts, whispering, 'Belter', as he went along. This was the version she had cleared with Hanlon the lawyer after much wrestling over points he said could land them in trouble. She'd lost on most of them, but she still had a cracking splash and spread about people-smuggling and the Hands Across Europe charity.

'I fucking love this, Gilmour. We'll go big on this one. I'm going to ask our marketing lads to get it on to radio to puff it for the morning editions.'

'Good.' But Rosie was a little uneasy. She knew the cops would be the first on the phone to see if she had names, and asking where could they find the illegal immigrants. And she knew that she'd be letting DI James Morton down the first time she was working with him. But she had no option.

'I know my cop contact won't be happy, Mick. He did give

me the heads up on the Morgan murder, but I can't afford to give him these boys. I can't betray them like that.'

McGuire nodded. 'Can't disagree with that. You'll just have to find a way to soft-soap your cop pal. He'll know he can't have it his way all the time.'

'I hope so.'

Rosie's mobile rang but no number came up.

'Hello? Who is it please?' She always answered the phone curtly until she knew who it was.

'Is that Rosie Gilmour?'

'Yes. Who's this please?'

'My name is Janey McCann. I'm Helen Lewis's mother. You know, the lady whose husband is missing – Alan Lewis.'

Rosie pushed the phone closer to her ear, and sat forward. She could see McGuire out of the side of her eye, watching her.

'Really? You're Helen Lewis's mother? I've been looking to talk to her.' She could scarcely believe that this was happening.

'Aye. Well. She wants to meet you.'

Rosie stood up. Somehow she could think better when she was on her feet. She paced across to the window.

'Is Helen in the country? After what happened in her flat, she seemed to disappear. I've wanted to talk to her about her husband. All the things that came out recently. Have you seen the *Post*?'

'Yes. We've both seen it. That's why she wants to talk to you. Can you meet her?'

'Is she there just now? Can I speak to her?'

'No. Can you meet her? We can go to another paper if you're not interested.'

Bitch, Rosie thought. She had all the moves, whoever she was. She didn't know anything about Helen Lewis's mother, other than what people had told her – that she was a chancer who was as wide as the Clyde.

'No, you wouldn't want to do that. It's the *Post* who have all the information on this story. We'll talk to Helen any time, and give her all the platform she needs to talk . . . Whatever she wants to say.'

'Right. That's good. When can we meet?'

'Whenever you want. Now if you like?'

'City centre?'

'Sure. Whereabouts?'

Janey paused for a moment, then said, 'There's a pub on Argyle Street. Just along from the Hielanman's Umbrella. It's called the Alpen Lodge. Meet us there at two. Is that all right?'

'Yep. I'll be there.'

'And you wouldn't be bringing any polis or anything?"

'I'm a newspaper journalist, Janey. I don't bring the cops when I'm going out to interview people. I'll be there at two.'

'How will I know you?'

'The Alpen Lodge? You'll know me, don't worry. I know what Helen looks like anyway.'

'Her hair is different.'

'Don't worry. I'll see you there.'

The woman hung up. Rosie looked at McGuire, all wide-eyed. 'Helen Lewis. Fucking seriously?' he said.

'Yep. She wants to meet.'

'Dancer! Take Matt with you – have him hanging handy for a snatch pic.'

'I will. This could be interesting, Mick. I wonder what she's got to say about the bold Frankie Mallon.'

'Maybe she'll confess she shot him. How good would that be?'

'Yeah. Well don't hold the front page till I see what she's like.' She looked at her watch. 'I'm going to grab a bite, then head up there.'

'Phone me as soon as you come out. There might also be queries on your spread, once they start working on it.'

'Fine.' Rosie was out of the door, her last big story now a piece of history at this moment, and her mind on her next splash.

CHAPTER THIRTY-FIVE

Rosie and Matt had entered the bar separately, Matt arriving a few minutes earlier so he could clock Helen Lewis and her mum once Rosie came in. From his perch at the bar, he gave Rosie a yes-this-is-really-happening look as she came through the door. It was exactly two in the afternoon and there was a karaoke in full swing. She glanced fleetingly at Matt, keeping her face straight as she took in the scene. The old guy on the karaoke microphone was belting out the Sixties classic 'King of the Road'. *'Trailers for sale or rent, Rooms to let . . . fifty cents . . . I'm a man of means by no means . . . King of the road . . .'*

The last line brought a couple of tables of middle-aged couples to their feet, raising their glasses as though the song was their mantra. King of the road. Aye right, Rosie thought. Depends on how long you've been in the pub and how many drinks you've knocked back to make you feel like a king in this part of the town. But what the heck, they were happy, singing, and at least they weren't fighting. Well, not yet. The Alpen Lodge was a peculiar name for a pub bang in the city centre, and where the only resemblance to anything remotely Alpine was that it was freezing cold. It had always been a mystery why they named it that, and even more peculiar was the thick Artex snow-effect on the outside wall, to make it feel like you were in some Swiss mountain hideaway. It was the kind of place you could easily go in to, and after a few drinks and karaoke, lose all sense of time, emerging blinking into the daylight the worse for drink, feeling it should be night. A very strange place to arrange a meet, Rosie thought. And it was packed to the rafters. Christ. She strained her eyes in the darkness and saw two women, one older and one strikingly good-looking younger one, in the corner. That had to be them. Helen Lewis was brunette in the photographs in the paper, but she was blonde here. They looked up, and after a few seconds, Rosie went across through the tables and stood by them.

'I'm Rosie.' She bent down, her voice low, not that anyone could hear much above the din. 'Can I get you a drink?'

'Hi. It was me who phoned you. Janey. This is my daughter, Helen.' The older woman looked up with a face that had been around the course a few times.

'Hi, Janey,' Rosie said. 'Thanks for getting in touch.' She turned to Helen. 'You look a bit different – the hair. But not that different. I recognised you from the photographs. What you having?'

'Jack Daniel's for me, please,' Helen said, ignoring Rosie's remark about her hair.

'Vodka and cranberry,' Janey said.

'Coming right up.' Rosie turned back before she went to the bar. 'A bit noisy in here, is it not – I mean, to talk.'

'It's fine,' Janey said. 'We had to find somewhere kind of out of the way. In case we bump into anyone we might know.'

'I see,' Rosie said. She went to the bar, ignoring Matt, who stood there sipping his pint. She returned to the table with a tray of drinks – a soda for herself. She set the drinks down and pulled up a chair beside the women, sitting close to Helen.

'Cheers,' she said, raising her drink. 'Good to see you. I'm glad you got in touch.'

There was a bit of a lull in the music as a woman murdered an old ballad, and Rosie glanced over her shoulder as she leaned in.

'So, how are you, Helen? How've you managed to stay out of the way of the cops? They're all over the place looking for you.'

'The cops are the least of my worries.'

Rosie raised her eyebrows but said nothing.

'Listen, Rosie,' Helen said. 'It was my ma's idea to talk to you, but I'm not that sure. But I've been reading your stories in the *Post* and, well, I need to make some things clear here.'

'Of course, Helen. Whatever you want to say. I'm here to listen to you.' She winced as the music started up again. 'But this is a helluva noisy place. Are you sure you want to talk here?'

Janey looked at Helen, who glanced beyond Rosie and past the toilets.

'There's a wee place at the back of the bar, with a pool table. It wasn't busy when I went to the loo. Let's go up there. It'll be quieter.'

They picked up their drinks and headed for the back room. It stank of beer and cigarettes. But at least it was empty, apart from the pool table and a few old-fashioned wooden chairs and three tables next to some wall seating.

'That's better.' Rosie plonked herself on a chair, and they sat with their backs to the wall. She leaned across the table, looking from one to the other. 'So. You were saying about my stories. It's been a bit of a revelation – all this scandal about the charity is awful. Unbelievable, really.'

She was about to ask if any of it rang true, when Helen interrupted.

'That's got nothing to do with me. I didn't know any-thing about it. It's all gone mental. And now this charity boss is found murdered. Christ! Makes me wonder who's going to be next.'

'Did you know him – Morgan?'

'I met him. Once. Over there. With Alan.'

'Really? Of course you'd have no reason to think he was involved in stuff like selling babies.'

Helen puffed. 'Are you kidding? Of course not. He seemed like a nice guy. I don't even know if he was involved in anything. I mean, how would I know that?'

She was defensive and flapping.

'Maybe he didn't know,' Rosie said. 'What about Alan?'

She bristled. 'Alan? Christ! What about him? He wouldn't do that. I can't believe he'd be involved. No way.'

'But you see from our story he was the charity's accountant. He would see the books.'

'Aye. Well, if he did, none of that shit would be there, would it?'

'But what about the wine-importing business? From my story, if you saw it, the wine business is a front for the adoption agency. I've been there. To their offices. The charity's office is in the same building, on the same floor. They're all connected. Some of the people on the adoption agency are named as directors of the wine business as well.'

'I know. I've been there. I was there when the partners in the wine business had some kind of wee reception for local businessmen. The town hall was there, and the police bosses.'

This was going better than Rosie had hoped. Helen wasn't holding back.

'Who were the partners? Alan's partners?'

'Them,' she said. 'Them guys you mentioned in your story. The Russian guy. I thought he was just a business-man. I mean I had no fucking idea. Pardon my French.'

'No problem. So Alan was in tow with this Russian guy and his company in the wine-importing business? And he'd be doing the books for them? Is that how you remember it?'

'Yeah, but I just can't see Alan knowing that they were into that baby racket. Alan was a nice guy. A good man. I'm his wife. If I even had a sniff about any involvement in selling babies I would have reported all of them myself. I love children. I mean that. I've none of my own, but the very idea of selling wee unfortunate kids for money or whatever reason makes me sick.' She swallowed, and Rosie eyed her curiously, wondering if the flicker of emotion was genuine. It seemed to be.

Rosie took a moment. Then she decided to throw something in to provoke a reaction.

'Helen, you said there, Alan "was" a nice guy. You say that as though he was dead. Are you now coming to terms with the idea that your husband is dead? That must be really hard for you.'

Helen swallowed and bit her lip. She turned to her mother, who put a comforting hand on her wrist. It looked like a little heartbreak scene, but Rosie's gut told her it was far from it. Top marks for performance. She was being pulled in here for their own purposes. Fair enough. It wouldn't be the first time that had happened. But Helen had a story to tell, and Rosie was happy to listen, regardless of her motive.

'I suppose . . .' her voice faltered a little, 'I suppose I have to think that maybe I won't see him again. I mean, why hasn't he got in touch? People, the police, they were looking for him in Romania, and here too. He can't have just vanished. I know he would have got in touch if he could.'

'So do you think he's dead? Maybe even murdered? Is it possible he found out about the baby scam?'

'I don't know. I really don't.'

Rosie was already thinking of this story in the paper, how she would write it. Helen was throwing in plenty of good lines here, but she needed a full story. From start to finish, how they met, their lifestyle. And, crucially, what had happened to Frankie Mallon in her flat. But this wasn't the moment to bring Frankie into it. Get the full story of Alan and their marriage out of her first.

'Tell you what, Helen,' Rosie said. 'I want to be able to tell your story. Your side of things. Are you living in fear at the moment? Is that what you're saying?'

'Yes. Definitely. Especially since the murder of that Morgan bloke. I'm worried that these guys are out to get me.'

'But why would they be?'

Helen hesitated for a moment and Rosie studied her face to see if she was lying. She was good. She was really good.

'I don't know. Maybe just because Alan was my husband. Maybe because I've made myself scarce.'

Rosie wanted to say to her that she had only made herself scarce after Frankie's body was found in her flat. Up until then, she was going about her normal business, playing the grieving wife every time a camera showed up.

'Sure. I understand that. But can we go back a bit? Go back to the beginning? Your life with Alan?'

'I just want to get my point across that I had nothing to do with this baby-selling racket. I want to let these thugs know that I didn't know anything about it. I'm scared I might be next. If they've killed Alan and then this guy, I could be next.'

'Yes. I see that. But for me to tell your story, and to allow you to say that, then I need to paint the full picture.'

Helen eyed her suspiciously, then looked to her mum.

'I know what she means,' Janey said. 'You know how you see these things in the papers, where the wife or man tells the whole story – where they met, their lives together. All that stuff. That's what you need to do.'

Rosie nodded. Janey was wide, all right, and well clued up.

Helen thought for a moment.

'Okay. I get that. You want me to talk about my life with Alan, how I grew up and stuff? You know I'm from the Gorbals. But I went to London when I was seventeen. Did a bit of modelling and stuff like that.'

'Yes. All of that,' Rosie said. 'That's part of the story.'

'Really?'

'Yes. Then how you and Alan went over to Romania and how he became involved in the wine-importing business. Tell me as much as you know about that. And about the charity, Hands Across Europe. What did they take over to Romania? Did you ever travel with them?'

'No. But I was there when they came one time.'

'Did you ever see them going back? I mean the aid trucks?'

'No. Why?'

Rosie shrugged. Her story of people-smuggling wasn't going in the paper till tomorrow, but she wanted to see if there was any reaction to her vague question on the trucks. There was none. She was satisfied that Helen knew nothing about that, and probably, as she said, knew nothing about the babies for sale. She would know that Alan was crooked. But to look at and listen to her, Helen was probably too wrapped up in spending her husband's money, and her trips abroad to notice.

'To be honest, I never really asked anything about Alan's work. He was an accountant. What was the point? I can't even count money in my purse. I was his wife. We went places together. He gave me a good life.'

Rosie listened. But there was nothing warm about Helen Lewis. No spark coming off her that made her feel this was a woman wronged. She didn't like her. She was a dame and a half all right. She put on a bold front, but given what

Rosie had learned of her background, she was probably also an accomplished liar. Not that she could blame her for that. Growing up in the Gorbals could turn you into anything. Some people emerged from it, studied at school and went on to become high achievers. A great many did not. And some who wanted the good life just took it. They learned how to live on their wits, deal with the people who ran the show, and slashed, shot or conned their way up the food chain. Helen Lewis had been putting on an act most of her life, Rosie decided. This was just another performance. There was no wave of sympathy washing over Rosie the way it often did when she came across people like this. But for the moment, she'd have to let her talk.

'Okay, Helen. Can we wind things back a little bit, and talk about you and Alan, how you met and your life here with him.'

Helen looked at her mum, who nodded in agreement.

'Might as well put it all out there,' Janey said.

'All right. I will.' Helen took a breath and swallowed a glug of her drink.

Rosie switched on the tape and pushed it across the table, reassuring them it was necessary for the newspaper's lawyers. They seemed to be placated by that. Then she listened as Helen spun her story of a hard life in the high flats, leaving to go to London, then meeting Alan at a business function. Rosie noted that she left out the fact that she had been a teenage prostitute in the Gorbals and perhaps an escort in London. She decided to let it go. It was Helen's story. Rosie would give her enough rope.

She finished talking, with Rosie occasionally prompting and asking for more information about Romania and the wine-importing business and the charity. Rosie had a good enough story. She decided it was time to talk about Frankie Mallon.

'That's great, Helen.' She sat back, but left the tape on, hoping they wouldn't notice. 'So, there are some other things I wanted to talk to you about.'

Helen nodded, sipping her drink.

'Fine.'

'Frankie Mallon.' Rosie let the name hang there for a long moment, waiting for a reaction. A little telltale flinch of discomfort flashed across Helen's eyes. But it was Janey who interrupted.

'Well, you'll have seen all that in the papers before. It was a break-in. A robbery.'

Rosie watched Helen as she shifted in her seat.

'Yes. I know he was shot. But I was wondering why in your flat? Did you know Frankie? He grew up in the Gorbals too.'

Helen examined the back of her hands, screwing up her eyes as though she was trying to recollect.

'I knew *of* him. He was a bit younger than me. A bit of a wee gangster. But I didn't know him as such.'

Lying through her back teeth. Rosie thought of Donna,

and of Helen parting with five grand of guilt money only a couple of days ago for Frankie's baby.

'But why *your* flat?'

'No idea. Why does anything happen to anyone? Who knows?'

Rosie sensed she wasn't going to get anything further out of this. Best to let her deny it and use her story. It might even flush out anyone in their crooked circle, or a contact of Frankie's to say a bit more. She had her story on tape. But she had to ask the crucial question, because if she went back to the office and hadn't asked it, McGuire would not be happy.

'Okay. Fair enough. That's all good what you've said here, and we'll give you plenty of space in the paper. I hope the men who you think are out to get everyone involved will believe you.'

'Yeah. Me too. I'm scared shitless.'

Rosie fiddled with the tape, checked that it was still running.

'Just one last question . . .' She paused for effect. 'Did you kill Frankie Mallon?'

It was like a bomb going off. The shock on their faces as though they weren't sure if they'd heard it, or how to react.

'What?'

'Frankie. Did you kill him? Shoot him in your flat? Listen, Helen, If you did, you might have had good reason. Who knows, he was a gangster anyway. I'm here to tell your story, so if you had anything to do with his death, this is the time to say it.'

'Fuck's sake!' She glanced at her mother. 'What is this? I mean, one minute you're all nice listening to my story, then you hit me with this shit? Accusing me?'

'I'm not accusing you, Helen. I'm just asking the question. Because the word on the grapevine is that you killed him.'

Janey slammed her half-empty glass on the table before Helen could answer. 'The grapevine?' she spat. 'That pish that people just make up? What grapevine? If I had to believe everything that was said about me over the years I'd have been dead years ago. Look, she's told you enough. We've said everything we want to say.'

Helen nodded. 'Aye. Too right.'

Rosie put her hands up. 'That's fine, Honestly. Perfectly fine. But I hope you appreciate I had to ask the question. Fair enough. You've given me your answer. So don't worry. I will say what you said.'

They sat in long silence and you could have cut the air with a knife. Eventually Rosie ventured, 'Helen. I'd like to get some photographs of you organised. How do you feel about that?'

'No. No way. You've got plenty of pictures. And anyway, you said you were not going to reveal where I am or anything. I'm in hiding.'

'We'll say that in the paper. I can still say it with pictures. It would be good to get a picture.'

She looked at her mum.

'I don't think so.'

'Okay. Well, what about one when you walk out of here, and you don't know it's being taken. You just walk down the road looking straight ahead. You won't even see the photographer. Or, I can take you somewhere else. Some place that won't be identified as Glasgow.'

'No. I think I've had enough.'

'Okay. That's up to you.' She looked from one to the other. 'It was really good to speak with you. And you've got plenty to say here, so I'm going to get back to the office and speak to my editor.' Rosie stood up. She wanted out of this claustrophobic dark place. 'I'll be in touch if I need to ask any more, if that's okay.'

'Aye. Fine.'

Rosie backed away from the table and opened the door to the blare of the music. She winked to Matt, then made her way up the winding staircase to the husky voice of a woman singing . . . *'Memories, light the corners of my mind, Misty water-coloured memories, of the way we were . . .'* Indeed, Rosie thought as she walked out, blinking, into the daylight, glad she was sober.

CHAPTER THIRTY-SIX

'I don't believe her,' Rosie told McGuire from where she sat opposite his desk. 'You know one of those people you meet and you take an instant dislike to? Well, a bit like that. As I told you, she managed to leave out sections of her life as a hooker. And also she claimed she barely knew Frankie Mallon back in the day. That's just bullshit. Donna told me all about her and him, plus I've got the nosy neighbour seeing him coming and going about her flat.'

McGuire nodded. 'And she bristled all right when you asked her if she killed him?' He chortled. 'That was quite ballsy, by the way, Gilmour, just to ask that straight out.'

'You told me to ask it.'

'Yeah, but I thought you might have put it another way.'

'How else can you ask someone if they've shot a person? What do you say – ask if a gun went off in the room? And anyway, by that time I was satisfied that she was lying through her teeth.'

'Do you think she knew all about the babies racket?'

'Actually, I don't think so. That's probably the only thing she said that I really believed. I got the distinct impression she was horrified at the thought of selling babies. In fact, that's why she got in touch – to clear her name on that.'

'Yes, because she knows the mob are bumping off everyone attached to the charity, and she's panicking.'

'I know. I'm prepared to believe she got in touch to tell her story in an attempt to save her own skin. That much I do believe. But I don't think she had anything to do with the babies racket. I didn't mention the people-smuggling to her yet, as I was waiting till we get it in the paper. Just in case she is at it, and was just fishing for information to pass on to the gangsters. You never know really what her game is. That's the thing with this dame, Mick. You just talk to her for five minutes and you know she's a chancer – and as for her ma, she's a bit of conwoman too. But I knew that before I went.' She paused. 'But, we've got a good story from her. It'll still be great in the paper – the wife breaking her silence, living in fear. All that stuff. And I'm sure that's true. But she's far from innocent.'

McGuire sat back and scribbled on his notepad.

'Okay. I'm happy to go with what we've got. You never know who it might flush out. But tomorrow is the people-smuggling story, so by late tonight, make a call to her and ask her if she knew anything about that. I know what her answer will be, but we have to ask.'

'Sure. I'll do that.' Rosie stood up. 'But we need to get the cash we agreed on to the boys – Viktor and Pavil. Are they sorting it out up in Accounts?'

McGuire looked at his watch.

'Should be. They told me this morning it would be there by late afternoon.' He thrust his hands in his pockets. 'I'm just uneasy about it, Gilmour. Are you sure these boys are okay? That handing them money isn't going to lead to all sorts of shit flying around? What do they do with the money when they get it?'

Rosie knew she hadn't told him her plan to get them to Europe, so she looked away from him.

'Gilmour, I can see from your face you're not telling me something. Come on. Out with it. I like to get a bit of warning in case any old something is going to fall on my lap.'

'It won't.' She hesitated, stood up. 'Look, I've got plans in place to get them over to Europe. I've got some contacts who can get them out of here and over in a lorry.'

McGuire threw his hands up. 'Fuck's sake, Gilmour. Your *own* people-smuggling racket. Christ almighty!'

'It's not people-smuggling.'

'It bloody well is. What do you call it if someone is in the back of a truck with no passport and smuggled through a border of another country? What do *you* call it? Hide and fucking seek?'

Rosie couldn't help but smile.

'It's only a one-off. I've never done this before.'

He shook his head. 'You'd better not have.'

'Of course I haven't. But I want to get these guys out of the country and over to the north of Spain. It's up to them after that. They'll be on their own. I'm sure they'll find work.'

McGuire lifted his papers and shuffled them as he headed towards the door.

'Right. That last bit of conversation, I'm now going to pretend I didn't hear, so don't tell me any more. Just get things sorted. But before you do anything, write up that Helen piece and have it over to me by tonight.'

'No problem.'

He left and she walked out behind him.

Trying to get newspaper executives to part with actual cash always involved a tussle of epic proportions. If it was a few hundred quid in cash to pay someone for a story and pictures, then that was fine. Even if it was a couple of hundred quid to take some contacts out for dinner, it was fine, as long as you filled in the form. The form in itself was a piece of nonsense, because there was no way in the world Rosie or any other frontline reporter would give the genuine name of a contact they were entertaining. But they had to go through the motions, and names like Jack Brown or John Smith regularly featured. Once or twice Rosie put down the name Hugh Jarse, so she could get a couple of hundred pounds to pay off a contact. The name of course would only sound funny if the accountant read it aloud. She was later taken to one side by the managing editor and told to stop taking the piss, but he couldn't keep a straight face. However, trying to get the accountants to part with five thousand pounds in cash almost involved being finger-printed. It had to be sanctioned by the managing director, then sent to London to their and the sister paper's head office and sanctioned again by their bean counters, complete with questionnaire as to who it was for and why it was necessary. As a result of all the hassle, she was told the money wouldn't be available until the morning. Now she had to go and break it to the boys at the hotel that the plans had to be put back. She knew they wouldn't be happy, but it had to be done. She hoped they trusted her enough by now. She hadn't heard from either of them for most of the afternoon, and when she called there was no answer to Viktor's mobile. As she drove towards the hotel, her mobile rang and she could see it was Bertie Shaw. She put it on speaker.

'Bertie. I was about to call you. I've been trying to get Viktor on his mobile, but he's not answering. Is everything all right?'

'Well, I don't know, Rosie. That's why I'm phoning you. There's been a bit of a development.'

Rosie felt her gut twist. 'What? Something wrong?'

'I'm not sure. It's the young fella. Pavil. He said he told you about his brother who he's been trying to contact and hadn't spoken to for a while.'

'Yeah. I remember he said. Saban. He didn't know where he was though.'

'That's right. Well, it turns out that the brother has phoned him on his mobile.'

'Christ! When?'

'About half an hour ago. He said he was in Glasgow.'

Rosie did not like the sound of this. A brother already here who hadn't talked to him in nearly two years, suddenly materialising as soon as he went off the radar.

'I don't like this, Bertie. There's something not right about it. What is Pavil saying? What does his brother want?'

'I don't like the sound of it either, Rosie. But this brother has got in touch, and Pavil is quite made up about it. He's very young, and I think he's a bit excited about the prospect of seeing him.'

'Seeing him?' Rosie was aghast. 'What do you mean?'

'Pavil said his brother is in Glasgow and was coming to see him to offer him some work, but Saban found he wasn't at his flat. So that's why he phoned. He told Pavil he wanted to see him. And so he has arranged for his brother to come to the hotel.'

'Christ almighty! That sounds like some kind of trap. What if Pavil's brother is working for the Albanian gangsters and just wants to dig up his brother for them? He might have been told to do this, to track Pavil and Viktor down. If he was, he wouldn't have much of a choice. You know the way these guys work.'

'That's exactly what I'm thinking. But what can we do? He's going to be here in about ten minutes.'

Rosie jumped a red light at the far end of Hope Street. She was only a few minutes away.

'Okay. I'm nearly there. I don't think there is much we can do. Has Pavil told his brother about talking to me?'

'Yes. He said he has.'

'Oh Christ! This is all a bit dodgy now.'

'I know.'

Rosie felt sick with nerves. She had nobody to back her up. She couldn't call her DI friend, because she was already planning to smuggle two illegals out of the country. Where was Adrian when you needed him? Then she hated herself for the thought, because as far as she knew, Adrian was still recovering somewhere after almost getting killed pulling her out of a hole. She hadn't heard from him since she'd got back. Jesus! Only one person she could phone now. She took out her phone and scrolled down.

'Jonjo, it's Rosie Gilmour here.'

'Rosie. I saw your name on my screen.'

'Jonjo, I'm sorry to ask you this, but I think I need your help.'

'No problem. Where are you? What's wrong?'

'I'm heading for the Crest Hotel. Can you meet me there as soon as possible? I think there's some trouble with these

Albanian guys I've been dealing with. It's a bit of a long
story. I'll tell you when I see you.'

'Don't worry. See you shortly.'

Rosie tried to compose herself as she got into the lift at
the Crest Hotel. As it closed, she could see Jonjo Mulhearn
and two of his henchmen sitting in the reception bar.
She'd had a brief five minutes to tell him what she was
doing and her fears. He thought it was a trap too, but
also told her maybe it wasn't, that perhaps Pavil's brother
just hated where he was and wanted a way out too. You
never know. But once Jonjo was assured that the police
were not involved in any way, he told her not to worry. To
play along with whatever was going on upstairs. If there
was any chance or danger, to have his number on speed
dial and ring it once. He would be there pronto. He'd
already posted a man on their floor, close to the boys' hotel
room. Rosie pressed the button for the second floor. What
the hell am I getting myself into here? she asked herself.
Her mouth was dry with anxiety. She could feel sweat on
her back and wanted to go back downstairs and phone
McGuire, the cops, anyone. This was madness. She was a
journalist, and she'd already crossed the line arranging to
smuggle these guys out of the country. Now she'd sum-
moned gangsters to help her out. Christ! She was behaving
like one of the mob herself. She quietly resolved that she
would never do this again once the current situation was

over. The lift doors opened and she stepped out and went down the corridor to room 212.

'Who's there?' It sounded like Viktor's voice.

'It's Rosie.'

The security chain was pulled back, and the door was unlocked then opened by Viktor, and she stepped inside. There were four people in the room – Bertie, Viktor and Pavil, but there was also a taller, slightly chunkier version of Pavil, with stubble and a mean mouth. Saban glanced at her and then at Pavil. In his new desert boots, leather jacket and jeans, he was better dressed than his brother. Whatever he was doing, he was not living on the bones of his arse like Pavil.

'This my brother Saban I told you about, Rosie. He is here. He contact me and he wants to go with us.'

Rosie glanced at Bertie, then at Viktor, who looked paler than normal. It was hard to read what he was thinking. He was a bit smarter than Pavil, she thought, and he didn't look like he was taken in by all of this. But he also looked as though he felt he had no choice.

'Hello,' Rosie said, crossing the room and stretching a hand out to Saban. 'Howsit going? Your brother and his friend are good people. What a coincidence you getting in touch as they are leaving.'

Rosie wanted it to sound exactly as it did, to let this guy know that she wasn't convinced by him, but she was big enough to take him on. She was jittery inside, but he wouldn't see any of that. He looked at her and smiled suddenly, looking more eager and youthful than that mean first glance she'd had suggested.

'Yes. They told me all about you, Rosie. You are helping them. They are leaving tomorrow. That is good. I am very lucky. I want to go too. I hate it here. Just like them. I am a slave. Can I go too with them? Are you okay about that?'

His English was much better than Pavil's and his tone was one of an excited young boy rather than a hard-edged Albanian gangster. But she knew nothing about him and what he had been doing here over these past two years. Right now wasn't the time to ask.

Rosie motioned to them all to sit down. She had to maintain that she was in control, which she was, as long as the brother didn't look like any kind of threat. And right now, he didn't. She was probably just being paranoid. Maybe he really *was* just a long-lost brother wanting to be reunited with his younger sibling. And she didn't have a lot of options. She could hardly tell Pavil's brother he couldn't go with them.

'Okay. The plan is to leave here early in the morning. We have to be at a motorway service station car park close to here. That is where the driver will be and he will be loading up, waiting for us.'

'What about the money?' Viktor asked.

All three of them looked at her, and she was more conscious of Saban's stare than the others'.

'I'll have it by the morning. Before you leave. It's a lot of cash, so it has to be signed for and that takes a lot of paperwork in London. It all takes time. But don't worry. It will be here.'

'You are sure?' Viktor asked.

'Yes. I'll be here first thing. Then we go. I'm coming with you to the service station to meet our contact.'

Pavil looked relieved and she saw him smile for the first time.

'That's good. You are very kind to us, Rosie.'

She nodded, still a little tense. She still wasn't sure what to expect in the next few hours. But everyone seemed fine with the arrangements. All she could do now was hope to Christ that the brother wasn't a plant.

CHAPTER THIRTY-SEVEN

It was early morning and still dark by the time Rosie and Matt were headed down the M74 motorway, sleet slapping the windscreen. She'd arranged to meet big Tony, a truck driver she'd encountered on a foreign aid trip a few years ago when she was part of a charity convoy. He was a larger-than-life ageing hippy with a lot of stories to tell. She hadn't been that surprised when he'd told her one night when he'd had too much local hooch in Budapest, that sometimes he drove 'other items' to and from Europe. He'd never confessed what they were, and she didn't push it, but she got the impression the he was dropping some cannabis loads off from time to time. People-smuggling was a different ball game, he'd told her. Gangsters did that, he'd said, and he didn't want to get involved. But he'd agreed to do it this one time, on condition, he'd joked, that when he was done with all this travelling, Rosie would write his life story.

They were too early for the rush-hour traffic and they were grateful that when they took the slip road off the M74 and headed into the service station car park there were only a couple of cars there. Rosie turned around to check that Bertie was driving behind Matt with the three Albanians. None of this felt good. She was clutching her handbag, which contained five grand in a padded brown envelope. She was about to hand it over to three Albanians who were to be smuggled out of the country by an illegal arrangement *she* had made. This was wrong on so many levels. McGuire's 'people smuggler' words rang in her ears. She had lain in bed last night twisting and turning, as sleep wouldn't come, trying to tell herself that she was doing the right thing. And deep down, she believed that she was. She'd been using these refugees to give her a story that would break open a smuggling racket, so the least she could do was attempt to protect them. If they'd agreed to go to the police as she'd wanted, it would have been more straightforward. But because they'd refused, she was left with no option. She couldn't leave them high and dry. Why not? she asked herself again and again. Because she felt guilty about some of the people she had used and then didn't take enough care of before, and even though she knew none of it had been her fault, she was constantly niggled by the voices on her shoulder saying she could have done more. No. This was the right thing to do.

'You're quiet, Rosie. You all right?' Matt asked.

'Yeah. I'm just not feeling good about any of this. I couldn't sleep last night for thinking about it. I mean, what am I doing, smuggling people out of the country?'

Matt sniggered, trying to lighten things.

'I know. And we don't even get paid for it. Maybe we should take it up full time.'

Rosie tried her best to smile, but her stomach was in knots.

'I just want this one time to see if I can do the best for someone I've used on a story. Sometimes I feel I let people down, and you know the bad things that have happened in the past that I blame myself for. These guys will have money, so once I get them away from here, the rest is up to them.'

'I know what you're like, worrying about things and people you've dealt with. But right now, I'd say we just get this done, and then we walk away. Whatever happens to them after this, it's not your deal any more. What you're doing is right. It might not be legal, but it's right.'

Rosie nodded. She could see three trucks in the car park, some of them parked a good distance away from the service station. Probably long-distance guys who had come from Europe, then stopped off for a kip before travelling further north. She rang Tony's number.

'I see your car coming in, Rosie, and the one with the boys in it behind yours. Just drive across to the back of the station. It's quiet there. I'll walk round and meet you all.'

'Fine.' Rosie hung up.

'Just up here, I think, Matt. Behind the station. Tony said it's quiet.'

Matt drove, and Bertie's car followed.

They got to a deserted place in the car park that was almost in darkness. Rosie's eyes darted around in case anyone else was there. She got out of the car, and when Bertie pulled up alongside her, he got out too, with Viktor, Pavil and Saban. The icy wind would have cut you in two, and she could feel the sleet on her face. The boys stood in the shadows, worried looks on their pale faces, and she felt a genuine angst for their plight. Whatever life had thrown at her, nothing could be as difficult as having nowhere to go, no certainty in your life, no idea where your tomorrows would be, or if you would even make it till tomorrow. Pavil and Viktor each carried a small bag, and Saban had a small rucksack. Rosie and Matt went across to them, then big Tony came swaggering across in his cowboy boots, his straggly blond hair blowing back in the wind, revealing his single gold earring. He came up to Rosie and gave her a hug, and she caught a whiff of tobacco and coffee on his unkempt beard.

'This is Tony,' Rosie said. 'Viktor, Pavil and his brother Saban.' She gestured to the boys and they all shook hands. 'Tony will look after you now until you get into Europe.'

The boys all nodded, shivering in the cold. Rosie could see Viktor's knees knocking. None of them were dressed for this weather. Saban was sickly pale. She went into her handbag and took out the Jiffybag containing money. She handed it to Viktor.

'You can look after this, Viktor.'

He took it and was about to stuff it into his bag when suddenly a car screamed towards them, lights flashing. It seemed to come from nowhere. It happened so fast, everyone was rooted to the spot, blinded by the light. Cops, was the first thing Rosie thought, then, as it screeched to a halt, she realised it was not. Her stomach dropped. Three burly figures spilled out of the car. She saw the metal of the guns in the headlights.

'Oh, Christ!' she heard herself murmur.

Then, from the back of the car, another figure emerged.

'Nobody move!' A tall, thin, well-dressed man in a black heavy coat came towards them pointing a gun, holding it with both hands.

Rosie glanced at Bertie, who looked stunned. Then at Viktor and Pavil. Saban suddenly looked as though he was going to be sick. The tall thin man with the gun moved towards him and grabbed him by the hair, then punched him three times so he was buckled over.

'Saban, you little shit!' His accent was strong Albanian, like theirs.

Saban was on his knees, then pulled to his feet by his hair, blood spurting from his mouth. He started to cry.

'Tears, tough guy? You double-cross me, you fucking little shit, you die. You know that,' shouted the tall man.

This is it, Rosie thought. These bastards are going to kill us all. Whatever was going on, they weren't going to leave witnesses. She glanced around, hoping that someone had seen the car screech in. She could see a couple of people at the pumps in the distance. Christ. She had to do something, say something.

'Listen,' she heard herself say, 'I don't know who you are. Please . . .'

The man abruptly stopped what he was doing and left Saban hanging there, snivelling. Then he turned, his face blazing with rage. Shit, he was taking a step towards her. He grabbed her by the hair, and put the gun to her head. The other thugs behind came a step closer, guarding everyone else.

'You. I know who you are. What the fuck you think you are doing?'

Rosie didn't know what to say, and for a second she felt as though she was hearing him in the distance. She bit down on her lip to stop herself from passing out.

'Please. Don't. I was helping.'

'Helping? You fucking shit. Helping these fuckers? They are *my* business. Not yours. You speak one more word and I shoot you like a dog.' He turned the gun on Matt and Bertie. 'And you fuckers too. Everybody shut it.'

'Erian. Please,' Viktor pleaded.

It seemed to Rosie they knew each other, and she wondered if he was some kind of enforcer in charge of the workers. One of the gorillas thumped Viktor on the back of the head with another gun and he crumpled. 'Shut up, I said.' Another of the men dragged Viktor to his feet.

'Give me the money,' the tall Albanian said. 'Hurry. I saw this bitch hand you something.'

Viktor glanced at Rosie, his eyes full of fear and defeat. He handed over the padded envelope. They stood watching as Erian looked inside. He threw it to one of his henchmen. Then he turned to Saban. He began to prowl around the three Albanian boys like a cat toying with its prey.

'So, Saban. You are given a job to do, and you cannot even do it. You were told. You knew what you had to do.'

Saban swallowed. 'I couldn't, Erian. He is my little brother. I couldn't.'

'Fuck you! You know the code. Brother doesn't matter. Blood is nothing. You have no family. This is business. Your brother betray us, like this piece of shit.' He pointed to Viktor, who stared at the ground. 'We bring them here, give them work, new life, and this is how they repay us. Talking to some fucking newspaper.' He glared at Rosie. 'My boss in Bucharest, he tells me to kill you, Rosie Gilmour. But I think not. Is not a good thing to do in your own country. You are very lucky to escape in Bucharest. Your friend lucky too. But we will find him in Bosnia.'

Rosie swallowed, thinking of Adrian. Then the rush of blood came to her head.

'Please. Let them go. They won't harm you. What does it matter if they are part of your organisation? Please just let them go.'

'Nobody is going anywhere till this is finish. Shut up.' Erian walked across to Saban.

'Okay. Do your job now. Do what you were told.'

Rosie heard herself gasp as Erian handed Saban a gun. He dragged him upright and forced his hand with the gun in it to his brother's head. Pavil broke down, trembling, his eyes shut tight, waiting for the gunshot.

'Please, Saban. Please don't kill me. Our mother, our father . . .'

Saban stood, his whole body shaking, the gun pushed to the side of his brother's head, and with Erian's hand still holding his finger on the trigger.

'I can't . . . I can't kill him. He's my brother.'

'You have no brother. Kill the fucker. Or I do it and you are next. Kill him and you will live. Do it!' he barked.

Everyone stood, open-mouthed, waiting. Rosie braced herself. Then came the gunshot. She closed her eyes for a split second, afraid to look. Another gunshot. And she felt Bertie grabbing her and diving to the ground. What the Christ! She was terrified to look up. She could see Matt on the ground next to her. More gunshots, ringing out, bullets pinging off cars, windscreens smashing. Then suddenly silence. Rosie looked up, and in the half light she could see one of Jonjo's boys. She got up on her elbow. She could see

Viktor, Pavil and Saban lying on the ground, huddled together. She glanced around and saw that the gorillas with the guns lay motionless. Big Tony crouched behind a car. 'Fuck's going on? I'm in the wrong fucking movie here. You okay, Rosie?'

'I think so.' She began to get to her feet.

Then, from the shadows, Jonjo came towards her.

'You need to get this moving fast now, Rosie. Quickly. Get these boys out of here. Cops will be here shortly.'

'Shit. How did you know I was here?'

'We were outside the hotel all day. We had a feeling something would happen.'

'Christ! Thanks. I don't know what to say.'

'Don't say anything. Just get these guys out of here before it's too late.'

He went back to his car with his men, then roared away. Rosie stood over the bodies of the three Albanian gang members, guns at their side. Viktor, Pavil and Saban slowly got to their feet. Tony came out from behind the car.

'Come on. Let's get the fuck out of here. My truck's over there. Follow me.' He headed towards his truck.

Viktor went across to one of the dead henchmen and pulled the envelope of cash from his jacket. Then he grabbed Saban, and held him by the hair.

'You came to kill your brother?'

'I knew I couldn't. But I said I would.'

'I don't trust you.'

'I would never hurt my brother.'

'You double-crossed us. You told them where we were. You shit!' He hit Saban in the face.

'Please. I want to be free like you. Please take me.'

Pavil turned to him.

'Please, Viktor. We cannot leave him. Please.'

'Fuck's sake, guys. You've got three seconds or I'm off.' Tony was standing at the back of his truck.

'Viktor,' Rosie said. 'Take him! Quick! There's no time for this. You can't leave him here. If the cops come you never know what will happen. Take him! You have to!'

Viktor stuffed the envelope of money in his bag and turned to all three of them.

'Let's go.'

And with that they were gone. He turned back to look at Rosie, but he didn't wave and his face showed nothing. There was no emotional farewell. This was about desperation, life or death.

Rosie looked at Matt and Bertie. 'We better get out of here pronto.'

'Jesus Christ, Rosie. I don't believe this! How are we going to get out of this?'

'We were never here. Nobody saw us.'

'Fuck's sake. What you going to tell McGuire?'

'I'll worry about that back in Glasgow. Come on.'

CHAPTER THIRTY-EIGHT

'Gilmour! Where the hell are you?' McGuire barked into Rosie's ear.

'I'm just on my way in to the office.'

'I've been phoning you for half an hour. What's happened? Please tell me the stuff that's coming in from the wires about a shooting incident at a motorway service station is nothing to do with you.'

'Well . . .' Rosie hesitated, knowing there was no easy way to say it. 'I'm not going to lie to you, Mick. It didn't go according to plan.'

'Fuck! What happened? The wires are saying police are there. Maybe three people dead.'

'Yeah. That's about right.'

'What the fuck, Rosie!'

'I know. Listen, I'll explain it all when I get there. It all went a bit tonto.'

'Who got shot? The Albanians?'

'Yeah. But not the lads I was dealing with.'

'What the fuck happened?'

'I'll be in the office in fifteen minutes. But bottom line is, the Albanian mobsters found out where we were. We got rumbled and they came with some heavies.'

'Jesus-Christ-all-fucking-mighty! Is it their bodies that are lying on the forecourt?'

'Yes.'

'Jesus! Who shot them?'

'Mick, I need to go. I'll see you shortly.'

Rosie had only stopped shaking after a mug of sweet tea and a chocolate bar. Matt had smoked two cigarettes one after another from a pack of ten he said he'd had in his pockets for weeks. They'd jumped into his car and sped off onto the motorway, heading in the wrong direction for ten minutes before they even noticed. Then Matt took the nearest slip road and they headed back, stopping at a café in the East End of Glasgow to get their breath back. Rosie was still pumped up and almost high on adrenalin. It wasn't the first time she'd seen a shoot-out, but it was the closest she'd got to seeing someone's brains almost get blown out at point-blank range. Her mobile rang in the car.

'You all right, Rosie?'

'Jonjo. Christ! I can't believe what just happened. I . . . I don't know what we'd have done if your boys hadn't turned up. How did you know?'

'Word was that there was a bit of aggro among the Albanians here, and talk about the newspaper story. I had no idea about those boys of yours until you told me, but once I knew there was a bit of heat, I just got the lads to stay around the hotel area till you left. Then we followed your cars. I have to say though, I didn't expect it to get this bad. These Albanians, they don't fuck around. You're lucky they didn't shoot you first.'

'I know.' It suddenly came home to Rosie how close she had been to death.

'Anyway, those lads you were helping got away and that's what counts. By the way, I'm sure they're no innocents themselves, but what the hell. Guys take a risk coming over here trying for a better life only to find these bastards have them in hock for the rest of their lives. That's just not fair.'

'I can't thank you enough, Jonjo.'

'You don't have to thank me, Rosie. Not ever. Go and get yourself a large drink. You deserve it.'

He hung up.

'Jonjo Mulhearn? Christ, Rosie! You're keeping some funny company these days.'

'I'm not keeping company. I . . .' She didn't know how to describe the relationship. 'We were in touch after Boag. I think he likes me because I didn't grass him up to the cops that he was there that day – as if I would have anyway. I mean, he saved my life.'

'I know. But you don't want to be in his debt.'

She looked at Matt.

'I don't think he sees it that way. For a crook, he's quite straight in a lot of ways, if that makes sense.'

'Aye. Well. You still want to watch what you're doing there.'

'I will. But, Matt, if I hadn't phoned him, we were dead meat out there. You know that, don't you?'

'I do. And that puts me in his debt too. I hope he doesn't ask me to go on the rob or anything.'

Rosie smiled. 'I don't think he does that any more. His businesses are all legit – at least on paper. He's made his money.'

They pulled off the motorway and into the office car park.

'As soon as the pub opens, I'm going straight there to drink four pints in a row.'

'I'll try to join you once I've seen McGuire. That's if he lets me out again.'

The editor was at the back bench, chatting to one of the assistants. He glanced up when he saw Rosie come in, and pointed to his office. He didn't look happy. Rosie crossed the editorial floor, where a couple of early reporters were working away quietly and gave her a wave on the way past. Marion was at her desk, getting her jacket off ready to start work.

'He's not best pleased, and the day's not even started. I've told him to be glad you're all right.'

Rosie smiled to hide her angst.

'Where would I be without you, Marion?'

'The wires said there was a shooting. Were you in the middle of that? I heard it on the car radio on the way in.' She glanced over Rosie's shoulder and she could sense McGuire approaching.

'Yes,' Rosie said quietly. 'But as you see, I lived to tell the tale.'

Marion sat at her desk.

'Aye, well, good luck with your man.'

McGuire strode past Rosie and into his office. She followed him.

'Fucking hell, Rosie!' he barked.

'Yes, I'm fine thanks.'

'Don't give me your crap. What the fuck happened out there? How did these bloody Albanians turn up?'

'I'll tell you what happened, Mick. If you just give me a hearing. It's not my fault.'

'Nobody said it is. But I just like to know what's happening.'

He sat down on the armchair next to the coffee table and Rosie sat on the sofa.

'Okay. Tell me.'

'Right. First up, is that the guys for our story managed to get away. None of them got injured. Well, one of them got a bit of a slap, but he's all right.' She hesitated a moment. 'I would have called you last night, but things happened very quickly. When I went to see them up at the hotel, I was a bit shocked to find there were three of them.'

'Three of them. What do you mean?'

She told him about the younger boy, Pavil, having a brother who had suddenly called him saying he was in Glasgow.

'So the brother was working for the gangsters and sent him to dig out his brother?'

'Yeah. Not just dig him out. But to kill him.'

'Christ!'

'But that wasn't how it looked last night. I would have called you, but it was half eight and I knew you'd be busy. The boys, Viktor and Pavil, had agreed to take the brother with them. Obviously he didn't say anything about being sent by the hoodlums to find him, he just told him he wanted to go to Europe – like them, he wanted out of here. So they bought it. Though I think Viktor was a bit suspicious.'

'Were you not suspicious?'

'Yes. But what could I do? He seemed all right, and there was nothing to suggest we were being led into a trap.'

Rosie described the scene as they were suddenly surrounded in the car park of the motorway service station.

'I kid you not, Mick. There was a moment when I thought the game was up. These gorillas had AK-47s aimed at us and the boss man was forcing the older brother, Saban, to hold a gun to his brother's head. If he'd pulled the trigger, I'm pretty sure we'd all have been shot straight afterwards.'

'Christ almighty!'

'Then when I heard gunshots I thought he'd done it. Bertie pushed me to the ground, and when I opened my eyes seconds later, there were bodies lying around.'

'Who the fuck arrived like the cavalry?'

Rosie took a breath because she knew what the reaction would be.

'Jonjo Mulhearn's boys arrived. They did it.'

'Aw, for fuck's sake!'

'They saved our lives, Mick.'

McGuire was quiet for a moment then sighed, shaking his head.

'Rosie. I'm glad you're not shovelled in here in a coffin, because I'd have a lot of explaining to do – apart from anything else. But Christ's sake. Mulhearn's a gangster, just the same as the Albanians.'

'Well, not quite.'

'Aye. Tell that to the cops. His boys just shot three people dead. And my investigations editor is in the middle of it. This is not Deadwood, Rosie. We have laws.'

Rosie knew that although the editor was saying this, he didn't really believe it, and she could tell he was secretly enthralled at the whole story. McGuire had never knocked a door in his life, but he loved the excitement of reporters on the edge. But she knew this was just a bit too edgy for him.

'What if the cops find out? There must be CCTV in that place.'

'We were round the back, about fifty yards or so away from the whole service station forecourt. So I don't think CCTV would pick it up. Anyway, Jonjo phoned me and they've already talked to the café people. They know him. The CCTV tape was broken, apparently.'

McGuire shook his head. 'Christ!'

'So I don't think the cops will even be looking in my direction.'

'Well, I sincerely hope not, because you weren't only in the midst of a shoot-out which the police will be all over, you were actually there to smuggle illegal immigrants out of the country. Can you imagine how that would look if it got out? And they're off with five grand of the *Post*'s money. Jesus Christ! Why did I even agree to that? Oh, I remember . . . I didn't.'

'Exactly. I did it off my own bat. And at least I wasn't smuggling them in.'

'Aye, very funny, Gilmour.' He ran a hand through his hair. 'So where are we on the story? Obviously we can't mention a thing about this shoot-out. Not ever. But we can still tell the story of the boys, and others, being smuggled into the country on the charity lorries.'

'Of course. I'm ready to write it any time.'

'And the cops will be down to ask us where they are.'

'We just say we don't know.'

'Christ. It's dodgy. We need to get Hanlon in to see where we stand. And what about my five grand? Don't tell me it's blowing all over the M74 in the middle of all this.'

'No. The biggest Albanian thug took it off me, but before the boys left, Viktor grabbed it out of the dead guy's pocket.'

He puffed. 'No fool he, eh? Right. Get the story they told us about them being smuggled here on the charity wagon, and any pics we've got. That'll be a great splash and spread. Have it ready so I can get it legalled tomorrow. We'll use it the next day.' He stood up, looked at Rosie. 'Go and get a stiff drink and get home as soon as you've done your story. The paper's looking great for tomorrow, with the Helen Lewis story all over the front page splash and spread.'

Rosie had told TJ she was too tired and stressed out to meet up for dinner, but he'd insisted he wanted to see her tonight. She was glad he'd done so, because now, half a bottle of wine and some good pasta later, she was finally able to relax. The first gin and tonic hadn't touched the sides as she gulped it down, describing the scene a couple of hours earlier. TJ had sat shaking his head, sipping his drink. But even though Rosie was so caught up in her own drama, she thought she detected a slightly detached look in his eyes. No doubt he'd heard all this before, as her working life was a constant drama. TJ always listened, these days not preaching to her to give it up as he had in the past, which had caused clashes between them. But there was something not right about his demeanour.

'You all right, TJ? I'm so busy running off at the mouth that I've barely asked how you're doing.'

He half smiled and fiddled with his wine glass. Something was wrong.

'I'm cool, Rosie. I'm just a bit perplexed that you risked your life again to that extent. You honestly need to stop and think about these things.'

Rosie felt a little uneasy. Surely he wasn't going to preach to her. She knew more than anyone that her life was chaotic, but it wasn't like that every day.

'Aw, come on, TJ. It's not like that every week. I mean, there's months go by and I'm just doing normal stories, investigations. I know sometimes it gets dangerous, but usually that's because something unforeseen happens.'

'Yeah, like taking on Albanian and Russian gangsters in their own neck of the woods. You know you were lucky to get out of that.'

'I know that. More than you.' She realised it was a bit terse, and she thought his face burned a little. 'Sorry.' She ran a hand over her face. She was tired.. 'I don't mean to snap. But please don't preach to me. I know you care about me and worry, but honestly, telling me what might have happened doesn't help.'

He pushed his hand across the table and covered hers.

'Okay, boss.' He smiled. Then silence for a moment. 'But, Rosie, these guys in London, you know the ones I'm doing the session work for? They want me to go with them on tour.'

'On tour? Like a rock band?'

'Well,' he smiled, 'more of an old farts jazz kind of thing. There's a lot of festivals that he's got lined up, and they like my work so far. So they want me to go.'

'Of course. You must go,' Rosie said too quickly.

'Dying to get rid of me?'

'No. Of course not, TJ.' She touched his face. 'But I . . . I can't say to you do this, do that. You're your own man.' Her stomach sank a little. There was no drama in this, not like the last time when he was going to the US for a few months. Maybe they had matured, maybe the relationship was bigger than a few months' absence.

'I fancy going. It'll be good fun.'

'How long for? Where will it be?'

'Actually, all over Europe – Germany, France, Austria and stuff. And they're negotiating some deal for concerts in the USA and Canada.'

Rosie made a whistling noise. 'Sounds like a long haul.'

'Could be six months at least.'

'Just touring all the time. That would do my head in.'

'Sure, you never sit on your arse anywhere for more than a month.'

'Yeah. But this is my home. I always come back. Do you not feel that way?'

He took a long time to answer and Rosie studied his eyes, waiting.

'Well. Sometimes. But the main reason I'm here is

because of you. But we're not going anywhere really, are we?'

His words hit Rosie like a punch in the gut. This was what it was all about. He wanted to move on. She felt her face burn. She took a gulp of her wine.

'TJ. Listen. We've done this before. I thought we were clear what we had here . . . how we felt about each other.'

'I love you, Rosie.'

'Yeah, and I love you too. But don't lay all that guilt stuff on me, that you're going on a six-month jolly around the world playing jazz because our relationship isn't going anywhere.' She tried to control her irritation. 'Christ, man. Where do you want it to go? I thought you were okay the way things are?'

'I am,' he said quickly. 'I understand your work is what you do, what you are. It will always be the number one thing in your life. I get all of that. And I'm not looking for a wife. But you have to understand that sometimes I get bored in Glasgow. I'm on the sidelines of your life.'

'Christ. What do you want?'

'I like doing gigs. I like the idea of getting out of here, making my life feel a bit more exciting. It's how my life has always been really.' He smiled. 'Why should you get all the excitement?'

Rosie couldn't help smiling. 'You can come along the next time there's a chance I'll get killed.'

'No thanks, darlin'. I've been there, taking a bullet for you.'

The atmosphere had turned a little, simmered down. She wasn't angry; she knew any irritation she had was irrational. She had no rights here. Neither did TJ. There was no commitment from either of them, and he was right. It did drift along. But he was the only real constant in her life, and she knew how bereft she was when they'd quit the last time.

'So, what do you want to do? Draw a line or something tonight?'

'What do you mean?'

'Do you want us to end this? Like, end us?'

He looked shocked. 'No. Christ's sake, Gilmour. No. I don't ever want that. I love you.'

They sat for a long moment saying nothing. Rosie emptied her glass and drank some water.

'Then what's to worry about?'

'Will you be here when I get back?'

'Sure. Unless somebody shoots me.' She looked at him. 'I'll be here. That's if you come back . . .'

CHAPTER THIRTY-NINE

Rosie drove to the office feeling as though she'd been hit by a train. So much adrenalin from yesterday's drama with the Albanians had sent her into a feverish nightmare when she'd finally dropped off to sleep. And when she'd woken at four in the morning, she'd lain there, pondering over TJ's words at dinner. The fact that he was so keen to go away didn't exactly flatter their relationship, but she knew that was her fault. He'd settled for everything on her terms – no real commitment, no moving in together, just go along and see how it goes. But maybe he did want more and if they were more settled he wouldn't want to go away. What also niggled her was that she wasn't upset that he was actually going. That was a real sign that whatever this was, it had perhaps run its course. Maybe she should talk to him about that. Perhaps it was time to be brutally honest. But the thought made her uneasy because she knew how much she loved him, and how much she'd longed to be with him when he'd gone away a couple of years ago, when she didn't think she would ever see him again. TJ brought some stability to her life. He was a rock for her, a refuge, and she did love him on top of all that. So what was wrong with her, that she couldn't just go the whole hog? She didn't want to, and she knew that deep down. Living a normal life with a family wasn't cut for her and she could never fit it. Rosie lived in the adventure, the excitement, the danger, the chasing of the story; all of that sustained her. But even though at times it didn't seem enough, that she'd pined for TJ when he'd left her for New York, it wasn't enough for her to make the leap from where they were. She pushed the thought away with the notion that even if she did, perhaps he didn't want it anyway. He did say he liked to go away. Maybe the truth was that he was just as restless as her.

The mobile rang on the passenger seat and she could see it was DI James Morton. She braced herself, knowing her story on the Albanians was on the front page.

'Jim,' Rosie said, breezily. 'How you doing?'

'Up to our eyes in dead Albanians, Rosie. I suppose you've seen it on the news?'

Rosie thought she detected a note of irony, but she told herself she was just being paranoid.

'Yes. I saw it on the telly last night. Some stuff. Are they dead?'

'Yes. Three dead. Shot. That's one of the reasons I'm phoning you. Your Albanian blokes in the paper this morning. The ones who were smuggled in by the charity. Great story, Rosie. I need to get a word with them.'

Rosie hesitated, feeling guilty, but cornered. She blew out a sigh.

'Don't know where they are now, Jim. I interviewed them a couple of days ago.'

Lies as blatant as that always bothered Rosie. If it had been some hoodlum or thug she was lying to it wouldn't have bothered her, but the big cop was just trying to do his job, and in reality he might have been able to do more good for Viktor and the boys than they could do themselves.

'Come on now, Rosie. I know you reporters don't just drop someone after interviewing them. Especially you, and with guys like that. Would you not even give me a mobile number to have a word with them? They're not in any trouble.'

'I think they'll be out of the country by now. They were going away, they told me.'

Silence. This was one contact she could quite easily lose, and she didn't want to.

'Look, Jim. I can make a call to them, but if I can't get them, then they're obviously gone. I'll do my best. But they have left the country, I think.'

'Okay. See what you can do. By the way, the other reason I was phoning you . . . I have a bit of inside information I think you'll be interested in.'

'Really? I'm all ears.'

'Alan Lewis, your missing accountant. He just walked into our Stewart Street police station last night.'

'What? You're kidding! I thought he was dead. Everyone did.'

'Nope. Very much alive. And very angry, with plenty to say. I'm sure you'll be interested in that.'

'You bet I am.' Rosie was shocked. This changed a lot of things. She had to get a way to talk to him. 'Where's he been? Is he talking about the baby-selling racket? About the gangsters attached to the charity?'

'I don't know about that, because I won't be seeing him till this morning. But I can tell you this, though don't use it right now – it's only for your information. He said his wife hired Frankie Mallon to kill him.'

'Christ! Where? How?'

'In Romania. Mallon left him for dead. And more than that, Rosie. He said he walked into his flat in the West End last month and Helen Lewis was standing over Mallon with a smoking gun in her hand, like some old movie.'

'Are you serious?'

'Deadly.'

'Can I use any of this?'

'Like I said, I haven't spoken to him yet. So, no. It was passed to us up at the Serious Crime Squad because of all the background and the charity he was involved in. We've a lot to talk to him about.'

'Is there any way I can talk to him? Is he under arrest?'

'No arrest. Not yet.'

'Is he likely to be?'

'I don't know yet. But tell you what: get me those Albanians to talk to – even if they're abroad. Get them to talk to me and we'll see what we can do.'

Rosie waited a moment before she answered. The Albanians were out of the country. The cops would surely not extradite them back in to accuse them of being brought in here illegally.

'Like I said, I'll do my best. I'll try to get in touch with them this morning. That's really all I can do. But I'm dying to talk to Alan.' She waited. 'And I might be able to help you back up Alan Lewis's story about his wife hiring Mallon to kill him.'

'How do you mean?'

'I talked to someone recently who said that very thing. That Mallon had been hired to kill him.'

'Really? You kept that quiet, Rosie. It's not even been in your paper.'

'Well, you know what it's like. Proving it would be a problem.'

'Okay. I'd definitely like to talk to that person too. So let's see how we can do this. And, Rosie? Everything I'm saying to you here is off the record.'

'Of course.'

He hung up.

'I knew Helen Lewis was lying through her back teeth,'

Rosie said aloud as she slung her mobile onto the passenger seat. Her initial instinct was to throw her to the police, contact Donna and get her to talk to the cops. But Rosie wasn't finished with Helen Lewis yet. She dialled her mother's number. It went straight to answerphone and she left a message saying she had to meet them.

'So she's a murderer, as well as a lying, scheming bitch,' McGuire said. 'So much for the weeping all over the paper yesterday.' He rubbed his hands. 'The Black Widow. I love that. I'm looking forward to hanging her from the rafters. What's your plan, Gilmour?'

Rosie sat back. 'I'm of a mind to set her up with the cops. They don't even know where she is, and they've been asking for her contact number, which I've told them I don't have. I hate lying to them about that, because the big DI has been decent with me.'

'Set the bitch up then. What's it to you if she gets dragged kicking and screaming to the cells?'

Rosie thought. 'I don't know. I need to think about it. But I have to get Donna, the mother of Frankie's baby, I have to get her to talk to the cops. The DI is going to give me a real inside track. But I have to give him something. He wants to talk to the Albanians.'

'Then give him their bloody mobile. Christ, Rosie! They're out of the country now. What do you care?'

'I know. You're right. But I do care.'

'You're a headcase.' He looked at his screen. 'Now clear off while I get ready for conference.'

Rosie spotted Donna in the café where they'd met before, and the toddler looked up and pointed at her when she came in the door.

'Bright girl, this one,' Rosie said, sitting down. She looked at Donna, her eyes automatically scanning her for any signs of a relapse into drugs. She looked good, clear eyes and skin, and was wearing a warm sweater and jacket. 'You look well.'

'I'm doing great, Rosie. I've been offered a part-time job. Two days a week, helping at the crèche in the community centre. And I'll be able to bring Amy with me. So I'm over the moon.'

'Good stuff. Everything going well with the new house?'

'Aye. It's great. Quiet street for where it is, but so far I haven't had any problems. I used some of that money I told you about – that she gave me – to get it decorated and things. But I've been watching what I'm doing with it. It's not exactly a million pounds, but it's a wee nest egg if I manage it well enough. I'm happy, Rosie.'

'Good,' Rosie said, waiting for the right moment. 'Listen, Donna. About what you told me. About Frankie Mallon and what he said to you about being hired to bump off Alan Lewis.'

'Aye.'

'I totally believed what you said. I haven't used it in the paper, because we've no proof, really, apart from you telling us. But although you said Frankie was out of his box on drugs that night he admitted it, you believed him, didn't you?'

'Aye. Definitely. He was quite clear about it all. He wouldn't make something like that up.'

Rosie paused a second, watching her.

'I think you should talk to the cops. There's been a bit of a development on that front, and what you say about Frankie kind of backs up what they've been told.'

She looked confused. 'I don't know what you mean.'

'I can't really say too much right now, but I have some contacts, let's say, with the cops, and I've been told that they have information that Frankie was hired to kill Alan Lewis. Hired by his wife.'

'How come? Who's said that? Was Frankie mouthing off to everyone before he got killed?'

'No. The information didn't come from Frankie or anyone who knew Frankie. It's from another source. But you don't need to concern yourself with that. The bottom line is it seems Frankie is dead because he got involved with Helen Lewis, and she's the kind of woman who used him to get to her husband – and probably her husband's money. She's a proper bitch. A conwoman and a criminal. And everything right now is pointing to the fact that she killed Frankie that day.'

Donna sat processing the information, holding the drinking cup for her little girl, and stroking her face.

'I always thought she did it. She's a bastard. Left my wee girl without a daddy. I know Frankie was a bit of a bad lot, but he loved the wean. He provided for her and he always would have. It's not fair.'

'Of course it's not. That's why I think you should talk to the cops. If you tell them what Frankie told you, then that would back up what they've just found out.'

She puffed. 'I don't know. That might involve me in a big court case. If she gets charged with murder, I'd be a witness, and I'd have to go into court and testify. I don't know if I'm up to that. I'm just trying to get on with my life and put a lot of things behind me. I did love Frankie, but once I knew he was running around with that Helen bitch, I just felt so bad. He really hurt me. But I'm trying to put that behind me. All the drugs, all the messed-up life. I don't think I could face a court case. I'd be scared.'

'I understand that. But you should definitely think about it.'

'But what if I went to court and told everything? That would make me a grass. Okay, she's killed the father of my child, but in the Gorbals you don't grass people up. I could get slashed just for doing that.'

'I don't think Helen Lewis is exactly queen of the Gorbals, Donna. Everyone probably hates her. I don't even know if she had many friends there, or even still has.'

She shrugged. 'Probably not. She was always thinking she was a cut above everyone.'

'She killed your wee girl's daddy.'

'She gave me money to help look after her.'

'It doesn't matter. To me that just confirms her guilt. Don't you think?'

'Aye. Definitely. But there was a scrap of decency in her for doing that.'

'She left your wee girl without a daddy because she was greedy for money, Donna. She's got off scot-free and has probably right now got more money than you can ever dream of. Not money she's earned, but money she stole from her husband. She deserves all the trouble she gets.'

Donna sat for a moment. 'And do you really think the cops have got something big on her?'

'They have. My information is they have her just about nailed to the wall. But your information might finish it. How about talking to them anyway? What do you think?'

She pulled her little girl closer to her and stroked her blonde hair.

'All right. I'll talk to them.'

'Good.' Rosie nodded. 'I think you're doing the right thing.'

The kid looked up, her bright blue eyes a little picture of health. So innocent and trusting, Rosie thought. The look we all had before life comes crashing in and sweeps it all away.

CHAPTER FORTY

Time was running out for Helen Lewis. She'd already stayed here too long, and what she should have done the day she escaped the clutches of her kidnappers was to keep on running. By going to her mother because she was so scared at the time, all she had really done was find a place to hide, but on top of that she had left herself open to these bastards tracking her down. She was safe in her mother's flat, and as long as she didn't put her face around the area, she'd go unnoticed. Most people she'd known would have either moved out of the Gorbals, or the ones who were there would have forgotten about her long ago. And anyway, she had changed her hair and looked different from the teenage girl who'd left all those years ago. But appearing in the *Post* had made her more edgy. She'd blown that cover and she knew she didn't have much time before she had to get moving. She would leave tomorrow. As soon as her mother got back in from the shops she would tell her, and they would go together. She went into her bedroom and began packing. Most of her expensive designer clothes were still folded and in the case – there wasn't much call for them, moping about this place. She heard the door open and her mother come in. Helen stopped what she was doing and went down the hall into the kitchen, where her mother was filling the kettle with her back to her.

'We've got a problem,' Janey said to her, without looking over her shoulder.

'What do you mean?'

'I bumped into Nora MacDonald up at the shops and she told me that wee scumbag Gimpy Jackson was asking about you.'

'Gimpy?'

'Aye. Remember him from years ago? His brother threw him out of the third-floor flat when he was fourteen for stealing his drug money. Left him with a bad leg. Brother was a drug dealer. You know the Jacksons. They were all related, and all scum.'

Helen remembered the family, hard as nails, who knew everything and everyone's business. They were moneylenders, and plenty of people in the Gorbals had been on the receiving end of a beating with baseball bats if they were late with payments. Helen had gone to London by the time they were making a real name for themselves.

'I remember them. But I was away, Ma. A lot of that stuff went right over my head. Anyway, what's the problem? What's that Gimpy been saying?'

'Nora says he told her he was working for some guys in the town now and they were in with these East European gangsters. I mean, Gimpy always talked the talk, but he's a wee prick, so he might just have been shooting his mouth off.'

'Christ, Ma. I don't like the sound of that. What did he say?'

'Nora says he told her that all that stuff in the paper was true, and that you were in with these gangsters too. But you stole all Alan's money.'

Helen felt a chill run through her.

'What the fuck! Where is a wee shite like him even getting any of that kind of information? He's just bullshitting.'

'Aye. Well maybe he's no'. So it's not something you can take a chance on. He says to Nora he heard you were back in the Gorbals with me. But he didn't believe it, because that would be just plain stupid as it's the first place they would look for you.'

'Christ. Maybe it was plain stupid. Listen, Ma, I need to get out of here fast. I thought when we talked to that reporter it would come across in the paper that I was a victim in all this. But if that's what people are saying, then maybe someone will find out where I am and I'm not safe here any more.'

'You're supposed to be seeing that Rosie Gilmour tomorrow. You told her you would meet her. What do you think she wants to talk about?'

'Christ knows. It was her who phoned me. Maybe I should just patch it, and get out of here tonight.'

'I don't know. I think you should meet her and see what she wants to ask you. You never know. It might be some more information about what's going on. You need to know everything before you decide to leave here.'

Helen didn't know if it was a good idea to even hang around till tomorrow; the thought that this Gimpy character was blabbing his mouth off made her uneasy.

'I think I should get out of here tonight. Why don't you come with me?'

'Me? Leave here?'

'Yeah. Come with me. We'll go somewhere. Spain. Start again. I've got plenty of money. Cash money, and I've got access to all these bank accounts. We won't have any money worries, and we can be out of here forever. We can go to some wee place where nobody knows us. Maybe get a wee café going or something. I'm sick of all this shit.'

Janey stood gazing out of the kitchen window at the blocks of flats in the drizzle. Then she turned to her daughter and sighed.

'You know what? I might just do that. When it comes right down to it, there's bugger all for me here. Hasn't been for years, and that's the truth.'

Rosie sat at the table while DI James Morton was at the counter being served. They'd come to the café round the corner from the police HQ as Rosie didn't want to go to his office to chat. They'd spent the last hour with Donna while she gave the police a detailed statement on her conversation with Helen Lewis. Donna had only agreed to making the statement and talking to the police if Rosie was going to be with her. The detective agreed to it reluctantly and she'd been with him as they sat in Donna's neat little flat up in Springburn. She was glad she'd done well enough and was taking care of herself, but Rosie was niggled by her conscience that she had talked her into speaking to the cops, in case anything went wrong. She noticed during her statement that Donna told the police about the money Helen gave her, but said she had spent it all. She was obviously worried they were going to hold it for evidence. Rosie had driven back to the city centre behind the DI's car.

She had to do her best here if she had any chance of a word with Alan Lewis, who was still with the police. Not under arrest, they'd told her, but helping with enquiries. Technically he was free to go at any time, but he was cooperating with them as they investigated the charity. Rosie felt she'd done plenty so far by giving Donna to them, but she had also spoken to the Albanians, who were now in Spain. Big Tony had phoned her this morning to say that he'd driven from Calais to Barcelona in twelve hours. He'd dropped them at a small hotel on the outskirts of the city, and the rest was up to them. He was off to the Costa del Sol to pick up some cargo. Rosie had spoken to Viktor and told him the cops wanted to interview them. He was totally against it at first, but Rosie reassured them that if anyone spoke to them it would be while they were abroad, and they would not have to be brought back here. She had to be given assurances by the DI that this was the case. And anyway, she knew that if they were under any threat, barring the cops turning up with handcuffs, the boys had the wits to make themselves scarce. She was determined not to compromise them, even though the DI had told her that, strictly speaking, she'd been part of an illegal smuggling operation by arranging for them to get out of the country.

The DI placed Rosie's black tea on the table and sat opposite her with a mug of coffee.

'That went well, with that kid Donna. She seemed all right.'

'Do you get the impression she is telling the truth?'

'Well, I think she's being honest enough about what Frankie told her. But at the end of the day that's evidence we cannot call on from a dead man. It's circumstantial, but on top of what Alan Lewis is telling us, then it's good.' He raised his mug in a cheers gesture. 'So thanks for that. But bear in mind, I could still have you arrested for people-smuggling.'

Rosie smiled. 'Yeah. Only if you can prove it, Inspector.'

He sat back and was quiet for a moment, studying Rosie's face.

'You love all this stuff, don't you, Rosie? It's what you live for. I kind of admire that.'

Rosie smiled. 'It's my life in so many ways. I think I've spent so much time in other people's misery or shitstorms here and abroad, that it's hard to get a sense of what actually matters outside of what I'm doing at any particular time. I live in a world of deadlines, pressure, fear sometimes.'

'The fear of failure?' he interrupted, looking her in the eye.

Rosie sat back. 'Christ. Is it obvious? No. I'm only joking. I'm not afraid of failing. Sometimes I do.' She recalled some of the people she'd let down. 'I don't fail on the stories as such. Or I seldom do. But sometimes I feel I failed the people I worked with. People I use on stories. Like Donna, for example. I've brought her to you because it's the right thing to do, but also because it's almost like a bargaining tool for more information. I don't feel good about that.'

'But you're doing the right thing.'

'Of course. I know that. But I was also doing the right thing a couple of years ago when I gave the cops a Kosovan refugee called Emir . . . he got shot under police protection. I'll never forgive myself for that. Others too . . .' Rosie's voice trailed off. She didn't want to go there right now.

He sighed. 'Yeah. I remember that guy. It was a terrible time. There were fireworks everywhere. I didn't know you at the time, but Don told me about it, and how awful you felt. I kind of get a handle on that, now that I've met you a couple of times.' He paused. 'None of my business, Rosie, but maybe you take on too much. Maybe you make it too much of your life.'

Rosie smiled and shook her head. 'I don't know any other way.' She changed the subject. This was getting morose. 'Anyway, let's not take the soul-searching too seriously. How about me talking to Alan Lewis?'

'He's not under arrest, so he can talk to whoever he wants.'

'But you've told him not to.'

'I haven't, but I'm sure my boss has. I think he'll be getting out of the police station today and we've put him up somewhere. I can ask him if he'll take a phone call from you.'

'Would you do that?'

He shrugged. 'Yeah. But talking of bargaining, what about Helen Lewis? You still haven't given me a contact number for her.'

'I don't have one,' she lied. 'They contact me. Her and her mother. I'm going to see them tomorrow to ask her about Alan – based on the new information I have from you. I want to put it to her. She lied to me. She's a scheming, horrible person and she lied to me – lies which I put in my newspaper, half of me knowing she was lying. So now I want to tell her what I know, and see how she reacts. I need to see the whites of her eyes.'

'I'd like to be there to see them too.'

'That would make me setting her up. Something niggles me about that – giving people up.'

'She's a cold-blooded murderer, Rosie. What part of that can you defend? And by her husband's own account, she sent a hitman out to murder him, while she looted his money. She's a bad lot.'

'Yeah. I know that.'

'When are you seeing her?'

'I'm still not sure on a time. I'll let you know.' Rosie looked at her watch. 'I have to get moving. I'll give you a call.'

He gave her a look that said he didn't believe her.

'I will. When I can.'

CHAPTER FORTY-ONE

Rosie was surprised and glad when the call came from Janey to ask her to meet them at the City Inn hotel near the Broomielaw. At least it wasn't in that bar with the blaring music again, not for what she was about to do. There was a little lash of tension in her stomach as she and Matt headed across to the hotel and parked the car.

'Do you think she'll go mental?'

'It's entirely possible. But we'll cross that bridge when we come to it.'

'Well . . . Bear in mind she probably shot Frankie Mallon because he was noising her up. I don't really want to make her angry.'

Rosie smiled at the way Matt always made jokes when he was worried something bad was going to happen.

'She's not going to shoot us, Matt. We're in a hotel in the middle of the city.'

'Okay. Well if she does, you'll never hear the end of it from me.'

'It'll be fine. She is a bad lot though, so we just have to see how it goes. Don't let her see you're edgy.'

Rosie might as well have been saying it to herself, because right now, as they went up in the lift and along the corridor, she was more edgy than Matt. She had to get this right for the plan to work. She knocked gently on the door.

'Who is it?'

'It's Rosie.'

The door opened and Janey looked from Rosie to Matt.

'And Matt. I forgot to mention I was bringing him – in case we need more pictures.'

Janey opened the door for them to come in and Rosie saw her looking at Helen.

'Why do you need more pictures?' Helen said.

'It's always better to have them,' Rosie said, hoping she wouldn't ask any more questions.

She looked around the room and saw cases packed. 'Are you going away?'

'Yeah. We're leaving. In fact we already left. We're only here tonight and taking the train to London tomorrow morning. Then France. Then who knows where . . . But we're not coming back.'

'Really?' Rosie asked. 'Why the rush? Has somebody found out where you were?'

'There was a bit of talk about it. My ma says she met some-one and he told her he was working for some nutters in Glasgow. Heard my name mentioned.' Helen looked anxious, her eyes tight under the make-up as though she hadn't been sleeping. She crossed the room and sat on the sofa, motioning them to sit. 'But it's not just that. All that stuff the other day I read about in the papers – that shoot-out at the motor-way place. Albanians. I just want to see the back of this place. I'm scared to stay around in case they find me. In case it's all connected. Simple as that, really. That's why we're going.'

Rosie hoped the wire Matt had put on her was picking this up. She sat in an armchair, opposite Helen, facing her so that her hidden camera could also pick this up on video. She glanced at Matt sitting by a table and he winked. He would take pictures later, if things worked out.

'So what did you want to see us about? I thought we said everything the other day. You've had it all in the paper.'

Rosie took a breath, waited.

'There's some other things I wanted to put to you and ask you about.'

'What?'

'It's information that has come to us in the last day or so. About Alan and his disappearance in Romania.'

'I've been over that a million times, with the cops and the press at the time. I've no idea why he would disappear, leave me high and dry like this. Maybe he's with one of his floozies. I wouldn't be surprised.'

Rosie waited a moment and watched her, then asked, 'Do you think something has happened to him?'

She shrugged. 'Don't know. Why would you say that? Do you?'

Rosie ignored the question.

'Helen, I want to ask you about Frankie Mallon and how he came to know Alan.'

'Why do you want to know that?'

'I'll come to that in a minute. But did Frankie do some work for Alan? I know you met him through Alan – you told me that yourself – but did Frankie work for him?'

Helen hesitated, and looked as though she was trying to remember if she had said this in past interviews with the police, in case she was incriminating herself.

'I can't remember.' She brushed it off. 'I think he did some work for him, but you know, Alan never told me about his work other than that it was boring accounts for companies. He only ever talked a bit more about the wine-importing business he was getting involved in, but he only told me that because he was going to be travelling to Romania a bit. And I went with him too a few times.'

Once more, Rosie waited and watched.

'Do you remember Frankie Mallon ever going with him? To Romania?'

The words seemed to sting Helen, and she shot Rosie as calm a glance as she could muster. But Rosie could see the little flush rising on her neck. She was rattled.

'I honestly don't know. But I don't think so.'

Rosie flipped back the pages of her notebook and screwed up her eyes.

'What about in September last year?'

'What about it?'

'Did Alan go to Bucharest?'

She looked surprised. 'Yes. Of course. That's the last time I saw him. Why are you asking me that? It's well documented.'

'Did Frankie Mallon go with him?'

Now it was an icy glare she shot Rosie.

'What? No. I . . . I don't think so. I wouldn't know. I mean, why would he?'

'Well, maybe he was working with him in other areas you didn't know about.'

Helen put her hand up. 'Hold on a minute. What are we talking about here? Are you saying Frankie was working with Alan in this babies scandal? Is that what you're getting at here?'

'No.'

'So what are you trying to say?'

Rosie took a moment.

'I'm asking because some information has come to us that Frankie was in Bucharest at the same time as Alan. That they were seen together.' Rosie paused to watch it registering before she added, 'They went out fishing in one of the lakes.'

Helen blanched and she glanced at her mother.

'What is all this? Why are you suddenly asking all this crap? What does it matter anyway?'

'It's just information we're trying to look at.'

'Well I don't know anything about that.'

Rosie waited. She knew she wouldn't get too much longer before Helen exploded.

'When did you last see Alan?'

'Aw, for Christ's sake. I've told that a million times. I last saw him the day he was leaving here to go to Bucharest. Last September. You can read that anywhere. What is all this?'

'Is that really the last time you saw him? Are you sure you want to say that?'

'What?'

Rosie let the silence fill the room, the air crackling with tension. Janey looked at the floor.

'Alan is alive, Helen.'

'What?' She managed to look genuinely shocked. 'Alan's alive? B-But . . . how? I mean, how do you know?'

'You know how I know, Helen.'

'What?'

'You saw him yourself. When he used his key and walked into your flat three weeks ago . . . And Frankie Mallon was lying on the floor, shot in the chest by you. Frankie was trying to blackmail you, because you had hired him to kill your husband. Does that sound about right?'

Helen looked as though she'd been shot herself. Her face flushed and she jumped to her feet.

'Wait a fucking minute. What are you talking about? Look, who do you think you are? Coming in here accusing me, telling me Alan is still alive. It's just rubbish. Now get out – before I fucking throw you out,' she snarled. 'You can't go accusing me of anything.'

Rosie knew she just about had her.

'What – you going to call the cops?' Rosie reached into her pocket and took out her mobile phone and pressed a key. 'You won't have to. They're right here.'

Helen looked at her in disbelief and staggered back as though she was dazed. She grabbed for her bag as a key was suddenly turned in the door. Then it opened, and in walked Alan Lewis, his face grey and his eyes cold and angry. DI James Morton was behind him, along with a woman detective and another uniformed cop. Matt started furiously snapping the scene.

'What the fuck! What is this? Alan . . . You . . . You're alive . . . !'

'I think you can cut the crap now, Helen,' Rosie said. 'The game's up.'

Her mother stood open-mouthed as Alan, hair shorter and cleaned up, walked across to Helen.

'I brought some people who want to talk to you, Helen. Believe me, you'll be glad it's them and not any one of these thugs who are currently scouring the city for you.' He turned to the inspector. 'This is DI Morton.'

The DI looked Helen in the eye.

'As Rosie says, Helen, the game is up. Your man here has told us everything. And I mean the lot – selling babies, people-smuggling, money-laundering. He'll get jail all right. But so will you. Because he's back from the dead, despite your best efforts.'

'Fuck this. I don't know what you're talking about.' She glanced at Alan. 'Selling fucking weans? Christ almighty.' Then she looked at the cop. 'I don't know any of this.'

'We'll let the courts decide that,' said DI Morton. 'But you did send a hitman to kill your husband, so don't even start denying that. Alan's told us all about that too.'

Suddenly Helen reached into her bag and brought out a gun. She furiously waved it around the room.

'Right. Everybody fucking just stand where they are. This thing's loaded.'

The DI stepped forward.

'Helen. There's no way out of here. Are you going to shoot us all? There are police outside the room and all over the hotel. Come on. Don't be stupid.'

'Helen . . .' Alan said. 'Stop. Just tell me why you did it. Why did you send Frankie to kill me? I gave you everything. I loved you. And you tried to get me murdered. Why did you want to be with scum like him, when you could be with me? I'd have done anything for you.' His voice shook a little. 'Why, Helen? Did you think Frankie was going to look after you? Christ! He told me out in the boat that afternoon, after he thumped me on the head the first time with the fire extinguisher. Yes. I'll tell you about it. I sat there, stunned, shocked, terrified. He told me that you sent him to do this. But that he was taking everything. He was killing me and conning you. How could you be so stupid?' He swallowed. 'I loved you.'

'Shut up. I've had enough of you. You lied to me, you cheated on me with whores every time you were away. You think I didn't know? What was I supposed to do?'

'I cheated on you?' Alan shook his head. 'Come on. Put the gun down before someone gets hurt.'

'No. Everyone just get out of my way and nobody will get hurt.' She turned to her mother. 'Come on, Ma. Let's get out of here.'

She kept the gun pointed at Alan, then at Rosie and the cops. Her mother didn't move. Janey looked around the room, and seemed to buckle.

'We're not going anywhere, Helen. Put the gun down. It's over.'

'Ma, don't say that. We can go.'

'No we can't, Helen. You need to face up to what you did. I've had enough.'

Helen began to shake, her face flushed, and her voice trembled, almost shrieking. 'You've had enough? You think you've had enough. What about me? You made me who I am!'

'Stop it, Helen.'

'No. You helped put me on the game, Ma. I was fourteen

fucking years old. I didn't know anything. You put me on the game. Where do you think that left me as a girl? Eh? You forced me to have an abortion. So don't you tell me *I* have to face up to what *I've* done.'

'Helen!'

'Shut up!' She broke down. 'Everything I did was to survive. Frankie would have killed me that day. He came to my flat to get all my money and he wasn't going to stop there. He would have taken my money and killed me. It was me or him.' She began to sob. 'Ma. Please believe me.'

Alan took a step towards her, his face suddenly full of concern.

'Helen. Give me the gun.'

She jerked away, pointed it straight at him. 'Get back!' she shrieked.

'Stop, Helen!' Rosie heard herself say. 'You need to stop now. You know what you've done and why you did it. So tell that to the police. You don't have an option here. You can't shoot your way out of this. Put the gun down.'

She aimed the gun at Rosie, her hands trembling.

'You set me up, you bitch. What kind of bastard are you?'

'Listen, Helen. I'm doing you a favour. Do you think these gangsters will ever stop looking for you? Look what they've done to everyone who has crossed them. You're a dead woman walking. Getting into police custody is your only way out. These mobsters will hunt you down no matter where you are. You stole their money.' Rosie paused.

'And, by the way, you left an innocent wee girl without a father.'

Helen looked at Rosie, her eyes full of tears and defeat. She suddenly dropped the gun and the detective was across the room in a second to pick it up. The female police officer was at his side, and in a flash Helen was in handcuffs.

Rosie looked at the DI as he came over to Helen.

'Helen Lewis, I am arresting you on suspicion of the murder of Francis Mallon.'

Helen's head dropped down to her chest and she wept. DI Morton nodded to the cops and they pushed her towards the door. As she got there she turned to her mother.

'Ma! Help me!'

Janey stood there, stony-faced, and said nothing. The officers ushered Helen out of the door.

Rosie pushed out a sigh as she looked at the DI. They both looked at Janey.

'Am I under arrest here?'

'No. But we'll want to talk to you. You need to give a statement. Helen has been living under your roof for the past three weeks, so you have been harbouring a murder suspect.'

'What was I supposed to do? She's my daughter.'

Rosie looked at her in disgust. 'I need to get out of here.' She nodded to Matt, then turned to the DI. 'I'll give you a call.'

'Thanks,' he said.

Rosie and Matt walked along the corridor in silence and got into the lift. Rosie stared straight ahead.

'I don't feel good about that, Matt. Maybe I should. But I don't.'

He put his arm over his shoulder.

'I know how you're feeling, Rosie. I knew it wouldn't sit well with you. But sometimes you have to do things that aren't always easy. But it was right. Just believe that.'

She nodded as the door pinged and opened for the ground floor. As they got out of the hotel, they could see Helen being bundled into the car, and as it drove past them, she looked at Rosie, her face streaked with tears and mascara. Somewhere in there was the angry teenage girl, confused, abandoned to predatory men by her own mother. How else could she have understood how she was supposed to fit in and live her life after that? Rosie turned away.

CHAPTER FORTY-TWO

Rosie left the editor's office with his usual 'you and your bleeding heart' quote still ringing in her ears. McGuire had punched the air in triumph as she'd described the drama with Helen Lewis and her arrest. No other newspaper would even have a sniff at this, he said, and it was almost too good not to use. But he knew the restrictions, because Helen was under arrest, and no doubt the Crown Office would be moving quickly to formally charge her and to have her in court for a first appearance, barring newspapers from mentioning any details of her alleged crimes. On top of that, Alan Lewis was also facing charges of people-smuggling and money-laundering concerning the charity. DI Morton had told Rosie the details of how he'd escaped and survived, and it was a fantastic tale that she was desperate to use. As long as the police investigation was ongoing she was restricted on how much she could say, but she knew she'd get away with mentioning how Lewis had stayed under the water after Frankie pushed him into the lake and could see him turning the boat around and disappearing, leaving Lewis to float to the shore. He couldn't rely on his gangster mates to get him home, because he knew he had also been conning them out of money in his accounts. He had to make it on his own, staying in farms, befriending a local and finally getting smuggled out of Romania once he was able to get access to some money. Rosie knew she had to tread very carefully as she knocked out her story, giving as much detail as she thought she could get away with for tomorrow's paper. The bulk of Helen's words couldn't be used right now, but would put the *Post* so far in front of the other media when all the background came out at the end of her eventual court case. Then, she'd be able to use the full interview, Helen Lewis's gun-wielding meltdown, and the police stepping in to arrest her, as well as Alan's full story. But that would be a long way off. For tomorrow, McGuire was delighted that the lawyers had okayed him to use a front-page picture of Helen coming face to face with her husband who'd been missing for six months. Matt's pictures were terrific, capturing her stunned expression perfectly. But Rosie had to play down the story of what really happened, by writing . . . *This is the heart-stopping moment when Helen Lewis met her husband for the first time in six months. Minutes before detectives moved in to arrest her, the woman was stunned when her husband walked into a hotel room where she was being interviewed by the* Post.'

It was great stuff, and Rosie should have felt like celebrating, but right now she felt deflated and just wanted to go home. But when the phone call came from DI Morton asking her for a quick celebratory drink, she knew she couldn't refuse. She had to keep this guy onside for the future. She was meeting him in Archie's Bar in Waterloo Street. She decided to take the car, because right now it would be too tempting to go into the bar and knock back three or four rapid gin and tonics just to kick out the blues. The car would keep her disciplined. She still had to meet TJ later – he was going on the night flight to London and although they'd said their goodbyes the other night, she wanted to be there to see him off when he stopped by her house en route.

There were no parking places in the street near the pub and rather than go searching, Rosie decided to go into the car park at Anderston bus station. She drove through, but couldn't find a space until further in, at the end in the corner. She'd been so busy trying to get her car into the tight spot that she hadn't noticed a car drive past behind her. She was quite glad. Car parks were eerie places at the best of times, and it was dark outside. It was good to feel that she wasn't alone. Rosie got out of the car, pulling her bag over her shoulder. She closed the door and began walking towards the light at the exit. Suddenly she heard footsteps behind her. Her stomach jolted a little. Christ, Rosie. It's just your imagination. Keep walking. She quickened her step, afraid to look over her shoulder. She was only fifty yards from the street, where she could see traffic. She could feel her heart beat faster. The combination of tiredness and paranoia was getting to her. Keep walking, she told herself. But the footsteps grew louder, closer, and she was so scared she started to break into a run. But as she did, a figure appeared from behind a pillar and suddenly she stood before him. She was too confused even to work out what was happening – a robbery, a junkie. But it wasn't. Her legs turned to jelly and she couldn't make another step. Then suddenly she felt a bag going over her head from behind and she was dragged roughly backwards.

'What the fu—What is this? Here. Take my bag. Take everything.'

She felt a single blow from a heavy fist to the side of her head and everything went black.

When she came to, she was trussed up in the back of a van, her face against the cold metal floor. Her head was pounding, and when she blinked, her vision was blurred. She felt sick. Cold fear ran through her. She tried to focus to see if her bag or phone was anywhere and she could see the phone among her things scattered on the floor. Perhaps it was a robbery and they would let her go. But she knew it wasn't. She lay there, terrified, barely able to breathe for panic. Then suddenly the doors opened and as she peered out, she could see the van was not in the car park. There was traffic. She tried again to focus, but something was wrong. She couldn't see properly, blinking, but everything was still blurred. She thought she could see the lights of the Kingston Bridge, so she must still be in the city. Then she was roughly dragged from the van. She tried to look at the man, but she was seeing double. This was serious. Whatever had happened, the blow to her head had caused problems, or maybe they'd drugged her. Her movements were slurred, like she was wading through mud.

'Wh-what . . . who are you? Please. Don't hurt me.'

She was pulled to her feet and felt the ties behind her back being cut and her feet released. But she could barely stand, felt sick rising in her throat.

'Please. I'm sick. I can't see properly. I need a doctor.'

She heard someone laughing. Then she saw his face for a moment. A man in a dark suit.

'This is message from our friends in Eastern Europe. We are here now. This is not your city.'

'What?' Rosie tried to focus.

She could hear water and, from instinct, she knew she was at the banks of the river on the Southside. She saw the silhouette of what looked like a huge warehouse she knew. Then she was grabbed on each side and dragged towards the water. She could see its inky blackness rushing past. Her body was icy cold but soaking with sweat and her head was thumping as though it was about to explode.

'You can swim? If you can, maybe you live. If not – is your problem.'

Rosie turned her head to make one last plea as they

dragged her to the edge. She pushed her hand inside her pocket and pressed the button to ring the last number she'd called on her mobile – the DI's. She could hear it ringing. But it was too late to matter now. She could feel herself flying through the air, legs flailing. The cold icy shock of the water on her face left her gasping for air when she came up for the first time. She'd never felt cold like this. Down she went, beneath the water, eyes open in the pitch blackness, the taste of oily, gritty water in her mouth, swallowing, choking. She kicked furiously with her legs to bring her to the surface again, but she was weighed down with her boots and clothes. Her arms and legs were getting heavier the more she struggled, and she sank again. The pain had gone from her head. But every survival instinct pushed her on. She broke through the surface, and could see nothing, just blackness. Her legs began to feel numb and she couldn't move them. She was going to die here, in this river, like this, alone. Nobody was coming. Nobody even knew where she would be. An image of her mother dancing with her father on a snowy night in their living room came to her head and she tried to kick her legs again – but nothing. Then she was below the water again and pulled her arms to try to come to the surface, but they felt so heavy. But again, the image of her parents dancing, the music, she suddenly felt the warmth of the house that winter's night, the crackling of the open fire, the old record blaring on the radiogram. Rosie felt her eyes closing. There was the warm embrace of something as the music carried her off and suddenly she wasn't afraid any more. She chased the warm embrace and she slipped away.

'She's fucking deed! Look at her, Terry! She's blue. Fuck's sake, man! Somebody get an ambulance or something. Get the polis!'

Rosie could hear voices in her dream.

'Up there! Go up to the Jamaica Bridge! Flag somebody down, for fuck's sake!'

'I'll go. You can hardly fucking stand up you're that wrecked.'

The voices came and went and Rosie lay on her stomach feeling someone punching her back.

'That's not what you're supposed to do, Dan. You're fucking punching her.'

'I'm trying to get the fucking water out her lungs, man. Maybe she'll come round.'

'She's dead, man. I think we should get out of here before the cops come. We might get blamed.'

Then silence. The sound of people moving, shuffling. Rosie coughed. Then vomited.

'Fuck me, man! She's no' deed.'

Someone knelt beside her and lifted her head back.

'Listen, hen. It's all right. Jamie's away to get help. You'll be all right. We'll no' let you die.'

Rosie slipped in and out of consciousness, freezing, shivering, her teeth rattling. Then more voices.

'Stand back, everyone. We've got this.'

She could hear sirens and see the yellow glow of jackets. Ambulance flashing lights. Hands and arms touching her, lifting her onto something. She was alive. She opened one eye as she was going into the back of the ambulance and suddenly she knew where she was. There was a two-seater sofa below the Jamaica Bridge, and beer cans and bottles strewn around. This was where down-and-outs lived and slept if they couldn't get a hostel. Christ almighty! They'd saved her. She felt tears warm on her face. Because part of her wished they hadn't. Then she saw them, unsteady on their feet, gazing at her with wide eyes.

'Is she gonnae be all right, boss?' she heard one of the voices slur.

'She's alive, anyway. Listen, you boys stay where you are. We'll need a word with you. What you saw.'

'Didny see anything, man. Just a body bobbing up and down in the water. She must have jumped. Poor lassie. We just dragged her out when she got close enough to the side. Fuckin' scary.'

Rosie heard the ambulance doors close, blinded by the light inside. People talking, asking who she was. Then everything went black.

CHAPTER FORTY-THREE

Sarajevo, four weeks later

The first week after Rosie got out of hospital had been spent mostly staring into space in her flat, and sleeping for hours on end. She'd never known such exhaustion. She was beginning to think she was sinking into some kind of depression, but her shrink friend told her this was perfectly normal. She was suffering from post-traumatic stress – probably had for a long time – but the plunge into the river and the near-death experience had pushed her over the edge, made it acute. Tears had come to Rosie's eyes when she'd confessed to him that there was a part of her that wished she had died that night; that she knew that the warm feeling she had had, which although she was trying with every fibre of her body to survive, was something pulling her to death. She was worried she was feeling suicidal, but he reassured her that was normal too. Time, he told her, is the great healer. Never mind the cliché. It was true. You need to rest, completely rest, he said. Get away from here. Get away from the job. Maybe even think about getting out altogether. You have your life to live, he'd told her. Rosie had listened passively, but the part that was Rosie Gilmour the journalist pushed him away and she knew she would be fine when she got back to work. He warned her not to: this was when she should stand back and take stock of her life. TJ had been right. She'd called him to tell him, but played it down. He was working and about to leave for a tour of Germany so she only told him half the truth. He seemed detached, and she wasn't quite sure how she felt about that, but it wasn't bereft.

The rest of the time she spent at home, watching old movies, reading, sleeping. Visits from McGuire, then nothing. She wondered when she would go back to work. He told her she was off for at least a month. She'd tried to phone Adrian, but nothing. Then she phoned his friend Risto, and he told her that Adrian was going to talk to her but there had been some changes in his life. He would like to see you, Risto had said. Rosie couldn't imagine what had happened. Was he ill? she'd asked. No. I cannot talk, he said. Why don't you visit? He is asking. Why doesn't he call? she'd asked. He said to visit. I can't speak any more.

Now she was in the car with Risto heading back to where she'd once felt happy and free, with the bracing air of the mountains in her face, and the safety of Adrian. Risto hadn't said much on the journey, and she wondered if Adrian had suffered some permanent damage. Perhaps he was seriously ill, in a wheelchair or something. Her stomach was in knots. They drove through lush valleys dotted with small villages. Then up to the house where Rosie remembered his mother lived. Now it looked exactly the same, with the smoke swirling from the chimney. Like stepping back in time, the small houses, farms, tight roads. In the garden, she saw Adrian's mother glance at Risto's car, then go quickly inside. Rosie felt sick with worry. She was desperate to see Adrian. There were butterflies in her stomach and her heart beat faster. They pulled the car up into the yard. Then, suddenly, Adrian was standing in the doorway, a smile spreading over his face. And a little boy in his arms. For a moment Rosie was dumbstruck. He hadn't told her of a relationship or a baby, but why would he? It was his life. Her head swam as she got out of the car and walked towards him. Suddenly, there was a flash of recognition, as she saw the baby closer up.

'Rosie. My friend. You remember this boy?'

Rosie was stunned. The little boy from the orphanage. The toddler in the cot who had cried and wailed, who had reached out to touch Adrian. She choked back tears.

'Jesus, Adrian! What? How! My God! You brought him home with you?'

Adrian grinned as the little boy snuggled shyly into his neck.

'Yes. I did. I went back and talked to the orphanage boss. So I made the decision. It's all legal. Not stolen or bought. The father is dead. The mother is gone – could not be traced.' He cuddled the boy. 'So he is mine now, Rosie. My boy, Jabir.'

'Jesus! Why didn't you tell me? I've been trying to get hold of you for weeks. I was worried sick. I mean . . . All the way here, I really thought something was wrong with you.'

He came across to her, put the little boy down and took her in his arms.

'I had to wait until I could bring him here. It took some time. Nothing is wrong with me. Not now. I am happy. This is my life now. I can give this boy a life he couldn't have. And he can have my life.'

Rosie scanned his face. The trademark dark shadows of a man whose sleep had been haunted by the demons of war and heartbreak and loss were gone. The pale, tired face she'd left behind in Romania was glowing with something much deeper than sheer good health. Adrian was happy, and seeing him standing here, remembering who he'd been when they first met, made her throat tighten with emotion. She hugged him and he held her tight. Then he pulled back and looked at her.

'You are all right?'

He wiped a tear from her cheek.

'I'm just so happy that you're happy.'

'I'm glad to see you, Rosie. This is a great day. Come. My mother has cooked. But first you can rest from your journey.'

The meal had been a feast prepared by Adrian's mother and sister, who'd joined them at the table along with Risto. Rosie listened to their stories as they drank wine and toasted absent friends, but also drank to a future filled with great hope. She closed her eyes for a second to take a picture in her mind of this night so she would remember it forever. Rosie had watched earlier as Adrian cradled the sleeping boy in his arms, then gently laid him in his cot in a room next to his. He has everything he needs, she thought, as he pushed the little boy's fringe back from his eyes. She was glad for Adrian, and yet somewhere inside there was a tiny ache that she had lost him, that whatever they had been to each other was over. There was no regret, no sadness, just an ache that she couldn't explain to herself.

Finally, there was just Rosie and Adrian sitting at the table, looking out at the blackness of the winter sky as the wind howled around the cottage. Adrian raked the flickering fire and placed another log on, then came back and sat at the table. He poured a little wine into both their glasses, and raised his.

'To you, Rosie Gilmour. I am glad you came into my life.'

Rosie smiled, and reached across, brushing his cheek with the back of her hand.

'We've had some times, Adrian. Truly. You . . . you mean so much to me.' She hesitated. 'Probably more than you know.'

They were silent for a moment, comfortable, two friends relaxed with each other.

'What now for you, Rosie? Another big story?'

She shook her head. 'Who knows. I haven't thought beyond this.' She spread her hands. 'Glasgow seems like another world.'

Adrian took her hand. 'You know, Rosie. You can stay here. I mean . . . longer than a holiday. I . . . I . . . What I'm saying is that my life is different now. I have my boy. I can see now clearly what my life should be.'

'You are very lucky to be able to see that, Adrian. I'm so pleased for you.'

Rosie looked beyond Adrian out to the darkness. She had never, ever been able to see what her life should be. It just was what it was. And it was really about work, and people she encountered, and relationships that came and went. She'd tried not to ponder too deeply on where she should be in her life, but she knew right now she was tired. Exhausted. Burned out. She saw herself drowning in the freezing river, and she shivered.

'But my life is not complete, Rosie.'

Rosie only half heard his words and she looked at him, surprised, but didn't say anything. Here, like this, with Adrian, was a feeling so potent that she was afraid to even imagine that her life could be like this.

'Rosie, why don't you stay here for a while? I . . .' He touched her face. 'Stay with me, with us, as long as you want.' He brushed her lips with his, and for a moment their eyes locked. 'Will you think about it?'

She could hear the urgent buzz of her mobile on Silent, and knew it was shuddering somewhere in her jacket hanging up in the hall. She let it ring . . .

ACKNOWLEDGEMENTS

When I began writing the Rosie Gilmour novels I only ever imagined doing two of them, and now we're at number nine – and who knows what will happen next!

It's been a wonderful, fulfilling experience for me, and I am grateful to so many people – family, readers – for all their support.

My sister Sadie, my greatest friend, who is ever at my side. My brother Des, who even in the most difficult times always finds time to ask me about my novels and takes a great interest in my work.

Matt, Katrina, and Christopher, who inspire and throw in ideas, and Paul who keeps my techno stuff right.

My cousins, the Motherwell Smiths, as well as Alice and Debbie and all their family in London. And my cousins Ann Marie and Anne.

I am lucky to have so many close friends: Mags, Eileen, Annie, Mary, Phil, Liz, and journalists Simon, Lynn, Mark,

Maureen, Keith, and Thomas in Australia. Also Helen and Bruce, Marie, Barbara, Jan, Donna, Louise, Gordon and Janetta, Brian and Jimmy.

In Ireland, I am grateful to Mary and Paud, for their support, as well as Sioban, and Sean Brendain. And in La Cala, Yvonne, Mara, Wendy, Jean, Maggie, Sarah, Fran, Billy and Davina. There are so many people who make a contribution to my life, and you all know who you are.

Thanks also to my editor Jane Wood, for believing in the Rosie books from day one, and to her assistant Therese Keating. Also to Olivia Mead in publicity, and all the top team at Quercus, who have been the best.